HOME IS THE EXILE

HOME IS THE EXILE

by
Hilary Masters

H. M.

For Bethany College —
with my thanks for
a warm + happy occasion —
Hilary Masters

THE PERMANENT PRESS
SAG HARBOR, NEW YORK

10 Oct 1996

Copyright © 1996 by Hilary Masters

Library of Congress Cataloging-in-Publication Data

Masters, Hilary.
    Home is The Exile/by Hilary Masters
        p.   cm.
        ISBN 1-877946-73-7
        I. Title.
PS3563.A82P5 1996
813' .54--dc20   95-16898
                                         CIP

Manufactured in the United States of America

first edition, August, 1996, 1700 copies

THE PERMANENT PRESS
Noyac Road
Sag Harbor, NY 11963

By Hilary Masters

NOVELS

HOME IS THE EXILE
The Harlem Valley Trio:
STRICKLAND
COOPER
CLEMMONS

PALACE OF STRANGERS
AN AMERICAN MARRIAGE
THE COMMON PASTURE

MYSTERY

MANUSCRIPT FOR MURDER
under P.J. Coyne

SHORT FICTION

HAMMERTOWN TALES
SUCCESS: New and Selected Stories

BIOGRAPHY

LAST STANDS: NOTES FROM MEMORY

Acknowledgment is due Carnegie Mellon University for its community. Special thanks to Marne Martin of San Miguel de Allende, Mexico, for her assistance in research on the voyage of the *Sinaia* in June, 1939.

For Kathleen

hardy's return

Veracruz
13 June 1939

For some reason, a man writing in a notebook is given privacy in public. That's been my experience. Everybody recognizes the guy's on his own, wants to be on his own for a little. Show me a notebook, and I'll show you a guy on his own. The waiter in this café just flicks at the flies from a distance — a member of the *patrulla mosca* ? Oh, McGee, you are a card, for sure. A *cerveza* has been deftly placed down at my elbow, but the waiter didn't pause, didn't peek at my memoirs. He tippy-toed away.

Yet, I feel like somebody's reading over my shoulder. Did old Montaigne feel like that? Someone is taking in this homely history of old Roy Armstrong, formerly Capt. US Air Service and late of the Patrulla Americana, Spanish Republic. The late Spanish Republic. And that's the whole trouble in a nutshell, Molly.

People have been buying us drinks since we landed. Tequila. Beers. The Plaza Armas is one grand party. Many of my fellow exiles have passed out in doorways, hotel lobbies, cantinas. Others have joined up with the native bands that are playing around the square. One or two have fallen into the marimbas. The Mexicans are beaming. It's hard to feel very abandoned in the middle of such a fiesta. These Mexicans are agreeable and courteous. Laugh a lot, but with a reserve in their eyes. All shades of browns and blacks — some a reddish hue. Indian blood, I guess. Long heads and a slant to their eyes. Very solemn but give them something to laugh about and the whole face opens up. But the eyes stay sad, watchful. And why not?

This Plaza I'm sitting in is where the US Marines set up their machine guns in 1914. This afternoon some of us went to a little museum in a building on the waterfront, and we saw photos of that adventure. Pictures of US Marines standing in these very porticoes behind me where I write. Thirty caliber machine guns on tripods, all pointing toward these same fountains where kids are playing tag now. Maybe pointing at some of the same citizens who are celebrating our arrival on the *Sinaia*. What were the Marines doing here then? Making the place safe for democracy? Wilson was President. Mexico was hard up for democracy. You lose track of the number of times we've saved people for democracy. Well, it's a job I know something about, I guess.

For sure, the natives down here must have their fill of it. Being liberated, I mean. First came Cortés, then the US Marines and now all of us from *vieja España*, like that poem said. Another invasion to be sure, even at Cárdenas's invite. Maximilian, etc. Hey, remember the Alamo! That's when we picked up Hollywood and some other real estate from them! The Grand Canyon? Mexico's been liberated a whole lot of times. It's a wonder anyone buys me a beer. But, then, they think I'm Juan Carillo from old Spain, though they must wonder at my *habla*.

So, we've come ashore at Veracruz. It's a coming back, a return for some of us — at least to the hemisphere.

A hotter day I can't remember. The sweat pouring down our faces and queasy from the harbor roll. Eighteen days on the *Sinaia* gives you an uncertain view of the horizon. Mexicans, thousands it seemed like, standing on the quay waving and cheering like we were bringing them pieces of the True Cross. Get it, Molly — the True Cross to Vera Cruz? Oh, McGee. Bands and flags and big placards that said NEGRIN TENíA RAZON. What was that politician right about? That we were losing the fight? You'd think after almost three years in Spain, I'd have a little more of the lingo, but that comes from hanging out mostly with Yanks and the Russkies. Little Nikki spoke only English with me too. A newspaper guy told me, she was pushed down that elevator shaft. A fifth columnist, they say. "Where do you fly this day, sweetingheart?" she'd ask. Madrid had gone crazy. Dogs turning on each other.

"I'm checking out," Frank Tinker told me that last night. "You ought to collect your money and get out too." We were having a drink after a sortie. I'd just heard about Nikki falling down that elevator shaft. Pushed. Tinker had been drinking a lot more than usual. "This war is over and we've lost. We were losers from the beginning, old sport." He has this Navy blue-and-gold way of talking. The fascists were running wild. Tink left for France the next day; picked up his US passport and prize money. If I had gone with him, I wouldn't be here now without a passport. Sans commission. Sans dough owed me for sending a dozen guys West. Only my Boy Scout honor, and I'm not so sure about that.

EL SINDICATO DE TORTILLERAS OS SALUDA. This big banner waving at us on the quay. Some country this is; to be greeted by the tortilla union. How many returning heroes get that kind of a reception? Cortés got gold; we get tortillas and beer.

On the *Sinaia*, some of the brainy types got up classes on Mexican history for the rest of us—since we were about to become Mexican citizens. Apparently, Cortés landed somewhere around here, what is now Veracruz, and Montezuma sent him gold. Maybe in the last five hundred years or so, the Mexicans have wised up a little. If Cortés had been greeted with a stack of tortillas, he might not have hung around. As for us, we got no place else to go — those of us on the *Sinaia* — so we take the tortillas. Muchas gracias. T'ain't funny, McGee.

Three years years back, I made this trip, going the other way on the *Normandie*. Getting off in France with Frank Tinker and Ben Lieder and the others; on our way to Spain to fight for democracy. Well, that's what it said in the program. Now, I've come back on this tub to Mexico. Lieder and most of the others wiped out. If Tinker got his passport , he's probably back in Arkansas. Nikki dead. _La guerra es así._

"Ooh, Wr-roy...you fill me hopefully," she'd say, stretching out all pink and white in the early light as I'd get dressed to get back to the field. "You must fly away so early. Where to now, my eagle?" She was a Finnish dawn stretching out over Madrid. The first air raid sirens going off. Condor Junkers making their breakfast run. I can't erase the awfulness of Nikki at the bottom of that elevator shaft. _La guerra es así,_ she used to say. Maybe she was giving me a warning, if she had been on the other side? War is like that. I guess, if given the order, she would have turned my lights out. What was it Ben Lieder used to say, "All the mothers of the world are weeping?"

Veracruz looks okay from what I could see, marching in that huge crowd of people. 1500 of us get off the ship. Seems like twenty times that of the locals. All I wanted was to lie down on a bed that didn't roll and pitch. Eighteen days in the hold of the _Sinaia_ is enough for any officer and gentleman airman. But, here we were marching along with workers, bands playing, people hanging out windows. Guys on horseback with great big hats, firing revolvers into the air, just like the movies. The president down here, a general named Cárdenas, has proclaimed almost a national holiday because of us exiles. We're the first boatload out — none of us any longer welcome in Spain. Nor in Europe, for that matter. Hey, we lost. Nobody likes a loser. Talk on the ship is that Cárdenas is the same as Franco but he's on our side. Which side is that? Tell me that again, Amos.

Last year, Cárdenas took over all the oil fields from the Americans and Brits. That's okay by me when I think of those Messysmiths chewing on my tail a few months back, all of them tanked up on Texaco. But he did get us out. Come to Mexico, he said. You're welcome in Mexico. We are automatic citizens of Mexico. Well, isn't that the cat's meow? But it's more than I can say for Uncle Sam. Here I was born in the state of Connecticut, and I end up with a stack of tortillas. This must be the colossal wallet loss of all time. I'm a nobody. An unknown soldier.

"Your passport has been suspended, Mr. Armstrong. To serve in the armed forces of another nation is to incur the loss of citizenship." I'm looking at this bozo across the desk. Outside the consul's windows, April in France — not Paris. Couldn't get there. Got stopped at the border. His little eyes set close together and he seems about to smile on every word, but doesn't. Ivy Leaguer. I sit there looking at this guy, thinking about how I had left all that behind in '17, all those types at Yale when I lit out for France — I was a couple of years away from becoming one of them myself. But, oh for the life in the open skies, fighting the Hun. I could have been on a poster. And, here I am sitting across from one of these preppies and the club has blackballed me.

"Hey, that was Juan Carillo," I say, trying to find some kind of humor in him. "This is me, Roy Armstrong, Army Air Service, an officer and a gentleman."

"We're aware of the aliases you people used, but that doesn't affect the legality of the situation." What's he so mad about, I wonder. That I didn't stick it out at Yale? "Moreover, the Republican bank accounts in Paris have been frozen at the request of the Spanish Nationalists. They've won the hand and can pick up all the chips." This imagery pleased him ever so much. "So you can forget whatever monies you may have had deposited there in your name—whatever name it might be." He looks happy and his nose stalls out.

Eleven thousand smackers exactly, one for every *fasciti* I knocked down. Confirmed, that is. But, more than the money, I'm taken back by his attitude, none of the old team spirit. Hey, I'm on your side aren't I? I wanted to say. Wasn't I defending democracy the last three years? Okay, for dough — but I could have flown for Franco too. What's more, does anybody do it for free anymore? In Spain, I came on the notion that there are sides within sides. Ivory soap. If you weren't 100 percent pure, by whoever decided what floats, you were taken out and sunk. Like Nikki, I guess. No matter how bad you shot up Franco's boys. Like some of the Russian guys in our outfit. They'd just disappear in the night; their own people taking them for a ride. And so, here's this stick-up-the-ass across from me, smiling almost when he tells me I'm no longer wanted in the cradle of democracy because I have been defending the stuff outside the city limits of Cincinnati. I don't get it. I'se regusted, Andy.

This big plaza in Veracruz has beautiful large trees, fountains and houses on all sides with porticoes and doorways open to show big bowls of flowers, yellow tulips. There are little cafes tucked under the porticoes around this plaza, their tables set out, crisp and cheerful in the sun and shadows of the overhangs. I'm sitting in one making these notes for posterity. For who, McGee? You remember Nick Posterity, Molly — he used to have that little shoe shop over on McAdoo Boulevard.

But, I'm alive and back home in the western hemisphere. On the doorstep at least. A newly ordained Mexican citizen. Level out, mister. Make a few phone calls across the border. Get back my Eagle Scout badge. Up on a balcony of what looks to be city hall — circa Cortés — is this official, who is talking for *el Presidente*, giving us *El Gran Buenos Días*, and talking about *el desamparo*—the abandonment.

El desamparo. To be abandoned by your country, to abandon your country , he is saying — I catch some of the words enough and I get even more dizzy and sick. He's talking about Spain and my fellow passengers, who are mostly Spanish. A few Russkies, like the general and Consuelo, who pretend to be Spanish. But I'm thinking about the US of A. Haven't I been abandoned too? It's the heat, I tell myself, and concentrate on the white bell tower on one corner of the building. It's not the fact that you are a *gringo*, all alone in this Mexican plaza, sardined by Spanish exiles who are weeping and cheering, your eye on a big pile of horse shit just a step away on the cobblestones, the steam of it scouring your sinuses, or that you might be stuck in this place, this

Mexico, for the rest of your life sitting under balconies in the steam bath of the noon hour, listening to mustachioed politicos tell you how honorably you've lost the fight — your name and place in the world. Maybe this is a kind of hell my good deeds have somehow earned me.

Understand what I'm saying, Molly? You've done all you can for the right side and you still end up on the *basura con los bolsillos vacios*.

Hey, I'm not complaining. I'd be on a list if I was still in France — no papers and a price on my head for shooting down Franco's Fiats and Messysmiths. Probably in one of those refugee camps the French had fixed up. Good night, nurse. And if it hadn't been for that woman who followed me out of the consulate, a secretary of a sort, and gave me that slip of paper with the Mexican ambassador's name on it — I'd be waiting to be sent back to Madrid and Franco's prison. Or worse. *Pour la patrie*, this woman says and darts back in quick. Or was that, *parti*?

You're no better than a goddamn Red, I can hear Uncle Billy say. In Spain, we'd been hearing about this Congressman Dies going after Reds. But hey, it's me, folks, old Roy Armstrong — defender of democracy — just an old cloudbuster for hire. I ain't no Red.

Over at the Mexican consulate in Marseilles, you'd think I was the greatest thing since pancakes. My name — Juan Carillo, that is — is on this other list of heroes somebody keeps — and the very reading of it sets off a celebration; smiles, handshakes, greasy embraces. You are welcome in Mexico, the consul says to me after several hugs. He tells me about the *Sinaia*, leaving from the port of Séte, down the Mediterranean. By Presidential decree, Alvarez del Vayo tells me, all Spanish loyalists are given Mexican citizenship. A fella has to belong to some kind of lodge. *Viva Mexico!!*

And it's not so bad in this café on this pleasant plaza in Veracruz, all of the noise and the fear and the sorrow far away now. The beer is tasty and cool. And free. So far. Somebody's buying us drinks. I sit on the shady

side of the plaza and watch kids play tag
around the fountain. There's some Pancho
Villas, tooting trumpets and sawing on violins
across the way. Just down from me, in front of
another cantina, a guy is setting up another
marimba, like he's part of the bill at the
Lowe's Palladium. This whole place is an open
air party. Dogs all over, shitting all over,
happily humping for the occasion. I suppose to
shit anywhere you want, just squat wherever the
urge strikes you, makes for a certain beati-
tude, a sense of well-being. Ah!!

Some of my former shipmates wander about —
now that the formal ceremonies are over—eating
stuff from street vendors. I see Gen. Avila and
Consuelo. The tortilla workers have been working overtime. Everyone's singing, holding
hands. Some wobbling. Some stretch out on the
edge of the fountains, on the pavements. Like
they've come home — a home away from home, I
guess. To rest. And what about me? Is this my
happy landing? Citizen Carillo. If I can get in
touch with Tooey Spatz, he'll get me out of
this place. Hell, the Air Service ought to
pullafew strings. Me and Rickenbacker. Doesn't
anyone remember me?

Just now, I see Gen. José Avila, the erstwhile defender of Madrid, and his lady friend
making the paseo on the far side of the plaza.
They parade like some kind of royalty, her hand
lightly on his left arm. She's a statuesque
woman — as well I should know, Molly. About my
age. At the moment — on the arm of the general —
she looks maidenlike. A little different from
when we went through the Gibraltar straits.

The whole shipload was weeping . The last
look of the homeland. *El desamparo*. Old Tony
Zozaya, the journalist. We gave him a party on
his 90th birthday as we passed the Azores — the
old guy bent over double at the ship's rail
with grief.

"*Adios, patria te alejas, adios,*" he kept
saying over and over.

Later someone wrote a poem and it was published in the ship newspaper. All kinds of
people on this boat: poets, painters, newspaper guys, intellectuals and *un tonto americano*
up a pear tree. This woman, Susana Gamboa, was

like a social director, organizing lectures on
Mexican history, art, politics. A lot of politics. The whole boatload did nothing but talk
politics. Course that's how the war ended, in
cafés talking politics. That's why we lost,
maybe. Boring talk. This Gamboa dame brought
a mimeograph with her and puts out a little
newspaper with articles and interviews on the
boat. No ball scores, DiMaggio. Nothing like
that. The same in Spain. These people were forever cranking out tons of paper blasting Franco
or that politician or general. Give them a few
minutes quiet in a battle and they'd turn out
a newspaper or a magazine. *Hora de Espana* was
always around the airfield. Nikki usually had
copies in her satchel. She helped put some of
them out. I never paid much attention to them,
being in Spanish, not all that easy to understand. They'd print cartoons and articles on
politics and art. And poems. Here's part of
that poem in the newspaper on the ship. I wrote
it down.

Como en otro tiempo por la mar salada
te va un rio espanol de sangre roja, de generosa
sangre
desbordada
Pero eres tu, esta vez, quien nos conquistas
y para siempre, oh vieja y nueva España.

It was because of that mimeographed ship
newspaper that I come to know the general and
his lady — Señora Consuelo Moreno. Mrs. Brown
to you — and if that's her real name, my name
is Juan Carillo. And I have Manny Barreclerna
to thank for that too. As we're getting on the
boat in Séte, he spots me. "*Hola,* Armstrong,"
he says. "*Viejo camarada!*" But we never flew
together. His squadron, all Spanish guys, was
north of Madrid. We used to meet in the bar at
the Florida Hotel, while I waited for Nikki to
get off work at the Telefonica across the
boulevard. Ah, Nikki, *makeisioni* — I guess you
taught me more than a few words of Finnish.
Anyway, I make the ship's paper — *The Sinaia*
Bugle, you might say. The social notes—Who's
Who on board...*Juan Carillo, el heroe de la*

patrulla americana...gave me credit for a few more kills than the eleven confirmed. Pretty lurid two or three sentences about my supposed exploits in the skies over the Ebro. Is that me, I kept thinking?

Next day, there's this little envelope on my cot next to the *Sinaia's* keel. All of us younger, single guys are down here in the ship's belly. *"Que es esto?"* Next to me, is this Mex painter Siquieros. He's one of those Reds you can't talk to. Narrow minded. A hell-cat of a fighter, I guess. In a machine gun brigade. *"Es una invitacion,"* he says and turns his eyes up. And it is. Formal and flowery. So, I go up expecting a little merriment in the first class to find just the general and Senora Moreno in the corner of a cabin on A-deck—the whole space divided up by blankets hanging on wires so to accommodate about six couples or families. The general's rank gets him and his lady the area next to the porthole and he seats me down on their cot underneath it. He takes the chair opposite me, so we're knee to knee. It's just the three of us — no room for anyone else. Like we're about to get into a lively game of patty-cake. As the *Sinaia* rolls and plunges up and down. On the bed are little pieces of bread and a hunk of cheese—spread out on a brocade hankerchief. His lady, Senora Moreno, is behind him, pulling the cork on a bottle of sherry. Which is going to make me sick, as it always does, but how can I refuse?

This General José de Avila turns out not to be Spanish. No big surprise. Is anyone on this ship going by his right name? He sounds like a waiter at Romanoff's in Hollywood; in fact, he will probably end up there, serving borscht. I can almost smell it on him. He knows a hell of a lot about me. My time in the War. Spain.

"Your valor is well known," he says. "But you have suffered much loss of friendships. Comrade José Lindo, *por ejemplo*. You were close?" His pudgy face goes sharp as he looks at me from one eye, sidewise. He ought to have a monocle. It is taking me a few seconds to match up Ben Lieder with the name they gave him in Paris. And it's been a while since Lieder took on a few too many Fiats, once too often, and piled his Polikarpov into a hill near

Jarama. "The flying photographer." Always giving us lectures, like these people on the boat. Being with him was like being with the Salvation Army. Always telling us about the workers' revolution.

"Sure, Lindo," I say. "He was a hot pilot. A little crazy, maybe." I get the hard eye. "I mean, he took a lot of chances, would fly right into a stack of Francos."

"A class hero," the general says solemnly and munches on a piece of cheese.

"He was classy, for sure," I admit, though that's a twist on what he's saying. Something nudges me inside. "Does the name Nikki Raimussen mean anything to you?"

The general pauses in his chewing of the *queso* and looks up at the steel overhead, but a little too long before he shrugs and shakes his head. "Consuelo, you must join us," he says like her absence is hurting his feelings, and she's doodling in the conservatory or something. In fact she's been standing just behind him, inches away in the little cubicle. Out of his sight, but not mine.

Before, I put the rest of this show down, let me pause for station identification. The general is a little guy, but trim and muscular. He's about 60-something, I'd guess, and balding. A neat little moustache like Adolphe Menjou. His eyes bug out sometimes as he says things — for emphasis, I guess. Now this Señora Moreno is what we would call hearty. Still in the running. Blondish hair is bobbed. Large brown eyes that sometimes have a gleeful look, sometimes commanding. Right now, these eyes roll around like they've parted from their strings.

"Come, Consuelo, please join us," Avila repeats.

"I'm comfortable here, Leo." She's just served up the sherry in little metal cups. Where was she supposed to sit? Her eyes do another snap roll and fix on me as she reaches up and slips her dress off the left shoulder. All this behind the general's back, mind you, while he is saying, "But you have a valuable skill. You are a superb flyer. How will you get on in Mexico? There is — there is some problem with your government, I suppose," he says sadly.

"They no longer recognize your citizenship. And you Americans are very — devoted to your citizenship."

He's taken out a thin metal case with black cigarettes and offers me one just as his lady is offering her left tit. I refuse the cigarette, and the general taps his on the case and lights up. He holds it, palm up, as if he's trying to catch the ashes as they happen. Consuelo has shrugged back into her dress; then, slips down the other side. I guess to prove she's got a pair.

"Your own country has, hypocritically, not honored your defense of democracy, your heroic acts against the forces of fascism." He waves the black cigarette in the air, dismissing Washington, Lincoln, and FDR, all at once. He takes a little puff. "But, perhaps, you will find something in Mexico. Someone as versatile as you will, no doubt, have...how say, *los enlaces* —Consuelo?" he commands without looking around.

"Connections," she answers smartly, demonstrating her right one.

Then the two of them chat for a while in Russian which leaves me out, of course. Finally he gets back to English. "Yes...connections," he smiles and looks like a barber. How about a dash of Lucky Tiger?

I tell him I know nobody in Mexico, trying to look him in the face. He's turned a little to one side. Meanwhile, the lady has proved her points, you might say. Why I'm getting this show is a mystery but it's having some effect. Old Jack Armstrong is giving it a standing ovation. The lady's looking straight at me, full of Christmas cheer.

"That is surprising me, Comrade Carillo," the General is going on. "But perhaps we can help you out. To reward you for your heroism — for our cause." I told him I'd been well-paid — even though most of the money was tied up. I still had saved a lot of my regular wages. The dough is heavy in a money belt around my waist. Mrs. Brown has put her dress in order but is feeling herself up, smiling and rolling her eyes, like she's absent-mindedly trying to find something she's lost in the material; say, a pin or a penny. The general, smokes and looks over my head and into the round light of the porthole.

"Still," he goes on, "what are friends about, as you Americans say. But tell me, Juan — if I may call you so." He takes another deep drag on the cigarette, his hand cupped under his chin. The smoke is making me a little queasy, along with the roll of the ship, the sweet wine —not to mention the lady's performance. Jack Armstrong is wide awake. Then suddenly, the General leans forward so his beak of a nose almost touches mine. "Tell me about Jean Harlow. Her death is surely a great tragedy. You knew her, yes?" Watery blue eyes bore into me.

Now, I is flabber-de-gasted, Andy! The only person I ever told about that—the only person in Spain who ever knew about me and Jean Harlow was Nikki. Some of the guys in the Patrol knew about me doing stunts in those Hollywood movies. They had asked the usual questions. But I never boasted to any of them about Harlow. The night her obit was in the papers, I had met Nikki at the Telefonica and we go to a little café in the Retiro. We had gone to a movie. Fred Astaire. This is two years back. I'm pretty low — just to think of that wild, funny woman dead. So I tell Nikki about our times together. "I am giving more pleasure?" Nikki says brightly, and I had to laugh. So, Nikki knew about Harlow and so does this Red General! What does that add up to, Molly?

Meanwhile, Mrs. Brown has continued her demonstration, or advertisement. As the general leans back, she's taken up a stance at the bulkhead pulling up her dress to reveal this bush between her legs. It's black. She looks down at it, then at me, then down at it again — like it was as much of a surprise to her to find it that color as it is to me. The general is enjoying his smoke and tells me about his crush on Jean Harlow. He'd seen a lot of her films and he rattles their names off. Her portrayal, he says, is that of a human being wasted and made idle by a corrupt capitalist society. *Devastado*, he says. I had never thought of Harlow as *devastado*. I can hear her snort and laugh at the idea. Señora Moreno gives me another angle.

"*Si, magnifico y devastado.*" He puffs out the words, agreeing with himself. His companion has just pointed her finger at his his bald pate, turned her thumb down and stuck out her tongue. With her other hand, she dusts off the plate where the General apparently has struck out. Jack is becoming a little rowdy. "Consuelo." The General starts to turn around, his neck glued on his torso. "Perhaps, *el capitán* could help us with Mr. Lund?"

"Of course, Leo," the woman replies, every-thing quickly put right just as he faces her. "A brilliant idea, as usual." She encircles his neck with her arm and hugs him. The two of them take up a pose, him sitting down, she standing beside him, her arm around his shoulders, like they are posing for a photograph — something for the history books. The Defender of Madrid and his faithful consort.

"Who is Mr. Lund?" I ask, standing up, the interview is over. I look down quickly. Old Jack is behaving himself. The Senora's been looking in the same direction, and she winks.

"An old friend of ours. Yes, an old friend," the general is saying with a curious smile. "We hope to meet him again in Mexico. Is not that the case, Consuelo?"

Consuelo nods. "Yes, we must not lose the sight of each other."

Now, you might think that I would have spent the rest of my days on the jolly ship *Sinaia*, polishing off some romantic moments with the general's lady, but that ain't the case, Molly. I couldn't find her, and you'd expect on a ship that small it would be easy, but I only catch a glimpse of them once, com-ing through a door, until just now, here in Veracruz, walking around the Plaza de Armas, arm in arm. Couple days after her Sally Rand act, I saw her at a party in the main salon. A baby was born midway across the Atlantic and the captain threw a party. Señora Brown was coming out on deck just as I was going in. I gave her my best howdee-do, and she cuts me dead. Like we'd never met, and us on such intimate terms too. Was that some sort of a fit, some peculiar brand of *mal de mer* that seized her in the general's cubicle? Maybe she thought better of her performance. She'd been carried away by my fresh American looks. My heroics. Maybe The Defender of Madrid had brought up a reserve that had changed her mind.

Mas cervezas. I am taking big lungfuls of air, deep breathing that leaves me calm and relaxed. At the top of a loop. At peace for the time being. All the fright and sadness of the last several years has been exhaled. In comes the fresh air. Though not always so fresh. Some of the corners in this place smell like a dump. But, out goes the bad.

Negocio importante. Here's a list of people to get in touch with.
    1. Tooey Spatz — still at Kelly Field?
    2. Jimmy Doolittle — Last heard from he's flying for the Shell Oil company.
    3. Roscoe Turner — maybe care of RKO pictures. Hollywood. They can forward the message. He's flying for some oil company too. What's the name?? All of them used to be down here too before the Mexicans took over the pumps.
    <u>Hey, boys—get me out of here!</u>

So, now, let's say you're about 28 years of age and it is June 1968 and you are standing on the steps of St. Pat's on Fifth Avenue in New York City and, as far as you're concerned, you've just left the rest of the American Century inside, stiff in a sealed box.

You look around at the other guys your age or a little older, like Frank Mankowitz and John Burns, and they're crying too, some of them with the little PT 109 clips on their ties, so you'd think they could handle it better since they went through it only five years back, but everyone's doing the silent manly bit. Tears making quiet tracks down the cheeks. Men who cry; it's supposed to be okay. It's the 60's afterall. And some of them look at you, but don't recognize you until you say, "Frank...it's Walt Hardy from Dutchess County," because you've never met most of them but for the last year or more you have talked to a lot of them on the phone at all hours, and, so, the arm goes around you, and you get the grip, because they know your name, recognize your voice. They know what you did, what all of you almost did—and that you are one of them. A funny kind of reunion.

It's hello and good-bye right there, right then, to men, one or two women that have been almost more than your family for the last year and a half, actually more important to you than wife and family—if you had one—because you have told each other all sorts of things at every hour of the day and the night. Maybe, you know more about them than you do about your own family. For over a year you've talked numbers, registration dates, primaries, committeemen—going over lists on little bits of paper; key words and names scribbled on backs of envelopes or in small books as you stood in phone booths, hotel lobbies, your own kitchen—names and numbers you all hoped to put together, to reassemble like some ancient scroll that was in pieces and scattered all over the state of New York, and each of you had found a scrap of it in your backyard and which, if you could piece it together, would give the ultimate truth, unlock the rightful destiny for the US of A. What you had begun to feel was going to be your one and only destiny. It had been a first and a last chance for many of you. And it almost happened too. It was just about pieced together, when someone took a wrong turn through the kitchen of the Ambassador Hotel that June night in L.A. and all the little pieces of paper were blown away; so now all of you are standing on the steps of St. Pat's a few days later with some of these slips of paper still in your coat pockets like Confederate money, worthless figures from closed accounts; a match cover with the one phone number that could have made all the difference in the primary.

Meanwhile, if you're Walt Hardy, you're meeting a lot of these people for the first time but you know all about them, because eventually during those long phone discussions, guesses and speculations, the other guy would pause and sigh like it was four in the morning in a hotel room in Buffalo—and it probably had been—and you'd say, what's the matter? So, you'd hear about their wives, about the secretary giving them trouble, about the crabgrass in their lawn, about an unsecured loan they had to cover, about the fucking contractor who fucked up their fucking driveway. On the steps, you see one of them chatting up John Glenn, one of the pall bearers, and you mentally pull the file on the guy. On the midnight after the Indiana primary, you had heard all about his father dying of cancer. How they had got finally close at the deathbed; how the old man had patted him on the arm. He'd done well. Next to him, is another guy wearing a gray silk suit like very fine armor. You remember this county chairman telling you about his son. *Walt, lemme give you the picture, Walt. My old man sold encyclopedias to put me through Fordham. You know, door-to-door stuff. I bust my balls to get the kid into Princeton, you know what I mean? And, I say to him , for Christ's sake if you have to suck dick do you have to do it in the men's room of the New York Public Library? And a cop's dick at that? And from the Times Square precinct? It's costing me a bundle, Walt. Do you have any kids? You're lucky.*

Earlier, you were all sitting inside, listening to Bernstein conduct the Philharmonic, listening to Andy Williams sing. Andy Williams? Someone asked Jack English about that. Andy Williams, for Christ's sake? and he shrugged. "It was Ethel's idea." So, you were all sitting there wondering what next. What next, is right—what is next after you had mortgaged the driveway and the house behind it, mortgaged the family, your children if you have any; the crabgrass and your very soul, maybe—and it all came down to the disposable remains neatly boxed at the top of the aisle. You had heard the sirens from a distance, and thought—life goes on in New York City. Here you were sitting in this still point of time in this phony Gothic cathedral but people are catching on fire, jumping out of windows in New York City. The world may have stopped for most of you inside this temple, but outside people are still coping with emergencies, distress calls are answered and calamities are being pulled back from disaster. But not in this place.

So, if you're Walt Hardy, you've turned to Celia, your wife, just as the sirens come right outside the front door and stop like it has been St. Pat's that had been on fire—these huge tall doors of the church manned by the secret service suddenly swing open—like the movies with Samson coming through, and there he is—Lyndon Baynes looking about twenty feet tall and you're saying to yourself as he comes down the center aisle like a mountain, like a President, goddamn it, we knocked off that sonofabitch and here he is back from the dead, pushing through the dazzlement of the doorway like being beamed-up-Scotty, and taking the center aisle in giant strides—that sorrowful look on his face as if he were enduring a monumental intestinal gas attack and couldn't let go a fart in company. He got us in this jam, people setting themselves on fire, cities on fire, Vietnam on fire, the whole fucking US of A going up the chimney and he was supposed to be finished and here he is, bigger than life, like nothing had happened. Like the last year had not happened, had not mattered. He was still the President and Bobby was up there in the box.

Then, if you're Walt Hardy, you understand something about power; how even if you want to give it up, even if it might be taken from you, some of it, the glow of it will still stick to you; the way the smashed splendor of lightning bugs had stuck to your fingers on summer evenings in Pittsburgh; cold and bright and mysteriously long after the insect was dead.

So now, it's an older Walt Hardy—some years after this sad demonstration—who stands in his Dad's apartment over the old carriage house, looking down on those grounds back of the mansion; the long colonnade painted white and overgrown by the thick grape vines where he used to pursue lightning bugs of a summer evening, chase after them until they escaped into the broad leaves, flying beyond a boy's reach, some of them. So, Walt Hardy has been trying to tell his father about that day in June at St. Patrick's Cathedral and he's started talking about fireflies.

"I'd come upon her down there," he says to his father. "Just before it got really dark when the lightning bugs would come out. She would appear like a ghost at the end of the arbor, just pop out and scare the hell out of me."

"She was one for walking the grounds," the senior Hardy says and pours them more tea. When they had got back from the cemetery, his father had removed his suit jacket and though it wasn't Sunday, the gesture had made it seem so, for this had been his way every Sunday that Walt can remember, coming up the stairs to the apartment after parking the Packard just below, after driving Miss Arnett back from Calvary Church, removing his suit jacket and making some tea, spending the rest of his day off going through the Pittsburgh Press page by page and, maybe later, his stamp collection in his shirtsleeves and with the dark blue tie still tight in place. Sometimes, if the Pirates were in town, they'd take a big orange trolley, a Hamilton 75, down to Oakland and Forbes Field.

"Like a popsicle—orange," Celia used to say, reminding him of a part of the story he had forgotten. Sometimes, it might have occurred to Walt Hardy that she had given up her own history, parts of it anyway, to cull a present for herself out of his past, but now—he was surely aware—she had been packing, preparing to consign their marriage to that past.

"Yes, orange like a popsicle," he had said. She had continued to fold her clothes into neat units and place them in her suitcase. He quickly inventoried all the old stories, hoping to come on one she hadn't heard so many times that she might pause, put aside the suitcase and stay. But she had continued.

Walt Hardy thinks his father's hearing has lost its edge though the old man's shoulders and arms looked no less compact, no less firm this morning than they had all those other Sunday mornings when he would sit in his shirtsleeves and vest—just the two of them together waiting for the day to unfold like the last page of the *Press*. Hardy. That's what Miss Arnett had called him—Hardy. Not Mr. Hardy or even Bill—but just Hardy as if he were one of a kind, or a minister in the court of the Virgin Queen, and even young Walt had referred to his father and eventually to himself by the family name because it had come to shape an image of himself as well; of reliability, of duty and loyal service; an image that he was to convey later in those phone calls he'd make all around New York State—and later in D.C. and then Central America. "This is Hardy," he'd say, and you might think he was part of some lineage that went back to the Normans or something, but the recognition had been quick. Always and no matter who or what time it was on the other end of the line. "Oh, yes—Hardy."

In fact, growing up, Walt Hardy sometimes felt that he was part of a family that, for some reason, had lost its place at the high table . It would be easy to feel that way if you grew up on the grounds of the Arnett estate in Point Breeze and, especially, after reading Sir Walter Scott. Coming across the leather bound novels in the library of the main house was like discovering ancient registries that revealed his rightful heritage though they never explained why he and his family had lost it to be banished to the apartment over the carriage house.

Crouched by the mammoth fireplace near the leaded-paned windows of the second floor library, he would come on what seemed to be intimations of his true destiny, and so he grew up with a hunger to join a nobility he had met in pages of a romance or, later, in the chapters of the histories and biographies he would read to Celia in their first years together. He never talked much to her about this sense he had of being set apart from a world that had been rightfully his—never had to tell her because, from the beginning, she had recognized him as someone who had always been on his own, and this view of him had turned up an unexpected tenderness for him within her. "You're like a cat that's been put on a winter doorstep," she used to say, and laugh.

One time, hoeing her father's garden behind the bookstore in Poughkeepsie, she had turned up an old Indian arrow head; its puzzling perfection so original and yet ordinary that she had kept it in her dresser drawer for years. But she would also chide Hardy for this badge pinned inside himself especially in recent years; try to kid him out of it, as if it were an embarrassing table habit he had brought to their marriage, but it was now time for him to put it aside. His "little match girl act," she would call it.

"Well, break out the matches," Walt Hardy had thought and laughed, freshly stabbed by Celia's departure as he stood on the steps of Calvary Church this morning. Also, in this brilliant sunshine, unusually brilliant for Pittsburgh, he had been thinking of that other funeral in 1968, other church steps, as he stood on these church steps but once again with strangers he strangely knows. His father had stood to one side, on the farthest edge of the cast stone arch of the entry—the faithful Hardy, and he had taken his place beside the old man in the servant section, you might say. Eyes had discretely inspected him , assayed his genuineness in the flesh as against the image seen on television, published in news magazines, or standing before those Congressional committees, raising a right hand to swear to tell the truth. Selective evasions, Celia had called it.

For just a moment this morning, Walt Hardy had felt the old chagrin, the weighing of his worth, even of his father's worth, on scales held by these people, Peggy Arnett's relatives, who chattered and pecked at each other after her funeral. All of them, you might think if you were Walt Hardy, put center stage by a fickle fate, an unearned casting, while he, Walt Hardy, having peculiarly proved himself before millions, had been shown his place by the funeral director, to stand in the wings beside his father. Much like Jack English had gone up to Joe Resnick in St. Pat's that June day to tell the congressman he wasn't welcome but that he could sit in a pew near the toilets. So, Walt Hardy took his place with his father, the old Pittsburgh protocol safely in place, to represent the family from the carriage house, from that far place.

Some of the dinners given lately in his honor applauded or gave a prize to the people who had come the longest distance. He and his father had come only from the end of the garden, but that was a far distance, yet they got nothing more for it on the church steps this morning than a nod, a half-handed grasp from the Pittsburgh well-to-do. He had kept this distance and smiled at Peggy Arnett's relatives; the nieces, and a nephew more his age, and their children who slyly looked him over.

Nor did they, he reflected, know anything about power, though they thought their checking accounts and bills of credit bought them a ticket on the train. That wasn't the same thing, he has been thinking as he looks down on the garden this morning, remembering the luminous residue that had stuck to his fingers as a child and which, now that he thinks about it, seemed to illuminate that moment more than twenty years ago when he had turned to his wife in St. Patrick's just as LBJ strode by. Cold fire is what it is—this kind of power, and—if you were Walt Hardy—you would have known, that moment in St. Pat's, that you had to follow that power wherever it would take you. If not with LBJ then whoever. You had come so close to it with Bobby, had made a bargain, you might say, and you couldn't quit. You couldn't shake the stuff off, and it illuminated, not just your hopes, but the vision you had had of yourself all along.

"Where can I reach you?" he had asked her. He had told Celia nothing she hadn't heard before. She was almost finished packing.

"Reach me? Why would I want you to reach me?" She was

taking very little and wants nothing sent. Even if she had an address.

"It's not like I was shagging some bimbo," he said.

"That would have some virtue to it. I could live with that. I wouldn't like it but I could understand it. No, this has been coming on a long time. Damn the Kennedys anyway. Some standard bearers, some torchbearers. All they ever passed around was themselves." The suitcase slammed shut. "Lying to Congress. Lying to me. To me. You know how I felt sitting here, watching you on the tube, saying things I knew not to be true. I've been sleeping with a stranger. I feel used, Walt. You've abused me, Walt. That hurts."

All this jargon—Walt Hardy would consider it jargon—delivered so calmly. Was this the same woman he had lived with all these years? He had given her this very set of luggage she had just packed. For an anniversary. But I don't travel much, she had said. We're going places, he remembers saying, just as his father turns from the stove.

"Here's your tea," the old chauffeur says, and Walt Hardy turns from the view of the grounds and all the scenes that had winked up at him from the grape arbor, the large leaves dappling under the bright overcast that has crept across the sky. The two mugs steam on the checkered tablecloth next to the heavy white sugar bowl and creamer. He remembers the breakfasts there. Wheaties, the Breakfast of Champions. "You'll be leaving when?"

"I don't know, Dad. Maybe tomorrow after the will business. Or maybe, I'll hang around. We could go to a Pirates game. I have to be in Kansas City next week." The older man nods and spoons sugar into his mug. One, two and then half of a third spoonfuls each carefully stirred .

"Houston is on deck and St. Louis will be in town Thursday," he says. They had baseball, at least. Words seemed always to embarrass the older Hardy as if their mere utterance were a biological phenomenon, a quirk of genetics he could not control and was somehow a little ashamed of. Sometimes Walt Hardy would think his ability to keep confidences came from the long silences he had shared with his father.

"So, what will you do now, Dad?" Walt sips the tea and looks around the kitchen. Neat and efficient, the room had the snug convenience of a small ship's galley; a practical facility where a single man prepared one-dish meals. The wall clock over the fridge swung its brass pendulum back and forth, a perpetual accounting of this solitary life. "We could fix up some room for you in Maryland, you know that." He still used the plural pronoun; in fact, he hasn't yet told his father about Celia. To do so might be a jinx, make her flight something that could not be undone.

"I know that." His father nods. "But I have this place. Miss Arnett fixed it so I can live here for the rest of my time." The words came quickly as if memorized from something on a card. "The whole estate is going to be like a museum and I'm to be part of it. An associate curator." The older man looks shyly across the table and straightens his shoulders, as if to prepare them for the new commission. "I don't want to leave Pittsburgh," he says quietly and blows on his tea.

"Great," Walt Hardy replies. But he was thinking of the neatness of it, the largesse of the rich and powerful that can transform a chauffeur into an associate curator, still keeping the man on the payroll, with just a change of uniform. His mother had escaped all that, escaped all of them to become part of a disappearing act with Hector the Magnificent, a Greek magician who manifested himself at the Stanley Theatre one week in May—he couldn't remember exactly for he had been little, not in school yet—to send back only the one post card from Lincoln, Nebraska. "We're closing the bill."

A few years later, Walt Hardy would leave the grounds of the estate , schoolbag on his shoulder, to join chums at the corner of Penn Avenue, as they idly hung around the bars of the great iron fence of the estate. If you were Walt Hardy you would have wanted to be with everyone else, to be like everyone else; but he had not been, and so he acquired a peculiar sympathy with his mother's flight. He grew to understand a difference between him and others, a distinction pressed like the tin ceiling of the Isaly's Dairy in Wilkinsburg and just as thin. For, every morning he left the mansion's grounds to join his schoolmates at the corner of Penn Avenue was to tell a lie that he was not responsible for, yet he could enjoy its spurious validation. He never had to say anything. Just to have the liberty of the manicured grounds within that fence, was to imply, without a word, that he belonged to its magnificence. Simply to walk through the front gate and meet his schoolmates on the corner was to suggest he had come from his own yard.

Every morning, he prepared for school as his father read-ied the Packard in the garage below for its daily rounds. Years later, Walt Hardy could still put together the stiff sound of the whisk broom brushing and brushing the tufted upholstery of the limousine's rear seat. He had gone over his morning's fabrica-tion with similar care. Something special to tell the other kids about breakfast, perhaps; the grapefruits had red cherries in their centers—he would say he didn't much care for the cherry, but the oatmeal with real cream was okay—or maybe he could say the governor had been to dinner the night before, as he actu-ally had. Some big shot. Such people came and went through the main house and special concoctions would be put together for them. Mrs. Jenkins would pull out the huge jar of maraschi-no cherries from the rear of the mammoth refrigerator and place one dead center in the halved grapefruits. He had watched her one afternoon. So on school mornings, he'd leave his father in the garage and double back around the carriage house, around the greenhouse behind the arbor and the reflecting pool so as to come out by the front steps with the lions and the unicorns on either side and from there to the main gate; an innocent tour around the circle of the driveway, the same route his father would negotiate in an hour or so behind the limousine's wheel.

"You don't live there." The charge had come one blustery morning in April with a suddenness that had almost knocked the wind from his lungs.

"Do so," was all he could say for the hurt had built up fast in his chest, his throat. Because he did live there, that was the truth; not a complete lie. Moreover, the accusation was made by a boy he especially wanted to be like, wanted to be liked by. Charlie Poremski. Black hair, green eyes, and muscular, Walt Hardy can still remember the kid. Poremski always made up the sides during recess. So, he had looked into the boy's green eyes and was sickened, skewered on their predator's gleam. "I do so," he repeated.

"You don't really live there. We watched you last week. You live over the garage. Your old man drives Miss Arnett around. He's like a nigger."

And so they fought, there on the corner of Penn Avenue against the bars of the iron fence and the great shape of the main house behind the huge rhododendrons. Wrestled more than sparred and punched at each other as the others scuffed their shoes, a few walked on. At last, he had to give in, to admit to his imposture, though they had no word for it then. He felt wrongly punished. He had never said he lived in the mansion. Even more, he was wounded by their betrayal of his innocent fiction; the idea that they had plotted and spied on him; had lain in wait to expose his innocent idyll. What harm had it done them? What harm would it ever do, you might ask, if you are Walt Hardy?

After all, he had borrowed that history, as much to entertain his schoolmates on their desultory ambles to school as to exaggerate his own life. For surely, only dull, threadbare narratives awaited them in class, and most of these accounts, they were to understand later, with as little truth in them as well. However, he had memorized the dates and names in those history lessons; when power had been acquired and by whom. And how. Miss Arnett sent him to Cornell. Charlie Poremski was to die later in Laos.

So he had borrowed a way of life, as he had borrowed a tuxedo from a friend of his father's, a butler at the Mellon's, to go to a dance at the main house. He himself had been borrowed, as the wealthy have a casual way of doing, to fill out Susanna Arnett's dance card.

This morning, a woman had come over to him on the steps of the church , a glow in her eyes similar to what he had seen in the green eyes of Eddie Poremski. She held out her hand as if she was offering him one more dance.

"Do you remember me, Walt? I'm Susanna." She blushed. Her plumpness had slipped into a powdery middle age. "My goodness, we thought you'd be in jail."

"We're appealing," he started to tell her but the details of his legal battle were not on her mind. Actually, she made it clear she had no patience for any answer. The rich have a way of controlling the conversation, mostly with a polished rudeness.

All the while, the concentrics of her pleasant face added up to a kind of amity as she added, "Aunt Peg would have been thrilled to have you here. For the will, of course, but even so—of all of us, you were a favorite, I think. So good to see you here. And you've become famous too." And she once again held out her gloved hand to him. Those white gloves, the delicious little eyelets sewn around the cuffs, the smooth texture of the linen passed from his grasp as Susanna Arnett, now Mrs. Clayton Pell III—he had kept track of her—turned back and down the steps of the church to rejoin her family, two sumptuous daughters and a strangely stooped husband, a manager of family foundations. His posture, Hardy would think, came not from his pro forma occupation with the Arnett enterprises, but from lugging the different women in his marriage from Pittsburgh to St. Martin's to Christmas Cove and back. From room to room. The strain will eventually kill him.

But, the texture of those white gloves on his fingers lingered like a half-remembered aroma, and he turned the feel of the material over in his thoughts, as Susanna turned away, this weave of her glove spinning out the memory of her plumpness that Sunday when she found him in the garage. Dressed for church then too; white anklets and white collars and lacy cuffs also around the stiffly pretty frock, though she was too old for anklets. At least, her chubby twelve or thirteen year old body looked older, more ungainly in this Sunday School outfit—soon she would wear real stockings and pigeon toe down the main aisle of Calvary on low heels—but this Sunday she was still between plump curiosity and voluptuous erudition, Hardy remembers as he looks down on the old garden. His father busies himself at the sink, turns on the water tap, then off.

"What is this white kick you're on?" Celia had asked him. She holds up the white stockings, white panties, white garter belt, and bra he'd brought her. She's ready to give everything a try. This was when things were going good, before that plane crashed in El Salvador, and he had just returned from California. The whole way across the country he had inventoried the contents of the package in the storage bin above his head, imagining each piece as she would put it on, as he took it off. "Something you're working out?" she had said with amusement.

Celia is very smart about these corners in him, it was part of her erotic kit, that intelligence. Her instinct could nose out the merest slip of a secret, turn over the most innocent seeming incident to reveal its actual motive, yen. This was a hard-earned skill, a craft even; something he respected and admired. But he had deflected her more than once, and this time with a tale so commonplace that she almost had to believe him.

"Miss Arnett had an upstairs maid who lived in a room with a dormer window that faced the garage. I would watch her at night undress." He adds one false detail, then another, as Celia holds up each article of white lingerie, puts on the white lace gloves and starts to remove her clothing . The ordinary origin of his fantasy had been protected, and he would not appear foolish before her. It has been so easy to lie.

Because the truth includes the same woman who had puffed a little as she put herself carefully into the front seat of the BMW at the curb below Calvary Church, looking back at her burly daughters in the backseat, as if they might have somehow changed into something else, or even disappeared. She had peered over the rounded rise of her shoulder to twiddle her white gloved fingers at him. That same woman, as a twelve-year-old, had poked her head around the open garage door one afternoon and found him in the backseat of the Packard, reading a book he had borrowed from her great aunt's library. *Green Mansions.*

He had become a little excited reading about Rima, the lithe, virginal huntress swinging around in the forest with hardly anything on, the muscles of her thigh tensed and kissable as she strung her bow and then this niece of Miss Arnett's pops in on him. He was afraid she'd tell about the book, afraid she'd notice the open fly of his trousers. But she tumbled into the backseat with him, unknowing and cheerful, like she has just come for a ride to the picnic, breathless and winning in her girlish way, and all at once it is still—only the voice of Bob Prince on the radio above them as his father listens to the Pirates game—they were in New York, playing the Giants. Now and then, a small ting in the hot and oily mustiness of the garage, like a tack dropping, as the Packard's engine continued to cool down.

"Sunday dinners with Aunt Peg can be a dread-ful bore," she had said, imitating some movie actress she'd seen. Katherine Hepburn, probably. But she had looked pleased with herself. "I know you—I've seen you around here. You're Walter, aren't you? Hardy's son."

"Walt," he had said. "Just Walt."

Hardy remembers her look of discomfort as she recognized she has interrupted something. Made a mistake. Her dancing school good manners told her something had been happening which she has just interrupted; something she hadn't yet learned the steps for. She shouldn't be there. She had left the mansion and wandered into forbidden territory. She had looked for diversion from the boring Sunday dinner at her aunt's table. Cold muffins left over from last night's meal, cold meat and soggy cream puffs, an array of Heinz condiments—the heiress to the Arnett fortune condemned her relatives to share her Spartan tastes—but little Susanna had wandered off and found him in the backseat of the Packard just about to free his newly risen cock from the corduroy.

And that's all that had happened which is why he had to lie to his wife, invent the story of the upstairs maid—poor old Mrs. Emerson, atrophied and fussy—because the truth of it had been so foolish, so innocent. This is a mistake people still make with Walt Hardy, reading the yearning in him to play a part in a history for the part he has actually played.

For nothing took place on the backseat of that Packard limousine. The girl had sat beside him for several minutes, thinking hard for some graceful way to get out of the car and leave him. He held the book on his lap and waited for her to leave. What was he reading, she had asked and then shrugged when he told her. She didn't know the book. The aromas of petroleum and wax coat the afternoon's rising heat. A streetcar ground by on Penn Avenue. He could tell she searched for some pleasantry, a line supposedly memorized for awkward social situations. Nothing to do but just get out of the car. She clutched the door handle. It had been nice meeting him, but she guessed she better go. She carefully closed the car door and left the garage almost on tiptoe.

Several years later, an invitation arrived to a spring dance in the mansion's upstairs ballroom. Miss Arnett opened the house up once a year to her nieces and nephews for the kind of gala her father and mother had given her. A small orchestra played Rogers and Hart, Gershwin, and, just for the novelty, a polka or two. Hardy can remember the borrowed tuxedo's tightness across his shoulders, as he stood in the line with the other boys. One or two said they knew him but couldn't exactly remember from where; so, without having to say a word, he carried off his imposture. Then, Susanna had approached with her dance card, a bountiful vision in green organdy, to further validate his invitation. She hummed in his ear, as he maneuvered her around the floor, not looking at the other boys now, not wanting to see their expressions, the smell of her coming up from her gown; a mixture of bath powder and sweat and something else he couldn't identify. She danced happily until she must have felt his discomfort, took it to be disinterest, and she excused herself from the next two numbers, going quickly toward the landing where the rest rooms were located. He had half-followed her trying to say something funny.

There, he came face-to-face with Miss Arnett. She was like an aged woman athlete, you remember her pictures; say, a famous tennis player or a golfer, but stiff and small and with a regality that had made her an equal to presidents and senators, if not kings. Or so Hardy would think. She wore a dress of dark maroon lace, he remembered, not like anything you could imagine being sold in Pittsburgh—or even New York for that matter—foreign. She also carried a fan of gray silk which she folded and tapped him on the chest with. "You must give me a dance, Walt," she had said.

Astounded that she pronounced his name so easily, as if she spoke to him every day and night and so addressed him that the very sound of his name became as familiar to her as that of one of her house servants. Indeed, as was the case, he would think. But there was also a levity in her voice, not directed at him, and walking onto the dance floor, a small, strong hand on his arm, she seemed to be playing a comic turn, one corner of her mouth slightly turned down in a kind of self-disparagement. The old heiress dancing with the kid from the carriage house. She stepped lightly and gracefully in his arms and followed his clumsy fox-trot so easily that she made him feel like Cesar Romero. She must have had years of lessons, he had thought. The floor seemed to clear for them as they turned and turned around it. Now he glanced at the other boys. Their expressions had been wonderfully stupid.

Band music marches from his father's room. The older Hardy had finished his tea and retired to pore over his stamp collection. He had given a shrug, a Pittsburgh gesture. Walt Hardy considers a stroll on the grounds of the estate. Maybe when the light failed, he would walk through the pillared alley of the arbor. Some of the wooden columns had split and would have to be replaced before the place was opened to the public. The grapes had gone wild. The forecast was for showers and so, later in the evening, fireflies might be out. But he would not try to catch them, nor be tempted by their luminous, inexplicable fire.

August 12, 1939
D.F.Saturday.

Yesterday, flying to Tampico, I was thinking of Jimmy Doolittle and how he got into that cockpit a while back, pulled a hood over his head and took off and landed without seeing the ground once. Flying blind, they called it. So, yesterday in the DC-2, I'm looking at all these instruments on the panel: Kollsman gauges, the Sperry compass, the radio gyro—flight indicators of every kind and almost more than one man can look at, and of course, I also think back to '18 and the two or three little meters jiggling on the panel of the Spad—compass and a fuel gauge, if they even worked, but *now*, thanks to Jimmy and a few others, I got all these gauges and dials in front of me and I'm still flying blind. I mean I don't know where I'm going, what my attitude is — where the ground is. You know what I mean, Molly? Where am I and where am I going?

Right now, I feel suspended in some episode that is not my doing. Roy Armstrong at the mercy of the winds. Like in a balloon but unable to return to earth. The view from my window on the sixth floor of the Hotel Regis. One more address for the record. Below is their big park. The Alameda. Goes way up towards the old center of town. Like Central Park in N.Y. The Avenue

38

Juarez. It's cooler here than Veracruz. A brochure on the night table says that the rail- road line from Veracruz to Mexico City follows the same route that "bold Cortés and his valiant crew took to attack Montezuma's barbaric strong- hold." Who writes this baloney? Valiant thugs is more like it. The first of many liberations to come. The trip took us twelve hours — all night — but it seemed as long as it must have taken el Gran Conquistador. Months, I guess. Up over mountains, around hairpin curves, down the other side — it was rougher than the 18 days on the *Sinaia*. You wondered sometimes if the train had run out of tracks and was cutting the trail as it went — like four hundred years back. Now and then, part of a moon passes from behind a cloud to make it almost bright as day. We're in and out of deep mountain passes, tunnels. Rough terrain. All around me in this upholstered par- lor car, people losing their cookies. A line has formed going out to the observation platform where comrades stand three, four abreast, spew- ing *la cocina mexicana* out over the tracks. Some doing it as they stood in line. Unable to hold back. Like a buffet on wheels, but running back- wards.

This guy sitting next to me leans over with a curious smile, likes he's going to say some- thing, then starts to choke. I push him away just in time and he nods agreeably, like I had helped him to the right direction, and pukes all over the fellow passed out on the floor at his feet. "Thanks," he says wiping his mouth, and he seems truly appreciative. He puts his hand out which I take carefully. A round, jack-o'-lantern face. "Cranston," he says. "Green Battalion. Artillery." He's waved away my introduction. "Everyone knows you. Armstrong. You're this miserable train's only hero. Everyone knows you. The returning hero." He smiles but sounds pissed at something.

He veers off again to deliver a dollop of half-digested frijoles on the guy below. We are like a couple of old vets on a park bench, just spitting and chawing over a recent battle.

This train is rocking us like something out of Coney Island. "But like all heroes, you have this brilliant simplicity. Or do I mean simple brilliance?" It's not funny. "I mean that as a compliment, old man, understand me. You really are a hero!" Now, he's almost laughing, covering his mouth up. Breath like a garbage pail. "Heroes never catch on; that's why they are heroes."

"Catch on to what?"

"That you never had a chance. Once old Joe sent in his goons, the Republic never had a chance. They knocked off Nin, didn't they? Fucked up peasant reform. Remember? That fight was about something else and it wasn't the Republic." He looks around the swaying parlor car. "Hey, you wouldn't have a smoke on you, would you?"

The guy on the floor rolls over in the goo, like he's part of a recipe, and my companion accommodates him, gives him a little more. He leans over to pull up another ingredient from his throat and spits it out. "It was a joke. Don't you get it? Where do you think Franco got the fuel to run those German tanks? Or the Stukas?" He looks at me with a bleary wisdom.

"American companies sold him the oil," I say. We knew about Texaco and such. No big surprise.

"Come now, Armstrong. American companies located in Tampico so as to circumvent Roosevelt's phony embargo act? And you don't think Cárdenas didn't know about it? Nor the US? Could not have stopped it if Cárdenas and Roosevelt were really *simpático* with the Spanish Republic? And Mexico got a cut. It was a cozy arrangement. Oh sure, Cárdenas took over the oil, but only after the war was over." He starts gagging again, but it is a false alarm.

"Heroes get ground up in the works. In their own good deeds." He looks proud of this insight, then starts coughing and coughing, dry heaves that turn him the color of Campbell's tomato soup. "You make more trouble on the ground than you do in the blue skies." His heaving brings up nothing more; his tank is on empty. "But I really like you," he says, a big smile on the pumpkin face. "Mr. Lund will like you too." There's that name again. Gen. Avila mentioned this Lund on the boat. What's this guy selling?

The same pinko baloney that Ben Lieder used to bore us with. How am I so lucky as to attract these soap boxers? Even with the train's windows wide open, the stench is more than a Christian can tolerate. Also, I've been getting a whiff of something else. While this jerk has been yammering in my ear, Señora Moreno's black muff has surfaced in my mind. The vision puts out a scent more powerful than the stench around me. Old Jack has picked up the scent and is nosing around in my pants. She's somewhere on the train. But there's more than 1500 of us packed on this express — even if I locate Mrs. Brown, where are we going to find the privacy to do the dirty deed?

"Don't go. I have to tell you something," the guy says but I push him away. He's like a drowning kitten. "Well, watch yourself," he says then dives between his knees once more. I step over bodies. It's like a battlefield before the burial details show up. Then, there's this car much like a European train with a narrow corridor on one side and compartments on the other. Some with shades up to show occupants sleeping. Some playing cards, talking. One with Gen. Avila in a packed group of a dozen or more — all smoking and talking. I recognize Siquerios, that painter who bunked next to me on the boat. Heads together, eyeball to eyeball. It's a staff meeting, plain enough, another losing battle being planned. I've sat in on enough of them to recognize what's going on.

I keep going. Then, I round the polished veneer bulkhead of the car's foyer and she's there. She's been coming from the other direction, from the head of the train. Against me, smelling hot and sweaty. A strong woman smell that makes Jack stand to attention.

"Oh, Juan..." She's reaching down my corpus, grabs hold of my thick money belt. "_Dios mio_"! An honest mistake, I'm thinking, but who am I set her straight? "I have just been looking for you, my brave comrade."

"And I you, baby." My hands are on her behind which is muscular and hard for its size. Her dress is thin and all she has on, I'm sure of it. "We got to settle this score," I say in her ear. She's licking my face, my neck.

The train jolts around a sharp curve and throws us against the other side of the companionway. Jack pokes into her and she lets go of my money belt and grabs the real McCoy. "Ahh," she pants. "What score?"

No time for translation. "How about the platform. Out there?"

"_No, no, no,_" She is breathing like a steamroller. Her tongue is halfway down my throat. I have a hand between her legs and she is going limp. I'm ready to do it right there in the corridor. I start to pull up her dress and she stops me. "_Espera...espera...aquí._" She pulls me around the turn of the paneling by guess-what.._"Aquí.Here...en el lavabo._"

The small door of the toilet is banging in time to the train's violent sway. Cool moonlight filters through a frosted glass window to highlight the round metal sink in one corner, the porcelain commode with a polished wood seat jammed next to it. I visualize her, see both of us, on that seat, on the sink, hanging from the metal basket bolted to the wall. Other interesting concepts. The possibilties turn up the heat. "I must making excuse to _el general._ Then, I come back _pronto, mi caballeriza, mi jaca_ and we have..." and she says something I can't make out because her tongue is straightening out my middle ear. But I get her meaning. She gives Jack a final squeeze and goes like silk unwinding down the corridor. I go into the W.C.,further reconnoitering the place for its usage. Not a lot of room but the challenge of its confinement will make for interesting inventions.

Suddenly, the thought comes to me: I never heard of any Green Battalion of artillery. Who was that guy in the parlor car kidding? But then something else hits me. It was like coming out of a 9-G pull-out—one where you leave your ass behind. The tail just came off — like the screw has dropped out, and your butt stays put as you zoom up and away from it. Except this time the pullout is accompanied by a hot stream, a jet of liquid, boiling and stinging, that had raced around the tight turns of my intestines and then peeled off for a dive straight down the chute. Like a Stuka. I just barely get my pants down and squat over the seat when the stuff shoots out of me like cooked lye. Suddenly, I'm sicker than a dog. The other end is busy too, and I find myself almost laughing as I throw up. Just seconds before, the same close fittings had inspired quite a different activity. But now, I'm thinking, how convenient. I can sit on the toilet with my head in the sink. Both ends of me working overtime. I had kicked the little door shut, and during this painful delirium, I saw the handle turn once and then again. Someone tapped, scratched against the door. If it was Consuelo, I couldn't care less.

Nor could I find her or the general in the Mexico City station in the morning. But I'm in no condition to look. My stomach was digesting itself and seemed ready to explode again. The sun had just been reinvented that morning, brand-new. I almost fall out onto the platform with my bags, one more victim to be sacrificed to Montezuma's eagles. And here's another. I'm pushed aside by some medics carrying a stretcher. It's the guy from last night. The self-appointed volunteer of the mythical Green Battalion. His little round head rolls back and forth and that big smile is on his face. You might say, he's grinning from ear to ear. Whoever handled the knife had nearly taken his head off.

One of Montezuma's warriors materializes before me. But he's wearing a little cap that has a crown on it and the name Hotel Regis. He takes my bags before I can hand them to him. "*Lo mas selecto, señor,*" he is saying and I couldn't care less. I can hardly walk. Select me there, pronto, I manage to say.

Then everything goes blank. I am part walking and part leaning against this little Mexican who huffs and puffs. Noise and noise and more noise. Whistles blowing, police whistles. I'm tumbled into a taxi, face down against the leather upholstery. I pass out again.

The car stops. My angel — and that's his real name — hands me off like luggage. Carried indoors. Front desk bells ting-ting. Whirrs of machinery. Lifted again and hoisted to this room that overlooks the Alameda where I make these notes.

Here's what started today's episode, boys and girls. Today's newspaper. They have identified the guy on the train. I recognize his picture. He must be important for them to have a picture of him. Same Halloween jack-o'-lantern. Another Huck Sawyer in banana land. What I can make out from the Spanish, he was cut up during a card game. No one knows who did it. But get this. He had never been to Spain! He hadn't even been on our boat! Some sort of sales representative for an engineering firm. He had been in Veracruz on business, the report says. You meet guys like that who want to be part of something, falsify their papers. His name wasn't Cranston either. "Watch yourself," he had said. Okay, pal. Thanks.

My copilot is a kid named Miguel Garro. He has only a few hours on multi-engine and comes courtesy of the Mexican government, representing the 90% of crew the local politicos demand. Usually, I let him take over once airborne. He watches all these gauges and instruments as if they are about to predict rain. Like the old signs in the guts of a chicken. He has that long-faced, dreamy look that most of them show down here, like the Aztec warriors you see in the museum. So, if these instruments are a difference for me of twenty years, what must this technology seem like to him?

Maybe the two of us are trying to fly our different ways out of the same dream. Or is it a nightmare?

Funny to see Junkers tri-motors hauling passengers around here also. This time last year, I knocked down my third one of those babies over Madrid and if I may remind the gods once again, my thousand bucks for that kill, along with the rest, is still impounded in a frog bank. The Germans are flying these Junkers on their own commercial routes down here, but they are no competition for George Rhyl with planes like this Douglas. We're beating them silly. We can cruise at 180 MPH!

—I'm sorry sir...George Rhyl hardly looks up from the papers on his desk...but we can't hire any more Americans for a while. —Gordon Berry is flying some routes up north. Try him.

—Who says I'm an American...I say to him and I put my papers in front of him. —According to El Presidente Cárdenas, I'm a Mexican citizen as of last June when I got in from Spain.

Rhyl looks over my papers. Couldn't care less. He looks again, then pushes back his chair. His eyes go wide. He's seen my name.

—Holy Smokes! It's you. Armstrong. I heard you were in the country, Roy — he sticks out his hand — ever fly one of these Douglas transports?

So, here I am, adjusting gauges and gadgets smarter than me. No wind in the puss. Trying to keep my horizon level with or without an instrument.

Yesterday morning we're nudging 12,000 feet over Lake Texcoco, on a course to Tampico roughly following the road to Pachuca. The engines are harmonious. All these modern conveniences are flying the plane. In back, one of the generals we are flying has whipped out a guitar and I can hear pleasant chords now and then. Miguel, sleepy eyed but alert to the quivering needles and gauges in front of us, folds his large hands in his lap. I take out the letter from R. C. Putnam.

Ground fire brought Putnam down in '18 and he spent the rest of the war eating knockwurst, so it comes as no surprise to me that he is now an aide to Tooey Spatz. He answers me and not Tooey. He's too busy to write an old buddy from 29th who has recently embarrassed the Air Service by flying for the forces of capital D-damn-democracy.

Putnam has no news. He tells me flying for a foreign country has cost me my commission as well as my citizenship. Same old story. But they are trying to help me. Congress is crazy for MacArthur and his tank people. Army Air is getting peanuts. And Roosevelt is an old Navy man. Flying against the new German fighters could turn me into a "consultant." But then there's the Dies committee that thinks I'm a Red. A disloyal American. The Service could maybe try the same angle they did with Lindbergh, he says. Meanwhile, stay close to the American consulate in Mexico City. Then, this final note: _I ran into Roscoe Turner at the Cleveland Air Show. He asked that I pass on his best to you. He told me a wild story about you and Jean Harlow when you all were making that war film out in Hollywood. Is true?_

That big-mouth Turner!

Lake Texcoco is not much of a lake any more, all dried up to a puddle of its original, outlines of which you can see, from this altitude; the darker greenness the old moisture still feeds. So big once that Cortés had to build sailing ships to launch his final attack on Montezuma. Then, just off to our right is Teotihuacan. Nobody knows much about this place, the people that lived there hundreds of years before JC—not even the Aztecs knew about this city. From 12,000 feet, boulevards laid out straight and square. Huge buildings like the pyramids in Egypt. I could put this DC-2 right down on that main avenue — it's like a runway!

The ruins of civilizations, dried up, overgrown and plundered by people like me who are the end result of those civilizations. Makes you wonder.

All those gigantic stone pyramids at Teotihucan, put together to make sense of the stars, the rotation of the earth and the rest of it ends up on this instrument panel in front of me; these fancy gadgets I can work because I've read the manual — but how they work or why they work, I'm as much in the dark as that Indian astronomer two thousand years ago who cut chicken throats to make the sun return. Well, who can say that didn't work?

I'm not so sure we've come so far from those sun worshippers down there in Teotihucan. We've risen higher according to our own altimeters but that's only due to a couple of Wright Cyclones. Nothing more. The whole eastern coastline of Mexico stretched out before me, and I'm riding the crystal clear air like one of Montezuma's warriors hoped to do when he came back as an eagle. Or was that a butterfly? Where are all these wonderful gadgets taking us? Not just to Tampico, I bet.

I put the ship into a long power glide that will take us in over the Carpintero Lagoon, the baseball field, the cemetery, and Gringolandia, as the natives call the American part of town. Dead ahead, across the Chairel Lagoon, are the lofty spires of Texaco and International Petroleum and Cherokee Oil. All taken over now by the Mexicans. We're letting down a little too fast — the field's clean pavements still a ways yet — so I nod to Miguel and he sets the flaps. Then, I pass him the controls as well. Take my hands off the wheel. The automatic pilot's off, we're back to the old ways. His eyes go wide — the first real expression I've ever seen him make. He didn't expect this — landing the ship himself. I'm not sure why I gave him the controls, not sure he could handle them — but it didn't seem to matter right then. You want to learn all about these wonderful gadgets, you want to run them, you want to become a hero like Juan Carillo, sweetheart? Be part of the glorious 20th Century? Okay, go to it. *Arréglelo, amigo.*

I couldn't have made a better landing. A perfect three-pointer.

Sept 5, 1939
Tuesday

Back in Mexico last evening — down here they don't use the *City* part of the name — I stop off at Sanborns for some eats on the way back to the hotel from the airport. This is about the only decent place I've found to eat in this burg. It's in a pretty building, all blue tile on the outside and quite old. The restaurant is in what had been the interior courtyard of a palace, built by one of Cortés's sidekicks, all closed in now but the fountain in the center bubbling and the hitch rings for horses still in the walls but the waitresses in starched dresses and little white caps like parlor maids. You can get a pretty fair meal here — even a hamburger that's not too bad. Apple pie.

You can bet, I'm an expert on pie crust, Molly. Oh, McGee, not that old beef again.

Raising dough, as Uncle Billy used to say of mother. Maybe raising daisies now as well. No word from the lady in a long time. The waitress who brought me my pie and coffee is wearing the same kind of apron and frilly hat as the waitresses in the photographs on the wall by the cash register, this earlier bunch serving some of Zapata's men. His army occupied the city during the Revolution in 1910 — several times — and it looks like they took their meals at Sanborns too. But a strange picture. These campesinos, one or two with wide straw sombreros clamped on their heads and the muzzles of their carbines leaning against the counter, being served *huevos rancheros* by women dressed up for a high-class English melodrama. They ought to be serving sherry.

This morning when I adjusted the throttles to put the engines into synch, if I could have adjusted the same kind of harmony within me and seen it measured by an instrument. See the truth of it quivering on the dash.

What am I really trying to synchronize? Not these Mexicans and their history. They're doing okay without me, *muchas gracias*. Because I'm thinking of another picture; one hanging on my bedroom wall in New Haven, long ago. The same uniform, cap, and apron, puffed out sleeves as on the waitresses at Sanborns. That picture cut out from the *Hartford Register*. It hung over my bed at Aunt Flora's.

Mrs. Horace B. Armstrong of New Haven, Conn. demonstrates her prize winning recipe for Hot Cross Buns using Fleischmann's patented Red Star Yeast cake.

I'd stare into those eyes, trying to look under whatever shaded them as she bent over the worktable. Women sitting around her, watching her demonstration. Looked like a school cafeteria. Hands deep in the sticky stuff. "She's out raising dough," Uncle Billy would say again and laugh and laugh. What a card! "Winnifred is just a wonder." He'd shake his head like she was one of these new—fangled contraptions — like this aeroplane of these Wright Brothers, for instance, that somehow worked but had no real future to it. Just another gadget, he used to say. Oh, my.

Dealing out the cards around the tall glasses of lemonade, Aunt Flora always told how her sister had gone down to the Fleischmann people in Peekskill, N.Y. and talked her way into a job. Just talked her way in — well, you know Winnie, she'd say, snapping the cards. Her idea was to use the Herrman family recipes to demonstrate this new product around the country. Fleischmann's Yeast. Home Demonstration Units, they called them, were all over the map. Mostly in rural places, small towns, showing farm women how to put up vegetables and fruits, make clothes and quilts, and why not how to turn out bread and cakes? Why not show these housewives the con- venience of using Red Star Yeast that came in the neat, tinfoil-wrapped cakes; each cake the exact measurement needed for a recipe? What an idea, they said! Where have you been, little lady?   Just come right in and put on this starched apron and this frilly cap to keep that high piled hair out of the way and get out there and show them how to use Fleischmann's Yeast. Sell it! Raise that dough!

   "Be my Valentine—your mother." The mucilage of flour and water has gone powdery and the paper   doily   came   loose   after   a   month. Underneath a recipe for Bohemian Houska.

   So, looking for diversions from these _pen- samientos serios,_ I leave Sanborns and go back to the Regis and stroll into the Don Quixote night club just as the first show commences. This dance company of about a half dozen dancers or so have been putting on floor shows at the Don Quixote for the last month, for the tourists. They do native dances based on some of the old legends. "The Childhood of Sun and Moon." "The Corn Woman's Marriage." "The Flood." And so on.
   Take the last one for example. It's about the lone survivor of the flood who has a dog that cooks for him. All the while this dog is grinding the corn to make the tortillas, pat- ting the meal flat on the _metate_   and putting the cakes on the fire.   One day this lone sur- vivor discovers that all this time the dog is actually a woman. Hot doggy! So he marries her. Men do not live by tortillas alone, it seems. That's the message, I guess. In any event, he doesn't want to lose the cook. Come to think of

it, this story sounds familiar. Might have been sponsored by Fleischmann's Yeast. Except, there's no yeast in tortillas. Anyway, they produce a new race of humans. So much for the program notes.

I know this number by heart, because I've seen it several times mainly because of the dancer who does the dog part. I've been watching her. She's in the other numbers, but "The Flood" is her big role. I take my usual table at floor side just as the number starts. Flutes and tiny drums and gourd rattles accompany the dancers. Not so much music as a kind of irritant in the ear; not entirely unpleasant. The program calls it "*música típica del Mixteco*". The waiters, mostly cousins of Angel, my guardian angel, all know me and think I'm a real culture lover. But it's the girl-dog. *Eso es en pocas palabras!* Or in a couple of nutshells.

Which she has on her fingers and taps together along with the flutes. Costumes look like the wall paintings, the stone figures in the Museo Nacional but made of papier mâché. And it's not like dancing you see just anywhere — very athletic and arms out, feet firmly planted on the floor. Smack. Smack. Arms out. There go the flutes. Smack, smack go the feet. Arms raised, bent at the elbow. Feet smack again. Here a rattle, there a rattle. Smack-smack. Flute and drum, another turn on the rattle. Smack-smack.

So, I guess it's her feet that get me. They are big feet for a woman. Long and flat. And narrow. When she strikes them on the floor, you know it! But they are strangely delicate too and take odd angles, the way the tendons come into the heel and the slope of the instep. The pinkish ball of the heel. Kind of sweet almost. What's that song? She wears boxes without topses...etc. The way they look when she's the dog laying out the tortillas on the *metate*, blowing up the fire to cook them — at these times these feet of hers become — well, how to say it? Strong and fragile all at once.

Not counting the big blocky headdress, a snake, and some large blossoms like zinnias,

she's still on the tall side. Her profile looks
fierce, not the banana nose of the Indian but
a long blade and with a flare into delicate
nostrils. Eyes of obsidian. Cheekbones high and
mouth wide, heavy lipped. There's nothing to
laugh about in these numbers so I've never seen
her smile. The costumes hide the rest of her,
but her arms are often bare. Strong looking.
She's of a coffee color. Her name is China.

T hough it is a Lincoln that Bill Hardy polishes these days;
that yesterday, if you remember, carried both father and son to
the church and then out to the cemetery in Homestead as Walt
watched his father, about to become the former chauffeur,
become the associate curator, methodically shift gears and
check the rearview mirror. Every moment reminded him of the
man's careful rightness behind the other mirror that turned in
his memory of other times. This morning, Bill Hardy has
parked the midnight blue limousine on the concrete apron of the
garage to dust it off and flick at the hood, the headlights, the
fenders with a soft chamois. Then, bending over to wipe around
one headlamp, and then the other, he becomes foreshortened by
the height and angle of the window from which he has been
watched by Walt who, at last, leaves the window to finish dressing. It is the same small bedroom where he had put on school
clothes, pulled on jeans for Sunday doubleheaders at Forbes
Field, dressed here every morning of his life down to that last
investment made for him, a tweed suit from Horne's which he
knew, even as he pulled on the scratchy trousers, would be all
wrong at Cornell; made him look like a junior member of a
Pittsburgh accounting firm. It would make him look different
from the other freshmen.

But Miss Arnett had taken him downtown and sat in a wing
chair in the men's department to give directions with her ebony
cane to the manager and clerks who had sprung from the racks
and cubbies with jackets and suits like courtiers who had been
entombed with a ruler and suddenly brought back to life from
their sealed off, worsted graves by this new ruler; as if only
waiting for this diminutive local empress to lift their spell. He

remembers standing by as entire outfits were put together that he would later sell in Ithaca to buy something more suitable, easier to wear. Sweaters and slacks, sport jackets, shirts and ties —everything matching, coordinated to some paradigm Miss Arnett had in her mind of what a young collegiate should wear. She seemed to have dressed him from the pages of an old *Esquire* magazine or from the glossy photographs that curled up in lobby displays of the Nixon Theatre, images of a young Robert Young or a Gene Raymond, holding slim-stemmed briars at the *V* of their cashmeres, eager to pledge their ukuleles—their everything.

"Where are you calling from?" he was to ask Celia.

"Don't try to find me." She would pause to laugh, because she had caught his thought in midflight. "I've been doing the books for a real estate firm here, but I'm getting itchy feet. Okay *here* is Indiana—not too far away from Pittsburgh. I guessed you might be going to the funeral." Then, as if to second-guess him again, she would add. "But, in fact, I'm leaving tomorrow—going west, like they say."

"Where?"

"Anywhere that's warmer than Indiana," she would continue pleasantly, and this sound of her pressed on the bruise within him. But she would continue, "...almost missed the obit in the *Times*. Not so very large as I might have expected, four down from the guy who did things with soy beans and a peculiar tone to it as well. Did you get that? The kind of spin they put on the reason for her making the *Times* at all? The last surviving Arnett, the last child of Pittsburgh industrialist and financier and the rest. Like she was the last of a parakeet species, the Monongahela Parochito, for example, to fall off its perch in the Pittsburgh Zoo."

No one talked exactly as Celia did, combinations of images that had always tickled him, language put together in such a way so it constructed a place for herself as well, a special corner within the conversation. In the old days, he had heard her perform this trick many times. He listened intently to the sounds of her voice in his ear, relishing the liquidity of the vowels, the lilt of line, as if these vibrations against his eardrum might transform themselves into something more substantial—something he could touch or hold.

"...and I thought I should call and offer my condolences—if that's the right word for it."

"I can't tell you how much..."

"Yes, I know. But I don't think we can be right any more, Walt. I think we were probably only supposed to have a hot week-end but it somehow stretched out to twenty years. That was bad luck, a trick of the gods." She stops talking, as if to let her words clear the apex of their pronouncement, then coast down into his hearing before she says anything more. When she speaks it is in the voice of a best friend, "Find somebody." But the sound is off-hand, maybe looking away when she spoke. Perhaps she has a dog or a cat, Walt thinks. Or perhaps she has found somebody. "You must have your pick of the Washington Groupie Pool these days. Those little twinkies break out into orgasmic hives just being around criminals like you. Sorry, that's not what I meant."

"Yes, it is." She was making him smile, even though the cool tenor of her voice had hurt him a little.

"Yes, it is." She would pause again. Some other activity off the phone has drawn her attention once more. He feels her being patient, as if he was the one who had called her, and she's waiting for him to hang up. He tries to furnish where she was calling from with items borrowed from their past, from the house in New York or Silver Springs. She'd be talking from a kitchen phone, probably next to the dish cabinet, near the sink. It would be, he subtracted an hour's time, a little after five there so she would be having a drink—a diet Coke. A twist of lemon.

"Well, I only called to offer, maybe condolences is the right word after all. And I promise not to keep calling you when I see obituaries of people we knew. But, I feel like part of the family too, carriage house division, you will say—and by marriage even, but it's something anyway. You see, Walt Hardy, I still love you, but I wish I didn't." She seemed to be putting something away, a belonging maybe. Her voice had become a little strained. "So, are you going to Pittsburgh for the funeral? Don't forget your raincoat."

"In fact, I'm on my way to the airport," he would say. He doesn't mention the will, the letter from the lawyers, the memorandum; all in the attache case Celia had given him. William and Walt Hardy, father and son, both named heirs and parties to the last will and testament of Elizabeth Spencer Arnett. "Celia, I'm going on to Kansas City and then Denver. Part of this chicken dinner circuit I'm doing, almost like the old days. How about meeting me in one of those places? You can do some shopping." Some of the old joke.

He was hoping to wake her feelings, remind her of the breathtaking circuit they had ridden in the 60's when everything was to be dared, everything seemed possible; crazy schemes dreamed in small towns in the Catskills and along the Hudson. She has been saying she hadn't liked the company he kept these days; the silver jowled men and their Nancy Reagan clones; so very different from the farmers, or the small town hardware dealers they used to meet in the back rooms of village cafés, or the off-season, closed-up, dark lobbies of resort hotels where these ordinary people would whisper, look around the vacant rooms like being in a spy movie they'd seen; then, signal their switch to the Senator, to vote in the committee against LBJ's stand-in; sometimes because of the war. "My grandson just got called up," one might say. Or, on other nights, Hardy had learned to sit patiently and in silence, letting the hate build up like river ice in eyes growing hard in the glow of a Genesee Beer sign over the bar, letting the general malaise that rose from the frost-held ground that spring find its way through a committeeman's system, a decent husband and father of three, maybe even the treasurer of the Cairo Rotary, until the anger came up like cold vomit. "That goddamn Johnson is turning everything over to the niggers. I'll go with Bobby."

So, it would have been for the wrong reasons sometimes, or what Celia said, all along, had been for the wrong means. But a vote is a vote. If you're part of a revolution, if you're 28 years of age—let's remember—and a small part of a revolution that was on its way to being successful (all the polls were pointing that way) you worry about the IOUs later. And that's probably how some of this business began, Celia would say later, when things had begun to go wrong for them, after the unctuous voices on the phone started to turn her stomach, and the stiff women she was supposed to be "just girls" with began to look to her like enameled lizards. "Aren't you worried about some of these deals" she had said a couple of times. But his focus those winter and spring evenings in towns like Athens and

Cairo, Red Oaks Mills and Monticello had been to put together a bloc of votes; say, squeezing some dairy farmer for a vote that turned out not to matter anyway, but then to get back to the motel where Celia waited for him, and all the rush and heat of that afternoon's small triumph still pumping through him.

So to do some shopping, had become their special joke, a code word, because usually these towns only had a Mayberry's or a local Home Demo Thrift Store, not always open at that. Celia would spend time with the wives, helping him without knowing she was, because of the way she had of sitting down with these country women and talking as if picking up on a conversation that had only been interrupted to say The Pledge of Allegiance. Then, the odd, dumpy motels. It had been very sexy.

The sense of power, of doing something really important, if you're 28, is hard to deny. Especially certain moments, like first thing back at the room, he'd dial the state chairman's private number, Celia waiting in the stiff bedclothes, as John Burns tells him he had done well with that Middletown committee vote. Little victories that had teased them all with the promise of the ultimate triumph. Until of course the night at the Ambassador Hotel so some of them—and Walt Hardy is one of this number—were left with their hands outstretched, the prize just a fingertip beyond their reach. Or like someone cast in a spell, he once said to Celia. "Wake up," she replied. "Strike a match, for Christ's sake."

Nor was anything to come of their happy embraces after he hung up the phone. It must be the chicken dinners, they had first laughed. It must be the altitude. It must be her. It must be him. It must be the times. Celia never got pregnant.

"No thank you very much," her voice will have been saying from Indiana. "I've done my share of those gigs. But I guess it's a living."

"I hate these appearances. But, you wouldn't believe my lawyer's fees," he would reply. Urgent suddenly, he has eyed a travel clock, thinking of his plane and then making the flight with only minutes to spare in order to face the plastic face of the Iron City Beer clock set askew on the bureau of this small room on the floor above the garage. He can't remember the space being so jammed with oversized furniture, all from the mansion. The hands of the clock are stopped at noon or midnight, but it is midmorning as he gets dressed, and the rain has just let up. He has returned to Pittsburgh and its weather.

Not so bad for the half-century mark, Walt Hardy thinks and checks himself out in the mirror as he pulls on his jacket. The wardrobe had come from the servants' wing on the third floor of the mansion, carried over to the coach house so it had not so much changed status as changed buildings. In fact, come to think of it, the day he started high school, all the furniture in his room had been changed, everything in one afternoon. He'd come home from those first day's classes in algebra and civics to find his room completely different. His father had smiled as if in apology; then shrugged and checked the meatloaf browning in the oven. It had been Miss Arnett's idea.

The small bed and chest and storage bins his mother had painted with bright reds and blues and yellows had been removed, exchanged for these somber oak pieces hauled down from the huge attic under the mansion's mansard roof. But the wardrobe had come from Mrs. Emerson's room on the third floor, and it still smelled of the sachet envelopes she must have slipped into the folds of her clothing like secret billet-doux. Miss Arnett had not replaced her when she died; an upstairs maid was no longer required—if she had ever been really needed.

Walt Hardy had been a scrawny kid in this wardrobe's mirror. His wiry build pleased him now, but back then he practiced Charles Atlas' isometric exercises. He had sent for the muscle man's program from an ad in the back of an old pulp magazine that had been his father's, G-8 & His Battle Aces. Bill Hardy had a stack of them by his bed, and he would spend rainy Saturdays in a used magazine store on the South Side, looking for more. Every morning, young Walt would dutifully pump up his thin biceps, looking vainly in this same mirror for the blush of a pectoral on his chicken rib cage. He faithfully observed the rules for a healthful, strong physique. Five minutes of deep breathing before the open window every morning. But, his father's cooking never included the grains and light meats recommended. Nor were the creamy leftovers sent over from the mansion acceptable. Sometimes they had apples but that was about all the fresh fruit their diet ever included. He did drink a lot of milk. Self-abuse was hard to avoid, and besides, wasn't it like exercising a muscle? This particular omission in the regimen eventually made him question the whole discipline. That Charles Atlas had not thought to apply his isometric procedures to the development in this area made young Walt look closer at the man's photograph in the booklet. All of the musculature stood out, splendidly enhanced by a wide-armed pose that seemed capable of grappling a bear. But the skin tight swim trunks showed less of a bump than what poked out from his own jockey shorts. Young Walt lost faith in the whole program.

Dressed for school in the wardrobe mirror, he'd turn away, not wanting to look too correct, but to leave something undone, so as not to stand out too much. But, on this particular morning, he carefully adjusts the slim lapels of a Brooks Brothers camel hair jacket and grimaces in Mrs. Emerson's mirror at the TV personality he has become. A reflection in the glass that was as fleeting as the upstairs maid's had been, he reminds himself. She's probably buried in Homestead Cemetery also, perhaps in a section near the Arnett mausoleum but off to one side from where they had gathered yesterday; an area where servants and family pets were buried. Unknown soldiers.

His father must have carried some of this heavy furniture over from the main house. Everything on loan. Ruth Hardy had long disappeared by then. He had meant to ask his father about that day when everything had been switched, but he had been afraid he might embarrass his father with the exposure; that afternoon when he had been reduced from chauffeur to ordinary handyman. What had happened to that bed with the bright flowers and the little girl with a watering can pasted to its headboard? A few clipped words from Miss Arnett. "Hardy, do give these fellows a hand. You know where everything should go." Something like that, and it was done.

So father and son, man and boy, and finally two men with all the different shifts and changes in between, the secrets of life and the simple routines that men keep secret from each other. Both of them getting out of bed in the morning to follow their different routes, standing before mirrors, pulling on socks and shoes. Moving through these four rooms on the second floor of the carriage house. They neatly shared the one bathroom, and sometimes used the same tube of Burma Shave. The apartment's interior was finished from floor to ceiling in narrow lapstrakes of oak turned black beneath generations of old varnish, so at night, lying in bed, Walt Hardy would imagine that he was inside the hull of a boat, a Viking ship that had been turned upside down to protect him from the elements. He had been landed, after a long and perilous voyage, and now slept beneath the same small craft that had brought him to this strange shore.

Food was also sent over as well as furniture. Hot, covered dishes from Mrs. Jenkins's high-ceilinged kitchen usually promised more than what lay beneath their silvered domes; something more exciting than the plain fricassees and New England boiled dinners that his father would uncover with a flair. Even then, he would wonder at Miss Arnett's tastes—she who could have anything to eat but preferred this tasteless food—but the hot rolls and breakfast buns were delicious. So, his father's way with a skillet became exceptional, and by comparison, even exotic as the two of them "batched it," to use Bill Hardy's term. His father would entertain him as he cooked for them, stories about his days in the West, planting trees and digging irrigation ditches.

"Hey, we're just a couple of galoots riding the rails" he'd say, twirling the frying pan and juggling two or three eggs in his other hand.

"Oh, Dad...don't...don't," young Walt would cry and giggle so hard he'd lose his breath, have to hold on to the kitchen tabletop. And Bill Hardy would stretch his eyes and obey.

He made a delicious hash from the beef of the flavorless boiled dinners sent over from the main house. For hours, wonderfully long hours it seemed to the boy, he would watch his father chop onions, potatoes, green peppers, and celery, then add them to the beef that had been put through a silvery meat grinder clamped to the edge of the kitchen table—Walt got to turn the crank—and then the whole gorgeous mess of it slowly cooked in the big skillet with paprika and black pepper,lots of pepper, so the hot, spicy smell, the greasy richness of the meat and the onions and potatoes coming together, started the juices in his mouth and set his feet drumming against the legs of the kitchen chair. It was a recipe learned in the CCC, Bill Hardy told the boy.

Sometimes, his father would make a kind of nest out of the cooked hash, and lay into it the neat, round jewel of a butter-fried egg. It was at moments like this, just as the yellow yolk ruptured and all its goodness flowed into the peppery melange that held it, that Walt Hardy imagined no better place in the world than this small kitchen over the garage, and no better companion than this man in his shirt sleeves and vest who methodically prepared and cooked such wondrous food. That Charles Atlas would declare such food unhealthy only raised more suspicions about the muscle builder.

Why had his mother left such tasty meals? Her absence caused him a little confusion at first. Then, he learned to slip questions he had about her disappearance into a kind of file within him. To be answered later. Sometimes, looking up at the great Viking hull above his bed, he would decide the Greek magician had hypnotized her; that she had gone downtown for an innocent diversion from her duties as Miss Arnett's housekeeper, had walked into the Stanley for the matinee on her afternoon off and the guy had put a spell on her as she sat there in the audience, nibbling a Reese's Chocolate Cup. She walked up on stage in a trance and out of their lives, never looking back.

So growing up was like being on a kind of camp-out; boy and man and then, the two men; keeping a strange sort of outpost together; isolated but maybe meant to be only temporary—perhaps the orders for their fort had been misrouted. The courier had been killed. He had seen movies like that with Victor MacLaglen and Gary Cooper. Even now, he can't quite put a name to it. "It was in the CCC," his father would say. "I took up cooking in the CC Corps." And he'd shrug and half laugh as he served up some more of the hash or maybe take from the fridge a cake he'd put together out of lady fingers from the main house and some Isaly's strawberry ice cream he'd picked up. The sound of the word—the corps—turned fancifully in the boy's imagination; basting the image of that camaraderie his father had known as a young man; the smell and feel of men cooking and living together as they pursued a common venture. Building reservoirs.

The two of them never lacked for anything; everything came from the main house. Eventually, even television. "Why don't we get a TV?" Walt asked one night when he was fourteen. He had finished racking the dishes on the small kitchen sink. Bill Hardy was adjusting the old radio on the side table next to his recliner. A program of music. "The Series is going to be on television. I'll give you points on Philadelphia."

"Well, Miss Arnett said she might give us hers when she got a new one," his father said and turned to the sports section of the *Press*.

"That's it? We wait for her to give us one? Like one of her charities?"

He had been reading *On Walden Pond*. Thoreau roughing it in the woods, answering and beholden to no one, had fired a revolt in him. Later, in a literature class at Cornell, a cynical teacher had suggested that the hermit sometimes walked home to his mother's house for supper. Hardy had felt a window close. But earlier, he was all on fire. "We can buy one. Do we have to wait for her to hand one down to us?"

"We're doing all right," his father had said and carefully unfolded the evening paper.

And they did get a television set. After Edward R. Murrow did his program on Senator Joe McCarthy, Miss Arnett gave them the small RCA model from her bedroom parlor. She got rid of all her television sets at the same time.

So, now, even in the passenger seat of the Lincoln, the same foreshortening trick of before seems to be played on his father. Bill Hardy seems to have got shorter than Walt remembered, more compact. Growing up, Hardy could never find himself in his father's stocky physique, never could he fit his own scrawny kid makeup within the man's stature, nor can he see any resemblance in their profiles as they drove downtown. "You took after your mother's side." Bill Hardy often told him.

"Never a word from her—not even now," he says as they turn onto Fifth Avenue. He could remember the mansions that once lined this boulevard, a Pittsburgh upper-class duplication of the New York street of the same name. Most of the old houses had been torn down, replaced by box-like apartments. "You'd think she might have seen an obituary wherever she is. Given you a call." Maybe call me, he thinks. Celia had called him.

His father continues to steer the limousine without speaking, letting the Lincoln roll along in the right lane at just the exact twenty-five mile per hour limit; no more, no less. He was the kind of driver that made his son grind his teeth whenever he got behind someone like him. After long seconds he replies. "I don't think she's alive."

"No kidding. What makes you think that, Dad?"

The other's shoulders raise slightly. "I don't know for sure. I used to get Christmas cards, you know, mailed from San Diego. No return address on them. This last Christmas, I got none. But then, she and Peggy Arnett didn't get on well." The familiarity reversed the roles, the employer put on the same nominative level as the servant; yet the name was pronounced a little too casually. "I think she left Arnett as much as she left me." He pauses, like taking his foot off the gas pedal. "Us."

Walt Hardy nods and looks back through the rear window. An impatient driver behind them, blinks her lights. When, she guns around them, the young woman flicks a finger, but his father doesn't notice.

He wears the black worsted suit of his uniform, a white shirt and dark maroon silk tie. He did not wear the black, hard-billed chauffeur's cap which normally was fitted squarely on his head. Sometimes, in summer, Bill Hardy would wear a pair of aviator type sunglasses of a bluish tint, his son remembers, and they gave him a rakish appearance the boy wished his father would adopt more often. On Sunday afternoons, when Miss Arnett did not need to be driven anywhere, the two of them might drive out to the airport to watch the planes land and take off. Young Walt would imagine that people would think this man walking beside him, in uniform, wearing a military cap and a pair of tinted sunglasses, was an airline pilot—not a chauffeur. Then, such a thought would embarrass him, and he would quickly take his father's hand, squeeze it.

"I had something to do with her leaving, I guess."

"Why do you say that?" Bill Hardy says and slowly lets the car coast to a stop at the intersection. The blonde who had passed them has also been stopped by the traffic light. Walt Hardy catches her eye and smiles cheerily. She sticks out her tongue and busies herself with something on the dashboard.

"I don't know. This morning I was thinking of that furniture Mom had fixed for me, those farmers and animals she painted on the bed and the bookcases and how all that was moved out and.."

"Well, that was long after Ruth left," the older man corrects him. He always referred to his mother by name, so sometimes it seemed they weren't talking about the same woman.

"Yes, I know. I know that." They were coming into Oakland now. Forbes Field, long torn down and replaced by U Pitt buildings. But inside one of them, inlaid into the floor in the exact spot, is the brass replica of home plate. Something to be said for a place with that kind of sentiment, Walt Hardy often boasted to people.

"This was before the war," his father is saying. "I was just out of the CCC." His right hand moved to the knob of the gear lever to shift down for the traffic. Miss Arnett had always ordered standard shifts. Hardy has continued. "I sometimes wish I had been different for you, Walter."

"How do you mean?"

"Oh, I don't know. More colorful or something like that."

"You've been first class. Hey, you're my Dad!" Walt grips the older man's shoulder. Still pretty solid.

In fact, Bill Hardy lifts that shoulder but whether to receive or ward off the honor—his son isn't sure which. "Well, anyway, I was about to get drafted. Ruth and I were just married."

"Then I happened, right?" The history was not new to him.

"...and Miss Arnett had been down in Mexico with her fiancé..."

"Hard to think of her with a fiancé. Or with a man at all."

"Oh yes. Charles Halstead. President of Cherokee Oil." Hardy speaks judiciously. He relates the circumstances as something memorized or gone over a lot in solitude—a tale not really requiring an audience beyond himself. And it is the same as Walt has heard many times before. "She hired us both. She was re-opening Point Breeze; needed a staff. She had been living in New York. Traveling in Europe. Her and Mr. Halstead. He was supposed to move in after their marriage. Like their two corporations merging. His oil and her steel. But, he died in Mexico. Actually, murdered during one of those uprisings they have down there." He spoke knowingly as one who reads both of the Pittsburgh papers front to back. "She kind of withdrew after that. Hired your ma and me. Mrs. Jenkins came over from the Scaife house. Cora Emerson was upstairs." It is like a staff roll call, and Walt Hardy looks out the window. A huge dog is pulling his master toward a tree by the leash supposed to check him. A moment of sharing, Hardy thinks. "She became the person you remember."

His father raises his chin, smiles and pulls his neck up and out from the starched collar of his shirt. As a boy, Hardy used to think the gesture was painful—flesh rubbed by the tight choke of starched material—and the tight smile that always accompanied the gesture suggested a discomfort accepted and endured. To see it now, as they drive through Oakland; the lift of face, the fixed expression and strain of flesh against the buttoned collar, also seems to suggest pride in a duty done. "Your ma was not happy as someone's housekeeper. Too adventurous of nature. But then you came along, and so I wasn't drafted."

The sharp angle of light cast by the sun sections the rear seat of the Lincoln and draws across the plump upholstery like a knife's edge; not to slice the fabric but to define the absence of a passenger upon it. Father and son, Hardy is thinking; side by side in the front seat. It must run in the family. Both men left by their women. Could he dare say, abandoned by their women? At what point of passage does abandonment begin? But, maybe they gave off a scent that drove women out of the camp; essence of hermit, the smoke from the bachelor skillet, raised a smell that repelled the female. Because his father had never spoken unkindly of Ruth. His remarks always carried a sad understanding of whatever it was that had driven his mother up on the stage of the theatre during that matinee, to lend herself to the magician's act, to be levitated or sawn in half or whatever. Bill Hardy never blamed her.

"And Celia?" his father asks as if he had just performed his own trick of mental telepathy and had read Walt's thoughts.

"She's fine and sent her love to you. She's been very busy these days. With the real estate business." Half a truth was a little more than what he was used to saying, he thinks.

"I would have liked to see her," the older man replies simply as he pulls the limousine out into the parkway traffic. The manouver had been unhurried and deftly done. The Pittsburgh skyline abruptly presents itself. "If she had come with you, you both could have stayed in the main house. I could have made arrangements. I know she feels cramped in the apartment."

"It wasn't that, Dad," Walt Hardy says. "She just got busy." Of all the skylines he had seen in his travels, the buildings that rose from the delta formed by the three rivers always stirred something in Hardy—he could never put words to it—like no other city's profile. The skyscrapers were not all that outstanding, not so tall as others nor their grouping so unique or as massive. A couple of times, crouched by a jungle airstrip in Central

America, he would visualize these ramparts of glass and aluminum and steel, recite the names of the rivers that girdled them—Monongahela, Allegheny, Ohio—as if the incantation of these ancient Indian sounds and the vision of those luminous towers could work a magic to lift him out of hostile surroundings. It had seemed to work. A little plane or a helicopter had always appeared over the tops of the jungle to take him away.

Beyond his father's profile, across the Monongahela River, was the long bluff that coursed to Mt. Washington and on the sides of this bluff, like the terraces of the ancient Mayan cities he had seen in Central America, were the neat rows of modest houses where mill workers had once lived, where many still lived or their families, though the mills had long gone cold and dark. Most torn down. The houses looked, Hardy would think, like the orderly arrangement a child might make of blocks, but their roof tops formed staves of circumflex accents like a musical notation that, if ever produced,would sound a monotonous, one-note of the work force that these roofs had sheltered from Pittsburgh winters. A dull note, in fact, that had amazingly pushed up the glossy skyline downtown. Celia always tied such things together.

"You have trouble with means to the end," she told him that last angry morning. Her suitcase was almost full.

"I know all about that, Cee." He hoped his private name for her might slow her down. "I read Tom Wicker—all the same people you do."

"Oh, crap!" she said. She pushed down on the suitcase lid, then pulled it open again. "You have lied. You have lied and lied. You have lied to me. To me!" She stopped suddenly to thwart her tears. "The whole fucking social contract is out the window. This kid was raised on different soup. I told you and I told you to get out. But the humming and drumming was too much for you, I guess."

Her seriousness almost made him laugh; her civics class earnestness. Had she always been that way? Living together for twenty years, he had been surprised. "Look, sometimes the circumstances demand you play by different rules. No one likes doing it. Do you think I wanted to do it?"

"I mean the lying. You stood there in front of millions of people watching you, raised your right hand and told lies. Just like that. And you were smiling like you used to..." She took a deep, ragged breath. "How about going somewhere, the mountains, a movie—anything, and you'd smile—just like that."

"I had to Cee. Don't you understand, I had to do it. We had to protect him." The reasoning was still working for Hardy, the imagery still moved him—the corpse of the slain chieftain borne by his faithful captains.

"Don't make me puke!" Celia had shouted. Fortunately, their nearest neighbor was a quarter mile away, because the windows were open. It was a fine spring day and too early for air conditioning.

"It's a long term thing," he finally said to her, wishing his words sounded better. "When you sign on, you sign on."

Bill Hardy has pulled off the Parkway at the Grant Street exit, and stopped at a traffic light by the art deco facade of the deserted Baltimore and Ohio station. The rails that used to stretch far back east have been taken up and the area made into a large parking lot . A new prison was going up near by. In the car next to them, also waiting for the light to change, a man picks his nose in what he assumes to be a special privacy. Windows rolled up, probably something pleasant on the radio, the guy attacks his nostrils, first one then the other, with an authority, a gusto that is audacious and clearly pleasurable. A virtuoso, Hardy thinks, and laughs.

Then, the private elevator that lifted them to the penthouse of the Arnett Building took them right into the core of that crystal which enveloped the city, and Walt Hardy was to think later about how the light outside the Gothic-shaped windows was another kind of luxury the rich and powerful of this city had been able to enjoy. He could remember, as a teenager, coming downtown on a Saturday, at noon, to walk in the taffy-like gloom of the murky streets. Streetlights would be on.

Often, depending on Miss Arnett's calendar, his father would change shirts three times in one day. But from the tops of such buildings as the Arnett or the Gulf or the Mellon, the air would be clear and limitless as it will be afterwards in the English garden of Susanna Arnett Pell's small estate in Sewickley.

"Are you hiding out? Back here behind the lilac bushes, and you—the man of the hour." Susanna chides him with an intimacy which might acknowledge a shared history but which, at the same time, doesnt really make him her equal either. His celebrity has put him in a special category, the kind of instant fellowship the well-to-do will sometimes fancy with the notorious. Especially, the indicted, Hardy muses. He would guess that some of the people in this formal maze of brick and roses, walled in by privet, had endorsed his earlier employment. Some may have even funded the effort. Just about an hour ago, the odd terms of Peggy Arnett's will had put another imprimatur upon him, and if the legal language had not written him into the family, the old woman's bequest had surely made him much easier to chat with in this suburban snuggery. "You need a fresh drink," Susanna is saying. "Having thoughts about the will? What will you choose?"

"Actually, I was thinking about the air and the light," Hardy says, looking into her face. Susanna is a pretty woman, and her regular features and complexion go with the pink roses, the sunny symmetry of her garden. "I was thinking of the smoke that used to hang over this city, and how clear the air is now."

"Yes, isn't it wonderful," she replies and breathes deeply.

"But then, it's because the steel mills have closed down."

"I know, it's awful, isn't it?" she says and snaps off a blown rose bud.

"All those men, thirty thousand of them, out of work. Never to work meaningfully again."

"Well, of course, I've read those same figures too, Walt. I expect they mean as much to you as they do to me." Her roundish face loses a little of its softness as she returns his look. Her point. Lately, too many of his thoughts came out like that. Testifying before Congress made for a kind of thoughtful sloppiness; dog-earred King James expressing the commonplace. "Come, there are just scads of people here that want to meet you."

He lets himself be pulled back toward the fish pond and back into the party of relatives and in-laws and functionaries who have been invited to celebrate the reading of Peggy Arnett's will. Hardy's share had been the only surprise; the rest knew what they were getting, even Bill Hardy who had discretely disappeared after the meeting in the lawyers' office. Right now, he pictures his father carefully pulling the Lincoln into the garage of the carriage house that was his to occupy, under the terms of the will, for the rest of his life. Would he change anything now that it was his; say, move the kitchen clock from one wall to another? Put the TV in a different corner? Moreover, the terms of his late employer's will guaranteed him an income as a so-called associate curator in the museum the mansion would become. He would sit on a chair in the foyer, direct tourists toward the front room where the tour would start. Hardy can see him greeting each one pleasantly but with a reserve that would establish the difference between them.

"Oh, here's someone I want you to meet," Susanna is saying, almost lifting his right hand up to take the one being offered by a well-knit man who wears a sporty waistcoat beneath a hunter green blazer. Hardy only half-listens to the introduction, and Susanna passes on to other guests. It was the graceful exit of a hostess leaving men to their serious talk; a turn practiced from her girlhood. Hardy attends the talk with hums and a nod here and there; it's familiar stuff.

Indeed, his contribution at such gatherings had been only his mere presence; a totem of some kind. It would be too generous to say, he represented their beliefs; they had no beliefs but held opinions. The confusion could almost be seen in their faces, a certain perplexed mien that gave some of them a thoughtful expression. Hardy would not kid himself. Whether the party took place in Houston or Lake Forest or Orange County, he was an interchangeable guest and, like Mrs. Emerson or his father, a loyal servant to their opinions. And always, after what seems to be a regular time period, the talking game is over and a hand would reach inside a coat, as the man he has been listening to is just about to do. "I've been meaning to send you something..."

"Oh, please. Thank you," Hardy stays the hand. "I can't accept any money." He looks around the garden with a farcical expression. "There might be a spy among you." The man laughs with him; at the very idiocy of the idea. "But here," Hardy presents a business card from his billfold. "Here's the place to send whatever contributions you feel you can make. What little I did, you understand, I would gladly do again and for no compensation. But lawyers don't think that way." His hand on the man's elbow steers them into a brief alliance, a common prejudice toward the legal profession. An old technique left over from those days in the Catskills. Sometimes, the strategy even worked with lawyers. "So, whatever you can do will be greatly appreciated." Hardy squeezes the man's shoulder. The squeeze of the clan, Celia called it.

"Don't worry, I will. And I won't be the only one," the man says heartily. He's been called to arms and courageously signs up. A servant has just offered a tray of canapes. "It's been my pleasure." The man puts forth his hand, shakes and leaves.

Hardy looks over the assortment on the tray held by the black waiter. The help are both black and white, a diversification that speaks well for the thinking here in Sewickley.

"You with a caterer or what?" he asks the young man.

"Yeah."

"Where you from?"

"Northside." The waiter looks over Hardy's shoulder, then to one side.

"What part?"

"Perrysville." He starts to move away.

"I know Perrysville," Hardy says.

"Oh, yeah?" the waiter says. "Try the shrimp puffs."

He goes to the fish pond. Ceramic dolphins, the size of lake trout, sport above the lily pads and the drowsy shapes of carp. He takes up a place, makes himself available for another guest to take a turn with him. He's grown adept at such staging. Yet, he's also aware of a difference in this garden from other places he's recently set up shop, if you will. Here, he is also the chauffeur's son, the boy from the carriage house, the kid that Aunt Peggy sent to Cornell and, then, amazement hits them, he is also the same one that—well, wasn't he just on the cover of *Time* magazine—who did that business. You know? Down there. And here he is! It was all too perfectly amazing. How were they supposed to treat him? Hero or someone from the servant's quarters? Some remembered him as a boy hanging around the kitchen of the main house in Point Breeze, waiting for scraps almost, or hiding out in the library or, when older, invited to fill out the dance cards of the Arnett sub-debs. So now some of these same people have approached him, hands out to pump his odd celebrity, titillated by the idea and perhaps enthralled by whatever miracle—let's do call it democracy— that has put him in the same Sewickley garden with them on this fine spring day. His very presence among them, rubbing elbows or whatever, somehow ennobled them, but assuredly, it was not to be a lasting relationship and, therefore, could be borne with grace and good humor.

Then Susanna Pell comes back to him. "Now you must give me some of your time," she says, almost hugging his right arm to her full bosom. He knows her to be in her late forties, about Celia's age, and her clear complexion, her plumpness lend a kind of arrested youthfulness. Or was it, Hardy wonders as they amble to a stone bench in the shadow of a tall hedge, the startled expression of an innocence fixed in aspic.

"Oh, Walt." She swells with the best of good feelings and all for him. "I am so happy for you and everything." What she meant by "everything" he cannot guess. At this very moment, he faces fifteen years in prison.

"There's that curious smile again," Susanna is saying and touches his arm when he stays silent. He considers she might be acknowledging that drowsy Sunday afternoon in the garage of the carriage house. She has been talking about Aunt Peggy's will and her strange bequest to Walt Hardy. What was he going to do, his future? Had he seen any of the clinics Peggy Arnett had established in Mexico and Central America? That's what her husband did, Susanna confides quickly, as if to get the man's obligatory credentials out of the way. Her husband manages the family foundation that funds these clinics. Hardy must have seen them, known about them, she asks hopefully, head tilted. Funny, wasn't it? Each in their own way—she means the main house and the servant wing of course— helping those people down there. She leans away from him with a speculative look as if measure the effect of this insight. They've shared the same interest, the same hopes for the people *down there*.

"If freedom could only be a vaccination," Walt Hardy says.

"Oh, yes, yes. Wouldn't that be splendid!" A hand goes to her throat. "What a marvelous way of saying it. I'll have to remember that."

Hardy has continued to engage the roguish stare of the dolphins. "Give me a break !!" he hears Celia say. Susanna Pell has leaned toward him, a confidential proximity.

"What will you choose?" She comes even closer for the secret to be passed.

"What?"

"From the mansion?"

"I haven't the slightest idea. I may not take anything."

"Oh, but you must. You must take something." His disinterest is about to ruin her party. "Take me with you, please. I've always wanted to poke around Aunt Peg's secret places in that house—and that's what you'll look for. Not the usual valuable junk."

"Why do you say that?" She has surprised him a little.

"Well, all that secret stuff you've been doing—I just don't think you'd be interested in jewelry or the Constables or the Watteaus. They're all supposed to be fakes anyhow." She dismisses the Arnett collection with a wave that includes the "stuff" he had been doing. Her hands are small and well-shaped.

"I have to be in Kansas City to give a talk. To look through the whole house would..."

"It wouldn't take that long," she argues agreeably. "Especially if you had a partner." She takes on a winning look, something she's practiced, he guesses, on all men, starting with her father. "Oh, it would be such fun too. Like a treasure hunt. I think Aunt Peggy meant it as such. I wouldn't put it past her."

The spare language of the will recited in the lawyer's office had nicked his curiosity *...and lastly, to my good, young friend, Walt Hardy, I grant the right, before probate, to look through my house, which he knew as a boy, that all of its bureaus and closets be open to him and that he have the right to select one item from those articles therein, whatever its value, which he may keep as a memento of our friendship.*

"Like Hansel and Gretel, you mean?" he asks Susanna Pell.

Later, when he would tell Celia about the next morning, he would leave out a few details. He did not list the textures and lustrous surfaces of the the mansion's interior, and how they had set a sensual frisson going within Susanna. He had met her in the leather paneled foyer. Celia would hear about the appearance of the sun in the hazy sky, how it hung like a large gold coin in the glass panes of the porch on the east side of the mansion. "It looked like a spotlight," he would say. The Palladium mirror beside him was struck full; the surface turned to molten brass in which he saw himself looking pleasant and interested.

Actually, Susanna had meant no harm, he would tell Celia. Sure, she would say and laugh.

"I haven't been in here for years," Susanna says. "Aunt Peggy became a total recluse, you know."

She has been looking up at the gold washed aluminum of the ceiling and then ran, almost breathlessly, across the hallway to the reception room where she turns and pauses by the Steinway, ready to launch into a few lieder, he would tell Celia.

"Oh, look! The Copeland Spode!" she cries from the dining room, and the level of her voice alerted the major domo who had met them at the front door. Both men watch her review the artifacts and antiques in the formal front parlor; an inventory of stones and shells made by a child on a beach.

"I much prefer the Spode to the Worcester porcelain," she tells them "What do you think?"

"All this will be put back to its original Victorian elegance," the man says. He has introduced himself as the curator of the new museum. His father's new boss, Hardy thinks.

"What you may remember, growing up here, the house was different from how it looked when Miss Arnett was a girl. Her will calls for everything to be put back to that time. Circa 1905."

"Oh, Walt," Susanna calls him to a corner of the dark room. Her round face had become cunning. "Remember this?"

He has no memory of the small painting. A young woman, being dragged through a museum by an old gentleman, surreptitiously eyes the lustrous limbs of a marble couple locked in classic embrace. "Something by Dornier," the curator sniffs. "Mr. Clayton Arnett's first art purchase, during a bachelor tour of Paris. Only of historical value, I'm afraid."

"And, look!" Susanna Pell exclaims as she came on yet another item. Her inspection has continued into the parlor. Through the large windows, Hardy again sees the enclosed porch; potted ferns stationed on the terrazzo floor, where he had often curled up with a book in one of the wicker armchairs, dozing off to the grind of steel on steel as a streetcar passed on Penn Avenue. He inhaled a dry, spicy aroma of different woods, a smell given up by drawers being opened for the first time in years. "These look like Peebles," Susanna is saying to herself and the curator clears his throat to agree. "Can you imagine getting comfy in these?" she asks and runs her hands over the crenelated tops of the furniture. She sits down in an armchair, just to see how comfy it might be, her ankles crossed. It is a pose of entitlement.

Hardy has walked away during a discussion on Rockwood pottery. Susanna's rapturous cataloging had drawn the curator's closer surveillance, so Hardy is able to slip through a pocket door and to stairs that led to the second floor and the family's "inner sanctums." The library was up here. Also the family salons and bedrooms. The industrialist's home office, a kind of message center with telephone and ribbon teletype, was tucked away between the two master bedrooms. Peggy Arnett's suite of rooms, so very differently decorated from the rest of the house, had been made out of her old nursery into something like a stage set or like the lobby of an old movie theatre. Art deco and austere. He remembers that's how it felt to him as a boy, like going onto a movie set.

This passage and these back stairs were very familiar to Walt Hardy; he could still trace them in his sleep. The route detoured around the front rooms and public salons of the old house to wind not behind their walls so much as within them; a house within a house, and the enclosure had fascinated the young boy Hardy, added fuel to those fantasies already banked by Stevenson, Dumas and Scott. And W. H. Hudson. Around every corner, a secret was to be revealed. Even the wallpaper smelled different, perhaps its bald patterns contained coded messages, a map for treasure.

He had assumed these passageways to be his special domain, and he became very comfortable on the back stairs, in the private corners where the Arnett family had loosened their public attire. He remembers moving through the rooms of this inner house with a peculiar light headedness, a giddy equilibrium; as if he were about to come upon something in one of them that would explain a mystery he had not been aware of until the moment of its solution.

Nor was Hardy even then unmindful of the shell game this complex suggested, and he would often talk to Celia about it— lecture might be more the word. We've all heard the story enough, the melodrama of America's greatness. How the dissembling nature of Clayton Arnett enabled his greed to operate privately within the public structure of his philanthropy; libraries and schools and museums—the duplicity of people like Arnett and Carnegie and Frick. And so forth. Great wealth sustained a bifocal view of itself. Examine the doors of the mansion through which Hardy had passed this morning. They exemplified this division in their very construction, a sandwich of different woods composed their manufacture. The door panels the family saw from within their private rooms were carved of mahogany, but the facades that faced the entrance hall and the formal rooms were a veneer of pine stained to look like mahogany.

But on this morning, if you're Walt Hardy, you still suspect another passage exists that will take you to an even more private room. The cozy library, its windows level with the lower branches of the old oaks outside, still make him feel as if he has climbed into a tree house. He used to think this other room he could never find would also rest in a bower, like the library, and if he found the right door it would swing open on a jungle where the white, elusive form of Rima swung up through the Edwardian prose, defending her jungle friends. Everything got mixed up. It was he, *'ardy*, as those little grunts called him, who swung down into the jungle, bringing hope and rocket launchers. If not democracy. Give me a break, Celia would say. How much of that baloney was he going to slice? How he misses her, he thinks, and turns another way.

But, as always, the hallway comes to a dead end, and Hardy goes back to the library to look for that old copy of *Green Mansions*. That's what he would take! That would be his chosen inheritance. Had he even finished reading the novel? He couldn't remember how it came out. Probably badly. His reading had been interrupted that afternoon in the garage. Maybe the book is still somewhere in the garage where he'd secreted it for another go at masturbation. Just now, he hears Susanna's heels tap along the parquet in another part of the mansion. She's still interrupting his browsing, Hardy thinks and quietly laughs. That afternoon, she had innocently distracted him, but had she also unknowingly misdirected the rest of his life? If she hadn't poked into the garage he might have finished the novel, put the finishing stroke to his reverie, let's say, and the rest of his life would have been quite different! That's right; it's all been her fault! Everything that's happened to him has been Susanna's fault, and he smiles at himself in the polished surface of the library table.

Yet, there were times he felt like the figure in a romance, a character in the sort of stuff he remembered Miss Arnett reading. Such self-appraisement is part of the gunrunner's kit, but if you were Walt Hardy, you might be aware of that sort of flattery. Let's give him some credit. He can recall the heiress surrounded by stacks of popular novels with cover illustrations of women imperiled by the elements, their clothing disordered by forces beyond their control. The books in the family library were not to her taste—he can never remember her reading any of them. Instead, her reading was shaped by the best-seller list. Had anyone used this library but him? Nor had a fire ever been set in the hearth of the large fireplace at the far end of the room. This morning, the stones and their mortar look newly laid.

Nor did Miss Arnett buy books. She rented them. Many times, he had accompanied his father in the old Packard limousine downtown to Kaufmann's where they returned a half-dozen novels to the store's lending library—ten cents a book per night—and picked up another stack to bring back. Miss Arnett seemed to have some arrangement with the book department that gave her the first crack at the new novels, and she never seemed to read them so much as inhale them along with the smoke from Dunhill cigarettes. He had often spied upon her as she read. She held a thin black holder with a smoking cigarette aloft, above her head as if she were hailing a taxi. Or conducting her concentration on the page. When she inhaled, the smoke disappeared like white streamers up her nostrils, like a dragon's breath going in reverse. She was a study in black and white, chrome and pearly luminous. Glossy like an old movie still of the 30's.

So the sets of classics had been his alone to read. Ornately bound volumes of Sir Walter Scott and Alexander Dumas and Winston Churchill, the American novelist, and James Fenimore Cooper. Row on row of complete works monitored by the gravely etched visages of Longfellow and Whittier and Carlyle. Carl Sandburg's biography of Lincoln. He had plowed through the biography's many volumes one whole summer and, for a long time, that folksy vision of Honest Abe had even influenced how he combed his hair for school. Does anyone read these books anymore? Perhaps, Miss Arnett's ignorance of them had put her ahead of her time. Clearly, he had been the first person to crack open the Sandburg volumes which had been a book club dividend.

On this morning, he comes on books he had never seen before, but it is clear, by their shelving and condition, they had always been a part of the library. They hadn't interested him then. Bought by the yard, like the famous Arnett collection of Impressionists, the guzzled acquisitions of the rich. *The Meditations of Marcus Aurelius*, *The Selected Speeches of Daniel Webster*—three fat volumes. At least two different encyclopedias. A whole shelf of books authored by someone named Henry Baldwin Hyde. Another volume promised *Scientific Whist* while, next to it, a slim, elegant tome promoted *Five Talents of Woman* or *How to Be Happily Married*. This book's pages were as freshly crisp as those of Sandburg's *Lincoln* had been. Maybe, the volume had been a gift, another manual, along with the lessons on whist, a kind of one-two punch for a successful domestic life back then.

But Peggy Arnett had never needed the advice, or had the occasion to use it. The murder of her fiancé in Mexico had sent her into seclusion in the next room, the art deco retreat that she had made-over from her old nursery. Hardy had only known her as an older woman, but he had seen pictures of her when she was young. On the small side but with a determined line of jaw. Her father's brow gave her eyes a covert look, as if she had just looked up from the ground where she had spied something interesting but wasn't quite ready to tell the photographer about it. She had always been turned out smartly in these photographs as if they had been taken for a slick magazine—and maybe they had been. Her pose suggested an energy at rest. *Stoppered* might be the better word and with its own curious attraction.

In recent years, Hardy has felt the curious heat given off by the wives and daughters of the wealthy men who have befriended him, a casual sexuality drawn from Swiss bank accounts and made into a shiny hotness which could gloss the plainest face with a sensuality no cosmetic could duplicate.

Something like that with Peggy Arnett probably, Hardy muses, just as he hears Susanna enter the old nursery next door. The woman's heels tap lightly and discontinuously on the bare floor. He pictures her going on tiptoe.

Miss Arnett took all of her meals in that old nursery, read her novels there and from there tried to influence the world events which she refused to watch happen on television. Pay them off or fund them, depending on their character. His father told him, she had sent large checks to Nixon during all of Watergate. It was in this other room where he heard Susanna rummaging about, at a glass topped copy of a Le Corbusier desk, where Miss Arnett also wrote out his birthday checks along with all the others.

Hardy saw this mammoth checkbook once. The large format ran six checks to the page, as if to keep pace with her munificence; to ease the pressure of the Arnett fortune pushing at the dam of its own accumulation. He had received one of these rose tinted checks on each of his birthdays, and each for the same amount. Twenty dollars. He had received such a check only a couple of months back, and, like all the others, it had been enclosed in a Hallmark card, this one featuring ducklings. He wondered if her view of him had never matured, or perhaps her interest in this particular investment had merely stopped growing.

Another disappearing act, Hardy thinks this morning; not with a Greek magician from the stage of the Stanley, but self-propelled and into the sleek chrome and frosted glass room within the ornate Victorian architecture of her father's house. Perhaps that was one of the five talents of women—he should have looked closer at the book. Talent No. Five—How to Disappear. Women leaving rooms and the life within them to vanish into thin air, with or without the help of magic; to disappear within their own houses. Within themselves.

He must remember this line of thought to tell Celia. Its sensitivity might win her approval, and his understanding of what may have happened to his mother (therefore, what could happen to *all* women) might start her return to him. Making this note to himself, he even thinks he hears Miss Arnett calling him. It is the same unadorned inflection he remembers overhearing as she talked to a servant—to his father. Or even to him if she knew he had been curled up on the window seat, reading in the library bower. She used to call to him, and, when he appeared, reach into the box beside her chaise and present him with a chocolate covered cherry. He hated the candy and always flushed it down the toilet in what had been her father's bathroom.

But, it is Susanna Pell calling him "Look what I've found,"

she cries. She is breathless with triumph and holds up a note-book. The bottom drawer of the desk is open.

"What is it?"he asks.

"A diary it looks like," she says, then her expression deflates—the find suddenly not so wonderful. She looks closer. "But it's not hers. Not her handwriting. Here's a newspaper clipping pasted in." She needs glasses, Hardy observes, his feel-ing toward her softening. "It's an obituary. An aviator."

"Let me see," Hardy says, reaching for the book. He only wants to read it, to read it for her. But she jumps away.

"Ah, no, you don't,"Susanna says, laughing. "Finders keep-ers." And she puts the notebook behind her. Her expression dares him to come get it.

"I just wanted to see it," he replies.

Susanna's breath has quickened and she licks her lips. A calculation has come into her eyes which takes him back a lit-tle. Just for a second, he wonders if she might want to continue their old history, like finishing off the Hudson novel—take up in one of the dusty bedrooms nearby what they had left undone on the backseat of the Packard limousine decades before. "I'll tell you what,"she says, after taking a breath.

"What?"

"I'll let you have it, if we finish that dance. Remember?"

So, they go to the large room across the hall and above the grand staircase, where that dance had taken place years before,and where she had left his arms with choked-back tears. Hardy takes hold of Susanna and twirls her slowly around and around, feeling foolish and laughing, feeling that he observed some sort of a pay back for a faux pas he must have committed but could not, for the life of him, remember. She assumes his laughter is for this little game she has thought up, and she hap-pily hums a tune to accompany the bald scraping of their shoes across the parquet floor. They would finish the dance, Hardy thinks, and that would be all there was to it. It would be like picking Rima out of the trees where he had left her in *Green Mansions*. He would find that book, and he would finish it, once and for all, and it would be like catching up with a narra-tive that had gone on without him; a history confiding in itself as it waited to be read.

Sept. 7—Thursday

About this girl — China. Suarez or something like that. Her daddy's a general, but so is everybody down here. One of Zapata's old side-kicks. Last night, I was trying not to clap too hard after her dancing the dog-cook number, because there's only a few tourists around, just off the Missouri Pacific. But I can see her black eyes look me over. Slide to one side within the ornate headdress. She knows me from before at ringside. I've been there almost every night when I'm not flying. But there's a lot of applause from a table at the far corner. Three or four guys, and I recognize Manny Barreclena, who came over on the *Sinaia* with me. An ace and a gentleman. He waves me over.

So, that's how I meet her. She joins us after she takes off her headdress which makes her only a little shorter. She's being interviewed by one of these guys who turns out to be from the NY *Times*. Reed Ansers. So, I find out a lot about her by just listening. Her daddy sent her to the States to a college called Bennington. Ansers seems to know about the place. That's where she started dancing. So her English is pretty good. She's dancing with a group called Paloma Azul, Blue Pigeons, put together by an American dancer. Anna Soco-something. Someone she met at this college.

I'm trying to listen to her give this inter-view while Manny and the others are talking about Hitler moving into Poland today. Those goddam Stukas again. We ought to sign up, he says. Yeah, yeah. This dumb Spaniard wants to volunteer, sign up with another losing side. Meanwhile, I steal looks at this girl. Her eyes are large and luminous and black, and I think she has been stealing looks at me. She is wear-ing lots of jewelry, earrings and trinkets around her throat and wrists that make tiny scratchy sounds when she moves, even her most casual movement is accompanied by a strange music.

Barreclena is a little soused — theres a bottle of tequila and many empties of beer on the table. He starts spouting poetry, a problem I always had in Spain with guys like him. Mainly, I guess because I couldn't remember any to spout back. But, I used to think that our side went down because most of them were always quoting verse or printing pages of the stuff. I don't think the Krauts over in the Condor Legion did much of that. Anyway, here goes Manny...

...como por un valle de duras rocas de sangre pasa un inmenso rá¡áo Paloma de acero y de esperanza

...which I remember from a lot of handbills.

"That's Neruda, isn't it," this guy from the *Times* says. He seems to know everything. He has a sharp nose and beady eyes and is dressed like a pimp. White suit with vest, dark red shirt, gold tie clip and cuff links like tiny tennis racquets. "Something about doves of steel and hope."

"Here, my friend." Manny leans toward me, and I'm afraid he's going to plant a wet smacker on me. "*Esta es una paloma de acero*." he grips my shoulder. "You should do the newspaper story with him. *Un piloto fantástico con la patrulla americana*. He shoot down many, many fasciti."

I note the girl kind of stiffens in her seat and looks at me. Something about the smell of old, dried blood on the hands raises the heat in a female. It's the truth, Molly. I've run into it before. Or maybe, she's upset that this old *gringo* is a killer. I'm making a bad impression and I think of her beautiful, big feet under the table.

"So you're an American," the *Times* guy finally gets around to me. I'm honored. "And you flew with the American Patrol?" I nod. "That makes it a little difficult for you, I guess." I nod. "I mean, you lost your commission? Your citizenship?" I nod again. "I guess you knew Frank Tinker. What do you think about him?"

"What about him?"

Ansers looks amused. "Your old wingmate blew his brains out the other day in a hotel in Little Rock."

"When?"

"Middle of June." About the time I landed in Veracruz. I remember Tink saying, it's all over. Better get out. I can see him flipping over on a Heinkel, holding his fire until he was in the Kraut's hip pocket. He must have got to Paris and picked up his passport and got back in the States. To Little Rock. Not the worst way to go, I guess. Do it yourself. *Saludas, amigo.*

This girl next to me has a blue rebozo thrown around her bare shoulders and arms, and she gives off an aroma of perfume and sweat that is pretty heady. Her arms are long and strong looking and shapely. The night club is stuffy. The small band starts playing a tango and Ansers asks her to dance. He doesn't waste any time. Her dance with the company was angular and jerky; now she moves around on ball bearings. Ansers has his rat nose stuck into the middle of her fulsomeness, you might say.

"*Ahora, amigo,*"Barreclena is saying. "Are you for some sport this evening? I know of a new *casa de minina, pajaritas muy frescas, y cantantes melodiosas.*" He kisses his finger tips. "In the Roma Colonia and very clean too." Normally, I might have been interested. Companionship down here is not all that easy to find, so I've had one or two turns with the professional ladies. But I'm watching this girl, China. Not with any design, mind you, but something in me didn't want to disappoint her. Shucks, she'd just heard what a hero I was and now the conversation has turned to whores. Manny is waiting for my answer. I tell him, not tonight.

She comes back to the table, breathing deep which does a lot for her appearance. She adjusts one of the thin straps that holds up her dress.

Manny gets up and says good night like someone
going off to parliament. Ansers stays on his
feet also. "I'm having an early evening too.
I'll call you when I get the piece together,"
he says to the girl. "And I'd like to do a
piece on you too," he says to me. "American
flying hero, trying to get back his commission,
his citizenship and so on. It's a good angle.
Maybe, it could help you." He has the smile of
an undertaker.

Then, the girl and I are alone. I'm trying to
locate my tongue. Finally, she speaks. "*So,
Capitán h'Armstrong*, you are not interested in
some *picante chilli* this night."I play dumb
like I don't know what the guys are up to. "Where
are you coming from, brother?"she snorts. She's
a lot younger than me, but seems to know about
things. I am watching the pulse in her bare
throat do little leaps and I feel like I did this
morning at 12,000 feet. I wanted to pull back
the control column and kick hard right rudder and
put that transport into a snap roll. Crazy.
Naturally, I kept on flying straight and level,
like I'm trying to do at this table with her.

"I must eat," she says simply. I look around
for a waiter. "Not here. You come with me?"
Foolish question.

She's got this little Chevvie roadster parked
behind the San Diego Church, so Daddy General
must have done okay in the Revolution. We wheel
through the streets, she drives pretty smooth,
and pulls up in front of a place on September 10
called Le Gourmet. She's well known in this
place. In fact, it begins to dawn on me, that
she's a little on the famous side herself. The
waiters greet her like royalty.

She really puts on the feedbag. Plates of veal
stew flavored with lime and orange, *chilaquiles*,
t*acos de barbacoa*, *tortillas*, soup with thick
macaroni like strings, chicken in chocolate mole,
rice and beans, corn meal *chabacanos*. Everything
washed down with iced pulque mixed with mango
juice. I wasn't flying today, so I dug in too,

but she's a champion. Both hands going almost at once, her cheeks puffed out like a squirrel's, and her eyes glow, black fire, like a panthers thinking of the next course. Is it me?

Each new flavor, each bite closes down these dark orbs. Juices and pulp savored, swirled around. Swallowed. She asks me questions as we eat. My time in Spain. How many planes did I shoot down? My answers seem to feed another appetite. Who'd I know in Mexico? Who do I fly for now? How did I get the job? It's a little like a job interview.

The questions are making me edgy. Another dame asked me questions like this. Nikki. And she was supposed to be a spy. A fifth columnist.

This kid's face changes as she talks. She goes from a *Vogue* cover to one of those Aztec masks like she had put on as the dog-cook. Come to think of it, maybe her role has made her hungry. Her features go sad and joyous. Ancient and girlish. How she looks and what she tells me. She's what? Mid 20's.

"You're not convinced, h'Armstrong?" she asks. Her cheeks are popped out with chicken *mole*. She's been talking the accepted pinko line about fascism, about the oppressors. Especially Hitler going into Poland. Chamberlain going butt up. Yes, the workers, etc. And et cetera. Yeah, yeah. Jesus, when are you going to turn off that radio, Molly. Hitlers run into Poland is on everyones mind; so I guess its understandable.

"Look," I say."I'm just a guy who flies for pay. I've been through one big war and two revolutions. Three if you count a little go-round in Mongolia. I was in the Big War that was supposed to end all wars. So, here we go again."

"The fascists will be stopped," she says, wiping her plate with a folded *tortilla*. Her dark hair is wound tight into a crown on her head, varnished and soft in the restaurant's light all at once.

"Hey, I've been fighting Germans since I was seventeen years old," I tell her. "Just 'cause Hitler and Company don't agree with Jefferson and Lenin does't mean they are going to lose. I

just came out of a war where the losing side was
supposed to win because it was supposedly the
right one. We were loaded with ideas of truth
and beauty. You get it? If you're thinking
morality and justice, Franco should have lost.
He didn't. He had the planes and the tanks and
the oil. And, incidentally a lot of his oil
shipped out of Tampico."She does have the good
grace to look down at her plate, if only for one
more bean. "So, don't talk to me about ideals.
I've seen the best of ideals blasted to
smithereens by Stukas. That stuff's for
Hollywood. Happy landings."

My declamation has even taken me by surprise
and we don't talk for a little. Fans whir up at
the ceiling and dishes clink back in the
kitchen. We're closing the place up, it looks
like. A squad of waiters stands at parade rest
by the kitchen door, and I get the feeling
they'd stand there all night for this general's
daughter if she wanted. Or maybe her fame as a
dancer. China has worked a mouthful of food back
around her molars and swallows. "Ha," she says
all of a sudden and bits of something splatter
the air between us. "Even jade splits."

"What's that, some kind of old time saying."

"A poem. In Nahuatl—the language of the
Aztec. Even jade splits...Even gold breaks...Even
the quetzal's feathers are plucked out...Not forever are we on earth...But only for a short
while..."

It's like some kind of a curtain line. The
waiters are happy as hell to see us go and a
couple of voices raise in song in the kitchen.
I peel off the *pesos* for the bill as China
stands to one side, one foot crossed daintily
as possible over the other. I think of a little poetry myself.

*Sardine boxes/without topses/Slippers for my
Clementine*. But she's damn interesting. Energy.
The way she goes at her chow makes me wonder
about the rest.

"I give you ride," she says smiling big. I
think she means to my hotel. The top is down on

84

her little buggy and the night air is cool and
sweet. The air in this city, seven thousand feet
up, is especially wonderful, almost like wine.
Sweet and clear. The earlier rain has refreshed
the ancient aromas of this city, brought them up
to the surface. I am thinking it must have
smelled this way to Montezuma — moist clay and
vegetation and blossoms. A wonderful heavy perfume. It's lucky I wasn't flying today. She
makes several passes around the zocalo, like
she's giving me a tour of the palace and of the
cathedral, and then she whips down Madero and
picks up speed when it becomes Juarez Avenue.
The streets are pretty empty and there doesn't
seem to be a speed limit, as far as she's concerned. So, in no time, we've zoomed past the
Alameda. The Hotel Regis has come and gone too.

"So, where are you taking me?" I finally ask
but in a friendly manner.

"Perhaps, I'm taking you to meet Mr. Lund."
She almost sings it out and laughs, head thrown
back. There's that name again. Gen. Avila and
his lady had talked of doing something with a
Mr. Lund. The guy on the train also.

She drives in a regal fashion, arms held out
stiff and straight as both hands grip the top of
the wheel. We're on the big broad Paseo de la
Reforma now, and she's doing a Barney Oldfield
on the Indianapolis Speedway. We have the boulevard to ourselves. Not even a tram in sight. I
guess they've stopped running too. If there are
any cops around, they must be like the waiters
in the restaurant — on the family payroll.

"I take you seeing sights, *mi turistito*," she
laughs and takes a corner on two wheels.   To
make this short, we stop off at a dive that has
a small combo. Everyone knows her here too. We
drink a lot of stuff and dance. Rather she rhum-
bas and I kind of stand in the middle and try
to hold on. Manny's talk about my exploits has
bounced her hormones. This is some kind of a
hero's reward, I tell myself. A whole lot better than that *Croix de Guerre* and I goddamn
deserve it. Pin it on me, brother!

Then, we're back in her flivver and barreling into the night. She's yelling poetry and all kinds of stuff in Spanish and other weird languages. She's told me, like a challenge almost, that she's half Indian. She even licks her lips, though I take this as an automatic gesture that has no immediate meaning. Her mother was Zapotec. They go back before the Aztecs. China is like a kid playing hooky. "We are making the sun," she says.

I'm half stewed, half nappy and after about an hour, she pulls up into a darkness that has only starlight to ease it. I make out campfires low in the distance, like tiny stars brought to earth. One of those clay pipes you always hear is tootling sadly. China is walking like she has x-ray vision and I'm trying to keep up. Then she stops me. "*Paso a paso,*" she whispers. "*Comprendes*?"

Sure, Im beginning to *comprende*. She's brought me to some kind of family celebration and I'm going to be the main course. Roasted Armstrong. "*Aquiá*" Her voice is is rich as one of those sauces on the *chilaquiles* at Le Gourmet. Peppery and hot. Her hand is strong and warm. A little moist. Maybe, the fascists are getting even with me. Or some faction of the Reds. She's been hired to lead me to my death. Nikki comes to mind. Maybe that's what she was about — her assignment was to kill me off in bed. She tried hard, come to think of it. Tinker does the number to himself in Little Rock and I get plugged in Mexico. The last of the *patrulla americana*. Can it be true? Something in me says, no. What I saw in those beautiful eyes tonight wasn't anything like that. I'm pretty sure. So, I follow.

Then, she stops and whispers, "Quetzalcoatl came here." I'm about to laugh — say something about George Washington sleeping around when it suddenly hits me where we are. She's brought me to that old city I fly over. Teotihuacan. And my eyes become accustomed just then, as if to prove the guess. The shape of the main pyramid rises up just in front of us like a great wall.

Like a huge, silent beast out of the past. The anonymous clay pipe continues to toot in the darkness. And then her mouth has found mine in the dark. A perfect fit. She tastes of chili pepper and a sweet hotness. Like warm fruit, and all the rest of her too, her lips are saying. This is the treat I get before my heart is ripped out.

Then she starts scrambling up the pyramid and I'm after her as quick as I can go, hands and feet. The victim running after his own sacrifice. Running up the steps. We get to the top. This old airman is not too winded, I'm happy to say. From here, we can see the light of Mexico City, faint and pulsing. In the darkness below, I can make out the lines of the older city. Teotihucan. Built long before the Romans and not even known to Aztecs or Cortés — so I've read. Which saved it from destruction. Its treasures are in the museum. A wide avenue, like a runway, leads to another pyramid at the far end. Ruins of other buildings on either side of the ancient boulevard.

Meanwhile, China has been humming to herself, unwinding the coil of her hair so it falls down around her face, down to her waist. She starts moving around me, her arms out like she is the dog-cook, but this dance is not so jerky. The top of the pyramid is flat and about the size of a tennis court. I can barely make out the edges of it. Straight down almost on four sides. Piles of rubble, a couple shapes that look like benches. Toppled columns. It's a special performance and all for me. She seems to move to the notes from the clay pipe tootling in the darkness. She dances to its slow melody. Her jewelry clinks and rattles a little.

The sky is getting lighter and my eyes play tricks on me. Certain moments. She looks like something off a vase. Her dress stretches around her legs, the rebozo arcs wide. She holds the material out to make wings; lets it loop and fall around her. In the glooming, the whites of her eyes become luminous. She keeps turning around and around. Her arms look shiny. She's working up a sweat. So am I.

Well, what can this officer and a gentleman say? My heart wasn't cut out. We made the thing work. We made the sun come up.

So, I'm out at the field this afternoon, still a little woozy and tingling with the feel of this strange girl. China. Even as I write this down, I can't quite believe last night. And, of course, I'm thinking of Nikki too, and the similarity. Still think about that possibility. One Finnish and one Latin or Indian, but their enthusiasms, politics, justice — a lot of similarities. Is this kid working for somebody else? Let's face it, Molly; I may be a hero but I'm getting on. The landing gear is beginning to creak when the wheels touch down.

This afternoon, we're putting some new instruments into the Ford Tri-Motor. These Mex mechanics are A-Number One, I trust them completely, but I want the new Sperry horizon in a particular place in the cockpit. Up front and not on the side with the rest of the instruments. So, I'm in the hangar and George Rhyl walks in with this guy.

"Want you to meet Chuck Halstead," he says.

"Heard a lot about you," the guy says. He's a little older than Rhyl and is dressed for the tropics. Outfitted by Abercrombie & Fitch, I mean. His hand is quick and dry.

"Heard you've had some bad luck. Your commission and all."

"Chuck runs Cherokee Oil down here," George says and slightly winks.

"Well, I used to," Halstead says and gives a phony laugh which we all join in. He refers to Cárdenas taking over the oil, of course. So, we stand around for a bit, like we've lost our scripts. The grease monkeys are jabbering and laughing in the cockpit of the Ford.

Then Rhyl says, "Chuck has that Beech Staggerwing" and nods to a little green ship parked over in the corner.

"Well, it's the company's plane,"Halstead
says quickly, as if I might be a stockholder.
"...but he needs a pilot," George goes on.
"Yeah, the guy who flew us down ate too many
tamales," Halstead says, wracked up by his own
wit. We all do the ha-ha again. Good old
Montezuma and his revenge—that sort of humor.
Yeah, yeah. The mechanics keep busy in the Ford.
If they know English they don't let on, but I am
still a little embarrassed.
"It would be okay with me," Rhyl is saying.
"And I thought you could use the extra dough.
After all, I know what I'm paying you." More
laughter. Ha—Ha. It's a merry occasion, and
George is having trouble with his eyelid again.
It's supposed to be a wink.
"I'll think it over," I say. I'm thinking
another job would take me away extra times from
this girl I've just met. A spicy dish I've only
just tasted.
"I still have a few things to clean up down
here," this Halstead is saying. "About a year's
worth, I figure. We could fit the times we need
you into George's schedule. I think we could work
something out," he says. "Think it over and let
me know."
Rhyl walks him back to this gray Dodge parked
outside the hangar, and I go back to helping the
mechanics with the Sperry. Then, my shoulder is
gripped. It's George again.
"For Christ's sake," he says. "Don't you know
who that is?"
"You introduced us," I say.
"It's not just the extra dough. It's the guy's
contacts. You've been filling my ears with wanting to get back to the States, getting your commission back. Here's you're chance. And what's
even better, his sweetie is Peggy Arnett."
"Is that so," I say and the dumb look on my
face sends Rhyl's eyes into a spin.
"Steel, you knuckle head. A&W Steel. She's the
heiress to A&W Steel. She's got more congressmen in her pocketbook than a *tortilla* has beans."

Well, I guess that do make a diffy-dence,
Andy. Tune in tomorrow, boys and girls.

celia's return

"I guess I'm a little like the member of the family who has d disappeared but who is talked about at every reunion—his very absence makes him a presence. Except this time it's reversed. I'm not a member of the Arnett family but I've kind of showed up and..."

"...and so now they talk about you as if you were," the journalist fills in Hardy's pause, nodding agreeably as he takes notes. Be my guest, Walt Hardy thinks, and looks around the barroom. Whatever he had meant to say had just come on its own glibness and stalled, an occupational hazard incurred, possibly, from talking to too many congressmen and Washington bureaucrats. His eyes take in the man across the booth with an expression he knew would appear to be both frank and reserved. Cee would say it was his I'd-like-to-tell-you-more-but-I-can't look.

"You got it," Walt Hardy finally says and twirls the ice in the scotch and soda with one finger, takes a sip. The reporter's head nods more vigorously. He's on to something. He's got a lead.

Somebody at the party in Sewickley must have tipped off the newspaper that he was in town. When Hardy walked back to the carriage house this morning, after the tour of the mansion with Susanna, his father had just answered the phone and handed it over to him. The reporter understood he couldn't say much, his case being appealed and all that, but could they meet anyway? Sure, why not, Hardy agreed, thinking some discrete publicity might bring in a few extra bucks. He had arrived at the restaurant near the newspaper office a few minutes early, a habit with all appointments, so he had already read the restaurant's history on its menu before the journalist came through the stained glass doors. The place had been a speakeasy and then a brothel until after World War II, so the interior had been partitioned into cubicles and small anterooms that gave off a slightly wicked ambiance which Hardy found quaint and amusing. At the long

90

bar, a group of neatly dressed men and women drank and joked, junior executives from nearby corporate headquarters, he figures. Their boisterous collegiality had a faintly erotic quality that went with the place. He has looked over the two women more than once. Only curious.

"What is it you do again?" the reporter is asking with slight apology. He shrugs and lowers one shoulder. "I mean in the real world. I mean your title."

"I was employed by the American Petra Company as a manager of technical information services."

"That's in the oil business?"

"It's a firm that puts together petroleum resources and their specific utilization into an assemblage of monitoring and consultative directives." It takes a while for the guy to write all that down. Two plus two comes out five, Hardy thinks. Or maybe zero.

"So when you were doing these other chores, let's call them, in Nicaragua and El Salvador, you were ostensibly checking out oil reserves and figuring out how to use them? That was your cover?" The guy was being all buddy-buddy.

"All that stuff is in the record of the Congressional hearings. You can look it up. I really can't add any more to it because, as you said earlier, my lawyers are preparing for the Court of Appeals."

"But you no longer are employed by this Petra Company?"

"No, I resigned about a year ago. Putting together my defense was a full-time job, and I could not fulfill the company's expectations."

"So, how..." the reporter almost blushes, though it might be the window light reflecting off his pink shirt, "...how? I mean, you are now appealing the indictment. You've got some high-powered lawyers working for you?"

"How am I paying for all this expensive legal talent? My savings at first. But they are long gone. Now, I must rely on the donations of the good people who believe in democracy and who support freedom and those who fight for it." It was risky to say something like that, one-on-one with a journalist. Such rhetoric usually went with a larger, more sympathetic audience, a group that had paid out money to be so stroked.

But the guy has laughed and picks up a thick slab of fried potato from the plate between them. He sprinkles it with vinegar from a cut glass cruet. In some of the odd places Walt Hardy had found himself in recent years, he would sometimes get a hunger for such hearty Pittsburgh fare. Sandwiches with the french fries stuffed into the roll along with the grilled kielbasa, onions and, peppers. "But, how about the Arnetts, have they contributed to your expenses? They have a history for supporting such causes. I guess you knew that old lady Arnett sent Nixon money all through Watergate."

The charge has become tiresome. Actually, Hardy had often encountered conservatives and liberals meeting at the same ideological crossroad. The political landscape was never neatly sectioned off. "On the other hand," he tells the man, "I just found out yesterday, that there is a family foundation that has set up health clinics, hospitals, all through Central America."

"Did you ever see any of them?" the man asks.

"No, fortunately, I didn't have to check any of them out," Hardy says and smiles over his drink. "I always boiled my water." The journalist gets the joke. One of the women at the bar has hooked the spike heel of one shoe over the brass rail which shifts her hips to one side, a Venus de Milo angle. Hardy looks back at the reporter. "So, if you're asking if I ever received money from Miss Arnett—I mean aside from an occasional birthday check—the answer is no."

"Not even in her will? Isn't that why you returned? Came back to Pittsburgh? Something about the will, wasn't it?"

"Yes and to see my dad. But she left me no money."

The reporter was about forty and with a disarming, or what he hoped to be a disarming yokel manner that Hardy had seen through immediately. Too much intelligent skepticism sparkled in the man's eyes. "Nothing?"

"Well, it is of a personal nature. A sentimental item of no material value." A book about a jungle girl, if he could find it. Or maybe this old diary of the aviator's. How would the reporter regard that? Hardy had looked at some of the journal before he came down-town for the interview. That this old account could be his inheritance was funny, and he is almost tempted to tell the reporter about it just to share the idea.

"You know this is quite a story," the reporter confides in him. "Your father was the chauffeur. And here you are, the chauffeur's son, returning almost like a hero. On the cover of

Time magazine. Almost a member of one of the great American industrial families."

"That's what makes America great, isn't it?" Hardy plays chicken with the journalist's stare. Finally the other man gives up.

"Well, you know what I mean," the guy says though still not entirely convinced of Hardy's seriousness. "How does it feel?"

He is a little sympathetic to the journalist's problem. There is quite a story here, but none of it was coming together for him, nor for his editor. Fittingly, the face of the clock over the bar is also screwed up, the hands reversed so they are a backward *5:45* which only looks normal in a mirror or maybe if you were drunk. Someone has told a joke and the group laughs uproariously. It's a diversified council of three-piece-suiters—two black guys and three white. And the two women.

"How does it feel?" Hardy repeats the question and looks down at his drink. "Verified. Validated." The words surprise him as much as they engage the reporter who writes quickly on his notepad. "Pittsburgh has a way of sifting the real from the false; a way of establishing identity. It must have something to do with the light."

"The light?" The journalist has flipped to a fresh page of his notebook.

"Yeah. I was thinking yesterday of when the mills were all going and the sky was full of smoke and soot, yet there was a wonderful light that would cut through all that darkness now and then. A little after dawn or at odd times during the day and the whole world seemed to be illuminated for the first time. Like—what was his name?—Gabriel coming down on a beam. At my school desk, dozing through civics class and suddenly this shaft of light would shoot through these very high windows—why those windows were so very high I can understand now—and strike the open book before me like a holy picture. It was pure magic."

"So rare that it was like magic," the reporter says.

"Something like that." Walt Hardy watches one of the women push away from the bar and walk toward the rear of the restaurant, toward a pay phone by the swinging doors of the kitchen. She wears a grey blazer, miniskirt of dark blue, and blue suede shoes. As she punches out the number, she slips one foot out of its shoe, rubs the underside over the instep of the other foot as the number rings. Then, she steps back into the shoe and says hello.

"Like what?" the reporter is asking.

Hardy has to think for a moment. "Because that sudden flash made you see things that had been there all along, and then it was gone—but you were left with this fresh image, the truth that had been on the page in front of you all along."

"A revelation, you mean?"

"Well, that might be overdoing it." Hardy laughs and draws one leg up so his foot is on the booth bench. It's a chummy pose; something a coach might use while talking to a young player so as to show a companionable limberness of limb. Story time; here comes the message.

Do you rehearse that stuff or does it just come out of you like toothpaste when someone squeezes you, Celia would ask? This was before she had got into her Civic and turned out of the driveway in Silver Springs She had played the part of the dutiful wife, not so much standing behind her man but sitting down for him at another chicken dinner—the more recent fare a little fancier than the simple plates they had been served in the Catskill hill towns. In those days, she had been his best audience. You should be the candidate, she'd say, not that stuffed shirt. But something about him, he couldn't explain, preferred to be behind the scenes. Not go public. Then, it had gone sour.

"Returning to Pittsburgh is for me like one of those beams of light striking something that's been in my life all along but that I didn't see; had got used to, I guess. I've been thinking about a guy named Eddie Poremski. We used to walk to school together—the old Park Place School. We played sandlot ball together. I always wanted to be on his team. Even bloodied each other's noses now and then. Just kids, you know. Eddie joined the Marines and was killed in Laos."

The reporter writes hurriedly. Hardy lets him catch up as he sips his drink and thinks of the next line. Going-home traffic moves slowly on the Boulevard of the Allies outside the restaurant, a congested memorial to World War I. Once, to close a deal in a secure place, they had all met in France, near Reims—to test the champagne, someone had joked. One afternoon, during a recess, he got away from the others and drove down along the Meuse River to where the World War I trenches had been dug. He'd come across a military cemetery of American dead, thousands and thousands of crosses and stars implanted in the smooth green nursery of a French countryside. Many, Hardy remembers, had been killed on November 10, the day before the Armistice. A peculiar anger had seized him, standing in that park of dead men, their abandonment so meticulously cared for, and that identical emotion has just slipped unasked into the small eulogy he has been piecing together for Eddie Poremski. It is a trick he had come on quite by accident, a technique actors might employ to give their lines authenticity, but—let's remember—if you were Walt Hardy, you would not always be aware of pressing that key.

"That was a while back—Laos, Cambodia," the reporter is saying.

"Yes, a while back."

"...and this guy Poremski?" He wrote out the name carefully on his pad for Hardy's verification.

"Well, I've been thinking that whatever I have done—right or wrong," he pauses to eyeball the journalist in an appeal for a little fairness, "has been because of guys like Eddie Poremski. It's like I was keeping my word to him. Check out those people at the bar. No offense to them, but people like Eddie Poremski are totally out of their picture—and as far the freedom fighters in the jungles of Central America," the image of that cemetery in France freshens his voice like a sudden spring shower, "I, for one, would not abandon them. We kept our word."

The reporter regards him closely with a half smile on his mouth, inspecting first one eye and then the other, and then back to the first, checking on the balance of sentiment in both. Would Hardy wink one of them? Was there more coming? Something to make sense of what he had just been told?

The group at the bar has also fallen silent, and Walt Hardy instinctively senses that something else is occurring. He's been spotted. Lately, a patch of sensitivity has grown on him, like a rash, that picks up a signal in a restaurant or sometimes on a street corner, as he waits for the light to change. It's like an itch he dare not scratch in public.

And sure enough, the woman who had used the telephone is coming their way. Her colleagues have turned toward the booth where he and the reporter talk , and their expressions are tinted pleasantly with anticipation, a speculation about to be verified.

"You're someone famous, aren't you," she says a little shyly. "A celebrity?"

"Ask him about the *Time* magazine," one of the men suggests, then takes the question himself. "You're the guy with that Contra business...Hardy. Right?"

"I guess the interview is over," the reporter says good-naturedly, but Hardy notes the man is still taking everything in.

"Isn't that right?" the young woman persists. "You're that guy on TV?" Her appearance has changed. She's a fan all of a sudden.

He's seen similar transformations in women. The way a man's celebrity hits some women, turns them on. It was an old truism taken for granted in the regions he has recently left, but that he, Walt Hardy—a middle-aged man of ordinary appearance—could rouse such appetites was a phenomenon that he had never been able to completely accept. For example, that interlude with Susanna this morning. He had taken her in his arms and twirled her around that dusty ballroom as part of a game, a friendly rouse that covered the social gap between them as it also made fun of that gap. In his mind that was all there was to it. And, in all fairness, he did owe her a dance.

"What are you drinking, Champ?" one of the men asks. "Another round." He turns to the bartender.

"No more for me," the reporter says, gets up and puts out his hand. "Nice talking with you."

As pained as he is by his barroom celebrity, Hardy is grateful to these new comrades for driving the reporter away. The man had begun to ask speculative, philosophical questions—a sure indication that the substantive part of the interview had dead-ended. What did he, Walt Hardy, think of this American penchant in politics to make people virtuous whether they liked it or not? Then, of course, whose virtue, whose definition of virtue were they talking about? Such questions always stumped him, made him feel akward or foolish when he tried to respond.

It's no better when he has posed similar questions to himself, usually after evenings with certain powerful guardians of the national virtue whom he had addressed to raise money for his defense fund, and—just to fill in the blanks—for whose particular ideal of virtue he had performed the very deeds which made this defense fund necessary. Round and round, it goes. The cycle seemed closed with no way out for the average citizen; a perpetual crusade fueled by a calling to remake the world in the images, the declarations of the Founding Fathers. Can we say, rules for conquest? The Founding Fathers. He first heard of that bunch at the Park Place School. "Our founding fathers," their teacher used to say. But whose Founding Fathers had they been talking about? If you were Walt Hardy, it was a team you had wanted to join ever since.

Hardy can remember a history professor talking of the priests who had accompanied Spanish explorers to the source of the Rio Grande; the holy fathers converting the Indians to Christianity, absolving them of their heathen sins, so they could enter heaven after the conquistadores blew their brains out. A kind of assembly line turning out new, virtuous souls. So, maybe it was the religion. He had encountered the same fervor in Nicaragua in a colonel who performed similar baptisms, similar absolutions on the natives of his own land.

"Hey, Champ," one of his new comrades shouted. "We're going around the corner for some grub. Want to come?" Hardy felt a kind of free-wheeling gyroscope spinning within him, a giddiness induced by the drinks with the reporter, but also a sense of being cut loose in Pittsburgh, almost a foreign land to him these days. So, the anonymity he had expected to enjoy in the rooms above the garage on the Arnett estate, having dinner with his father in the kitchen, became something he could do without.

The young men and women wheeled and chattered around him like sea birds as they led him to their next hangout, another part of the beach. Apparently, this group drank in one establishment, then moved to a second for food, though what hunger for food they may have had was instantly blunted by the presence of some Houston Astros celebrating an unexpected victory over the Pirates that afternoon. The ballplayers lolled in their triumph at the bar when Hardy and his group came through the swinging doors. The young pitcher Pittsburgh had brought up from the minors had been overwhelmed. Photographs of athletes, trophies, and sports memorabilia crowd the walls. The bar is stacked four deep and the atmosphere roils in the vapor given off by well-toned bodies at ease. Hardy's erstwhile friends dive into this stew to feed another kind of hunger, leaving him alone at a corner table to order a New York strip steak from a waitress who calls him, "Hon."

But he does not feel slighted by their desertion. The informality of the waitress, her Pittsburgh mode of address, made him quickly at home in the lively place. The tight fist that had gripped him since his return to Pittsburgh and the reunion with his father, has just come undone in the charged ambiance of this restaurant. The reporter's unanswerable speculations had put an extra twist upon this tightness, a spin on the gyroscope inside, yet the guy had helped by going too far. Hardy felt loose for the first time in months. *Cool*, as the revelers at the bar might say. He casually spreads soft butter on a piece of roll, evening off the edges all around and then takes a bite. To hell with cholesterol, the bread and butter are delicious.

This morning, his father had shuffled between refrigerator and stove and then table to set down the expected meal before him.

Juice, eggs and bacon, toast. Yet, Hardy had left the kitchen table unsatisfied. Now that the funeral and reading of the will were over, he had hoped he and his father could sit, take a breath and just talk easily over their coffee mugs. Man to man. Catch up with each other. In all the years and miles put down, Hardy would often create such talks in his head, and in these scenarios, his father would say something wise; then, lean forward to listen carefully to his side of the conversation. The dialogue for these fantasies escaped him, they remained a schema only, an outline of the two of them sitting together and talking; yet, they had made him feel close and at times a little sad to be so far away and, usually, in places very foreign to Pittsburgh.

But he's come back home, and Bill Hardy has yet to bring up the subject of his part in the Contra business. This morning, all the formal reasons for his return out of the way, Hardy had hoped they might talk about it. Get down to it. He had looked for his father to put a hand on his knee and start the conversation. "Answer me this," Bill Hardy might start, pulling up his chin and scratching speculatively at the wrinkled flesh of his neck. Questions would follow. Hardy would talk it out. Their coffee would grow cold, untouched. Perhaps the old man's eyes might glint with an unspoken accusation, look sidewise at a judgment. Yes, why not a judgment? But, his father had said nothing; only stirred his coffee and looked pleasant. As Walt Hardy waits for his meal in the noisy restaurant, he figures that he had wanted his father to call him to account, help him to an explanation for a lot more than his current difficulties, and it had been too much to ask of the old man, of anyone. No wonder he hadn't said anything. Where to start?

A third scotch has given Hardy an Olympian perspective. The father had no questions about the son's activities, because that was his training. Had he ever questioned Miss Arnett's attitudes and opinions; her business dealings with A&W Steel? He had turned away from such conversation with a servant's decorum. It wasn't his business. Yet, Hardy lays out the counters of his indictment on the checkered tablecloth anyway. He had committed perjury before the U.S. Congress. He had cut deals with several international villains. He had bribed and conspired. Forget why, whatever the reason. Call it democracy, call it conquest. Call it business. A felon to some, a hero to others? What of that, Dad? How about that? In his mind, he sees his father carefully fold over the newspaper to the sports section and continue reading. The man's unquestioning confidence, so silently registered, was hard to take. At the bottom, it was a lack of recognition of what he *had* done—however it might be valued—that bothers him. Take that nasty newspaper cartoon. All of them—North & Company—swinging from palm trees in a jungle of conspiracy. Walt Hardy with a simian brow hanging from one of the limbs. Hadn't his father seen it in the evening paper, in the editorial section? The cartoon had been syndicated, appeared everywhere. Surely, the Pittsburgh papers had used it. But Bill Hardy had never mentioned it.

"The Pirates are bringing up a young pitcher from Carolina," was all that he had said this morning as he poured more coffee for them both. So that was the level of their conversation. Nothing to fill in the empty baloons tethered to their silhouettes in Walt Hardy's imagination. The digest of their dialogues might fit into a sports almanac. Save for the time his father taught him how to handle the clutch and gear shift on the old Packard. But would that count as a conversation? But he would remember the lesson, unfold it more than once in memory to look for fresh lines in the seam of the event. Also, the stories of his father's days with the CCC, planting trees and swinging an axe. Digging ditches. The old man's shoulders looked solid enough to do that job even now. Then, the subject of his mother, her whereabouts. Why she had left them? That made for a lengthy discourse. How they had met and got married was something out of an old movie, and he sometimes found himself casting their two parts with different actors—say, Veronica Lake and Alan Ladd—to give the same lines different interpretations. The waitress from the Grand Junction Greyhound terminal restaurant and the guy just out of the CCC in Colorado. He had only seen her that once, he would say, that morning. She had put down the plate of ham and eggs, rye toast on the side. Splashed more coffee into his cup and gave him an extra jelly.

"I saw her with this small bag, come out of the terminal and get right on the bus." Hardy knew the scene by heart. "She came right down the aisle and sat down in the seat next to me. And there were empty window seats, too." His father would smile at this point, raise an eyebrow. " 'Where're you headed?' she asks. I tell her Pittsburgh. I had heard from my mother's uncle who was the head gardener. Miss Arnett was coming back from Mexico and needed a chauffeur. 'That sounds okay to me,' she said and pushed her seat back, got comfortable."

The next was Walt Hardy's favorite part, and he would play it over and over, trying to make out their voices. Especially his mother's. "When we got to St. Louis, we got off the bus and got married and made the rest of the trip by boat. That was her idea," Bill Hardy would say with a shrug, then laugh open mouthed, head raised back. His own brief wildness still suprised him. "Lots of river steamboats in those days. We got on one in St. Louis and went down the Mississippi to Cape Giradeau and then turned into the Ohio at Cairo, Illinois. They pronounce it like that," father would tell son. "Like the syrup—*KAY-ro*."

Yes, Walt Hardy would think and breaks off another piece of roll. His colleagues from the other restaurant have just waved at him and disappeared into an inner dining room. There's a town in New York with the same name. Cairo. In Greene County. In his former life, the county chairman who lived in that town was up for sale. On the take for either Republicans or Democrats. LBJ's people. The guy could be had. What does he want, the Kennedy people had asked one evening? Hardy knew the man's wife needed a hysterectomy. Okay, they said. Throw in a job for him in Albany, he had said. Sounds fine, Steve Smith had said. Good work, Hardy. Take care of it. Just then, Celia had come back into the motel room from the bathroom. What's that about? she wanted to know. It's about a kind of syrup, he had told her. *KAY-ro.*

As a teenager, if he found himself downtown, he'd sometimes walk over to the waterfront, to the Monongahela, and imagine his father and mother getting off the paddle-wheeler in 1940. Sometimes, a riverboat would be tied up there, and he wondered if it was the same one that had brought them up the Ohio to Pittsburgh. Coming all the way up the Ohio to get off in Pittsburgh, excited and in love, but later, he would also think how they had entered the compound in Point Breeze, had all but disappeared into this small apartment over the garage. Landlocked. That would explain her restlessness maybe. Was it Santa Barbara? The last place his father said he had heard from her? A California woman, his father often said, they're never happy anywhere else. What if he should show up in her living room. in Santa Barbara. She had read about him, seen him on the cover in *Time*. Hey, Ma—what do you think of your blue-eyed boy. He had a hunch this disappearing woman—for in his mind she was always in the act of vanishing, stepping up on the stage of the Stanley but never completely gone—that this forever retreating mother would have a definite opinion about her son's recent history. Unlike his father, she'd tell him what she thought of him. He just knew it.

The sizzle of the steak precedes its appearance, and the rich, greasy aroma of the meat puts spurs to his appetite. Side dishes of baked potato, the ubiquitous iceberg lettuce salad, and a grayish whipped vegetable were set down in order. "What's that?"

"Parsnips. You like parsnips, Hon?" the waitress asks. "It's one of the chef's specials; pureed with cottage cheese and a little nutmeg."

Nor was it half-bad, Hardy admits, once again taken by the eccentric ways of his native city—even with parsnips—and an immense longing for Celia suddenly swells within him. She would be amused by this dish, even the unabashed macho tone of the restaurant, and certainly the waitress's direct manner. Driving himself downtown in the Lincoln, the western light had etched the Pittsburgh skyline, the apartment buildings and houses of the inner city as they appeared from the darkening green folds of hillsides and foothills that came down to the edge of this ancient river basin. Hardy was struck again by the sylvan nature of this city, how the steel and concrete structures of it, no less sophisticated than those in New York or Chicago, seemed to rise from a virgin forest, with neighborhoods of more homely rooftops showing above the vegetation. When he looked on this prospect it was with the sense of a déjà vu, as if he had seen this same combination of structures and lush vegetation in a period that preceded his own history; stone temples and the remains of rude houses overwhelmed by a rapacious jungle.

But today, that aspect could have been part of an essay that he and Celia might have put together during one of those long drives to a village in the Catskills, say Cairo, on their way to a political meeting when all had seemed possible. In the eloquence of his whiskied fluency, he scripts the conversation they might have had about Jefferson and his ideas on a rural democracy, the importance of that rural character to a democracy—we all know about that—and then comes A. Hamilton and the urban Federalists. Country gentleman and city slicker, you might say; it's been the same argument back and forth. A couple of times during his torturous sessions before congressional committees, Hardy thought he could hear the lines of this old dialog in the mouths of the politicians who pressed him for answers he would not or could not give. But wasn't this view through the Lincoln's windshield this evening just what Jefferson might have appreciated—a city with all the advantages of the wilderness? And, come to think of it, had he not reviewed this visual synthesis from an automobile named for a leader who had attempted to keep this union of urban and rural ideologies together? Hey, there's a metaphor you might want to remember, if you were Walt Hardy, an artful figure of speech that could open up checkbooks in Chicago. Land of Lincoln and, and let's not forget, Carl Sandburg. And so forth.

Ha! Cee would respond. Just name a few of those wilderness advantages. Outdoor plumbing and bad teeth. And their exchanges would become fun, exciting both of them as a kind of foreplay, almost, that would find a happy resolution in a motel after a firehouse barbecue or chicken and dumplings with a town committee. Hardy stops eating, his feelings have choked on a chunk of memory.

"How's everything, dear?"

Fine, everything's fine, he nods to the waitress, for the steak is done just to the grade of pink he appreciates, but his appetite has gone. Celia has gone. If she had been with him today, instead of Susanna Pell, he might have found some clue as to what old lady Arnett's will had wanted him to take. Funny that he would put it that way—what she had wanted him to take. It was his bequest. An odd old duck, Peggy Arnett, to make his inheritance a kind of scavenger hunt. She would have remembered his ways as a boy, poking around the mansion, picking up books, trying on their various fancies for size. That had been her reason. But, Cee could spot things, in an argument or on a shelf, that his observation sometimes passed over.

Certainly, Celia would have fended off Susanna, let him enter the place by himself. Let him make his own choice of memorabilia rather than this flyer's journal. Roy Armstrong. The woman had shoved it into his hands. "But I had to take it," he would say to Celia. He often calls up her spirit for comfort and advice. Hardy wonders if these imagined intimacies were not the richer part of their marriage, and the idea makes him a little uneasy. He reaches for his drink.

"Had to take it?" she would ask, her eyes going wide with amusement.

"Well, it was just a joke, really. But something in her expression."

"Something in your pants," Cee would say. "Not just in her expression, boyo. What did she want in exchange?" Her mouth would become tremulous, nervously ready to smile. He could remember the look. They could have been talking about a county chairman, someone not to be trusted. "What was your half of the bargain?"

"Only a dance. An old joke. So I danced with her." He savored the watery scotch as he imagined Celia's laughter. Anticipated it. Like a balloon bursting. All out, all at once.

"Give me a break," she'd say. "Only a dance? That suburban matron had gone gooey over your criminal past. She had grabbed up anything just to rub up against you..." But this speech embarrasses him, for the language was his own, put into

Celia's phantom, and he brushes some bread crumbs together into a neat, tiny pile, pinches them up and drops them onto a plate.

He always took pride in his faithfulness to Celia. He held this loyalty aloft, like a banner, and especially in places like this bar and restaurant which seemed to be training camps for what a senator of his acquaintance called "sport fucking."

But Hardy, like most men, never considered whether he tested his fidelity in such atmospheres or whether he teased the corruption of his innocence. Both could be enjoyed. Let's give him some credit; now and then he wondered if this sense of loyalty was not just a little self-indulgent, a little too self-congratulatory if not gratuitous. Because his true-blue faithfulness seemed to make Celia uncomfortable at times, like something she had not expected, a clause in the fine print of the contract that she had not counted on. In fact, she had seemed a little disappointed that the political scandal around him had not involved some sexual high jinks as well; perhaps, not so much to explain his involvement as to complete the picture of it she held in her mind.

And, in truth, he might have got the better part of the unusual barter this morning with Susanna Pell. The sections of the old memoir he had read so far were fun to read, like pulp fiction, like some of his father's old magazines. Armstrong had been a soldier of fortune, a rather romantic figure, according to his own lights. The figure who appeared in the pages just browsed appealed Hardy. The pilot's footloose idealism. Also, the journal mentioned places in Mexico that Hardy knew. He had been to some of them. Armstrong's life picked at his curiosity. But why would Miss Arnett have this notebook in her desk? Charles Halstead, her fiancé, had already made an appearance in the journal. His father had said Halstead was killed in Mexico but here he was alive in these pages. Strange, Hardy thinks, to encounter a person living in another's history, someone you knew to be already dead. It was like knowing a truth about that person, a secret truth unfairly known, as in Halstead's case, yet irrevocable. How things were to come out in a play though the actors, reading their lines, would be unaware of what would bring down the curtain. They hadn't read that far. Celia would know the term for that sort of thing, and Hardy longs for her to be there beside him, in the bustling sensuality of this restaurant. But she is not. He scoops up the last of the parsnips, wishing there had been a little bit more.

Miss Arnett must have kept the journal as a sentimental souvenir of that time. He's amused to think of that spry old lady he had waltzed around the floor, flying around Mexico, hob-nobbing with Mexican generals and soldiers of fortune—being someone's "sweetie." She must have been around thirty-five. And none of them, he reflects in the warm haze of his Olympian perception, knowing their pages were numbered.

Hardy waves for the check with a light headeness not com-pletely due to whiskey. He's suddenly eager to read the rest. He would drive back to Point Breeze, get the journal and read it in the backseat of the Lincoln by the light of a flashlight, skip to the good parts, find out about Halstead and Arnett. Whatever Armstrong might know. He nearly knocks over his chair as he gets up, and the waitress regards him warily. You had to have been there, he almost tells her. Had to be in the backseat of that other limousine that Sunday afternoon; have one book substi-tuted for another by the very same person who had interrupted his reading of the first. It was like fate. Something like fate, anyway. Therefore, only right to read the journal in the backseat of the Lincoln. Rounds everything up, ties up loose ends, he reasons, and pushes his way out of the crowded barroom, smil-ing in such a way as to make the couple entering the bar won-der about him.

However, only the kitchen light burned in the second floor of the carriage house when he parks the Lincoln and turns off the ignition. The mansion is dark. His idea has lost its heat on the drive back. Where was he to find a flashlight? Just looking for it would cool his impulse even more. Why do you need a flashlight, his father would ask, awakened, and the whole enter-prise, his enthusiasm would be braked. Stopped short. A bluish refridgerant glow suffuses the grounds of the estate as the hard light of a full moon above Pittsburgh is filtered through river mist. Not the wisp of a cloud in the sky. The round blimp of the greenhouse behind the colonnade pulses with the unearthly illu-mination, as though the moonlight has passed through the frosted glass panes to undergo a peculiar photosynthesis within, and is then pumped back into the night air with even a greater intensity.

Not ready for sleep, Walt Hardy strolls to the end of the colonnade. The windows of the mansion and carriage house face each other. He thinks of his father behind the dark window of his bedroom stretched out like a stone warrior atop his tomb. Slightly snoring. Lights in the kitchen. A plate of something left out for him on the kitchen table; probably a piece of cake. Behind him, the mansion looms like an old cargo ship run aground. Tree frogs harmonize. A whine and screech of cats from across the street. The heavy breathing of a city sleeping.

The eerie light plays tricks upon him. The moon shadows of the colonnade lay down a lattice upon the ground, like a ladder on which a slight form seems to be climbing toward him. One too many scotches, surely; one too many glimpses of Rima swinging through his thoughts. Had he unknowingly sum- moned ghosts? His mother? Peggy Arnett? Celia? Because the shape continues to advance, earthbound but steadily; finally to materialize before him.

"Yes," Celia says. "It's me. I thought you could use a buddy."

Sometimes, Celia wondered if men saw themselves at all when they looked in a mirror, actually looked at themselves and not some image placed on the glass by vanity or some notion about themselves that filtered out their true reflection. Why are you taking so long, Walt used to say as she inspected her face, as she leaned into a mirror to number the changes around the eyes and the mouth, that he never seemed to notice. As a mat- ter of fact, he must view her with the same sort of efface- ment—if that's the word—or maybe it was a kind of amnesty that men practiced in marriage, that refused to account for the flaws their wives could clearly see in their own faces. Or maybe, they just didn't care.

When she was fifteen, she took money saved from baby- sitting chores and bought a full length mirror at Kresge's that she hung on the back of her closet door and that her mother would sometimes use to check a dress hem and the two of them, mother and daughter, would be like sisters for a few minutes, enjoying a conspiracy with the mirror against the man who never seemed interested in his own reflection, save while shav- ing every morning, and even then she knew her father never really looked at his face. She had come upon him more than once in the one bathroom of their apartment over the art supply and book store, eyes focused on the Gillette razor doing its work through the lathered flesh of his cheeks and jowls; never really looking at himself. She had thought the process so dangerous that it demanded all of his concentration. So, just this mirror on the bathroom medicine cabinet, a small looking glass fixed into a mahogany frame on her mother's bureau and then the long one from Kresge's that she had mounted on her closet door and before which she practiced the Twist to the muffled exhortations of Chubby Checker on the Poughkeepsie radio station. That's all they were allowed. Only the first two were necessary, her father said, since pulling on the same clothes through the seasons, you already knew how they looked, you didn't need to see yourself full-length.

This disinterest in how they looked—no, it was more than that; it was a peculiar self-denial men had that went beyond vanity or was an ultimate vanity, but here Celia would catch herself in a mire of speculations and suggestions that were sometimes too much for her and which would catch her up short with questions as to how she had become lost in such ideas, and where did they come from anyway? But, just the ordinary damage control check that women make of their faces is construed as some kind of narcissistic endeavor by men —something that came with the plumbing, as her mother would say— by men who never recognize their own images; therefore, believe everything is okay. So who is the realist and who is the romantic? Does Teddy Kennedy know what he really looks like? Celia didn't think so. In a mirror, he probably still sees that young kid his brother, the President, put into office and which his other brother, Bobby, had invited to that breakfast meeting she'd gone to with Walt; slim and endearing in a gawky manner, eyes wide and eager like a polly-wog's. But look at him now.

She'd read somewhere that evil spirits, devils and monsters, could not see themselves in a mirror, that the glass never gave back their appearance, and there might be a practical reason for that which she would have to think about, but more likely the mirror did reflect the monster standing before it; all the shaggy outlines, the loathsome wens and sores clearly defined. It was just that the monster saw himself as a normal being, did not see his monsterness and, maybe, that was part of being a monster.

Just outside Little Rock, Arkansas, she had come on this idea. It had appeared in the long reflection she had entered into when she left the outskirts of Amarillo, Texas like a road sign that had been passed too swiftly so that its complete message was not comprehended at first. To locate her thoughts on a map did not verify them so much as it made her comfortable with them, knowing where they had appeared to her if not where they had come from.

So, appearances and reflections. The colloquium had occupied her solitude all the way across the country, once she decided to get back on the road. Pursue the sun. She had never really been warm enough—here's another idea that had come to her just as she drove away from Indiana, not daring to look in the rearview mirror because Walt's shrunken figure might be stuck on it. She might have paused had she looked, but then she got mad all of a sudden and for the silliest reason but there it was, goddamn it, she was tired of being chilly and then cold and then chilly again, so she had turned toward Arizona and the desert. She kept going. She was tired of shivering and headed for heat.

Well, it was much more than that, of course. The heat business was just one more of those half-glances at the truth that had become second nature. And where had all that begun? This technique or habit or style of tossing a piece of the truth into the larger lie, like seasoning. Stone soup. Somewhere she had stopped for gas and to use the rest room, and several truckers had stopped talking when she walked by, went silent to sight her over their styrofoam cups of coffee like it was hunting season, all of them husbands and fathers, and one of them young enough for her to be his mother, she told herself in the toilet's mirror—not bad, not too damn bad.

Maybe if she had been a mother, had been able to have children, they'd still be in Red Oaks Mills worrying about the crabgrass and what to do with the family room, now that the children had left the nest. Maybe the children would have traveled west by now themselves instead of her making the trip all alone. That was funny, wasn't it? Walt would have his own engineering firm and they'd still be going to conferences around the state, the country, like they did when he was moving up in the Jaycees, but they'd be mining and industrial conventions and the first thing she'd do when they checked into the hotel room would be to sit down on the bed and call one of the children in Seattle or San Francisco. Both would be in college or maybe one of them was already out, working. Yes, Daddy is here, she'd say, and pass him the phone, moved as always by his squarish face going soft like he was about to cry as he put down the notes for his speech and prepared to talk to one of the kids.

Then, of course, they did go to other conventions and meetings, and other phone calls did come at all hours of the day and night, but these meetings and these voices on the line were very different. More serious and tired and—well, ugly, too. And all men. The wheeling and dealing, the pockets full of slips with numbers and names scribbled on them, the whole structure like a tree house boys might put together of a summer out of scrap lumber—all the same as when Walt was doing the Junior Chamber of Commerce bit, but the whole enterprise had become—well, serious. The phone calls were from Washington; men she had only seen on television spoke to her familiarly like a daughter or even more so. A disturbing intimacy. It was no longer make-believe. Put on the black velvet, Walt had said one time. We're having dinner with the Senator in Albany.

You've broken your father's heart, she heard her mother say and she drove beyond her exit off the circular around Indianapolis, missed the turn because of her mother's voice, and had to go all the way round the city again, to come back to Route 65 going south, to Louisville, Kentucky, where it might be warmer, pulling off the highway to check the map and get her bearings. Locate herself on the Interstate as well as almost twenty-five years back. Can I be of assistance, ma'am? This tall, handsome Indiana State Trooper had leaned down smiling, the image of the good-looking ex-athletes that surrounded Robert Kennedy, bodyguards and such—and little good they did him after all. So, you're Walt Hardy's wife, Bobby had said, taking her hand that night in Albany. He was shorter than she had supposed, but very broad shoulders and cold blue eyes that seemed to appraise her with a sound of distant laughter, and she had then wondered, later even more thought about Walt requesting the black velvet outfit which was the shortest skirt of her mini's.

All the awful rumors about Marilyn Monroe came after; that is, came to be known after, and that may have already happened when she had given RFK her hand. That poor woman already dead and yes—fucked-over. No other word for it. Fucked-over. So what was the point? She had let herself be used, like Marilyn, for everything was to be traded, even a glimpse of your wife's tush. How could she complain? She had known the score by then, had pushed Walt into the game, in fact.

The trooper got her back on the road and headed in the right direction to pick up Route 65 going south to Louisville, and Celia picked up her mother's voice again at the junction where she had left it. Your father has worked all his life for you to go to law school. It's different these days, Mom—these days and nights of riots and burning cities and the faint vibrations of what was to become that awful din—Vietnam. It was all different, Mom. We have to get out and do something. We have to do something about that war—stop it before it happens—that was her best argument, Walt's too. He said it first as they talked long after closing time in his one-room engineering firm where she'd come to do the books, one of her clients—he was then—her part-time bookkeeping service that was making tuition money for Albany Law. That had been the idea.

Rolling down the windows on the Honda Civic south of Indianapolis did no good. The aroma of that small office in Wappingers Falls next door to the barber shop flooded her memory. Powdery smells, tonic and talcum, and old linoleum and the spoiled milk mustiness of the latex paint Walt had rolled on the walls. Clip-clip went the scissors next door—sometimes she'd look up from his company's scanty ledgers and expect to see the points of the barber's shears poke through the plaster-board of the thin wall between the store fronts. The barber was the landlord.

But she'd see Walt Hardy studying books; reading biographies, histories, memoirs as he waited for her to tell him how he had really come out that month, and they would talk, or he would talk and she would listen. Never about himself much beyond being from Pittsburgh and that his father worked for a wealthy family—a chauffeur. His mother had disappeared when he was a child. Instead, he'd give her long reviews of the biography he had been reading or the nature of the history that had occupied him while she balanced his books—facts and accounts not all that strange to her for books had been her playmates and siblings as she grew up over the bookstore, and her father had pushed her to read and to read and then read more. Sometimes, Celia would wonder if he had not started the book store just to avail her of an unending supply of reading material.

Perhaps, her father had wanted to push her away from that mirror on the back of her door—which he must have known about—to push her away from herself in it. Did he think the reflection was destructive, self-limiting? So Walt Hardy's summaries of his readings of history had fascinated her, not for their content, but because of the tantalizing look on his face when he spoke as if he were leaving out some very relevant detail, a reference to something that had never actually happened, but, if included, the detail would make the whole account different, more accurate. Maybe, his own place in that history.

She had figured this out by the time she had sat in audiences and watched and listened to him speak at political functions. His place. Where he might have been or should have been in those events and in that other person's life; an anonymous actor in that long-past and irretrievable scene whether it was with Wilson at Versailles or Truman at Potsdam.

Recently, she had seen G. Gordon Liddy on television and she had been struck by the smug peace of mind the man had radiated, and she was certain his composure came from the certainty of his place in history, sordid and as nefarious as it might be. If he had remained an assistant DA of Dutchess County, an erstwhile candidate for higher office; eventually, becoming an ordinary citizen who, now and then, fired off a cranky letter to the editor of the *Poughkeepsie Journal*; well, what's the point? She was getting in deep again. He would be cranky, that's the point—he would never be satisfied, he would not have followed his particular, unholy star.

Oh, it was somehow not fair to her the way this earnest, hopeful and boyish search had swelled up in Walt like the floor of his small office next to the barbershop. An ancient and monumental frost had pushed up the middle of the floor so that the linoleum had cracked at the crown of the upheaval where she sat doing his accounts, her feet flat down on the floor to keep the chair from rolling away from the desk. She should have put a similar brake on her feelings.

But it hadn't been easy to see this need rising in his eyes as he talked of the sacrifices made by the few, chosen by history, to benefit the many; described the glorious junction in a road when all had seemed lost for humanity, for the Union, threatened by the forces of repression, of tyranny, of intolerance. Pick one. The orations were too large for that small room. To see the need in this orphan face. She had stopped outside of Louisville, headed back west now, and counted up all that language, those phrases and lofty pronouncements. They had come to nothing. Zero. Like his one-man firm's accounts.

But Walt Hardy could put a luster on them; they came out moist-eyed and that hadn't been fair either for, she learned later, he had really been talking about something else though, to let him off the hook a little, he never knew it himself. It wasn't a conscious effort—not at first anyway. Like looking in the mirror, he never saw what was there, only the image on the surface of the glass. Was there a space within all mirrors where the true images were stored? The truth? Like all of us, she had had a childhood by Disney.

Balancing the double cheeseburger with fries and the chocolate malt in her lap, Celia wheeled out of the fast-food bay and back on to Interstate 65. She had decided to eat nothing but junk food all the way across the country. A kind of perverse cleansing of her innards. She might just get really fat. She wanted to take in as many calories as she could hold and then some, pack them into every corner of her person until she filled out like one of those thick sausages served at the firehouse barbecues they used to go to in the Hudson Valley. Splitting apart over the coals and bursting with greasy goodness. She was going to be warm and fat. Oh, boy!

Once, one of her clients, an insurance agent who routinely cheated on his tax returns, gave her a couple of tickets to a dinner for the local congressman and she had mentioned it to Walt and he had said, sure, it's a free meal, they could leave after dessert and before the speeches. Looking back through the rearview mirror, the interstate had cleared out behind her—not one car or semi to be seen and the whole sequence from that dinner down to the Congressional hearings looked just like that—clear and a straight line all the way. They had become lovers by then, that need she saw in his eyes, in the pursed gap of his lips, she had mistaken for a place he might find in her, if only a part of her, but that had been wrong too. Also, her book-

112

keeping talents had proved his one-man engineering firm was not doing so well. Only the barber, the landlord, was making a profit.

So, Walt had smooth talked a gauge company in Poughkeepsie into taking his company over—"One more example of corporate piracy," he had joked and they had giggled and got cozy under the covers. After the fact, like the road map beside her on the Civic's seat, the directions of their life looked logical and clearly laid out on that part of the highway.

Because they hadn't left the dinner after dessert but had sat through the boring speeches, the town and county politicians rising and falling back at the head table like the pockmarked line of tin targets in a shooting gallery. "You could do something like this," she had whispered in his ear, "and better." Just like that, it had come out of her, and not even now, driving sixty-five miles per hour on Interstate 64 can she think of where it came from. Out of some dissatisfaction before the fact of what their life was going to be like—her going nights up to Albany to law school, Walt a permanent vice-president at Mid-Hudson Tech Gauges. Or more likely, the sadness in his voice as he had described some historical injustice, a moment when some poor devil had been pushed around. The temper of him as he came in from the garage, complaining of taxes. Firing off a cranky letter to the *Poughkeepsie Journal*. She had seen all this happening in their future.

"You can do this," she had whispered and just to test the odd notion that had crossed her mind, she had put her hand on his thigh under the table, and it was as she guessed. He was half hard, so who nudged who? The pudgy congressman boasting about what he had done for local farmers had turned him on, and Walt's face had become luminous, upturned like a dish about to catch the purest rain. He looked like that when he talked about Lincoln and Jefferson. William Jennings Bryan.

As Celia crossed the Wabash River into Illinois, she honked the Honda's horn to sound some kind of triumphal fanfare of her passage, one more division between herself and the deceitful landscape she was leaving behind, though she had been telling herself that she was a little bit responsible for everything that had happened since that chicken dinner in Hopewell Junction, the first of all those chicken dinners they were to attend. Eventually, they would be seated at the head table and Walt would be the speaker, the introducer, his face glowing and his lips shaped to fit around the appropriate word. The master of ceremonies but never the main speaker—the fixer, the go-between. Can-do Hardy. All the accounts of him in the newspapers, that article in *Time* or was it the *New York Times*, made much of that expression—his Huck Finn look, they called it.

Years later, she would think that actually more than one funeral was being held that sunny day in June of 1968; one of them had been RFK's and at least one other had been Walt Hardy's. All of his hopes, a boy's tree house of dreams brought down in one night to abandon him, she remembers the picture vividly, on the steps of St. Patrick's Cathedral, him going from one politician to another like a petitioner of some sort, cut off from a destiny that had seemed like a sure thing as the votes had come in from the California primary only a couple of nights before. She sucked the last of the chocolate shake through the straw.

But his destiny had not been her destiny. No prince had run around with a glass slipper in her shoe size. She had stretched out her hand one morning in bed to find his side of the bed empty and she had reached this conclusion instead. She remembered where he was, one of the trips he had begun to make to Central America and which was the beginning of this trip she was now making to Arizona, though she couldn't see that far ahead then. All the late night phone calls had started up again, and some of the familiar voices from '68 introduced younger voices and then Walt said they had to move to Maryland as if to make the distance if not the intervals between the calls shorter. It was like a corporate takeover—though not like the innocent silliness when Mid-Hudson Tech Gauges had assumed the bad credit rating of W. A. Hardy Associates.

"I must confer with my associates," he'd say and nuzzle her breasts, fastening his lips around a nipple and here she was, almost to the Mississippi River, one more crossing to put behind her and she could feel herself becoming tense and heavy just with the memory of it. "Going perky," Walt called it and she had never cared for the expression. His mouth—that Huck Finn look trying to find the right word to announce his innocence in an evil world—seemed shaped just to fit her there too and she sometimes felt she suckled all the children they never had.

But it hadn't been silly nor innocent though there actually had been a firm called American Petra taking over Mid-Hudson Gauges. No main office but an elaborate telephone hookup to different offices all over the country—one-room outfits mostly, so he was back to a one-room operation, but a pretty snazzy one and with no barber next door but a secretary who dressed like an expensive call girl. W. A. Hardy, Consultant. W. A. Hardy, Mgr. Technical Information. Mr. Can-do. Do me, she joked once in his office with his new title stenciled on his door. Every time she went into Washington to meet him, it seemed he'd have a new title or a new firm on the door. A new secretary, too, come to think of it. But the old fervor was back on his face, a light sheen like the sweat of a saint in the making, and so the references to "freedom fighters" and keeping his word went past her. After years of coasting on a kind of flat plain, like the one she was driving through in southern Illinois, their marriage suddenly got going again. Put on speed. Walt was like a man who had renewed himself, and, in fact, that had been happily true. He had been after her all the time.

So, she had reached out this one morning in bed, a little horny; then, sorry to remember that he was away on one of his trips—Guatemala, wasn't it?—and her disappointment settled into something else a little more thoughtful. Something was wrong. Off-center. Law school had been put off for good; she just didn't have the lust for it. So, then what—flower arranging? A chain had bought her father's store, and she had put that money into CDs for an emergency though she couldn't imagine what kind it would be. Walt had handled everything well. All contingencies had been anticipated and planned for. Their life had become like a military exercise; neat and with little wasted effort or material. Walt would return from his consultations like an athlete coming to the sidelines. We are winning, he'd say almost breathlessly. We just need to get supplies to these people. We're going to finish the job, he'd say, and he'd get that sad kid's look on his face, his John Wayne look she'd call it, as when he described something out of history to her, Lincoln being shot or Wilson failing to get the vote for the League of Nations; something like that, and she'd forget to ask about the job and who was paying for it, who had ordered it. The why of it. There was laundry to be done, just like her mother!

But on this particular morning, she had sat up in the empty bed and began to ask questions. Something wasn't right. Maybe it had been the softness of her stomach or the view in the bedroom mirror—a whole series of mirrors Walt had had installed on the bi-fold doors of the wall closet. She was a fairly usual looking woman, clean and nice—as her mother would say—whose breasts had settled a bit lower on her rib cage and whose upper thighs were looking just a bit dimpled. She'd have to double the aroebic sessions. She'd have to ask her husband about what he was doing. Really doing. She had long figured out the American Petra Company was some kind of a front. The two suggestions had posed themselves, just like that, in the mirror as she peered over her shoulder at herself.

It began to sound like he was working for another government when he answered her questions. Not a foreign government, but another one right here in the US that was some how connected but wasn't either; that ran inside the one everyone voted for. Who elected these people, she had asked? Where did their authority come from? His authority? They had the authority, he told her. Not to worry. Couldn't have a better authority, she remembered him saying. Well now wait a minute, wait just a goddamn minute; no, trust me, he had said. Trust him. We're in a mortal conflict with people that don't go by our rules. We have to do it differently. We're forced to do it this way if democracy is to have a chance. That's all.

But it wasn't all, of course. Like that piece of tape on the door that had tripped up G. Gordon Liddy and Company at the Watergate. That plane had crashed in the jungle and then the odd news note—not even in an American paper—and then came all the journalists at the front gate, the FBI, the Congressional hearings. Magazine biographies of Walt appeared in every waiting room of America. She didn't always recognize him. One time, at her doctor's, she came across some surprising information in a _People Magazine._ Can you really speak Spanish, she asked? My fluency in Spanish, he joked, is second only to my facility with Yiddish. And, you've been to Tehran—way over there? And listen, Buster, you make a trip to France and you don't bring this doll any perfume? She had tried to joke. He had only shrugged. He'd become very distant.

The bridge at St. Louis over the Mississippi was too large and not combustible, and that was a pity, because she wished it could be burned just to protect herself against herself, for about then, she had begun to think about turning around, going back. Something about him still got to her and she was sorry for it, angry with herself when it happened. Like the last time they made love, the night before he was to stand alongside Oliver North and MacFarlane and Poindexter and the others and raise his right hand to swear to tell the truth. They all had.

This night he had set all the closet doors at an angle so their lovemaking would be caught in different, multiple reflections. Not the first time he had done this with the mirrors, like a boy's project, more sweet than erotic, and he had been so earnest this particular night arranging the reflections of the orgy the two of them made. Lately, she has wondered if that same kind of industry, the same keen appreciation for a complicated assignment, to do it right, had not also made him lose sight of the nature of the assignment. She would raise this argument within the court of her hurt and anger.

For he had lied so effortlessly before the committee the next day. Technically correct but specifically evasive. Sitting behind him and to one side, she knew she appeared to be the faithful Washington insider's wife, knees primly together and on the edge of her seat with his celebrity, but she had been able to pick apart his testimony herself—a date here, a place there, and there must be lots more. Who was he protecting? Where had she been when the coffee burned? Reagan? Bush? Who? Was this the message of all those books he had quoted to her? To lie before Congress like that? Would Jimmy Stewart have done this in that movie he loved to watch—he had a tape of it and played it over and over. The climax with Stewart on the floor of the US Senate reading telegrams from kids begging him to stand firm against the crooked senators. The fat cats, as he called them, who couldn't care less about the little guy, the freedom fighters. Walt's eyes would get a little blurred sometimes seeing that part of the movie. The script had got turned upside down.

But he looked like that sometimes, like the actor. His voice caught the same way. Had he studied this pose? And it was the same look, the same catch in his voice and visionary stare, when he talked about values and that the person he was about to introduce, whether the local candidate for dog catcher or, even, Robert Kennedy that time in Albany; firehouse barbecues or black tie dinners, it was all the same to him. All the same before Congress as at the Jaycees conventions or that dinner for the Salvadoran Ambassador. What in hell did she think was going on? They sat at the head table with the Kissingers! Did that happen with just anybody? Any other assistant to the associate-associate for whatever? Had she never wondered how come? What a dope!

You know it's too bad your mother took off with that magician, she said to him once. They had been driving back from Greene County, crossing the Hudson River—another river crossed, Celia thought, as she checked the map for a route south from Interstate 44, from Missouri into Arkansas, still wanting to be warmer. If your mother was still around, you could throw her into your talk and you'd be the candidate rather than just the guy who makes the introductions. Every candidate needs a mother he can mention, maybe introduce at a dinner or a county fair. Walt had said nothing, and it was dark and she couldn't see what his face looked like. She had hurt him a little, she knew. They both knew he was a better man than the candidate.

So, when she came down from Missouri, from the north into Arkansas and Little Rock, getting ready to turn right on Route 40 and pick up what used to be old Route 66, celebrated in song by Nat King Cole, and she tried to whistle some of the bouncy melody, Celia had been thinking of how Walt Hardy looked when he stood up to talk, to swear before God that what he was about to say was the truth, the whole truth. She had wished he could see himself.

Somewhere on the outskirts of Little Rock, she wanted to say to him, okay, I guess maybe I'm a little to blame—I got you into this with that dumb chicken dinner. But maybe I can make it up to you. Maybe there's a mirror I can hold up for you so you will really see yourself. Maybe, I can do that, Celia thought as she headed toward Arizona. Maybe if they had had children, he would have sought his place, found his generation, there. So, she had pulled off the side of the road, counted to ten, and turned around.

"You know that's the funniest thing," Walt says in the morning. The phone had rung in the kitchen of the apartment over the garage, so when he returned to the bedroom, Cee is stretching drowsily, looking very appealing in his old bed. They had made quite a night of it; first in the garden in the moonlight and then in his room, whispering and muffling their cries so as not to wake his father.

"What?"

"That was the widow of a guy I went to school with here, grade school. I gave an interview yesterday and mentioned him and that was his widow on the phone. She just read it in the morning paper. Eddie Poremski was his name. He got killed in Laos."

January 5, 1940
Oaxaca

Just now, I look up from my notebook, and there is a dog looking at me from across the square. The *zócalo* here in Oaxaca is very pretty with a fancy iron bandstand in the center of it and shops and cantinas set up around three sides, under the porticoes of the old whitewashed adobe buildings. The cathedral is off to the fourth side, pinkish clay flaking off and the massive sides shadowed by tall mesquites and jacarandas turning purple. An Army unit has just raised the flag across the *zócalo* with a slam-bang blast of trumpets and drums, so it must be around eight as the eastern sun slants in from behind where I sit in this cafe having my bread and coffee. Like a spot light hitting a vaude- ville act, the sun beams strike this mutt full in the face. Two days here after flying China and a couple of generals down to see her old man.

This dog cocks her head to one side, and there's no doubt she's looking at me, like

she's been trotting around Oaxaca all night,
looking for me, and here she finds _El Gringo_
sipping his coffee in the Café Excelente and
taking the morning airs. Her head is set, fixed
on the right ear, like she's listening to some
sound I'm putting out that only she can hear,
that the sleepy waitress cannot hear, nor the
guy at another table, a salesman looks like,
dipping his _bunuelo_ into his java. She has little pointy ears that fold forward, a head and
muzzle small for the body which is the size of
a Labrador's — smooth, short hair. But the head,
still held to one side as if questioning my
presence here, resembles the little dogs that
the Aztecs raised to eat — or so China told me
at the museum the other day. Then, as I'm writing this, like she had posed for me long enough,
the dog moves down the street and I see that one
of her hind legs has been injured, and the bones
have re-set so she carries the foot an inch or
two off the ground, never touching. She does
okay on the other three.

Some things I can't quite put together.
Halstead seemed more than eager to loan me the
oil company's Beechcraft to fly China and these
generals down to this to-do at her daddy's
ranchero. China put me up to asking him since
I told her about flying Halstead and his girlfriend over to Guadalajara last month. I don't
like him that much. This rich dame, his girl
friend, doesn't say much. Stays in the background, always reading something. Shy straw.
Peggy Arnett. I'm thinking Halstead's generosity has something to do with him trying to get
his oil business back from the Mexicans. China's
old man is mixed up in politics, the upcoming
election and all that. He might even be a candidate for the presidency. Oil is poured over
everything these days in Mexico. Old Trotsky has
his say about it almost every day in the newspapers. The oil companies are still looking for
some way to reverse Cárdenas takeover of the
fields.

"Why, of course, old man," Halstead says when I ask him, like we are members of the same club and I've just asked for the salt. "I know General Suarez very well. A hero of the revolution. Please give him my warmest regards." I've looked Halstead up at the fancy layout he keeps in the Colonia Roma. Big rooms full of light and air through huge windows. His girlie is sitting in one of these open windows, her back to us, reading. It's a big place, several bedrooms. It looks like she's just shampooed her hair because there's a towel around her shoulders. Her hair is bobbed.

But what am I doing here? The whole world is at war, and I sit in this café, in this small Mexican town like a shirt too old for the laundry — like that big green, white and red flag across the way, hanging down on the pole and lifeless. The Russians jumped Finland in November and are taking a licking. German battleships are blowing up in Montevideo harbor. England and France and Germany are mixing it up. And here I sit, the Scourge of the Skies, like a fly stuck in molasses. In fact, it could be a sweet life down here.

Yesterday afternoon in the hotel, China rising above me as the sweat runs down between her breasts. The electric fan humming in the corner circulates the heat. The look of her eyes when she listens to my stories, warm and so very serious. Not the killing parts, but the stories of flying, the taking off and landing in different places. Looking down at the earth. Different planes. The close calls and the three-pointers. She wants me to teach her to fly. Like a child, that she almost is, she listens to these fairy tales. Even to me, my life sometimes sounds like a pulp magazine.

Then, there's the way she walks, floats is more like it. Her feet. The odd, touching positions they take when she stands to talk, to look at something. One foot placed over the other or even-steven. More still than still when she thinks about something, looking down as she works it out, putting whatever it is into the pattern

of her own ancient history. At those times, she
looks down centuries. She could be modeled in
clay, a figurine in a museum case. Then she looks
up. At me. _Hola!_ This kid has walked into my
heart! Hard to believe she is happening to me.

She talks about dancing the way some of us
talk about flying. She tells me her ideas for
different dance numbers. She wants to reinvent
the old legends, the Indian myths, she says,
all by dancing. And all for Mexico. Her country.

"Before Cortés, before the Aztecs even there
were people that were one with the earth.
Anahuac. I wish to go back to them, bring them
alive back," she says and takes another bite of
the _pambacito._ Like Frank Buck-bring-'em-back-alive?
We were having a snack — an understatement, of
course — in a little spot near the Bellas Artes
after the premier of her dance. It was a big hit,
standing ovation. That's mostly what we do; eat
and go to bed, and she does both with the same
appetite.

China's dance group, the Blue Pigeons, did
the show at the big Bellas Artes, and it was a
helluva difference from the shows at the Club
Quixote — more intense, serious. Art with a Big
A. Standing ovation, like I said. She's hit the
big time, for Mexico. Hard to believe it was
her on stage, the same girl who talks to me in
a restaurant, jumps on me in private. She is
talking to me like one of the footnotes in the
dance program. I'm getting used to these lectures. Quetzalcoatl, the hero, born of a piece
of jade placed in his mother's belly, rubbing
chili peppers into the wounds of his enemies,
then he becomes the wise instructor. Knows about
corn and the stars and such, and then disappears
into the East. When I say her group, it isn't
hers, nor is she the main dancer. An American,
Anna Sokolow, started the outfit, but tonight
China's dance about Quetzalcoatl was in the
spotlight. She made it all up. Isn't that something?

I'm suddenly sad in the restaurant as her excitement and pleasure includes me. I'm part of both. Her black eyes burn with a fever. Big, toothy smile, and the coca-coppery color of her throat and face going to a deep rose. Like a large flower has unfolded within her bosom, her throat. I'm sad, because all this time, part of my head is still trying to figure out how to get back to the States. Get my bars back.

The other night, the El Gourmet was full of theatre people. It's a late-night spot for food and drink. Dancers are always hungry, eat like stevedores, and China is the champion chow hound. People come over to our table to con- gratulate her on Quetzacoatl. Wine, flowers are sent to the table. Even a big flan. The waiters seem doped up, jazzed by the excitement. It was like a new government has just been pro- claimed, free elections and flans for all. China is *La Presidenta*. She is glowing, a silly-happy look on her face I've seen in other circumstances with just the two of us. And I am cynical, thinking if it could only be this easy to change history, to make things right by danc- ing about it. I danced on the right side in Spain, so I'm told, and where did that get me? Well, McGee, for one thing, into this beautiful girl's arms.

But I am also thinking of how I can get out of this very booth we are sitting in, laughing and being in love like school kids; high on her night's triumph while at that very moment I am figuring how to get back to the States. I've been talking a little to Halstead about what strings he can pull for me. Rhyl has filled him in on me. I feel like a piker because of China's success, something she has been honest about and has worked hard for. And part of her happi- ness, this moment, is that she is with me, Juan Carillo, el *heroe de la Patrulla Americana*. It is clear to see. She is showing me off like I'm part of her curtain call. Which is okay by me.

But all I can think of is the disappointing news I got from Tooey Spatz's deputy over at the Embassy.

"Your   name   has   turned   up   on   the   House Un-American Committee list of communist sympa-thizers. So, in addition to serving in a foreign army   in   the   Spanish   war,   you   have   that   mark against you. Your re-instatement has become a political   question   now.   And   now,   you're   a Mexican citizen! But Spatz is working on it." Political question? What in hell do I know about political questions? The embassy shave-tail that gave me the dispatch kind of smirked. He had read it, for sure. I'd like to catch him in a turn at 12,000 feet!

So it's a kind of treachery I'm committing — to be here and not to be here; to be kissing China, to lavish myself between her cinnamon scented breasts, to feel the soft saw of her breath on my neck as she sleeps so trustingly in my arms, to be made special by her laughter, while this other part of me is planning how to get away—get back to apple pie and the red, white & blue. Just now I have an image of how China's arms lift above her head, about to embrace me or rising above me, astride me, like something off an old vase; hair uncoiled down her back and her face turned to one side, shyly, as if the feeling has taken her by surprise, she's looking sidewise at the feeling because it's too strong to go face-to-face. Or she does-n't want to scare it off. And I want to take a powder? Cripes!

But what is my citizenship? Where do I belong? Since I left for France in '17. Can anyone prove where I, Roy Armstrong or Juan Carillo — either one of us — belong? Just a child of the century, that's me, lacking one year. Flying through the century from those War crates up through this snazzy DC-2 with all its instruments and gadgets. Variable pitch props. Now I tell you, isn't that just the cat's meow?

Even on this Beechcraft I flew here to

Oaxaca, the prop automatically changes pitch with the drag. "You don't mind this extra job do you?" George Rhyl asks with a smirk. He knows about me and China of course. It's no secret that Cherokee Oil has money in his airline. Everything is all mixed up down here. Me and the Beechcraft are on loan, you might say, but to whose benefit? So, I fly two of her old man's cronies. The general Jesus Suarez, *el heroe de a Revolucion, amigo de Zapata, et cetera and la et cetera*—flying his pals down for a powwow out at the ranchero.

Just now, a warm pressure on my thigh under the table. It's this gimpy dog that must have circled around and come up behind me to lay her head on my leg. Close up, the muzzle really does look like one of those little dogs the Aztec had on their menus. *Tepexcuintl,* they were called. China spells it out. ("Why you always writing this down?" she asks in the museum last week. "You have this little book with you. You write me down *tambien*?") She was wearing a bright orange blouse that put a reflection like pollen on her shoulders, her face, and she was a blossom for sure. Even in the gloom of the Museo Nacional, she had this light about her like one of the corny paintings we had just seen — Mary getting the word that she was mit kinder.

So this mutt has just stretched out at my feet on the flagstones with a deep sigh, like she's been wandering through all the back alleys and plazas of the world, not just those of Oaxaca, and has at last found me. There's something final about that sigh, the way she makes herself comfortable. The one stiff leg stuck out straight from her body. She's a pretty animal at that.

I stay at the hotel on the square and China's at the ranch because *el jefe supremo* is in the dark about us. We hope. It's supposed to be a reunion of Zapata's old bandido buddies. An anniversary of some kind. I suspect something else. I listen to their chatter as we fly around Popocatepetl's snowcap — a hundred times more impressive than the glass curtain at the Bellas Artes. I catch some of their lingo over the drone of the Pratt-Whitney. The nearness of China's honeyed thighs beneath her vanilla muslin skirt makes me dopey and I drowse like a fly trapped in a sunny window. Just next to me. So, to change the subject, I tell her to take over the controls of the Beechcraft. I keep a feather touch on them, of course. She sits forward, wrinkles her brow. The pulse in her neck jumping. Serious and excited to be flying the ship. She's got on big gold earrings. Young as she is, she looks like one of those Mayan goddesses. Cut from stone. I wonder if she's thinking about what I'm thinking about. Wanna bet? How lucky we have this time together.

But, Congressman Dies says I'm a commie and for all I know China, this luscious daughter of Montezuma who has been teaching me her version of the corn ceremony, is getting me into deeper trouble by getting me to fly some of these cactus pinkos down to Oaxaca for a confab. Her daddy is mixed up with American oil, Mexican politics, and land. T'ain't funny, McGee.

Stupendous mountains, some of them still active volcanoes. Snow at the higher elevations, near-desert below. It's the kind of landscape that makes for really bad paintings. The General's La Salle touring model drops me off at the hotel in town and the rest tool out to the ranch. Later China slips back into town and comes to my room. She glides over to the window that looks out on the square and lowers the blind for our siesta. She gives the simplest chore an elegant turn. "I show you how to make Tequino, my captain." This kind of talk always starts us giggling. "First the ground is swept clean and the seed is planted and when the corn sprouts—ah—it push up and is taken from the sand and ground to *metate*, then cooked and fermented in gourds...oh, it is so thick and sweet to the taste. Hmmm...*sabroso*." Ingrate that I am, right then I start thinking about the cannibals somewhere in her family's background. All the while she has this silly, happy look on her face which the mirror over the bureau shows me doubling up.

"Why do you smile, Roy h' Armstrong?" China asked me in the El Gourmet restaurant last week. After her premier.

Well, I had been thinking that despite all our ceremonies to her different gods, we are going to go our different ways. Was I smiling? No, more of a grimace. She doesn't know me well enough to tell the difference. I am sitting in this restaurant being treacherous to this girl who has shown me how to breathe at 30,000 feet without an oxygen tube. Since that night out at Teotihuacan, the act of breathing out and breathing in has become a rare experience. I say no more.

She takes a couple of spoonfuls of beans and rice. I'm smiling, I tell her, because we seem to be doing some kind of a dance ourselves, like the one she just put on at the Bellas Artes. A playing out. Isn't this just like Cortés and the Aztecs? Hell, I even landed in Veracruz like he did, came over the same route he did to this ancient city where I am plundering their women, like he did. One of them anyway. I don't say that exactly, but she is nodding and looking thoughtful. Something wrong with the beans maybe. Look at my skin and look at hers, I say. Blue eyes and hers the color of midnight.

Like a child following instructions, she soberly puts her arm alongside mine on the table. Her face gets longer and the nostrils flare like she was smelling the difference in us as well as seeing it. "I'm no different than one of Cortés's galoots." I add the final indict-ment. "And I do it for money just like them. I fly for whoever pays the bill." She had just laid out the itinerary of this Oaxaca trip; how her old man has temporarily hired me away from the airline. Fixed it up with my boss who, I guess, was paying off Halstead in some way. Everyone doing the next guy a favor. I'm the marker that's passed around. "That's me, Roy

Armstrong, loyalty and citizenship for sale."

But she puts her fingers across my lips. "Not true, h'Armstrong. You forget I went to school in the US. I know who you are. I meet some like you at the Williams College. Full of the ideals and no place to put them down. There is no nice clean place to put down the ideals, so you hold them to yourself where they eat out your stomachs." How old is this kid, anyway? Her hair is pulled back tight which draws the lines of her face so she looks ageless; she looks very much her mama's side of the family. Nothing to fool with but my sweet discovery. Eyes take up more of an angle above the high cheekbones. And I'm grinding corn with this Indian? "I know you well, carino. You talk with the cynicism but your insides are pure. The fascists paid well, too. You could have flown for them in Spain."

"Hey, look," I say. "You're not turning out to be one of those dames that fall for guys on the losing side, are you?"

"You...you...you..." but she can't find the right words and goes back to her plate of *clemole.* I've hardly touched my stew. She's has a couple more spoonfuls. Her eyes have a black dullness in them as they level me. "*Qué significa* — galoots?"

I start to explain, but she waves me off and launches into a long history about her father. Much of it, I've heard before, but she's giving me another lesson. I must have missed the point — that's her manner. Her mother was pure Zapotec — they go back long before the Aztecs. A wave of her hand dismisses Montezuma and Company. Her father is from an old creole family, Spanish landowners. As a young man, he was a rebel, joined up with Zapata to fight against his own kind, his own background. Land reform was the cause — his ideal. She's rattling in Spanish now, and I'm listening hard to keep up. She can't seem to make up her mind as to how she feels about her old man. His *idealismo;* she uses her hands for emphasis. Then, she talks of the hard way he treats the peasants, *los campesinos.* Her father's family in Oaxaca go back to Cortés when they took the land away from the Mixtecs. With the help of the Zapotecs, incidentally. An old grudge. Therefore, her mother's side go back to the sun's creation. Well, we know about that, don't we, McGee. Meanwhile, her father lives through the revolution, becomes a general. Zapata is knocked off and his body hung in the public square. *El general Suarez* survives and goes back to his ranch, his *milpasos,* and puts up No Trespassing signs.The Revolution Stops Here. But the *campesinos* still think he's the cat's meow because of his daring-do on their behalf twenty years ago. So does China, I think. But she also speaks sarcastically about him. She has become excited as she gives me this history lesson. A rose-colored bruise creeps into the dark skin beneath her eyes. Her spoon picks up speed. Then she is quiet for a while, breathing deep.

"My father's ideals—he is betraying them," she finally says in English. Very seriously. Her eyes become huge, pink around the edges. She's ready to cry. She shakes it off. "Not like you, h'Armstrong. Not like you. You are no loser, you...*eres honesto.*" It sounds like a threat of some kind. Or a command. I am not to become like papa. So then, explain to me, Molly, why she gets this *honesto americano* to fly some of her old man's pals down for a powwow? Who was she working for? Who am I working for? That's always been the question, Father Barber. What man's family do I belong to? Am I involved in a plot against Cárdenas? Something to do with the elections? Always some such skullduggery going on. It's in the papers.

But, for me, it's a little holiday with my sweetie, and I get to see another part of this beautiful country with a five hundred bill besides. Whatever China's involvement. She reminds me of the women Jean Arthur or Katherine Hepburn play in the movies. Daughters of rich men who work in the soup kitchens as plain Janes, organize the workers, but go back home in Westchester on the weekends in time for the tea dance. Maybe China hasn't found a place to set down her ideals yet, either. I change the subject.

"You know this painter Rivera?" I ask. She's been inspecting the large flan an admirer has sent over to our table. "You seem to know everybody."

"*Si. Por que?*"

"I'd just like to meet him. I was looking at his murals up on the third floor of the Bellas Artes this evening, before your program." The paintings were strangely noisy, loud. Hundreds of people: Indians, Spaniards, white and brown and red all crowded out from the wall. A din of Mexican history and present times. Heroes and villains. Juarez and Diaz — incidentally both from this town of Oaxaca where I am writing this. Also modern faces. Joe Stalin and Rockefeller. Lenin and some other Reds, including Trotsky who is living right here in DF. Doesn't that make you want to stop and think. Trotsky? Anyway, machines, mills, tractors gears. Whores and saints and automobiles. Tanks and planes. Peasants in white pajamas. The whole kit and caboodle like a big orchestra gone crazy, blowing their brains out on a painted wall, out of tune but in harmony too. Silent and a blast all at the same time. It's the way I feel sometimes. My whole history. Like I've been dropped into a great madness, an awful, enormous party and I can't find the door. So, a guy with a vision like Rivera's I find very interesting.

China shrugs and replies in Spanish, something she's been doing more often, though she knows I can't always follow her especially when she gets excited. She gets tired of English and dives back into the pool of her native sounds. As for me, it's sink or swim. Other times, in bed, she will mouthe a lot of round vowels that I take to be Zapotec. No need to translate. But, right now, she is saying in Spanish; yes, she's met Rivera. He and his wife, also a painter, live out in Coyoacan and she's been to their house. Has posed for him, in fact. They have parties she's been to. Where she has met Señor Lund. That guy again. She turns her eyes around and looks in a teasing way — the way she did yesterday stepping out of the bathtub, holding the towel before her, like a very tasty *torreador*. Or would that be *torreador-a* ?

"So, who is this Lund?" I ask her. She's serving the flan. Again, I wonder how she works off all the stuff she puts away. I've put on a couple of pounds since we've been together, but she stays lanky and firm. Not an extra ounce on her. All that dancing. She's like an athlete always in training. Constantly practicing, exercising even when she's not performing. And eating. Just yesterday in the hotel room, she went through some of her exercises—*au naturel*. Well, I guess! So who is this Lund?

"*Es un grand filósofo*," she says very seriously. "*Un grand hombre*." She taps her forehead with a finger. A small morsel of flan has stuck to one corner of her mouth. I want to lick it off — even in this restaurant.

I look around the room, as if I was really going to give China a big buss on her sticky sweet mouth, and I see them. They are coming toward our table, too. *El general* José de Avila, the sometime defender of Madrid and his lady — the ever lovely Consuelo Moreno. Mrs Brown, to you. She precedes him, weaving through the tables like a blocking back leading the way through the line of waiters who hold trays of dishes high over their heads. And the general has that kind of quick, small but mean character of a tailback except he's lofting, like a RDF, this black cigarette in a long silver holder. There's no doubt about their direction. They're on a beam right down to landing on us. They have this pleased look on their mugs, about to favor us with their company.

Meanwhile, I'm trying to think fast. What to say to China. I'm remembering the time on the *Sinaia* and later on the train with my hand down Mrs. Brown's pantaloons, and here I sit with China, the first good luck in my life in a long time. I'm about to be punished for all my foolishness — lose all my good fortune. Because right then — as they walk from the rear of El Gourmet toward us — in just those few seconds, the news suddenly breaks on my dumb head.I have been absolutely, totally, completely happy with this beautiful *mestiza* sitting across from me, this zany spirit who has, as the Spanish would say, eaten me up and passed me through her bowels. Now all that is to be taken from me because of a drunken, stupid manoeuvre six months back with this lady who is fast coming toward us like a wagon load of bad eggs.

"Ah, it is *el Capitán Carillo,*" Consuelo Moreno is saying; smiling, rolling her eyes and one hand already presented like a royal fin. The general behind her grins like he has a gas pain.

"...and...*atención*, José..." She steps back to give him room enough to properly appreciate China. "*La hora del brindis!*" In fact she looks around our table, for a glass of champagne to raise in China's honor and is clearly saddened not to find one. Her inspection lingers a bit too long over the remains of the flan. "Your dance this evening, *La Paloma Azul, simplemente magnifico, señorita. Brillante, emocionante.*" She's got one hand plastered against her bosom, and it looks like she's pumping up for a Jessica Dragonette. The general has been puffing and nodding. His head is on a spring coil.

When I start the intros, they quickly sit down like someone in the place has pulled a lever; the general next to me and Consuelo shoving in beside China. So we're suddenly a foursome,like we've been playing bridge together for years. The two women start gabbing in Spanish *come tornado*. Avila puffs and smiles benignly. He also eyes the half moon of flan on the table. "Your former employers are having their hands full," he says slyly.

I think first he must be talking about the Spanish Republicans, but he means the Finns. So also he knows about my time there in '22!! "Joe Stalin made a big mistake pushing them around," I say. He puffs once on his silver holder.

"They're tough." And that's true. All four or five of the Russian attacks have been pushed back. Gruesome pictures in the papers of piles of Russian soldiers, frozen dead and stacked like cordwood in the Finnish snow. How does he know about me in Finland?

He seems sure the Russkies are going to win.

So for the second time that night, this lead ball rolls back and forth in my stomach, because Avila's probably right. Fair play and justice and — what China had been calling "idealism" — all that is about to be crushed once again, tossed aside by the sheer weight of the Russian army. Overwhelming numbers. The number of tanks. How many Stukas you can put on line. So what's new? Socrates won all the points but ended up drinking the poison. "What do you think of old Joe Stalin signing up with Hitler?" I want to nick this little runt just a little.

Meanwhile, China has summoned a waiter who brings extra plates and forks and the general and his lady dig into the flan like it's going out of style. It makes me wonder, whoever bought them dinner, must have kept them on the *plato del día*. The ceiling fans slowly turn in the bare lights of unshaded fixtures. Greasy paper streamers in the national colors tremble, flutter, keep the flies circling.

Avila is still holding his cigarette with one hand while he shovels in the flan with the other. "But tell me, how is your job with the air company? How difficult it must be for you, superb warrior that you are, to be exiled and disowned by your own country when your skills could be used against the very forces you have so out-standingly confronted..." and on and on he went, neatly picking on the scab of my feelings. Snob, he is; but dumb, he is not. Carefully, he mouthes the last bite of the custard. "You and Senorita Suarez must pay us a call. We are at the Shirley Tourist Court in the Cuauhtémoc. A temporary but suitable arrangement," he says, daintily wiping his mouth with my napkin.

Yesterday afternoon, here in Oaxaca, I lay on the bed and watched one of these little lizards that Mexican hotel rooms seem to come equipped with. China was drawing a bath. They call them *quijas* and they eat mosquitoes and flies like gangbusters. They are part of the hotel service, you might say, keeping insects under control. Anyway, *esta pequeña lagartija* gives me quite a show as I listen to China happily humming to herself in the bathroom. He's been called out of hiding at the top of the window drapery by the tempting buzz of a plump horsefly that is skip-pity-hopping back and forth across the curtain rod, like one of those bouncing dots at the movie sing-alongs. Back and forth, zooming up and down on some kind of scale, sometimes hit-ting   the   ceiling,   then   richoetting off...bzzz...bzzzz...bzzz. And all the while, the lizard is straining its tiny dinosaur head this way and that, following the fly. Sometimes he makes a quick dart from one side of the cur-tain rod to the other, a vain attempt to catch the insect which seems oblivious to the threat. Each time the lizard is caught out in the open, a little embarrassed by his failure to grab a snack.

Of course, the lizard just looked embar-rassed. After running the whole length of the curtain rod, he has to watch the fly casually gun its wings, dive down and then peel out the open window. Gone. *El quija* looks around, hop-ing no one has seen what a sucker he's been. But was he embarrassed? Can lizards be embarrassed — and if so, would he be anyway? This little routine must take place countless times, day and night, and the lizard has to win a few. But he must also suffer many such embarrassments, many misadventures in the hunt. So, where's the shame in missing a few? It's part of the game. Who cares how foolish you look, or how impossible a particular hunt might be? Darting back and forth across the curtain rod, your hunger becomes an obsession. An involuntary response to a pass-ing attraction. You're part of a food chain that has only one genuine, blue-ribbon embar-rassment. Starvation.

Then, China is standing in the doorway of the bathroom. How long she's been standing there, I don't know. She is holding the towel before her and looks over it. "You think I am pretty?" she asks. She has the good grace to blush at the question.

Only ten years ago, Lindbergh flew the first Mex Aerea route from Mexico City up to Brownsville, Texas, and it took him six hours! I go back and forth to Merida in a couple. That Clipper flying boat just made it across the Atlantic, to Portugal, in thirty-six hours!! Somehow Texas is getting farther and farther away from me even as I fly a whole lot faster than Lindy. I'll never make a three-pointer on native soil again.

"You must walk carefully here on the ground, *mi aguila.*" China says the other night. "It is not like your sky where all is open. I love you with my heart. I love you with myself. You must be careful." Her arms raise and she plants one on me. Well, forget Texas.

The sun has risen hot on the back of my neck. This dog at my feet stretches and turns over to her other side, like she's with me forever. The *portales* around the square are mostly open, ready for business. More cars passing through the Oaxaca *zócalo.* The cathedral's bells strike the hour—nine o'clock. Not only tell the time but own the clock as well — or used to in the old days when nobody owned a watch. Not so much a service, you might say, but the authority, an influence and a reminder. A notice posted in the air every hour on the hour — Hey, boys and girls, we just struck another hour off the ones you have left. Counting the hours to Final Judgment. So, shape up, everybody.

And, it is time for me to mosey back to the hotel. China is picking me up in a half hour to take me out to her old man's ranch for a fiesta. Even the backstairs help is invited to this one.

So, I get to meet the general, the hero and the traitor of the Revolution.

January 1940
San Luis Potosí

First things first.

I get this letter from Jimmy Doolittle, saying yes he did indeed remember me from the Thompson Race in 1932 and he was glad to hear I had got out of Spain in one piece and was doing so well in Mexico. Then he says,

You're exactly the kind of guy we need, Armstrong, to teach these young kids the ropes. You and I are old roosters, too old for the fight that's on its way. And we'll be in this war, for sure. But we have some know-how to pass on—you especially. The goddamn politicians keep poking their noses in. I'll do what I can about your problem. I'm seeing Hap Arnold next week, and I'll bring up your situation. Also, there's an outfit being put together — all volunteers — to fly for the Chinese. Claire Chenault is doing it. Might be a way for you to get back in. Meanwhile, happy landings...
Doolittle

Forty and I'm an old rooster. Cock-a-doodle-doo. T'ain't funny, McGee. These oilmen I flew up here from Tampico yesterday didn't think I was so old but Miguel seemed nervous and I am thinking it is because the airline has rolled out the rickety Ford Tri-Motor for us to jockey these American and Mex big shots around. New instruments put into the dash in front so we don't have to crane our necks to the side. Miguel talks suspiciously about the oil guys in the back. The Mex Supreme Court just upheld Cárdenas's takeover of the American oil companies; so what is all this hocus-pocus with the *gringo*? he wonders. For the moment, I'm not a *gringo*, not part of the hocus-pocus, as far as he's concerned. Like I'm on the same side of the border as he is. It's a beautiful day for flying. The colors of the earth are heartbreakingly beautiful. Some turbulence.

Miguel rattles on as I fight the headwinds coming off the Occidental. And speaking of old-timers, the three Wasp engines on this tin goose sound like they're going to come off their mounts at full throttle. The one in front of us sprays the windscreen with oil. Miguel chatters as I'm hoping the compass on this old crate is reasonably accurate and that we are heading in the general direction of San Luis Potosí where there is a pretty modern airfield built by the strongman Cedillo. The government hunted him down and knocked him off last year. His name came up at the fiesta in Oaxaca ten days ago *(much more on that, much more)* and all this while, my copilot is becoming hostile about our passengers who are, he says, plotting to steal back the oil which the Mexicans have just appropriated. Get the picture? I mean is this a crazy place or what?

Look, *amigo,* I say to him, we have this job for which we get paid pretty good pesos. He sends a whole bunch every month to his family on the banana farm, doesn't he? What's he crying about? Who rides in the backseat is none of our business. He doesn't know about that, he shrugs and looks down at the landscape. His long, sleepy face looks unhappy. His eyes shift right to left like he's trying to find stray goats. We've got pretty close flying together.

He puts a hand on the throttles and readjusts the synch on the three motors, though they sounded okay to me. I check the manifold pressure on the new gauge in the panel and try to get a little more altitude out of these mixers. Then this passenger pokes his head through the curtain.

"Excuse me, Captain." Round, pink face and a voice that shows he can be pleasant with employees like Miguel and me. "There seems to be a problem with the toilet. The lady with us is having a little...difficulty." His tone riles me too, because he's a little too apologetic for the woman — like if it was one of them, they could stick their dingo out the window and let go, and not interfere with our crucial navigation and flying, but you know how women are, he is almost saying.

"See what I mean?" I say to Miguel when the guy returns back. I unbuckle and start to get up. "_También, operamos la letrina._" And I'm happy to bring a smile on his face as he takes over the wheel. It's the same clownlike grin I see on China and the ancient clay figurines in the museum. One thing about the people down here, especially the Indians, is that they have had this centuries old stone face on them that can look mean or suspicious or immensely sad but get them to laugh and it's like the sun coming up for the first time.

The passenger section of the tin goose has been carpeted and provided with rattan seats and two small divans of wicker that are bolted to the ship's sole. A couple of small tables are fixed in the different groupings and little red draperies swing and sway from rectangular windows that can slide open for a little breeze if wanted. The crapper is aft, on the starboard side, and I only nod to the passengers on the way. Halstead's woman is dressed in white slacks and a blue jacket and sits in a chair away from the men. Nose in a book.

Normally, the toilets on these Fords are just privies, just a hole through the plane, which affords you a view of the landscape as you get your relief. But when Rhyl fixed this plane over, he put in a small boat toilet with a hand pump from a tank of water. And that's the problem right there. Someone had forgot to open the petcock of the water tank and painted over it. When I come back from the cockpit with a small wrench, Halstead sticks out a hand and stops me. "Have a drink with us, Cap?" They're passing around this silver flask. I tell him not on duty, and keep going. His sweetie goes deeper into her book, like she's trying to keep a distance. Embarrassed, maybe, for all the fuss on her account. Having to use the toilet and the like.

It doesn't take much, and with the water running, the whole rig works just as nice as you please. On my way back, she gets up quick, like she's been waiting for everything to be okay. Not a word of any kind as we pass each other; no recognition from before. No thanks. She looks to one side with the barest line of a smile. Her mouth turns down a little comically, a kind of apology, I guess, for having to obey nature. On the seat is the book she's reading. Capt. Horatio Somebody. Cover is a picture of a guy at the big wheel of a sailing ship, and it's blowing hard.

"Well, sit a while with us, Cap," Halstead grabs my arm. Like we're old pals. "I guess Pedro hasn't tanked up on the cactus juice too much so you can let him drive this plane a while longer." The others join in the joke. Five of them all together. All very jolly. These dumb Mex's and so forth.

"Miguel is a very fine pilot," I tell them. Maybe they ought to see how good he is. How confident I am with him. So I stretch out in the chair.

"Taught him all he knows, I bet," says the guy who brought the news about the stalled crapper.

The company encourages a certain amount of socializing between crew and passengers, especially passengers like these. Then there's Halstead's dough in the airline. Several reasons for me to sit down. He's pretty influential. But, I'm holding my breath because I know what happens next. They've been talking about the Mexicans taking over the oil business — everywhere you go, it's the A-1 topic, places like the Bristol Bar, The American Club in MC—but I'm about to be a change of subject.

"Captain Armstrong is a famous pursuit pilot, three times over an ace and in two wars at that," Halstead says to them. I'm the freak to be trotted out. Sometimes I think the company must print my life story on the puke bags. Four, five sets of eyebrows all lift, pulled up by the same string. It's old news for me. Some people like to hear about men killing other men. Almost as good as sex stories for some of them. All I ever wanted to do was to fly, to be neutral in the air. Free of gravity, you might say, and to step back a little and look at Mother Earth. The war business was exciting and it enabled me to fly, to break free of the ground. But the killing? That was something else. I think guys on the other side felt the same way. Some of us were lucky, that's all. People like Doolittle and Roscoe Turner want to go faster and faster. All I ever wanted to do was to just stay aloft, and I guess some of us would kill, if we had to, just to stay aloft. And some of us did just that. It's that simple. Introductions have gone around.

I tell the big shots to fasten their seat belts. We're getting closer to the Occidental Range and the ride will get bumpy. I wonder about the woman in the toilet and hope that she can hold on to something. I've been fielding the usual questions. They ask a lot about the Nazis — what did I think the Germans were going to do next? It's been pretty quiet overseas this month, but for the Russians and the Finns. The Italians. The English and the French are digging trenches all across Belgium.

"Chuck has the inside dope," another said, laughing, and he almost puts a grip on the guy's skinny shoulders. We were bobbing up and down right merrily now. If we had been in the DC-2, Miguel could have put us up another five thousand feet to get above some of this rough air. But these Fords don't have superchargers on them and fly a much lower ceiling. I hope the lady is holding on.

"Chuck Halstead has it all," another announced, and they all laughed, pleased and happy to be in this oilman's company. Their eyes have slid over to where his woman had been sitting, like she was still in her seat and part of his take.

"What do you think?" Halstead has quickly turned toward me. His eyes are light blue, washed out. There's a flurry of whiteness just behind the rim of my sight. His girlfriend has made it back from the rest room and has taken her seat behind us. Gone back to her book. What do I think, I repeat the question.

"Yeah, about the Germans. You've been there. You know them as adversaries." He goes on before I can say anything, even if I wanted to. "I was having lunch with Joe Daniels the other day, and he told me the Gestapo is flooding Mexico with so-called tourists and businessmen. Trotsky may have dreamed up this oil takeover, but the Nazis are taking advantage of it. They struck out with Cedillo but they're still ready to move in. Others are ready to take his place. This guy Almazan up in Monterrey, for instance." Everybody nods. "Then, there's Suarez down in the South." He's swung around and looks at me like we share a secret. "You know about him, of course." I get a little chill.

"Yes, we like Almazan too," one of them says. Who the *we* might be is not clear.

The talk goes on but I'm listening with half an ear because I was thinking that if Halstead can have lunch with Joe Daniels, the American Ambassador, then Rhyl may be right. He just might be the guy who can get me out of this place. But, I don't like him. Strange bedfellows and so forth. Get it, Molly?

Anyway, the engines begin to whisper and the plane veers off to port. Miguel is making his approach so I leave the big-shots and hand over hand into the flight deck. My copilot is all business, and I just sit down and buckle up for the ride back to earth. Always a sad occasion for me.

Later I'm sitting in the inner court of the hotel in San Luis Potosí that we have put up in. The fountain is splashing, and a couple of the help are softly murmuring in the pantry. Going back over my notes. To leave Mexico would be to leave China and that doesn't set right with me.

Now that I'm back on the ground. These times we're apart have a strange kind of melancholy that is almost pleasurable. Because, I know we will be back together in a day or even within hours. Her kiddish high jinks. Her elegance when she talks about Mexico — even the blues that sometime come over her like an overcast — sitting here in this hotel's inner courtyard, I hurt with the thought of losing all that. If I vamoosed, would she leave with me? I don't think so. And now we have a dog too. The animal has adopted us. Old Armstrong is settling down. "Dalias," China says the other afternoon, coming through the door, her arms full of gorgeous blooms, cut from her roof garden. Orange and magenta and brilliant red. I have her write the name down. She's written her name in this old notebook. On almost every page — like a kid. China. CHINA. C-h-i-n-a.

This aged tequila is as good as any French brandy I've ever had. The fountain goes splash-splash. It's become nicely cool. Miguel's in his room practicing his navigation problems. His homework. The Arnett dame has been restless; she's come out on the balcony outside her room several times. Halstead and the others are meeting with local big shots in town, maybe visiting a *casa chica* later. A couple of them asked Miguel about women, like he pimped on the side. Right after we landed. Not even a thank you for a nice landing, but right off — where's all that chili kept? They look pleased with themselves, but he looked blank and smiled and shrugged them off. They didn't see his eyes. So, Halstead's lady is upstairs sawing through that fat novel.

Footsteps up above me. The waiter has brought me another one of these smooth tequilas and there's more clatter from upstairs, over my right shoulder. I look around. It's her. She's come out of her room again to take in some of the night air and stands on the balcony that looks over the patio. The rooms here are small

and stuffy. She's all in white; a different outfit from the plane. Like the floppy pajamas
Harlow sometimes wore. She looks bored. Maybe her
book has bored her — the hero has to manoeuver
that square-rigger through the Straits of
Magellan. I can feel her looking down on me as
I write these lines. Her regard steady and
thoughtful. She is very fair and her eyebrows so
light she pencils them in. She's come out for
air. Then, click-clack go the sandals on the
marble. The door catch releases, the door closes. All done unhurriedly. Splash goes the fountain. I think about the thing in Oaxaca. General
Suarez. China.

Then. Clack-clack. She's back out again as if
she forgot something. Her footsteps on the tile
steps from the balcony. She's taking a walk.
Then, she's standing beside me. Her perfume is
lemony.

"Sorry to bother you," she is saying. "But I
can't seem to get the fan in my room to work.
You seem to be handy at fixing things. Could you
help me? It's so hot, I can't sleep."

She's looking at me directly, like a librar-
ian. Looking up at me almost, like she's just
seen my name on the overdue list. Her eyes are
light gray. They shift to one side; she's embarrassed to need my help. Again. Her hair has been
pushed back behind her ears which are small and
pink. There's a glisten of moisture above her
top lip, and she has this funny smile on her.
Turned down and a little clownlike. Her problem
is just a trifle boring, her expression says. I
follow her up the stairs to her room. The pajamas are loose and clingy all at once. She's a
small woman but plainly all there.

"My name is Elizabeth Arnett," she says when
we enter her room. "But friends call me Peggy.
I hope you will call me so." She's forgot to
turn the little switch that makes the fan
rotate. I guess the fans in Pittsburgh don't have
switches like this. "How perfectly simple," she
says, bending over the table to get a closer look
at the gear. More lemon flavor rises from her
throat. The pajama top has fallen away and I get

a view of her small breasts, a glow on them from the bedside lamp. I find myself thinking, this lady is worth millions of bucks and but she's made just like every other woman. "I feel so awfully dumb," she says and sits down on the bed and puts her head to one side, shakes out her hair a little. She still looks amused. "Would you like a cigarette?"

"Never took it up," I say.

"No bad habits?" she says, her lips curl down in that throw away smile and her eyes do a sideslip. Then, she is aiming this cigarette holder at me. "Chuck is very fond of you," she says, taking a drag. All businesslike. "And I admire you very much, too."

"Oh yeah," I say. I feel like I've sneaked into the dorm room of a ritzy girls' school. I shouldn't be here, but it's kind of interesting.

"Yes. You are a man of special talents. Brave. Idealistic. Courageous. Risking your life for a cause you believed in. Where did you go to school?"

So, it's maybe a job interview. Her nod approves of my Yale credential. I tell her a little about joining in 1917 but her expression says she's found out all she needs to know and cuts me off. She's crossed her legs and one of the clogs dangles half off her foot. Her heel and sole look naked, a child's foot after a bath. Her suitcase is open in the corner. Thin, sketchy undies hang over the sides —s o under all the yacht club garb, she wears Frenchy frilly stuff.

"Well, thanks again. What shall I call you? Roy?" So, I've been dismissed, you might say. The night has become more humid. China's on tour in the sticks with the Blue Pigeons. One of her friends is looking after the dog.

"It always looked so beautiful, so peaceful what with the farmers out in their rice paddies and the oxen, ducks—and the green of it. The green of it. The green could hurt the eyes. I see it in my sleep. You never got there?"

The question has lifted lightly within the man's reminiscence and turns to rest upon Walt Hardy as if only then did the speaker understand, and a little startled by the understanding, that his audience had not shared this part of the world, this history with him. And actually, Clarence Adams did seem like an old shipmate in conversation at slack water, engaging him in a reunion on the change of tide. Hardy looks away into the adjoining dining room. Paper flowers in glass vases. A pewter tea service of elaborate fashion. A dusky harem girl holds up the empty brass socket of a lamp on the sideboard. The two men lounge in the front parlor of the small house. Cee has accompanied the other woman into the kitchen to help with the coffee. A very large television set in the corner, its sound muted, displays a wrestling match, and above, a prettily painted Jesus stretches out His arms. Wings flutter near the front window where a canary makes broken flights within a cage hung next to the drapes.

"That was the peculiar thing about it," Adams continues. "Because that green grass could cut you to ribbons." He was a large man so when he crossed his legs and looked beyond Hardy's head and out the front window, the mere act proclaimed a self-measured importance. Hardy guesses he was about to hear part of a memoir that had been given on many occasions; yet, the words sound freshly minted as they are pronounced; their significance only, just then, made out. "Peculiar, like the peacefulness could all at once shatter—like jade splinters. No warning. Fragments of green. None of us expected such things. It was pretty weird. We never got used to the beauty of it and its meaness."

"Yes," Hardy replies. He is a little sorry they have kept this appointment. He and Cee have but little time together and much to work out between them. But she had insisted they accept the invitation from Eddie Poremski's widow. The old mill town of Lawrenceville was a part of Pittsburgh she had never seen, she said. But to herself, Celia had argued the visit might be a neutral interlude, a moment in which neither had much investment.

"The old social contract," Adams has paused to look down at his feet, and a big toothed smile apologized for springing such a term, perhaps for even knowing the concept. "The old social contract was out the window. We're not the same anymore. Not since Nam."

Here Hardy is persuaded to nod and take his place in what must be that larger audience Adams has addressed over the years since his return to Pittsburgh, to Lawrenceville, and to the widow of Eddie Poremski. Hardy imagines the man as part historian, part eulogist, reciting these narratives in union hall and neighborhood tap or VFW Post. A kind of mill town Homer. His broad face gleams with pleasure, with authority; a genial, all-weather narrator, Hardy thinks—a big black, mill-town Homer, a replacement to that pale, green-eyed Eddie Poremski who had tormented him so in grade school. He holds back a laugh.

"You smile," Clarence Adams has just said.

"Though not with humor," Hardy replies, looking Adams straight in the eye. "Recognition of familiar terrain, you might say. Your landscape and mine were separated by a hemisphere. But hostile jungle is hostile jungle no matter which side of the world you're on. Beautiful and deadly."

"Yeah, that is the truth," the other replies thoughtfully. "I read about you." Adams seems a little anxious now, as if he feared Hardy might start telling his own history. In the kitchen, at the rear of the house, the two women talk as distant cousins. "But nobody goes to jail."

"I'm sorry?"

"I see that, in your case, that immunity business you got from the Congress might throw out the case against you."

"It's not all that certain," Hardy says and turns away to look out the window behind him. Traffic on Butler Street is backed up by trucks.

"Oh, I think it will occur," Adams says pleasantly. "I think it will be certain. None of you will serve time—and that's cool. As it should be? You were on the right side. The side of freedom. You were serving your country, doing your duty. Just like me." Adams pauses to nod judiciously and Hardy expects something more.

"How did you and...and...Shirley meet?" He hopes the question sounds okay.

"In church, actually," Adams replies and recrosses his legs. The gesture reestablished an ownership of the recliner and all else in the small living room, including the narrative. He wears soft-looking slippers, and his manner clearly signed the expectation that this visit would only briefly interrupt what had been a serious relaxation. His eyes slip back to the television across the room and Hardy, with some expertise in such semiotics, summons a certain respect for the man. Even the fuzzy footwear affirms Adams's comfortable possession of the room, the house and everything within it.

"...the proverbial battlefield conversion," Clarence Adams has been saying, and his smile becomes huge. "Eddie, of course, was from Point Breeze, like you. My people lived in East Liberty. So, worlds apart, as they say. Eddie was at the USX in Homestead. I was in the wire division—across the street." His head indicates the direction. "Yes, worlds apart. Shirley and I met at a Saturday eve Mass at St Mary's. I was just back and things were copacetic. Plenty of overtime. It was a sweet life." Again his look passed through the white lace curtains and out of the room. He appears expectant, prepared to see something different from what lay on the other side of the curtains. Hardy turns to follow his stare. Across Butler Street, the gigantic black facade of the derelict steel plant looms like the wall of an ancient city. Just beyond, the Allegheny River flowed toward its rendezvous with the Monongahela to form the Ohio.

This morning, he had taken Celia sight-seeing in the Lincoln, and they had crossed the West End Bridge over the junction of the three rivers. "This is where it begins," he had said to her. "This is where the Ohio River begins. Think of that." And Celia had known he had wanted to stop the car. He had slowed down, so the truck behind them had blared its air horn. She knew he had wanted to stop and get out to look at the water as they used to do in New York. All the rivers they had crossed, the many times they had driven back and forth across the Hudson, she thought, and he stills gets excited, like a boy almost, and for just an instant she had almost forgiven him everything. The love she still held for him had threatened to come loose. "There's too much traffic," she had said, squeezing his arm. "Show me another time."

"You and Poremski were in the same outfit?" Hardy asks without turning around; a sociable inquiry only. He continues to look at the rusted hulk of the mill. A slight wisp of steam plays from a slender stack, as if one last fire was kept going, hopefully and at little cost.

"I'm a little younger than Poremski was," Adams says pleasantly. "But that's all right. Shirley kind of appreciates that I'm younger." His laughter is feathered deep in his throat. "We get along, as they say. Yes, we do well enough. My Nam time was what brought us together. Shirley ran this ladies group in the parish that helped vets get back into the stream." His language unfolded with a worn dignity, old material carefully unrolled once more. "She would listen to the tales I had to tell and sometimes they'd make her cry. Not that I was a hero, but that I had done certain things or that certain things had been done to me. Just ordinary stuff. That I had lived so close with death. All that made her think of Eddie; that he had done the same, been done to the same. For he did die. They never saw each other again, after he left the Burgh. So it was when first we met; she listened to my stories and imagined him. She would cry about the both of us, what had been done to both of us, but her tears fell only on me. Like they say, man—the rest is history." Adams stretches out his legs and shifts his arms along the sides of the recliner. He lightly taps the toes of the slippers together. "That's where I made my mistake. I should have stayed in the service."

"Why is that?" Hardy is ready to go along as straight man. It is already after four o'clock and the twilight game of the double-header with the Cardinals starts at six.

"Two mistakes actually. The mill was paying seventeen-fifty per hour, more for overtime, when I got back. So, I went back into steel. It was too sweet. Then Shirley had granted me the honor. So, we were a unit, you know? A family almost." He spoke as if the last morsel of a delicious meal has just passed over his tongue. "When everything went bust a few years ago, my GI re-train had run out, so today I am what the people down at Unemployment call unskilled labor. That's my speciality. I'm an unskilled person. I made all kinds of steel wire. I made some of the new cables for the Golden Gate Bridge. In San Francisco. But I'm an unskilled person." Adams held out his hands, palms up, and Hardy expects to see the welts and scars of such awesome braiding. The bird chirps and nervously tests another perch inside its cage; returns quickly to the first one.

"But we are doing nicely. Yes, indeed," the big man continues. "Shirley is a dietitian at the junior high." It was something more than a job description. "That handles the mortgage. Then, from time to time, she gets some hours down at the mall. At the Hill's Department Store. I do a little carpentry with my uncle, paint houses; he's a contractor. So, we're doing all right, heads above the big muddy." He laughs and hums to himself. It is an unsettling sound.

"What about another place...out West, for example?"

"Ah, yes, Mr. Greeley's good advice," Adams says and brushes at one trouser leg, pulls at the crease. "Did you wonder that nobody ever said, Go East?"

"Here we are at last!" The kitchen door swings open. Shirley Adams carries a tray with cups and a china coffee pot. Celia follows with a plate of cookies. "We just got gabbing. Sorry guys." Her voice is strong and forthright—a Pittsburgh sound.

"Mr. ...hey, I call you Walter?"

"It's just Walt."

"Walt has just suggested we might relocate," Clarence Adams tells his wife as she sets the tray down carefully on a glass-topped table. She straightens up, perhaps to seriously consider this possibility for the first time, and fixes a strand of straw-colored hair behind one ear. Hardy imagined her when courted by the late Eddie Poremski, but even now, she could model for one of those dolls he remembers from school fairs, perfect pink circles painted on round wooden cheeks. Maybe it was the cookies, encrusted with sugar and gemmed with citrons, for as Shirley Adams passes them around, she looks "old world." Polish Hill.

"But, you see, Shirley has people here. Has people buried here, and so do I." Adams says with deeper emphasis. "Then, again, painting houses or pumping gas or doing a little yard work would be the same for me in California as it is here. Unskilled labor is the same everywhere. I expect in California, the verdict at McDonalds is the same too—they're into hiring young dudes. Your Dad was a working stiff, wasn't he? A chauffeur, I read in that newspaper article, for the Arnett family?"

"Yes, that's right," Hardy replies and looks intently at Celia. He holds her gaze, afraid the laughter within him might burst through. He has just remembered the late Eddie Poremski's taunts about his father. *Your old man drives Miss Arnett around. He's like a nigger.*

"Something will work out," Shirley Adams is saying as she pours coffee from an ornate porcelain pitcher; no doubt a family piece. "You're too good a man to be passed over for very long."

"You see how she cossets me," Adams says, his expression at once pleasured and knowing. Celia looks preoccupied, distracted by something beyond what was happening in this room. For reasons she had not or could not explain to Hardy, she had made a big U-turn in Arkansas and retraced her route. Now, something tells him, she's decided returning had been a mistake.

Yet, last night had been very special. Their love making had been lavish, and she had seemed eager to pleasure him. Her own pleasure had been intense, like the old days. But such frenzy could have been fired by all kinds of frustrations. So only a truce of bodies; a temporary splint of the fracture between them that he had caused. He dared not regard last night as anything more but he still felt all could be set right if he could only come up with the word, perform the act. But what was the clue?

Sounds like—he played charades with himself as he had shaved this morning and had been instantly ashamed, quickly turned on the tap and flushed away the lather. Such smart-ass cleverness had driven her away. She has been observing Clarence Adams with that clear-eyed, all-encompassing attention Hardy knew so well but hadn't seen in a while. So, looking at her from across the room was like seeing her almost for the first time, the slender neck curved slightly as she concentrates on a conversation. She is a woman he wanted to know.

"Our happiness," Shirley Adams is saying, "does not depend on the steel industry. Men do not live by bread alone." The old wisdom has inflamed the woman's cheeks even more, as if the simplicity of the axiom has embarrassed her. On the fireplace wall, hung several framed photographs, some looked quite old, and the faces were foreign and pious, but Hardy can see a resemblance in all of them to Shirley Adams. A small detail of her husband's relatives are ranked on the mantle commanded, you might say, by a separate picture of Clarence Adams standing stiffly in uniform but smiling.

"I sometimes think we have been conditioned to look for happiness in the wrong places," Celia says finally. "I mean in institutions that are supposed to guarantee happiness but cannot or do not. Like the unions."

"Amen to that," Adams says. His eyes flick over to the television set that glimmers like a fire in a hearth. A team tag match is in progress; bodies fly through the air, bounce off the ring ropes. "The good old International."

"Or even in politics and government," Celia adds. Hardy wonders if she might have come across these opinions as she drove west to Arizona; say, like on billboards. He had been listening to too many congressmen lately so he has begun to think that ideas have become sized down to a bumper sticker standard. For a quick read at turnpike speed. Something to think about while looking for the next rest stop. In this small living room, the talk has unaccountably entered a serious study—not just the steel mills folding in Pittsburgh, but could any of it be put into a few words? The man of few words is extolled, but how many ideas does such a man have? Maybe only a few. Has anyone lately sat down with the speeches of Daniel Webster? Daniel Who?

Celia has placed that level look upon him, how she used to look as she was about to tell him his accounts receivable were not square with his firm's expenses. "How can freedom or happiness or democracy be guaranteed to anyone, least of all people who cannot feed themselves or their families. These cookies, by the way, are wickedly good. I can't stop."

"It's an old Polish Hill recipe," Shirley Adams says and starts to give the details as she hands the plate around once more.

"But you weren't in the service," her husband says softly to Hardy. He speaks delicately over his wife's voice, not meaning to disturb the women's conversation yet somehow insuring their privacy. "What exactly did you call yourself. Not with the government, were you? The CIA?"

"I facilitated different parties that ordinarily might not get together. All in the cause of freedom. A kind of broker."

"A broker of freedom." Clarence Adams relishes the language.

Hardy was sorry for his own words; they had just popped out. Fashioned to slide off the teflon walls of Congress or the media, they sounded out of place in this earnest living room? He noted Celia's eyes had slightly enlarged, though her attention to Shirley Adams had not wavered. A mote of caution had widened them, like the eyes of an animal startled by the sound of something behind it. Danger. He was not supposed to talk about his case, but the large, unassuming presence of Clarence Adams deserved a little consideration.

"A broker." The black man has nudged the word again, rolls it over. "Like in the stock market?" Celia's attention has shifted back, and he can feel her calm regard. Hardy does not want to meet her eyes. "I guess I must sound like one of those congressman. But who paid your wages?" Seemingly, the question has only just occurred to Adams. "You weren't in the service."

A huge man with long golden locks has lifted himself from the wrestling mat, crying with rage—the anguished spectacle of a child being unfairly punished. Hardy had been reviewing the usual answers that had always fitted this particular question and found none of them right. Certainly not in Lawrenceville. Finally, he says, "Frankly, I guess I'm not sure where the money came from." Though this morning, in Peggy Arnett's desk, he had learned where some of it might have come from. Breath, held and released, sifts among them. The sigh might have come from Celia, it might have come from himself. Still looking at the controlled mayhem on the screen, he saw from the corner of his eye that Cee has moved slightly—a nod of approval?

"What you said to that newspaper was so very sweet," Shirley Adams speaks hurriedly, as if she might be playing a conversational trump too soon, but the party was getting glum. "It was like Eddie was back and together. Oh, I love my man, here." She puts an arm around her husband's broad shoulders, leans forward and kisses his cheek. "He's my man. So, don't get me wrong. But seeing Eddie's name in the papers and all like that this morning was like he had been given another chance. And to have his name said by you, Wally, who is well—famous, I guess you are famous aren't you—well, it was like a special memorial. You know?" she pauses as if to confide in Celia. "His remains are still over there somewhere." She is strangely positive.

"Wally!" Celia laughs suddenly. "You called him Wally?"

The spots on the woman's cheeks become pinker. "Don't you remember?" she asked Hardy for verification. "I was a class behind you and Eddie. My family name was Laskovich. Shirley Laskovich." She nods; some sort of assurance.

"But Wally," Celia persists. "You never told me that."

"Well, not everybody called me that." Hardy hopes he sounded pleasant—a good sport. Poremski had made up a ditty for recess distribution. *Wally, Wally—plays with a dolly.*

Poremski had hated him on sight, and the unfairness of his scorn, its unreasonableness, could still rankle, because—even after all these years—he still wanted to make it up to Poremski, still wanted to be on his team, and that also was unfair, because it was impossible to do. Despite the years and their different fates, he couldn't put down this urge to dissolve Poremski's contempt in some brand of intimacy of fellowship. He had proved his worthiness. Hadn't he proved that he didn't play with a dolly? In this plain living room, he could call up Poremski's round face screwed tight around a cold mockery, recall the light that kindled the greenish eyes. They looked at him as if through a steel visor. Later, he would encounter that same expression in others, and he always responded the same way; reaching out a hand to that hostility, to placate its inexplicable scorn. Once or twice, Oliver North had scrutinized him the same way.

Shirley Adams has continued to tell Celia more of their history, as if she were welcoming a newcomer into the family. Celia half expected her to pull out a photo album, class pictures from the Park Place School, and she would not have been sorry. Hardy had few pictures of himself as a boy; his father had never thought about making a photographic record. "Since he lived in that big house, the Arnett House—well, not in it, but you know what I mean," Shirley continues, " but we all thought he was rich and snobby. Your clothes were so nice, Wally—especially I remember your sweaters. And that tweed cap you had that you gave Eddie. How he prized that cap. Do you remember?"

"Yes, I remember," Hardy replies. The bird in the cage balances on a bar and chirps once, then again. Adams held a mug with an antique auto logo beneath his chin and dunks a hard, square cookie into the coffee, lifts it to his mouth. He takes a similar communion with the television program.

In fact, Poremski had swiped the tweed cap off his head on their walk to school one morning and placed it on his own soup bowl head with a challenging, mocking expression. The cap had been brand new that week, something brought back from London by Miss Arnett and much prized for its material and workmanship. For its origin. But, the boy Hardy had let the theft become legitimized, hoping to barter the cap for friendship. He had even reasoned the cap had rightfully belonged to Poremski from the start, somehow his tormentor had earned it. "Whatever happened to that cap?" he asks.

"Eddie kept it," his widow replies proudly. "Of course, it got too small for him, but he kept it in the top of the closet. I'd come on him sometimes looking at it. Remember him, he'd say, meaning you, then he'd laugh and toss it back on the shelf. The hat meant a lot to him; that you had given it to him."

"Kinda like a souvenir, I guess," Clarence Adams says in his heavy voice. "School days," he adds and hums a few bars of the sentimental ballad. "Good old golden rule days." A winner's arm was being raised in the ring, but a fight breaks out. The decision is contested. "Yes, indeed," Adams concludes. "Good old golden rule days."

"Sometimes Eddie would play a guessing game with me when we drove past the Arnett place. There used to be a good pork butcher in Wilkinsburg," Shirley Adams explains to Celia then turns back to Hardy. "You had long gone by then but Eddie would say, that's where what's-his-name used to live. He'd pretend not to remember your name, and I'd have to give him hints. Just a game. Then, he'd say—oh, yeah, Wally-Wally. But he hadn't forgot you. And now here you are. Right here."

Wally-Wally is indeed here, Hardy agrees. In all his disgrace and with all his problems—he was here! Poremski, what was left of him, was on the other side of the world, but he—Walt Hardy—was sitting in the man's widow's house so the bitter thoughts about his old schoolmate, his adversary, were wonderfully sweetened. I've won, he wants to say to Cee. He has won that fight that Poremski had picked with him, and so if you were Walt Hardy at this moment, you might feel just a little triumphant and wonder if the gods had not put something special in your coffee; but, at the same time, be just a little ashamed to enjoy the taste of it all that much.

"Did you ever do that number in grade school?" Adams has surfaced once more. A car commercial has come on. "Ever do that number where you'd stand up and say what you want to be when you grow up? Remember? I can't remember what I said. Do you?"

"Not exactly," Hardy replies easily. "Probably a fireman or a flyer."

Adams's laughter is full and deep. "I probably said—unskilled labor..."

"Now, sweetheart." His wife places a hand on his arm.

"It's a funny thing," the man continues smoothly. "If you're not working, you're a nobody, and if you're working..." He turns one of his hands over, palm up, and looks big-eyed at his guest. The bird flutters its wings and chirps. "Well, anyways, nobody here is going to jail."

"We're going to be all right," Shirley Adams tells her husband. She seems out of breath. Her arm has gone around his neck and she presses her cheek to his. "Don't you worry now, you can't keep a good man down."

"You see what's happening here?" Adams asks. His eyes turn in a roguish manner though the light in them was not merry.

"You see what's going down?" And he smiles broadly, as if someone had asked him to smile for a picture, for the record. Like the photograph on the mantle.

The top of the Cardinals' batting order came up in the eighth inning, and Langford drove the first pitch directly at Bell at shortstop who snapped the ball out of the air like a fresh handkerchief to be smartly pocketed. Next came Ozzie Smith. The Pirates were in a one-zip game and Leyland had brought on Rodriguez to save the shut-out. The Mexican left hander worked the Wizard to two-two and then became a little careless with a high fastball that Smith rocketed past Merced and into right field corner for a stand-up double.

"Oh dear," Celia exclaimed and laughed. "Hope your Dad didn't see that."

"They have TV monitors everywhere." The senior Hardy

had gone to get them beer during the seventh inning stretch. "There's no escape. Must be a long line at the refreshment counter."

"Who's up next?

"Perry. He can be dangerous."

"So, do you think men live by bread alone?" Hardy cracked the shell of a peanut and divvied the contents between them, his attention kept on the field. The pastoral quality of the ball field below them, its greeness, and the clean, straightforward rules of the game are working a spell on him that he was unwilling to leave. The atmosphere in the bleachers especially appealed to him. They sat high above the third base line and though the community here might be as artificial as the turf below them, Hardy felt a release within this ticketed fellowship from the uneasiness seeded in Clarence Adams's living room. Celia persisted, "Agree or disagree?"

Perry took a second ball and Ozzie Smith casually strolled back to second base. "You want me to agree—to say, everything comes down to a full belly."

"I want you to say what you think. Really feel." Ozzie Smith stretched his lead off the bag. "What you feel, Walt? That immunity those congressmen gave you can only go so far."

"What's that supposed to mean?"

"I mean, you seem immune from a lot of things, especially your feelings. I can remember your feelings." She might have gone too far; so, she waited for him to say something; finally continued. "Those books you used to read to me, the places where Lincoln or somebody would do something; take a chance. Stand up for something. You would get all worked up. It was almost sexy. Well, it was." She laughed and hugged herself.

"That's what got me into trouble." Hardy also laughed. He wanted to say more, go beyond the snappy answer, but no words came to him. In any event, Celia seemed to have changed her mind. She gently shook his arm and smiled up at him. Hardy wondered if this might be part of that test he would have to pass. First question for twenty points: What did he really feel about things? Second question, for the balance. What was he going to do about it? Crazily, a hotness for her flooded through him right there and then. What could he say that would bring her back? If he and Clarence Adams had met by themselves; say, a chance encounter in a neighborhood bar—Hardy puts together the scene in his head—they might have been able to talk it out. Come up with a reason or even an excuse that would sound as good as a reason, and which, after the bar closed, they could take home to their wives; the right words that usually did the trick.

But the women's presence had affected their talk, made them shy of their own histories; no, not the histories but their accounts of those histories and the way they exchanged them. Perry had gone for a mean slider. Strike one.

"What about it?" Celia insisted. She was still smiling and her mouth was so very appealing, the lip line trusting and sensual all in one.

"Bread or no bread—I've seen both. People with no hope of winning, let alone eating, still putting their lives on the line." And this was true, absolutely true, so how could he cross out this line from the new handbook she asked of him? He even felt his throat thicken around the words as he spoke them. "People chose up sides according to what's put on the table in front of them. So, you take your pick, I guess. It's an à la carte menu."

"Same people sometimes?" Celia looked down into the deep ravine of the ball field. Perry had set up in the batter's box; Rodriguez started his wind-up. Smith took another cautious step toward third.

The assurance in her voice, the matter-of-factness of it, reminded Hardy of their early days, when she had come to do his books. She had never been judgmental but just added up the figures to their immutable truth; two plus two—profit or mostly loss. A dispassionate analysis of his failing business. "Yes, the same sometimes," he said finally. More times than not. Two plus two again. Though what he wanted to say, make particular, was that the same people became different, when offered a little bread so they actually were not the same. The bread, to use the vernacular, he had put down for a couple of airstrips in Costa Rica, for instance. How the landing fields were used was another broker's business. The whole deal had been compartmentalized in case of a breakdown, as happened when that guy got shot down. And, at first, the operation seemed recoverable. But that's beside her point. Perry was chatting good-naturedly with the umpire as groundskeepers cleaned up some debris fans had tossed into left field. He had told the truth. His part of it. That it wasn't the whole truth wasn't his doing. He hadn't known the whole truth, so how could he tell it? He had known nothing about the cocaine and the rest of it. He just transferred the money. Got some airstrips cleared. He had been only a broker.

But these specific evasions, as she called them, came apart under her persistence; these tests she had started giving him. Her committee of one had no rules of procedures, no Fifth Amendment to protect him. No glossy counsel telling him how to answer in their bedroom or here in Three Rivers Stadium. *"Mr. Hardy, you'll excuse me for saying so,"* the committee *counsel said into the microphone, "but I think you are not completely forthcoming."* Lives on the line. All the ringing phrases. Actually, wasn't it like the old rum-molasses-slave trade combination he had learned at the Park Place School? The original triple play that had made this country great. Miss Darnell was the teacher's name, and he remembered her leaning over their indifference like a parson on Sunday. Stand up and tell what corner of the trade-off you want to be when you grow up. The rum, the molasses or the slave.

His assignment had been to negotiate for the airfields. Lay them out in the bannana groves. That's all. A middleman and an engineer. That some people had been corrupted, some governments turned only meant they were not A-Okay to begin with. Those little guys, some not as tall as the guns they carried, had not hungered for democracy. They couldn't even spell the word. They had no word for it in their language. He felt the old sentiments swell within him. They had put their "lives on the line" for power or revenge, or for something to eat. So much for that, Hardy reasoned, just as Perry looked at a fastball. Strike two.

"You want me to say that we corrupted those people. The money, the bread; created a hunger that wasn't theirs to begin with?" Come to think of it, Armstrong's memoir told the same story. The flyer sounded a little too innocent, too shocked by the deals cut in Mexico fifty years ago. The oil bigshots buying the Mexican government, the revolution—everything had been for sale. Nothing had changed. Supply and demand, an old formula. They called it *la mordida.* The little bite. It's still happeneing.

"Say what you wish," Cee had replied rather stiffly. He had missed the question. She followed the action on the field. Perry had stepped out of the box and walked about in self-chastise-ment. Rodriguez was patiently waiting on the mound. Smith, one foot on second base, was talking amiably with Jay Bell. Rather than opponents, the two ballplayers looked like they might be exchanging news of friends or relatives; opinions on restaurants in St. Louis or Pittsburgh.

Hardy looked down the steep aisle that rose to their row of seats, but his father was nowhere in sight. The old man had gone to some trouble to get these game tickets for them, and it was obvious that he had meant the outing to be a family event. He had taken their orders for beer and kielbasa with a heartiness that had nearly put off the somber livery of his usual manner. They had smiled, heads together, as he walked carefully down the steep stadium steps. He had lived his life with the same care, the same slow and studied thoroughness by which he had polished and maintained the Arnett limousines. The devoted retainer. And he had driven those limousines through the streets of Pittsburgh in the same way he had raised his son; at a steady speed, obeying the limits of the mechanism, the handbook. Nothing more and nothing less.

"What about this flyer, Armstrong?" Hardy had asked his father this morning. Celia was taking a shower. "Did Miss Arnett ever mention him to you? "

"How do you know about him?" Bill Hardy had leaned back in his chair.

"We saw pictures of him this morning in an album. And I came across his diary yesterday. In the main house. Susanna Pell found it and gave it to me. Who was he?"

His father thought for a moment and then stood up to take their dishes to the sink. "He flew Mr. Halstead's plane for the oil business in Mexico. Before Halstead was murdered."

"Probably why she had the journal?"

"Might be the case." He came back to the table and lifted his pocket watch from his vest. He checked the time and then looked at the kitchen clock. "Like a souvenir, I guess. She and Halstead were about to marry when he was killed. It was a very sad time for her. More coffee?"

But here's what Hardy wanted to say to Celia. His father's sense of loyalty, that earnest pursuit of duty that was rare to find these days; that even went beyond the grave, even to protect the reputations of those in that grave—those were qualities that he, Walt Hardy, had learned to admire. Wanted to emulate. This model of behavior had been a gift greater in value than any cap brought back from a rich woman's European jaunt. Nor could these examples be taken from him. The father's goodness overwhelmed the son, and the solitary way the man had gone about that goodness, stuck to its principles, both as parent and servant made an impressive record, he always thought. After his mother had abandoned them, his father's sense of duty had been a guidon that he had followed all the way into the jungles of Central America. He couldn't really explain it, but if he could, maybe Celia would not be leaving him. Even at this moment, he knew she was waiting for this elusive answer, and even if he had the answer could he phrase it so it didn't sound like a press handout? Hardy turned to her and their eyes met as Perry, down below, connected with a pitch. The ball lined toward right field in a flat, mean trajectory.

Martin had to scramble and nabbed the ball neatly enough, but his throw was across his body, a little awkward. Ozzie Smith had already tagged up and was half-way to third base before the relay had got back to the infield. The Cardinals had put the tying run on third. Still one out.

"Who's up?" Celia asked.

"Todd Zeile. Third base. Impressive RBIs."

"Oh, dear."

The man next to them leaned over. "And yeah, if Bonilla had been out there, Smith would not have gone to third. Wouldn't have chanced it."

"That's for sure," Hardy said, an alarm going off within him. Too late. He shouldn't have been so agreeable.

"So, what do you think of that coon getting thirty million from the Mets?" Hardy glanced quickly at Celia. He felt responsible for the man's language—after all, Pittsburgh was his city. But then, this sort of thing could have been said anywhere. He looked sharply at his neighbor. The man's face was cheerful, pink and Irish. "Hey, don't get me wrong," the guy continued. "I'm for him getting whatever he can. Hell, I'm just a working stiff myself. We're all in the pot together, right? But, thirty million—jeez."

Hardy hoped something in his expression had challenged the man, had made him pull back a little. He wanted to think that. When Zeile stepped into the batter's box, the field suddenly became saturated with an intense color, as if the high-intensity lights that were to dissipate the oncoming dusk had also drawn the green dye, deep in its fiber, to the surface of the artificial turf. It was an unnatural, an unfair green, like the colors Clarence Adams had described earlier; how those innocent, vernal tints had camouflaged sudden dismemberment and death.

Because the whole argument, the game itself had become unfair; that is, played without any rules whatsoever. Directly below, Ozzie Smith elegantly paced off of third base, sure of himself; certain that he could steal home if given half the chance and tie the game. But, more easily, he could be wiped out in all his elegance and ability in a flash. What if Hardy, from his high vantage, dropped a brick? Took aim with a rifle? Called in air support? Game over—we win. It was like that. Not a fair competition of skills or of ideas. Of principles. But a quick leveling. You won when you eliminated your opponent, using any means to do the job; put more bread on the table or more missiles down the chimney. It had nothing to do with ideas or justice. Nothing learned in school. In the old flyer's journal, the same complaint was being made fifty years ago! As if it had been anything different before his time. Saluting your adversary as you shot him down. Or, as he shot you down. Bullshit, Hardy thought, and turned back to the homely contest being played out below them.

Here, at least, was a game originated and played in pastures by farm boys for shoe money, which had rules framed by honor and integrity, and which still had some of that old magic; that image of those old values—a transfer from old stones though the cost of that rubbing had got out of hand. The man sitting next to them would surely agree. But, for a time, say two or three hours, it made you believe in the rest of it—the old social contract, as Clarence Adams had called it.

Then Zeile took the first pitch on an easy swing to lift the ball high toward center field. Henderson stood transfixed on the track near the fence and whacked his glove against his thigh once and then again, looking up into the evening sky. A line of clouds lay along the western horizon. The ball rose into the pale amethyst dusk, as if ready to cross the Ohio River and bounce off a rooftop in Mount Washington, and then it paused to hang on the hook of its arc. The ball became another Sirius, a second Dog Star to accompany the translucent wafer of the moon, and if it could only have stayed there, Hardy would think later, suspended in the purity of that twilight and in the brilliance of Mr. Edison's imagination; the two elements together might have worked a third kind of magic so that there would be time for the confusion and soilage below to be flushed away. If it could only have hung there for a little while longer, a sort of clutch engaged in time's momentum, so the thing between him and Celia could be ironed out. So Clarence Adams could relocate his pride. His importance. Let the planet coast along without all of them, without any of their mistakes and horrors, so, before the ball returned to this artificial surface, the globe could have turned back a little toward innocence, the earth freshened, as a polluted body of water, if left alone, will purify itself.

And how had Clarence Adams actually made steel cable? Did he weave the strands with his bare hands? Hardy would remember the man holding his hands out. Did the thick grayish brown fingers still vibrate from the old task? No doubt Zeile's hands must tremble from the bat's contact with the ball. Even Ozzie Smith's whole being seemed to shiver, holding at third, waiting for the ball to come unstuck and drop, so he could add one more run to his record.

The whole day had shaken Hardy, and the hour or so with Clarence Adams had tappped even more of this wayward energy. Some hard lines remained standing after the quake. What he had only glimpsed in doorways and anterooms was clearly revealed in the shadowless field below. Some of the things in Armstrong's diary pestered him, not so much the reports of ancient betrayals but the man's misplaced idealism, his blinded innocence—why couldn't he see what was happening? Couldn't he see the way he was being handed around? It was pointless to be concerned with the aviator's confusion. It had all happened fifty years ago, and all the players were dead. It was history; an old story even then. But some of the coincidences of that past and the present made these accounts intriguing.

At Park Place School, Miss Darnell had lectured them on the evolution. Those Founding Fathers had been corrupted from the very beginning; the whole thing a matter of trade, tariffs. Wealth and property in charge. Doing business with slave dealers; then, with robber barons like Frick and Arnett. The teacher had been from Johnstown and had lost some of her family in the flood of '88. She had told them about the rich of Pittsburgh, not caring about the faulted dam above Johnstown, as they boated and played their summer charades around the artificial lake that eventually broke through the dam. In college, he would read that novel by Fitzgerald that described how the rich can drive over such things, leaving the mangle of their negligence behind. Two thousand people wiped out in Johnstown, a whole city destroyed, and the philanthropists like Miss Arnett's father turned their backs, broke up their camp. Oh, yes, Carnegie put up a library. Some payoff. And here comes this knockabout flyer, sucked into the whole contract. Here comes Walt Hardy. He wanted to shout at the pages of the journal—don't you see what's happening?

Who, come to think of it, who had employed Armstrong in Mexico? Halstead, the oil man. Cherokee Oil owned part of the Mexican airline as well. Hardy recognized the arrangement. The same kind of deal that had paid his own wages, as Adams put it. Wages—that good old union term which sanctifies the performance of a job nobody really wants to do. "Nobody goes to jail," the ex-steelworker had said, but what he meant was, only nobodies go to jail. He thought he might say to Celia that he had done what he did to give comfort to the man sitting next to him; a quick pop of righteousness. Sure, she would probably answer, while the store downstairs was being robbed.

This morning, when Celia had pushed him over to the main house, it was obviously her strategy for them to spend some time together alone, to share an activity, and maybe give him an opportunity to say something, clean up the air between them. "C'mon, let's get out of here," she had taken Armstrong's journal out of his hands. She was rosy from her shower, girlish, and Hardy was sorry his father was tidying up the kitchen on the other side of the bedroom door. They could hear him clearly. Last night their lovemaking had been surreptitious, perhaps made more exciting because of it, so he had almost reached out for her this morning.

"What's so interesting about that old diary anyway?" Celia asked. Her mind had quickly turned elsewhere.

"He's a funny old guy," Hardy replied and opened the window beside him. The air was deliciously heavy with the aromas of spring. Down below, a gardener pruned rose bushes. "He talks about places where I've been. It's like a history, that's all." He shrugged.

"Maybe you shouldn't read it," she said. "Like going into that old lady's privacy. Anyhow, now it's my turn to dance." She zipped up her slacks and pulled on a sweater. "I want the same tour as you gave Susanna yesterday." They walked through the garden toward the mansion, hand in hand.

Hardy could remember his benefactor's diminutive figure sitting at the art deco desk in her study, pen in hand, reviewing ledgers and check books, doling out the family treasure. Oftentimes the radio would be playing. Each of the manila envelopes he was to come across had been folded over their contents and securely taped to make packets of different thicknesses. All had been labeled. *Household. Family. Staff.* Surprisingly, one had *Lindbergh* scribbled on its face. Then, more bundles with proper names on their surface were stacked in a bottom drawer. *Thurman. McCarthy. Nixon. Bush. North.* What was that one? Did he see it straight? Clearly, the bold marker spelled out *O. North.* He had wanted to call to Celia in the next room. Hey, look! She had been paying some of that salary too. Without either of them knowing it, she had put him on her payroll!

Because each of these envelopes contained canceled checks sorted in the sequence of their printed numbers and bound together by red rubber bands. Other envelopes bore acronyms, codes of some kind, and the checks inside made out to associations, institutions, obscure societies, think tanks. Over the years, he figured, millions of dollars. Then, his name showed up on one of the fatter envelopes. *Walt Hardy.*

Not to be opened until after my death or after the death of Walt Hardy and the death of his children, if he should have any. Elizabeth Arnett.

The large looped handwriting filled the entire area of the envelope's face, a suggestion of haste in its raggedness, like a scrawl against time. Hardy had hefted this bulky package several times from hand to hand and each time had been about to jam it back into one of the desk's cubbies but then, he thought, what would one more offense matter. He ripped the tape apart.

The rubber band that held the checks together broke as he pulled at it, so the checks spilled into his hand like an unruly deck of playing cards. Most made out to stores, others to Cornell University and more—he didn't need to count them to know their number—were dated on his birthdays. Each for twenty dollars. Even her most recent remembrance, he had cashed it with a wry amusement only just a month ago, had been put into the final place of the sequence. The first check of this series, on top of the pack, was made out to his father. *Pay to the order of WILLIAM HARDY...Ten thousand dollars and no cents...Elizabeth Arnett.* April 14, 1942. Maybe she'd set up a trust on his first birthday. He made a note to ask his father about it. If it was still active, the interest would have turned it into a fair sum. He'd sign it over to his father. The old guy could travel, take a Greyhound bus around the world!

The birthday checks became the tabs on a business file that marked off different payments to Horne's or Kaufmann's and other stores and enterprises in Pittsburgh. The range of the sums were wide; from five dollars and change on up. An overcoat had cost $76.99. A pair of shoes, $12.75. The nature of each purchase had been carefully noted on each check, and the handwriting of this bookkeeping became more and more slovenly; a peculiar picturing of time's effect. He had rippled the checks so the handwriting became animated, a scribbled cuneiform wriggling like a virus under a microscope.

Suit with vest. He remembered that suit. He never wore the vest and sold the whole outfit to his roommate for a weekend splurge.

Two ties...sweater...handkerchiefs...underwear...dictionary... buckskin shoes...stationery...fountain pen...picture ...two boxes paper clips...luggage ...

Paper clips?!

The record of her generosity was almost cruelly complete and made clear for anyone who might review the extent of her philanthropy. It was like coming on an ancient tomb meant to be looted for its mummified account books rather than the magnificence of its occupant—or perhaps the two were interchangeable. But who would even care about these payments of petty cash? Her father's donations had been as grand as his business practices had been vicious. He had hired goons to beat up his workers. Local lore assumed he had paid for the strike leader's assassination. Then, like Frick and Carnegie, he had endowed a museum, an opera; set up a hospital. His daughter had no public image to improve. Her generosity was less lofty; funding a president or two, a chauffeur and his son. A laundry list of petty gifts.

The canceled checks had stunned Hardy. Some bequest! Had she hoped he would add up all these five and three dollar markers, the small change—to sum up her gifts, a bequest already made and used up? But, he wasn't supposed to have seen them. Another, after his death and his childrens' death—the thought gagged him; even the unborn made dead by her scrawl on the envelope—was supposed to come across these cancelled notes of her beneficence. Hundreds of checks written out to him from that six tiered checkbook he could remember her using. Think of the hundreds of bank statements she must have sifted through—fifty years worth—to abstract and collect these proofs of her generosity!

The morning outside had clouded over, and he had to switch on the chrome desk lamp. So, if you are Walt Hardy, some fifty years of age, you might feel as if you had been leased, as it were, for a couple of ties and some boxes of paper clips—for twenty bucks a year. He and Joe McCarthy and Richard Nixon and the others. All of them had been on Peggy Arnett's dole, recipients of her tidy gifts. Celia's quick footsteps crossed the bare parquet floor in the next room. Hardy had stuffed the pack of checks into his pocket and closed up the desk drawer just as she came through the door.

"Find anything?" she had asked. She held a large portfolio in both hands.

"No, nothing," he told her automatically. A career of dissembling had made the response easy and natural. The expertise saddened him, and—just for a moment—he wondered if these accounts might offer a reason to start over again. But, he had also been shy about revealing what he had found; one more embarrassment of the life lived in the apartment over the carriage house. Give me a break, Celia would say. Another sad story about that little apartment over the carriage house? Pass the matches! In any event, the moment passed, pushed aside by her own discovery. "What do you have there?"

"A photograph album. She certainly knew a lot of famous people. Look, isn't this Douglas Fairbanks and William Hearst? And Mary Pickford?" They turned the pages of the large book. Peggy Arnett peered out from many photographs, her expression more reserved than shy though something of both. She looked, Hardy felt, pressed. In some of the shots she looked away from the camera, her mouth set in a droll expression, as if she had been a little amazed to find herself in the same picture with these celebrities. Can anyone take this moment seriously, her expression seemed to ask. She might just dance out of the picture, do a Ruby Keeler buck and wing, before the shutter clicked—even as she linked arms between Ruby Keeler and Al Jolson. "Look." Celia had turned the page. "This must be your man Armstrong?"

Peggy Arnett stood beside a sporty looking biplane in six or seven pictures on the next page. *Cherokee Oil* was painted on its fuselage next to a profile of an Indian like the one on the old nickel. A single feather poked up from a head band. A cloth flying helmet, goggles pushed up, was fastened tightly under Arnett's chin to frame her face and squeeze out a sweetness similar to a nun's face confined within a cowl. She looks radiant. She resembles an old time aviatrix about to set a record. The man standing beside her appeared dressed for a movie part himself; whipcords and boots, a straw sombrero in one hand. Dark sunglasses obscured his eyes but the lower part of his face, the mouth set humorously, looked expectant, good-natured. Nothing special happening here, his stance suggested; about to shrug off any compliment. Hardy liked his looks, and he tried to dress the slight physique with some of the exploits he had read about in the man's journal. The two appeared at ease, like a couple.

"Think they had made it into the sack when this was taken?" Celia asked. "She looks like a big game hunter with a trophy."

"He's got a girl. A dancer. And Arnett was engaged to this oil man."

"You've got to be kidding?" Celia laughed and leaned down to look closer.

"What is it?" Hardy said after a little. Celia had become very interested in one photograph. She looked up at him, her eyes going to his face. The album lay open between them.

"You've cut yourself shaving," she said. "There." And she touched him just above his mouth.

The ball drops into Henderson's glove as a light drizzle begins to fall. Bill Hardy has appeared at the base of the steep grandstand stairs just as Ozzie Smith touched up and sprang from third base toward home as though he had been released from a catapult. Thirty thousand people jump to their feet, in full throat, as the center fielder takes one, two steps and hurls the ball homeward. The crowd has risen as one, and Hardy stands to see the play, then on his feet, he hears himself shouting. He has joined the roar and the excitement. His pulse races. He feels pumped up, out of himself. Right and wrong is about to be decided. Cee is looking at him, and her eyes glisten.

Bill Hardy has disappeared in the roaring crowd, and Hardy is alarmed for him because of the fragile cardboard tray he carried in both hands with its load of beer and Polish sausage. The old man could have been knocked over by the surge of fans, knocked off balance—to his knees even—but he would still try to keep the tray and the beer and the sausage level. Not spill a drop. Safe. Knocked over but keeping his balance. No matter what might rock or batter him, he would be steady, follow the map. Carry out his job. Hardy sees everything; all the history and the causes for everything; why his mother had left them, and why he would probably lose Celia.

At midfield, Henderson's powerful throw whizzes past Jay Bell. The ball strikes the earth six feet before home plate and glances precisely into Slaught's mitt. Here comes Smith full out, already in the dirt. The catcher's tag is perfect. Out. What a play! The crowd goes berserk. Hardy kisses Celia. She kisses him back, hard. His father abruptly appears from the melee, smiling and clutching the cardboard tray of food. He looks triumphant, a diver emerging from the depths with treasure.

168

"Hey, they had pirogies too," he says gaily and presents the beer and food. The crowd quiets; the inning is over. "What happened?"

"A great play." Hardy gives the details. Celia opens the umbrella she had brought, and the three of them get cozy beneath it, happily eating the greasy food and enjoying the game. The Pirates will win. It is almost in the record books. It is, in fact, already in the record books; never to be changed. Smith has been put out at homeplate, and, unlike so many events in life, that event cannot be taken back. Misinterpreted; spinned. The possibilities for the Cardinals were over for this inning, if not the whole game. It is history.

25 May 1940
Guanajuato

In this dream, China is some kind of animal grazing on big, juicy leaves, but what kind of animal can't be seen because I am looking at her head-on so it is only her face but not the rest of her I can see. But I know she's standing on four slender legs like a deer or an antelope. Her long elegant face, big dark eyes angled above the cheekbones, and her nostrils flare out and in like the gills of a fish as her tongue wraps around a particularly luscious leaf and pulls it into her mouth. She's foraging and has that dreamy look in her eyes that she gets when she is eating something particularly tasty. I've seen her like this across the table from me at a restaurant, lifting the food into her mouth, or sometimes looking down at her in bed as she takes me in.

Save, in this dream, we are somewhere on this high plateau, barren and rocky and before the rainy season, like right now in Guanajuato, and everything is washed out, the palest excuse for colors — but not where China is grazing which is lush. And I say *we,* because I'm watching her eat, watching her from behind a bush or a rock, and I'm not alone. She knows I'm watching her as she eats, and she keeps on eating, a wary eye out, because she also knows I'm there, watching her. And I'm suddenly a dog like Tonantzin with her leg all fixed up or maybe there's two of us, Tonantzin and me, both of us wild dogs or dogs gone wild and we know that China knows we are there waiting to spring out at her as she is eating, snuffling and swallowing all she can get down in that moment, as we crouch in the underbrush and bide our time. Then, we're off; running after her and snapping at her legs and sides. And all the while, I have this picture of China's face, trusting and beautiful — never asking for anything much more than to enjoy a quiet meal which we have interrupted. Then the other dog looks me full in the face. It's Peggy Arnett.

It has been just about a year since I landed in Veracruz. If I'd been able to pick-up my passport in Paris like Frank Tinker, then none of this would have happened. Of course, I might have blown my brains out, too. But then — no China. No Tonantzin. We're like a family almost, the three of us. Ungrateful wretch, I should take the hand dealt me. Who has a better life? I get paid in American bucks for doing what I love to do best. I have this beautiful woman at my side who thinks I'm the hottest number since Quetzalcoatl — old blue eyes has shown up again! China's at the theatre rehearsing for the performance tonight, Las Palomas are on tour and I've become a kind of Stagedoor Juannie. Right now, I'm sitting in the central square, *el Jardín de la Union*, of this small city, and very pretty it is with palms and birds of all colors and song. I'm having my boots polished by an Indian as I write in my journal and sipping a Carta Blanca. I got these boots made in Madrid three years back and now they're being worked over by a native here in New Spain for a few pesos. So, not all that much has changed, if you get my drift, Molly. I mean forget Juarez — the theatre tonight is named after him — and forget the Revolution, Zapata and Villa and the rest — it's all the same: some peon on his knees cleaning up the gringo's boots.

But, I'm uneasy about the place. Mexico. And I guess the business at the Suarez ranch in January still bothers me. What kind of place it is. If only China said something about it, I'd feel better. Her silence makes me confused and sorry. I want to keep remembering how she looked when she picked me up at the hotel in Oaxaca. I have looked out the lobby window just as she strides across the plaza. Her old man's LaSalle is parked behind her. She was wearing one of those white, white cotton dresses the local women wear in Oaxaca. Brilliant embroidery all over the sleeves, around the hem. Fanciful designs of birds and flowers. Legs bare and those long, strong feet in sandals.

We act like strangers in the lobby, for the benefit of the hotel people. Well, not strangers but hired hand and the boss's daughter. I want to grab her. This dog had followed me over to the hotel from the café and we talk through her. That's where the dog gets her name. "Es Tonantzin," China says, stroking her muzzle. And the dog starts wagging her tail like she's been the Mother of Gods all along and has been waiting for someone to recognize her. Naturally, it would be China. The desk clerk grins. China resembles the Indians down here; her people after all. You see it when she's standing next to them; not so much in the capital. Cheekbones and tilted eyes, like some of the Finns. All Mongols, I guess. But we have to be careful in Oaxaca. She's the *hija del cacique*. The big shot's daughter, and I'm the *gringo*. Not like in the DF where we can do what we please. The day before, she had to come up the backstairs, paid off the maid. *La mordida*. A bribe.

I had only seen the territory from the plane when we flew down. Driving out to the ranch, I get a ground view. Another reason I could almost live here. The country looks hot. Washes of color going from browns to grays to pinks. The mountains purplish green. Some still smoking.

171

Snow on the summits. Fire and ice. Fields of
corn and beans. At the crossroads, little domi-
noes of adobe houses. Up to our right, the old
Zapotec capital they've found on top of a mountain. Digging it out. China's people.

"Yesterday was *muy peligroso,*" I remember her
saying. "But you make it so hot for me,
h'Armstrong. *Mi sangre es fogosa, caliente.*"
Her black hair was full of the lustrous colors
of high grade oil. It spills around her shoulders, screens her face in the slipstream. She
flies the LaSalle more than drives it. "*Pero,*"
and she draws a finger across her throat. I get
the message. If Pappa-Generalisimo finds out, my
hide will be tanning on one of the racks we
have been passing.

China gets her height from her old man. Her
long aristocratic nose too. He looks pretty
grand in black and silver buttons, full charro
regalia. He wore a big ivory handled revolver,
and he's as fair-skinned as I am. His moustache
is white and about as big as the horns of the
steers on his ranch. A huge place. Guards at the
front gate, guns everywhere. He's what they call
a *gachupino*, a wearer of spurs.

It was a big party. All kinds of old revolutionaries, politicos. Lots of eats. Ten degrees
cooler inside. Big mesquite trees hanging over
the patio and fountains gushing everywhere. And
these fountains in near desert territory. Get
the picture, Molly? China told me he had been
a pal of Calles, the general thrown out by
Cárdenas. Now, he's supposed to be OK with *El
Presidente*, but why this big gathering?

Angel Dorantes, my guardian angel at the
Hotel Regis, told me a joke that sums it up. The
only party down here is the *Partido Nacional
Revolucionario.* So much for democracy. So much
for the revolution. Anyway, PNR for short. But
Angel tells me, the initials really stand for
podemos robar, nosotros? Can we rob? Do they
ever.

A mariachi band's staccato is nailing everything in place near tables loaded with food, tequila, and beer. An entire pig is turning over a pit. Several Indian women crouch under a portico, patting out fresh tortillas. Others are slicing up cactus leaves and throwing them in a simmering pot. I smell cilantro. Lots of back-slapping, talk. Some singing. It's a like a frat party. A national convention of some kind. And *el jefe* moves around. Politicking.

And who should show up but the *New York Times* guy, Reed Ansers. He came down by train. His rat nose is almost quivering like he's smelled cheese. "Do you understand what's happening here?" he asked me.

"A big fiesta. The General's feast day."

"Which the Nazis are probably paying for," he said. "Don't you get it — we're observing a plot to overthrow the government."

Then he launches into a history lesson. Cárdenas, the oil cartel, the fascists,the communists. He mentions Trotsky, Cedillo. Gen. Almazan. I can't keep up with the names; anyway, I'm looking for China. She's disappeared into the women's part of the hacienda. Ladies not invited to this barbecue.

"Your sweetheart's daddy is a strong choice. Did you know that Juarez was born in Oaxaca too?" He adjusted the little tennis racquets in his shirt cuffs, then makes a grab at a tray of chalupas. "Me? I'm just on the job," he said like he had heard the question in my head. He's taking little rat nibbles around the corn cake. "Like you. Though I expect your job has compensations mine doesn't enjoy."

So I felt like decking him right there. But something had happened. The band had stopped. Talk breaks off. A guy stands up on the fountain edge and shouts. "What's happening?" Ansers asks. His Spanish is only fair. It was something about people from the *ejidos*, the co-op the Government has set up nearby. Peasants. A bunch of them making a complaint. "Let's go," says Scoop and we follow everybody.

And here is the hard part. Here's where China and I have had hard words. Worse — silence.

There's a bunch of peasants on horseback down
below the hacienda. Big mesquites casting a
shadowy net over all. It's hot and dusty down
here. The landscape looks ready to blow away.
The whole scene looks like one of Rivera's
murals. About a dozen campesinos on horseback,
big straw hats, white pajamas and carbines.
Around them; Suarez's bodyguards and the party
guests. El grand papa stands in the center, elegant, in command. Like he's a movie director. In
fact, it looks like a movie. The older man on
horseback has a moustache equal to the general's. On either side, two younger guys on skinny nags. One of them a hairless kid, and his
sombrero seems too big for him.

"What's he saying?" Ansers asks. He's got out
his notebook.

I tell him it's about water. Always about
water. These are cotton farmers. They've come up
from their communes to pay respects to el
cacique on his saint's day and to ask him to
turn on the water. Their cotton is drying up.
Their horses have a powerful smell and flick
their tails, stamp the hard earth. They have
brought their own flies with them. In between
the courtly speeches, the flies buzz and buzz.

Suarez is patiently explaining to them the
sad circumstance. That when the government set
them up on their co-ops to raise cotton, somebody forgot that the water ran through his land.
A terrible oversight. Just like the bureaucrats
now running things, Suarez jokes. The _campesinos_
do not smile. They've all heard this tale
before, but the party guests think it's very
funny. They nod and rub their bellies, approve
his mastery of detail, his way with the peasants. His sorrowful understanding of their circumstances.

"See? It's like an audition," Ansers said,
taking everything down as I translate for him.
And he's right. Even the stance Suarez had taken
is something off a postage stamp. One hand held
up like Columbus greeting the natives, or Cortés
or Porfirio Díaz. Whoever. Yes, he was saying,

it was a bad time for everyone. And he understood that their cotton was drying up like the
husks of their ancestors' *cojones*, but there is
a larger picture. One that only he can see.
"That's a good one," Ansers said. He misspelled
the word for *balls*. But will the *N.Y. Times*
print such lingo?

The general had been saying that he person-
ally was going to give money to their local
priest for prayers for rain. Out of his own
pocket. He acted it out. And all of a sudden it
did smell like rain, that copper metal smell and
taste in the air, though it is something else.
I've smelled it many times. The armpits of Sgt.
Death.

It's like everyone is a cutout in a pop-up
book. Illustrated and not real, even the POW of
the .44 is like a cork popping. A kid's toy.
Simultaneously, the rider next to the old guy is
yanked off his horse, as if he had been lassoed.
It's the boy. He hits the ground with a comical
bounce and jounce.

"Holy shit," Ansers says. Pistols and rifles
of every description have been leveled across
the afternoon. Suarez hasn't moved. One of his
guards must have got an itchy finger. He stands
with his weapon in hand, ready for more. Maybe
a horse jumped from a fly bite. Anyway, the
bodyguard had just pulled out and fired.

The old guy is off his horse and blubbering.
Mi nieto...mi nieto. His grandson. The oversized
sombreo has fallen off the kid. He's a boy of
around nine or ten. Round pretty face, long
lashes. There's a big hole through a wad of
tortillas he had stuck in the sash of his pants.
Maybe his mother had pushed them in there for
his lunch. Going with grandpa up to the big
man's hacienda. Okay for lunch but not much to
stop a .44 slug — those tortillas. One rope sandal had fallen off a foot. The toes were pinkish. The old man was weeping and hugging the
dead boy. One, two, several guns cock in the
silence. It's tense. Then the General started
talking again. What he says is so outrageous, so
ridiculous that it makes for laughter. Crazy

under the circumstances, but it eased the tension. Reduces everything — even the dead kid — to nonsense.

Well, of course, we shoot your grandson, he said. Why would we shoot *un viejo cabrón* like you? Your horizon has few suns behind it, but it is your grandson who will rob us and violate our women. So we must shoot him. He waves his big revolver like a baton. Any more grandsons in your party? We might take care of them right now and save trouble later. No? Then, turn around and get back to your cotton fields. Some water may find its way into your miserable fields. To honor his saint, they might get a little water. The old guy has lifted the small body onto his saddle and mounts his horse. His shoulders convulse as he bends low. The mariachi band has started up. They've followed us down to the place. They dash out a peppy tune. The kid's hat remains on the ground. The *campesinos* turn their nags around and slowly depart. "Wow," Ansers said. "What a story. This guy could be the next president of Mexico."

Around me, around this very park in Guanjuato, are beggars, signs of great poverty. Centuries old poverty. And this is true everywhere, not just a provincial capital like this one. It's like those photographs of Villa's men riding into Mexico City on horseback under trolley wires. Served lunch at a tony restaurant by waitresses in frilly caps. A few lines of the new technology strung out over the old streets, the old violent intersections of Mexico. The wide gap between most of the people and the few like China's papa-general is like the distance to the moon.

"I don't get it," I tell her yesterday. The hot breeze through our train compartment's window made us sweat so then we cooled off. We've been on this train since before daybreak. "Don't you feel anything about it? He was just a kid. A boy."

She's been cutting my hair as we track through steep gorges and dry canyons. We're snug as bugs in this overstuffed compartment. The great Díaz might have ridden in this compartment on his way to dedicate the Juarez Theatre he'd just built in Guanajuato. That's where we're headed too. She's wearing a white cotton slip and is barefoot, pressed against me as she goes snip-snip around my ears. Outside the jacarandas are fading, the countryside is losing color. The rainy season is a month away. Inside this compartment, cut glass mirrors, prints of women with parasols, walnut paneling.

Tonight, China's group will dance in the theatre the old dictator built and they'll be lucky if they have a hundred people in the audience. The government has sent the entire *Orquesta Sinfonica* along to accompany them. But the whole country is like that, an orchestra waiting for an audience to show up.

But yesterday, China standing behind me trimming my feathers. When we go through a dark canyon, we are reflected in the window glass. A homey scene. "You think Mexico is a museum, h'Armstrong." Her voice is humorous but not funny. Snip-snip.

"Yeah, but Jesus H., China — how about it? Shooting a boy? That was murder. And nothing done about it." It's not the first time, I've brought the subject up.

"Unfortunate." She shrugs. "What do you know about how we do about it. These are peasants that have no right, in the first places, to take that land. The government set up these farms for them. Making them more capitalists. It is bad land. And so my father is supposed to donate his water, to make the land better. He is supposed to do what the government did not do. That would make his land poor. So, what has been gained? Meanwhiles, he has helped *los campesinos* in the many ways."

"But you described him as a creole fascist the other night. That's what you called him, remember?"

She shrugged a bare shoulder. "This is a complicated matter. It is the history for these peasants and my father to face each other. They are to destroy each other. *Una fuerza necesaria*.. Then...then, we start new. We build a great Mexico then. After *la fuerza*."

La fuerza. Where have I heard that talk before? In Spain. Red baloney. A kind of purplish darkness had spread just below her eyes, down over her cheeks. Like a bruise. She looks Indian, but talks like a graduate of that fancy school in the USA. A couple of nights before, we were out at Rivera's house in Coyoacan. She was another person. She spouted all this political lingo. They all did. And then, the great *filósofo* shows up. Mr. Lund. I finally get to meet Mr. Lund. Who turns out to be none other than Leon Trotsky. He's on the lam down here — just like me. I heard the same thing from all of them that night. How peasants and people like Suarez will destroy each other, the class war stuff; the government will step in — then, the revolution comes. The workers will take over and run things. How many workers do they have down here to run anything?

But does this old bolshevik Trotsky talk like that to me? He's heard of me, the hero of the *patrulla americana* and so forth. He looks like Barney· Google. Wiry hair sticking straight out. Thick glasses. "You like rabbits?" he asks me. "You should come visit me. I have a Patagonian buck that is quite splendid." And this is the Number Two Red? No wonder this girl who is giving me a trim is confused. Her slip is white against honey-brown skin. Her bosoms peeking over. "*Es simple para ti.* You take it straight, your idealism," she said. "Without the chaser. I love you for the way you follow the heart. But here we make the pots for *turistas*. *Nada auténtico.*"

My heart becomes one of those clay pots, because I haven't mentioned Peggy Arnett. She's been showing up at the field. Always looks surprised to find me there, like when she looks up from whatever she's been studying on the ground

and — gee whiz — there I am. That apology of a
smile. Oh, you work here? She carries little
bits of news. A new gallery opening. Lunch with
Dolores Del Rio. Gossip about some foreign
ambassador. As if I'd be interested in any of
it. Then, the other afternoon, we had just come
in from Tampico. Miguel was doing the paper work
in operations. Arnett strolls into view.

"Oh, I'm so glad to run into you," she said.
We're in the middle of the auxiliary runway. She
has this flinty voice. But it's relaxing to
speak to someone just in English for a change.
Not all this translation I have to do. China is
speaking more and more Spanish with me. Some I
get, some I don't. Then, thinking this makes me
feel sorry. "I have some information that might
be useful." That's another thing. Arnett sounds
like she's speaking to the board meeting at her
steel company. So you want to take a second
look, as the fella says, Molly. All that steel
moola. Her steel and Halstead's oil — that's
some arrangement, a marriage that might have to
be voted on by the stock holders!

"I've discovered quite a decent veterinarian
in the Colonia Obrera," she told me. "For your
dog, I mean." She smiled slightly, one corner
down like she's sucked on a lemon. "To fix her
leg."

Now China and I had been talking about
Tonantzin, her three legs. She gets around quite
well on them. We've joked about putting up a
milagro for her in the cathedral. One of those
little tin replicas people hang up for different cures. Could we find one in the shape of a
dog's leg? Gives us the giggles. Tonantzin gets
up and wags her tail, looks questions at us. All
this at China's apartment. It would be a test of
faith, China had said, taking a breath, suddenly straight-faced. Sober Indian.

So, this time — about three weeks ago —
Arnett's looking across the field at something.
Nothing. Waiting to be thanked, I guess, which
I do. Take the vet's name and address from her.
The Douglas has been been pulled in for servic-
ing. Her boyfriend's green Beechcraft is parked

inside the hangar. We seem to have said everything but don't know how to do *good-bye*. She's tapping one of her low-heeled shoes and peers out from beneath her brow. I am wondering what she might be wearing under her usual country club costume — those lacy undies spilling out of her suitcase that night in San Luis Potosí. Five months back, and I can still see her spilling out of her pajamas. She might be recalling that moment too, because her face is turning red and she puts a hand up to her front, to the very place. The color does something for her.

"Another thing," she said. Her features twist a little to one side, like it's difficult for her to ask. "Do you ever give lessons? Flying lessons, I mean?"

Last week: "Where were you this afternoon?" China asks me. She knows my duty roster by now. I told her I was doing a sight seeing job for Halstead which, in a way, was the truth. In another way — a lie.

Then, yesterday, the train comes around this curve and into the station at San Miguel de Allende. China has fallen asleep on the floor of the compartment. Arms, legs unfolded trustingly like a child's. Well, she is almost that, I remind myself. What are we doing together? Anyway, I look out the window. A few people getting off. But one person I recognize. I almost yell at him out the open window. But something about the way he moves keeps my mouth shut. He doesn't want to be seen. He jumps into a car across the platform that starts up, pulls away fast. It's Siquerios. That painter who bunked next to me on the *Sinaia* a year ago.

Nextday,
Guanajuato

It's become immensely hot in *el Jardin de la Union*. Like a Bessemer has tipped over in Pittsburgh. Hey, that's an interesting way to put it, McGee.

Anyhow, I'm having another shine as China sleeps off her triumph last night. Flowers and many curtains calls. She was magnificent as the sorcerer Tezcatlipoca in a number on Quetzalcoatl. "Is there anyone here who does not know the story?" one of the dancers kept asking the audience. Not a bad audience either. A lot of university students. Free tickets.

But, the big news in the papers is that someone tried to bump off Trotsky and his wife night before yesterday. They got into the fort he lives in and shot the place up with Tommy guns. I say "someone." They do know that my old bunkmate, Siquerios, was one of the gunmen. So, when I saw him yesterday getting off the train in San Miguel, he was on the lam. A funny country. Painters running around with Tommy guns, shooting up old revolutionaries. Can you see Norman Rockwell pulling such a stunt? In Spain they called Siquerios "the little colonel." But he's no Al Capone. No one killed. Not even a rabbit. The Bolshie's grandson got nicked. It's like Spain all over again; Reds knocking each other off. Or trying to. The paper says Trotsky's house was riddled. Siquerios, come to think of it, was a machine gunner in Spain. Another reason we probably lost that fight. He must be a better painter.

The rest of the news is not so comical. The Germans are half-way through Belgium, heading toward France. The same route as 1914. Stupid French. Their army locked up in those Maginot forts. So much for that great idea. Ansers says the English are supposed to be asking Hitler for a peace parley. The Nazis are pushing them into the sea. But I'm cornered too. I should be back in the Air Service. I've got to get out of this place. I've got to get back into uniform.

And China?

Last night her bare, beautiful feet stomping on the stage. Sorcerer or rain god or whatever part she played. Her bare feet turning the whole theatre into a corn lot or an ant hill or the tomb of a Mayan princess. And she would be

something else too, changing herself. I guess
that's one of the benefits of what she does. She
can change her history, be someone else.
Something I've tried, but can't manage. A trick
I may never learn.

Lately, her future appeared before Celia like a long plain
that had to be crossed; not like the prairie of the old pioneers but
one defined from the smoldering piles of apple orchards in the
Hudson Valley that permeate the air every spring; even here in
Pittsburgh, this sweet smoke of winesap rose in her memory.
This country was not turning out the way it was supposed to.

And for the last couple of days here in Pittsburgh, Celia could
not get the image of Joan Kennedy out of her head. Ted Kennedy's
wife kept standing in her memory as she had stood beside her husband in that receiving line in Albany some twenty-five years ago,
patient and looking a little nervous, to shake the hands of local
politicians and their wives. "Their lovely wives," to recall the language of those introductions from the dais, and she guessed they all
had been lovely, lovely enough. Joan Kennedy had worn an
orchid-pink dress with large round buttons down the front and
cut off a foot above the knees. Celia remembered the woman's
long slim legs were sheathed in pearl white hose. She was an
exotic bird that had mistakenly flown down into that provincial
capital to startle the natives with the fact of a singular migration
happening over their heads. Joan Kennedy had made all the
other women that evening look dumpy in their minis, like players in the wrong costumes and on the wrong stage.

Or maybe all of them, the women of her generation, had not
been ready to wear that abbreviated style; the fashion had come
on them before their minds and bodies could carry it off. Or too
late. Except for Joan Kennedy and a few others, but even she
had looked a little incongruous in the short skirt, though Cee
understands now that there might have been other reasons for
the woman's expression, the glassy smile fixed within the
blonde parabola of a lacquered bouffant. Maybe, it had taken a
further evolutionary turn of the female mind and body for the
style to look right because short skirts were back, and the young
women wearing them today looked just fine; at ease and comfortable.

Whatever. Politics and government and all the stuff of history books was something like that—a fashion that had to fit the citizen body just right or people would feel odd, left out and just a little frustrated. Sometimes angry. Yesterday, she and Shirley Adams had interfered with male talk, with the male silence as Walt and Clarence Adams shared the rehearsed violence of the wrestling match. But still she had tried to say something. Ideas had taken shape in her mind like the clouds she had seen one day in Indiana, developing on the windshield of the Honda like a photograph. Yesterday, these ideas had made her feel awkward.

What had she said that was so awful? Something about institutions not guaranteeing a person's happiness. Boy! Didn't she sound like her father, and, for a moment, Clarence Adams had looked at her with that same perplexed generosity, a suspension of the rules, that had been in her mother's expression before she would turn back to the housework, had disappeared into the basement under the bookstore to do the laundry.

Walt had got that look on his face, part impatience, part amusement. A familiar sign. Perhaps she had used the wrong words, maybe she had always used the wrong words, and she reviews her language and what she might have said as she gets her clothes and belongings together. But the review didn't matter anymore because listening to Walt and Clarence Adams talk yesterday, she understood it had been a mistake to come back; a foolish gesture she'd come upon at the bottom of her heart like a crumpled receipt from K-Mart. She's leaving for good this time; here she goes again. It's like being in a home movie being rewound and played back. See Celia pack. Let's see that part again! But she's made breathless by her journey's prospect; thrilled and scared all at once.

Yesterday, she could have said something snappy that might have grabbed their attention during the commercial breaks; pulled them up through the hazy bonhomie of a beer commercial—where, by chance, a single black actor guzzled with four or five white guys to endorse the product as it falsified an ideal—just like that, she should have said. Like what, they would have looked at each other, tickled by her voice going higher. There, on the screen. Didn't they see?

She could have said, "You pay your dues but you don't

something-something..." But this morning she still couldn't finish a commercial for that betrayal, for the disaffection that had come to her as she had driven west a couple of weeks ago. Mile after mile, something inside of her had been pulled out as the wheels turned. The words she had for it were out of style. Sometimes, she pictured herself standing before a jury, as her father had hoped she would, making a summation. "America is an argument that was framed and formulated within a specific setting and for the exercise and enjoyment of a specific group, but others, because of their race or gender, have no part in the discussion." That's what she had wanted to say yesterday, and what she had put together on I-40, as the talk shows on the Honda's radio aired the angers and frustrations of the disenfranchised. She would have made a terrible lawyer afterall. After all—are you listening Papa?—because she would have annoyed judges and alienated juries, lost clients, by her picky passion for what should be rather than getting along with how things really were. Here comes Suffering Celia, they'd say, set up the podium for the lecture. She laughs as she folds her clothes and places them in the two suitcases on the bed.

She can hear the faint stir of her father-in-law in the kitchen, the discrete sounds of a domestic. Indeed, wasn't that the truth of the man? Without a word, without her saying anything, Bill Hardy knew she was in here, in his son's old bedroom, packing up to leave them forever. It was as if he had read about her departure in the morning *Post-Gazette*, maybe a small item on the sports page, where he had also read an account of last night's game, the one they had all seen; studiously reading every word on every inning; not so much to find a discrepancy but to verify what he had witnessed. And he had come across the notice of her departure, so it was already a fact, like something that had appeared with the sunrise and had been set down into its determined place in the sky; so it couldn't be discussed or argued. Nothing could be done about it, he'd think. Walt had that same subservience to events, to go with the currents that had become rapids which carried him from the hill towns in the Catskills down to the jungles of Central America. It was a peculiar kind of run off that had eroded much more than soil.

That's why she had turned around in Little Rock. Just maybe, she had thought, he might perform one modest act all his own. Really do something this time and not carry out orders.

Nothing so grand as a response to the injustice and cruelty that the voices on her car radio screamed about, wept over or, even worse, had cataloged with a sardonic artlessness. No, nothing so grand. Just something simple, one human being to another kind of thing with no gain, no edge. No IOU.

"He's got IOUs he can call in," Walt used to say about certain politicians or about one of the men who later would stand accused with him before Congress. All their IOUs called in.

"How so?" In those days she had been thinking about going back to school, maybe even law school, so the workings of this world interested her. She'd have to know the strategies, how things were done.

"Oh, these guys pass around favors like catsup at a barbecue." He had laughed and blushed a little, shook his head, as if there had been much more to tell but she wouldn't understand the rest of it. Not for her tender ears. He squeezed her arm or some other part, and that had been okay for awhile, because the sex had been pretty good—no complaints there.

No, it was the way he would blush when they got to these specifics: how things worked. Like a schoolboy. First, she thought her questions had interfered; her curiosity became a nuisance. Or, she was asking him to divulge campaign secrets, how he had made a deal for delegates in the back room of a village hardware. Later, the same technique was used in more ambitious deals. How did the money get from the Middle East and down to Nicaragua? From here to Sadam?

"A phone call, that's all. He'd pick up the phone, say a few words and, then, invite the undersecretary to lunch. That's all it took."

"But what?" she would insist. "What did it take? What, for Christ's sake, did they have for lunch? Can you tell me that?"

Walt would blush and turn away, seem to deposit her query in a dead letter bin he kept in his head for such awkward questions. Like a schoolboy, yes, but one who had not done his homework. Caught out. "He'd say," she heard him as she packed, "he'd say—we got our can-do guy ready to go. Hardy."

It was this lack of petty information that had finally failed her. Not just the overall job. In the last look at it, he had not been able to tell her what she needed to know about the world he lived in. Almost a tribal error; something missing in the hunter-gatherer's quiver. They all had a dream, but had she ever been in it?

Celia sits on the edge of the bed, between her two suitcases. One of these days, she'd be really finished packing. In the mirror of the heavy oak wardrobe she sees this woman in transit. She could be someone waiting in a train or bus station. She had not been the only woman going somewhere on I-40. She had passed or been passed by other women in cars, some with children in the back seat, or with another woman, or alone like her. Women of America, on the move. Start your engines, ladies! Ta-dah!

"It's not giving them the vote that's the problem," her father used to say. He would be winding the stem of the large gold watch, tightening up the old joke he was about to spring. "It's teaching them how to drive." And she used to laugh along with him, both of them enjoying her mother's faint, accommodating smile. When had she become one of *them*, Celia asks herself; when had she learned that she was not on her father's side of the joke and the choice had never been hers? He had been winding up this joke, kept it running, all along. Her father had prepared her for Walt—must it always work like this?—for she had sensed the same need in him; this yearning he had to be a part of something that always denied him membership.

So, the dimensions of her journey ahead were not just measured in miles. She'd have to cross another kind of prairie, create her own version of the frontier spirit that had become diluted in the very romances meant to depict it, a way West disremembered. She might take a more northern route this time, I-80 maybe. Last night, when they got back from the ball game, she had looked at the road atlas she kept in the Honda. Right then, she had already made up her mind. "Are you coming up?" Walt had called down to her, ready to celebrate the Pirates' victory, but part of her was already half-way across Iowa; Colorado and the Rocky Mountains just ahead. Then she would cut down to Las Vegas where a pretty good accountant might find a job. The old Pace method was still basic, and she could brush up on the new rulings to pass the CPA boards in Nevada, where a still nice looking woman might get a tumble. A game of chance, as W. C. Fields used to say.

Menopausal Sex—How About It? Like some program on TV, and she might be one of the women sitting on the dais, answering thoughtful questions from the audience. Yes, she would tell the audience—just between us women and the million or so tuned in—she might have made that U-turn in Arkansas because she had been thinking of Walt's hard, pretty cock. She would say that and bring the house down. And it would be partly true. Partly. Hadn't she given up wanting to be part of the team? The Original Team. And last night, when she had put the map away and come upstairs to this bedroom, she had fucked his brains out but with an odometer already turning in her heart. So, she would say to the TV audience (APPLAUSE), Walt Hardy doesn't have the only cock that can rise up and say, "Good morning."

Anticipating the road ahead brings her to her feet and she resumes packing. It would be a freshening, a renewal. She could become a dealer in a gambling casino. She could put together her knack with numbers and the pleasing, unchallenging look of her and become a blackjack dealer. She had read that certain casinos ran workshops to train new dealers. They'd be looking for a more mature person these days; not a showgirl type but more of an older sister who might tease a gent to go down-and-dirty, take one more card and bust. She'd take her fair share of tricks, if that's the way the game is to be played. She'd become something of an outlaw. Just a little bit. She'd find her place in the desert, become a card-carrying member of a cardsharp union. A full citizen.

A sudden stab of regret shivers her. Not over it yet, and the old vulnerability still not grown over. She clicks close the fasteners of the larger suitcase. Snap-snap. Just like that. That's how she has to do it. They had had a dream and she was sorry to wake from it. Pack it up.

Yesterday, Clarence Adams had leaned back in his lounger and said, "There's nobody up on the stars calling for us to come up, nobody wants us up there, but we are determined to go. It's a dangerous place to be, on those stars. Deadly." He had smiled wonderfully. "We want things that don't want us."

But the man's smile had annoyed her, smug in his satisfaction with less. Whatever happened to Malcom X? Whatever happened to Walt Hardy and Celia Dutton? Whatever happened to a fair deal and a five-cent cigar? her father used to ask.

From the beginning, Clarence Adams and she and—yes, Joan Kennedy too—had never been included, had not been meant to be included. No wonder they all looked uncomfortable standing around in Albany twenty-five years ago, the breeze fanning their butts. They had been the parsley on the fatback in the counter. Walt Hardy, the broker, showed to fix things up, join up the parts that didn't fit or look right when snapped in place.

"Freedom fighters? Give me a break." She had confronted him once when everything began to come out. "Do you really believe this crap?" They must have been dressing to go to a banquet. One of the things they still did together. Another meal to raise money for legal expenses. She had put on a couple of pounds which also annoyed her. The chicken dinners had become more elaborate, fancy sauces and puff pastry. The lawyers got it all. The house in Silver Springs was all but gone. Her delphiniums gone. She had raised those delphiniums from seed, too. She wouldn't forgive Walt for those delphiniums either, and she finds herself laughing over the trivial indictment. Moreover, at these dinners, she was always put at a table with men whose eyes seemed to be pasted on. Zombies, who said things like, "Oh, rea-ally," and then turned over the lettuce of their salads when she joined the conversation.

Nor had she felt like getting dressed up the night she met Joan Kennedy. It was two hours to Albany and two hours back. She had spent the day with her mother who had started chemotherapy that afternoon. She had begun to tire of these pilgrimages. So, why did they have to go up to Albany that night? If they had dumped the reception, would it have made any difference? She could have claimed a crusher of PMS. He had been needed, Walt said.

"The O'Connell machine is restless," Walt had told her. "Bobby can't leave the Coast—the primary in California is just a week away. New York's primary is next week, and one of LBJ's boys has been pissing in the well. So, we're bringing in Teddy to stroke old Dan and his Irish boy-os." He was so sure of everything .

"What should I wear?" She wanted to go to bed. Watch television. Eat junk food. Tune out. "Is it going to be very formal?"

"Go short," he had said. "That black number you wore the

time before has a classy look."

Classy-assy, she thought. But, the idea that something could be done, still be done, had turned them on. What was that quote of Bernard Shaw's that Bobby Kennedy was always saying, *I dream of things that never were and ask, Why not?* Potent stuff. So they had to go to Albany because something could still be done. Why not? The cities were on fire but something was about to done. King had been murdered in Memphis, but something could still be done. The butchery continued in Vietnam but something was about to be done. If they could just get through the California primary. Then, get through New York—then. Then and then and then—something could be done. What was it Clarence Adams had said yesterday? We want to reach stars that don't want us.

Celia sits down again on the bed and consults with the woman in the wardrobe mirror. Not really so different from the other woman who had checked her hemline a quarter of a century ago; just a different mirror. In fact, she could probably wear that same "black number" as Walt had called it, if she still owned it. Inside, she was many sizes different, while, come to think of it, that Albany ballroom had become tacky.

The rapture of that evening could have been worn like silver lamé. It was a turn-on. Eyes shone. Their voices rose to tremble the dusty chandeliers above. The latest polls from California were going their way. Gene McCarthy had bought it, he had told her over the din. They had him and Paul Newman and the rest of that glitzy crowd by the short hairs. A young, slim Teddy Kennedy threw back his head and laughed and laughed. A deep, rich caramel of a laugh you could hear from wherever you stood in the crowd. Probably, Celia thinks, he has not laughed like that again. It had been a long, last cheer sent up to drift out the hotel windows on the thick June air of 1968 and down the Hudson Valley to blow across time and caress her memory in Little Rock a week ago. She had pulled over, put the Honda in neutral to consider this curious zephyr that had caught up with her. She had put the car in gear and turned around.

When the dream burst, she had cried not for Robert Kennedy nor for the country nor even for the injury done a people, but for Walt Hardy. Suddenly, he had been stripped of a future that would have been just right for him. His style. She remembers him on the steps of St. Patrick's, moving from one politician to another. He had looked naked. Whatever he put on afterwards never quite fit. Not quite what he should be wearing, not so much out of date as tailored for another, but as close as he could find to what he had almost worn.

Yesterday at the Adams's house in Lawrenceville, she had witnessed all the old gestures and hand signals still serving as genuine motions. He couldn't break the spell. He was like the unicorn, so enthralled by his own image that he had fallen prey to the dogs of old dreams.

"Thought maybe you could use a cup of coffee." Bill Hardy has appeared softly in the doorway, a mug in each hand. "A little milk, no sugar, if I remember."

"Yes, thank you." His eyes pass over the suitcases on the bed, as he goes to the wing chair in a corner. An old pennant from Cornell, like a grave accent, is tacked on the wall above his head. He looks at the window for a moment, opens it slightly, then sits down. "I'm sorry about this," Celia says. She has become a little nervous; talking to a father figure again, is it? She quickly sips some coffee. "I've left Walt a note." She sets down the coffee mug on the bedside table, next to an envelope. "It won't come as a surprise to him." Bill Hardy nodded solemnly. "Maybe, it's not forever. I just need to do some thinking on my own." Her father-in-law nods again.

Bill Hardy's sober response was the way he acknowledged all new information; as if nothing could surprise him or put a dent in his chauffeur's decorum. In his job he had witnessed all matter of faux pas. Nor, from what Walt had told her, had the man ever put off his muffled manner in their everyday life; he wore the dark broadcloth suits of his calling in their apartment. Any wonder his wife had taken a walk? Celia thought. He has continued watching her pack with a little interest; an activity, it occurs to her, his own wife had denied him the opportunity to experience.

And why should she have done so? Celia turns to the wardrobe mirror to present the other woman's case to the jury she had been addressing most of the morning. If she had got the same silent treatment Bill Hardy was giving her, had given his son, everybody—why wouldn't she leave? It seemed to Celia

190

that talking back and forth automatically establishes a community, made a family a family. Look at those immigrants shouting at each other over the dinner table. God knows, her father had talked enough, but that had been lectures, not conversations. She and her mother would have been happy with a little more silence. So what did she want?

She could never picture the three Hardys living in these tight quarters. This roof over their heads and all their needs supplied by Peggy Arnett—the old manor dole. Not just food and housing but identities as well. Then just father and son—more room anyway. She could recall stories told by the children and grandchildren of servants to the old Hudson Valley aristocracy; the Rogers and the Roosevelts, the Delanos and the Hoyts. Years ago, several of these descendants had been her clients, a car dealer in Hyde Park and a couple of merchants in Staatsburg, and these men recalled how their families, these families of servants, had depended on their employers for everything. If Mrs. Roosevelt happened to be in India during Thanksgiving, then no one ate turkey that year. It would never occur to them, one told her, to acquire their own bird.

Her father-in-law has been fingering the pockets of his vest as if looking for a toothpick, or maybe a scrap of conversation. Celia fits a packet of hose into a corner of the suitcase with a satisfying rightness. She already feels far removed from this place, from Walt and his father and their droll history. On her way. "Well," the old man finally says, "Walt says you came came across some interesting photos yesterday."

Half awake, she had heard Walt leave this morning. When he kissed her, she had automatically put her arms around him, kissed him back, let him hoist her off the mattress. In her drowsiness, she had heard him speak softly to his father. A kitchen chair scraped. She pictured them circling each other like smoke. "Something I have to do," he had whispered against her ear as she hung on him, and the important urgency in his voice had made her smile sleepily. Something to do—that old verb again. Though she had not been altogether sorry to let him go, for she hadn't yet figured out how she could pack in front of him one more time. This could become a really bad habit. She wanted to do it this time without him standing over her.

"Yes, pictures of Miss Arnett and this pilot in Mexico. Did they have an affair?" She has only asked the question to try to shock him a little; if the old man knew, he wouldn't tell her. She has taken some moisturizer from a kit of toiletries and applies some of it to her face, around the eyes and chin. Just a few tucks here and there—specialists galore in Las Vegas. Yes, she goes on, they had come across a lot of wonderful things Walt could have taken. Nice china, though a little ornate—she almost says, for them. She might have chosen a crystal pitcher, an early Steuben, under different circumstances. She leans into the mirror for a closer look. Maybe she had made that decision about the pitcher and her future at the same time. The language of the note on the bedside table had come so easily this morning; it was a message she must have revised many times in her mind without knowing it.

Walt had looked for this particular book, *Green Mansions*, but didn't find it, she told him. That's all he had really wanted —an old novel! Then these old photographs of Peggy Arnett as a young woman. Bill Hardy sips his coffee and looks out the window. Celia goes on. "He also came across the flyer's journal in the house. He's been reading it."

"Yes, he told me."

"It's right there. On the table. Next to you." The old man turns stiffly in his chair and stares at the leather bound notebook as if it has mysteriously materialized on the table behind him. He picks it up carefully and turns it over without opening it, as if to inspect its manufacture. Perhaps, its authenticity. Celia watches him through the wardrobe mirror, the reverse reflection giving her a different idea.

"So, you knew about this diary?" A tingling goes through her and she leans against the bed. "Who was this Armstrong?"

The old man's eyebrows crimp and relax as if to exercise the thoughts behind them, work them out before they are let loose. Celia has guessed what they might be; the tangle of the story is coming undone. He continues to stare at the floor beneath the bed. He massages the index knuckle of his left hand, and Celia feels she is seeing him for the first time. What she had always regarded as a kind of straightforward staleness of spirit, the ubiquitous white socks, his correctness at all tasks, opening windows a crack, shifting gears—all of that had been the marks of a special discipline and a peculiar loyalty that came with the job. Clearly, Walt had learned from him.

"It was a very difficult time for Miss Arnett," he says, all the words lined up finally. "Her fiancé had just been murdered in Mexico."

"When was this?" Celia sees pages in a calendar flipping back, a visual movie stunt. She knows where they will stop. She already knew the year.

"1940." He regards the journal in his hands then returns it to the table. "She told me about this book once. And Armstrong. On Sunday drives."

"This pilot was blackmailing her."

Bill Hardy slowly shakes his head. "Not to my knowlege." Days from now, she will drive through a line storm sweeping east across Iowa, and she will think of the old man, sitting in that chair by the window. All those years he had smoothed out a history, working and reworking the events as he tidied up the kitchen, performed his daily chores, turned the radio and then the TV on and off. He had been like a craftsman of some sort, reworking leather or a carving. The circumstances had been recorded as he would score a ball game so the whole history could be replayed for anyone interested; inning by inning, every strike and error. She will remember that when he finishes the story, she leans forward and puts her hand on his. It was all she could think to do.

"It's been a great heaviness upon me, Celia. I've come close to telling him many times." He turned to face her. "He was such a little boy when Ruth left, but he felt her gone quite much. He cried at first. A lot. Called for her in his sleep. Sometimes, in this room, I'd almost tell him. But wouldn't that give him another knock, harder than the first? Don't you see? What if I had come in here one night, sat on that bed there to comfort him and told him that his mother had not left him? That his mother was just across the garden, sitting up in her bedroom in the main house. Reading. Also by then, I'd found a feeling for him. I felt much like a father to him, if you know what I mean. I loved the lad."

"What was she like? Ruth."

Bill Hardy had stood up and gone to the room's other window, recessed in a dormer of the lapstraked ceiling. Celia will remember his figure, as she speeds west on I-80; an old man in shirtsleeves and vest, pants hanging loose, and a slight hesitancy of movement. His answer surprised her, and she will laugh at her surprise as she changes stations on the Honda's radio.

"She was a hot ticket, I want to tell you." The agility in his voice took a few years off of him. Not one to let any grass grow under her feet. Not Ruth, ha-hah! Should have known, her being a California woman. They'd met in Colorado as he was getting out of the Conservation Corps. The story had fallen into the familiar lines Walt had told her. The bus station restaurant. The bus ride to St. Louis and how they got married there and then made the rest of the trip by paddleboat.

Had that been the first and last time Bill Hardy had acted impulsively? When he had recalled that last part of the newlyweds' journey, he had pulled at his neck and looked sideways, almost roguish. For a brief moment, Celia could see herself with this young Bill Hardy, being footloose and foolish. Making him do something outrageous.

"'I am with child,' she told us that first interview. Came right out with it. That's the way she was—Peggy Arnett. You knew where you stood with her." Yeah, on the far side of the carpet, Celia thought, but continues to listen. So, she had made them this proposition. She had been too far gone to risk an operation—even the best surgeons her money could buy. "Also—and I remember this especially—she said she wanted the experience of giving birth. With Halstead dead—well, with us, she could keep the child close by as—"

"Like a souvenir," Celia broke in. She had been suddenly very angry. Of course she would have that experience— Peggy Arnett had been denied nothing. Her anger was pointless, Celia will decide later.

"You have to remember the times, Celia." Bill Hardy had come back to the chair, held onto its back. He seemed to enjoy a startling fluency.

"The war was coming on. Things were unsettled. She was —frantic. I expect she could have found someone in her set to marry but then the secret would be out. My aunt knew a midwife in Clairton, up river. Word was put out that she was visiting relatives in North Carolina. Recovering from Halstead's murder. Which she was, of course." Ruth went with her to make it look right. That was part of the agreement. He laughed and shook his head. "She even fixed up all the papers, birth certificate and such. Her lawyers did." He sat down. "She said it would be just temporary. Let the war get settled, and we could start our own family if we wished. We'd have these jobs for life. This place or something larger. She gave us a very handsome sum to start with."

"To keep quiet."

He had ignored her remark. "Meanwhile, I'd be deferred from the draft. She fixed it up. Later on, she might adopt the boy. Ruth got to name him."

"Wonderful."

"Yes. Ruth read poetry."

"Whitman. Walt Whitman."

"That's the fella. You knew this?" he asked.

"Just a guess." Getting close to Des Moines, she will feel her eyes become wet when she remembers this exchange. Then, a dull ache, like a flash of dysentery, had shot through her.

"It became too late to change," Bill Hardy had gone on. "To tell him. I'd got close to him and he to I. She let him have the run of the mansion. Just like it was his. All his clothing. Education. Everything he could ever want."

"Everything he could want," Celia repeated and her father-in-law had nodded; not catching her tone at first. Then, he looked up. . She put the tube of moisturizer, the last of her articles, into the kit and zipped it shut. "So, tell me, who was his father?"

"Why, Mr. Halstead." The question had turned him around. "And he was dead. That was the problem."

And dead several times over, she had thought. In Walt's time in politics, she had learned that a story can be so handled and polished so many times that it becomes an artifact, unquestioned and its place in truth undisturbed. Who or what was to be gained from disclosure, Walt used to say. From the truth? In any event, she already had the answer. The day before, leaning over him as they looked at the old picture album, she had made the connection. "So what about this flyer? This Armstrong?" It had been a shameless question, like asking a child about Santa Claus.

"I don't know," Bill Hardy replied. "He must have sent her this journal."

"One more souvenir," Celia had said, not sorry for the

sound of her voice. She zipped up the small bag. "Quite a collection."

"I want you to know," Bill Hardy had said as he stood. "I want you to know that I've come close to telling Walt many times. As a boy and as a man. Every time I wondered how this would change us. He worked so hard at everything he put his mind to. He was a good boy, a dutiful son. He is my son. What's the difference?" Bill Hardy's watery eyes had looked into hers.

It is only midafternoon, but Celia will decide to locate a motel. More than the monotonous driving, her sympathy for Bill Hardy has worn her down. She's only just left Pittsburgh a few hours ago, left the old man standing in the bay of the garage and, she would guess, about to pick up a chamois to dust off the Lincoln when she passed around the driveway. He had tried to place the secret upon her, like a garment to be adjusted with a servant's finesse, not just to share the secret, but to encourage her to exchange it for the apparel she had been fast undoing and packing. But she just wouldn't feel good about it—the marriage no longer fit her. Anyway, she had already guessed the secret on her own—at least his part of it. "Can I take that suitcase down for you?" Bill Hardy had said. He may have hoped her head would shake. "Very well." She heard the subtle change in his voice. He was no longer family but family servant.

As he descended the stairs to the garage below, Celia almost wondered if he might expect a gratuity of some kind. Yes, he probably hoped that she would tell Walt what he had not been able to tell him. That was what he expected. She had visualized him standing by the Honda, her suitcase not stowed but waiting for her to call him to bring it back up. He had been given her time to change her mind, for her to see the unfairness of it. One more woman leaving Walt Hardy. Was this fair, he had been asking?

She looks for a good place to spend this first night of her freedom. Unhappy, maybe wretched—but freedom. She can see Ruth Hardy making the same decision and living with it. She sees Peggy Arnett doing the same. It must not have been all that easy for her either. The hard lesson of abandonment is that someone has to go on. Has to leave. She is tempted, once she gets settled in her room, to take her notebook and rewrite the story. Get hold of Walt. But then, she'd probably turn around again. Who do you have to fuck to get out of this turkey? The old show business joke. Who told them that? Was it Shirley MacLaine that time at the Waldorf? She is suddenly weeping. She cries for all their years. Even for the goddamn delphiniums, she is crying. She takes a tissue from the box on the console and wipes her eyes, blows her nose. So that was done. "I'll be right down," she had shouted after Bill Hardy. In the motel room, she will shiver with an excitement and a promise. She's just a little nervous for the first time in years, and it's almost fun.

27 May 1940
D.F.

"Why do you call this part Jack?" China says. We were on the train returning from Guanajuato. We had locked the compartment and lowered the shades and are having ourselves a little fiesta.

"That's Jack Armstrong, the All-American Boy," I say. She is looking dumb. "You know — Wheaties? Breakfast of champions. You mean they never let you listen to the radio up at that artsy college?" I tell her about Jack Armstrong and his brother Billy and how they are always rescuing Betty from evil-doings inside of pyramids.

The Jack in hand is getting her attention; then, the light goes on. "Ah, so these Mollies and MaGees are the same programs. These Amos and Andy? These peoples you talk to?" The train's sway through the mountain passes has put a spell on us. The breeze through the open window plays along our skin.

The performance at the Juarez Opera House was a big success but the attack on Trotsky was what everyone talked about at the governor's party afterwards. China didn't seem too interested, and that's peculiar after the way she flirted with him at Rivera's party. But she was pretty exhausted after her performance. On the train, she falls asleep after our loving, curled up in one of the purple velvet armchairs. What a picture!

Lately, I feel like a truck driver, flying these routes to Tampico and Merida and back. It's slowly driving me nuts. I get a terrible urge to put the transport into a snap roll, but it probably couldn't take it, not to mention the passengers. I want to screw myself into the sky. Do a few loops, defy the grim reaper. A little Waco sport model landed at the airport the other day. A Hollywood type, just passing through. It was like seeing an old girlfriend on another guy's arm.

Telling China about those radio programs also calls up the ghost of Harlow because she and I listened to a lot of those shows. Well, let's be truthful — this Arnett woman in her white silk pajamas also made me think about Harlow. Harlow called me Ace. "Turn off that radio, Ace, and get over here," she'd say, already down to her skivvies.

Howard Hughes had signed up a bunch of us to do the flying for this war film and Harlow was in it. We weren't in any scenes together. Flyers were all out at the airfield in Burbank, doing stunts for the cameras in old Fokkers and SE-5's and some biplanes fixed up to look like the War crates. The real actors were acting miles away. Some days I was a German flying a Fokker and other days I was a Brit in a SE-5. Roscoe Turner and I put on a terrific dog fight for the cameras one day. I had him in my guns a half dozen times — these racing guys can only fly straight. It was a strange experience, pretending to be something I actually had been. Funny.

I feel sorry for Turner even with all his trophies. He got into the War too late to see action. Fixed himself up with a fancy uniform and a commision of Colonel from the so called Nevada Air Force. But, it doesn't satisfy him, I think.

Nothing old-time about this blonde that showed up at the field one afternoon. The picture people wanted to do some publicity photographs of her and us pilots standing in front of these old planes. "So, you're a genuine ace," she said after we had been introduced. We were waiting while the photographer reloaded his camera. She was just a kid. Not more than 19 or 20, I'd guess, but had already been married and divorced and done a few pictures. She had this flat Missouri drawl, a sad kind of voice that put too much know-how on her young frame. But the way she talked to me, like she wasn't taking this hero stuff too seriously. I liked that about her right away.

Then Roscoe comes up all charm and derring-do, white silk scarf over his shoulder, and that little moustache of his atwitter. But she doesn't give him the time of day, doesn't even stir but raises one hand in his face — without even looking at him — keeps looking up at me, waiting for an answer. What was the question? Something clicked, and it wasn't the camera. We have this romance.

Of late, I've thought it wasn't so much the war stuff that made her interested as that she might have seen something in me that she saw in herself — the fact of a fame unearned. Am I making sense, Molly? Like China, Harlow first had been attracted by my boy scout exploits, but then something more. A few unlucky souls had slipped under my guns at the wrong time, that's all. The six or seven sure kills I had then, a few more probables (before Spain, of course) was something that had taken place — achieved to use the official lingo — while all I was trying to defy the law of gravity. That had been my main purpose all along.

And Harlow recognized this right off. In her own way, Harlene (Harlene Carpenter was her real name, from a good family and went to poshy schools, like China, though you wouldn't know it from her screen roles) had defied a kind of gravity too. Became a Hollywood star, a kind of royalty. A matter of chance, all that. Her personality, something in her eyes, the way she stood. Then there was her body. She had been born with it, not worked for it. Not really earned it, you might say.

I felt a little funny thinking about Harlow with China sleeping across from me, curled up in the chair, all coppery brown within the purple velvet. Like a gem. Trusting. The breeze through the train window settles several ebony strands of hair over her face and, in her sleep, like a child, she pulls them away. A couple beads of sweat on her upper lip. I want to lick them off. Eliptical eyes closed. All of a sudden I see her in one of Rivera's murals. In fact, she's posed for him, for his wife too, and I can place her in a couple of his paintings. She's one of those Indian women curled up down in the corner of the painting, enduring the crazy history of Mexico. So, it made me feel a little peculiar looking at this sweet woman just across from me as I'm thinking of Harlow's body long gone and buried.

Let's face it. I've been thinking of Peggy Arnett lately too. Her unearned millions. Does that fortune make any difference in how she looks underneath? I mean how she's put together?

"What's a matter, Ace, you never see a naked woman before?" Harlene asked that first time. She had borrowed somebody's bungalow over in Malibu for our first fling. Well, no, not exactly like her nakedness. In fact, even if I had been Casanova, doing his memoirs in his dotage, I'd be unable to put the way she looked into words. My heart stopped for a couple of rpm's when she dropped off her duds. Talk about defying gravity. Her bosoms stuck straight out, all on their own! She told me Hughes had designed some kind of brassiere for her to wear in *Hell's Angels* so they'd jiggle a certain way when she walked. Like putting wings on a dirigible, I'd say.

Then there was the rest of her. Slim waist and a child's belly, perfect legs and a derriere like what you might see in a French museum. She used to waggle her behind around and it did have a special virtue all its own — but she'd make a comical use of it like she never took her perfection seriously. That's what I'm talking about — she wasn't to blame for the effect of her perfection on another. That was their — or *his* problem. It was unearned and didn't seem to mean all that much to her.

China mumbled in her sleep. Rarely in Spanish. She dreams in Zapotec. Mayan. She wasn't surprised that Siquerios, the painter, had tried to knock off Trotsky. She only shrugged. "My poor country," she said.

Several times, Harlow and I flew to a place the Union Pacific had built south of L.A. A resort called Rancho de Santa Fe. We had to keep our romance on the quiet because the studio had her hooked up with a leading man — who couldn't care less about how she looked, if you get my drift, Molly. Being able to fly places was something the studio bosses hadn't counted on. She'd meet me at the field, wearing a dark wig, and we'd take off in a buddy's Aeronca. He ran a flying school in Inglewood. One Friday, she had on a man's suit, a fedora and a black moustache like Chaplin's. "How's this?" she asked deadpan. No way of disguising those curves. She climbed into the rear seat of the little plane. "Should I leave on the brush? You'll get to like it, Ace."

We'd spend a couple of days at this resort in a little house that had its own small pool, kitchenette, radio — everything you'd want. She'd read scripts and I'd listen to the radio, then we'd hop into bed. Have a dip au naturel. Then, we'd order food sent over from the main kitchen and go back to bed. Or just roll over in bed. It was a dream, for sure. I remember thinking I had been dropped into some kind of a Valhalla for old warriors and dropped in while

I could still make use of my reward, you might say. Whenever she came into view, doing little chores around the cottage, picking up her silks or leaning into the mirror to check her hair roots (she wasn't really all that blonde) my needle would go off the altimeter. We both understood we were borrowing more than a room, or a plane, or a few days. We had a way of multiplying the time into a larger sum of days and hours than it was. We chewed it down to the marrow.

On this weekend, she was in bed studying her script. I was sitting across the way, listening to Rudy Vallee. I was sipping a cocktail, sent over in a silver-plated shaker from the main house and looking out the open French doors onto the patio. I remember thinking of this balloon I was riding in, this basket of suspended honey, and being grateful to whoever was responsible. Doing deep thoughts on the turns of life. The usual review a person makes when feeling satisfied and replete. To feel almost immortal or rather not to care, for the moment, about being mortal — another break with gravity, so to speak — because you knew, you'd somehow sneaked into the pantry and drunk from the same cup the gods use.

"You like that dope?" Harlow asked. She had finished her homework. She'd been watching me from the bed.

"Well, it's free," I said. Rudy Vallee's orchestra was a little corny for sure but it was contributing to my flush of the moment. Also, Fleischmann's Yeast sponsored Vallee's program and that was a funny connection. All that dough dear mother had raised for Fleischmann. Harlow had her secrets; I had mine.

"Free!" She laughed.

"Yes, free," I said. "Radio's a great invention. Music, sports, entertainment — all free."

"What kind of toothpaste sponsors Amos and Andy?" she asked.

"Pepsodent," I said. I could feel myself in her sights, and the rounds about to hit.

"And what kind of dentifrice, my hero, do I

see in your little kit bag?" Well, no way to get around that, so I said nothing. "Something else," she said. She had got out of bed, nude, and was straightening the sheets out, smoothing down the coverlet — offering a spectacle not meant for mortal eyes. "You know those guys, that Amos and Andy? They're not coloreds."

Now, I had known about Pic and Pat and the Two Blackbirds and some of those other entertainers in vaudeville, white men singing and dancing in blackface. Not exactly wrong, I guess, but peculiar, so I'm a little disappointed. "Amos 'n Andy are white guys?"

"Yes, white guys," she replied, her arms out and shaking her head for emphasis which set everything else in motion. Then she snorted and laughed, but it was a strange sound.

"What's funny?"

"Oh, it's just that you're a kind of innocent dick," she said and plumped up the pillows and stretched out. "Turn off that radio so we can concentrate."

Actually, the radio was already off and I was on my way, but our loving became different that day. We did all the manoeuvers we liked but did them with a sadness, like we had unexpectedly come on something in ourselves that we were sorry about, a fact we had been trying to ignore. At one point, her tears fell upon me. They were cool tears and the rest of her very hot.

Then, it was over just like it had begun. Quick and without an explanation or an apology on either side. She went on to stardom and I messed around in Manchuria. I came back to Hollywood a couple of years later to fly in another movie about airmail pilots. One evening near midnight, the phone rings. "Ace?" No mistaking that Missouri twang. She sounded like she'd been running. No how-you-been or how-are-you but just straight out, "Can you fly me somewhere?" I could imagine her eyes, searching, each one an arrow.

She was shooting a picture on location in the desert with Gable, supposedly set in Africa, and she had an early call. Could I fly her there? She sounded in trouble and, of course, the whole ache of her suddenly found a space inside of me. I didn't stop to think that she had all the studio resources she needed to get around. In the couple of years since *Hell's Angels* she'd become a big star.I thought of the days — time we had stolen. That she had called me, out of nowhere. And that I'd see her again.

I phoned the field and told them that I needed to take the plane up for a test. Some night landings and so forth. This airmail picture supposedly was using the same Swallow biplane that Lindbergh had flown on his mail routes, though I suspect this to be studio puff. For sure, it was the same kind of plane, a sturdy ship with no cowling on the radial and an extra-large cockpit up front for the mailbags. Harlow had beat me to the field, and she looked like she'd just come off the golf course — sporty skirt and blazer, two-tone oxfords, bare legs. She had a scarf wrapped around her head and most of her face for disguise. She hugged me. "Hiya, Ace. I'm much obliged." Over her shoulder, I saw the car that had brought her drive off. Her Jap servant behind the wheel.

It was like old times and like old friends. We were easy with each other. While I signed out the plane in the operations shack, Harlow stayed in the hangar gloom. The plane was already out on the tarmac and had been warmed up. She was very anxious. Nervous. Worried about getting to the film location on time, I guessed. She had a reputation for being punctual, very professional. So, she kept pushing me, telling me to hurry, as I gave the exterior of the plane a walkaround. Finally, I said, "Oh, just keep your pants on, Harlene."

She made a funny sort of snort, and when I rounded the nose of the ship, everything okay, she was straightening up, stuffing the article into her blazer pocket. They were always such wispy things. "You are still the funniest dick I've ever known," she said, giggling like a school kid. And I laughed too, because I had had the same idea and maybe sooner than her.

So, instead of getting into the front cockpit, she climbed into the back one and straddled me. I pulled the belt up over both of us and took off. By the time we got to three thousand feet over Riverside, we had managed the number. I did a few wing overs, climbed up to six thousand and dived straight down to pull up into a complete loop. Then started another and rolled out in an Immelmann. Harlow was holding onto the cowling, the scarf whipped off by the slipstream and her platinum hair like a banner. She screamed like a banshee. It was a joyous occasion all the way up and around.

I never saw her again after I landed and helped her down out of the plane. "Thanks for the lift,"she said out of the corner of her mouth and kissed me. That same night her new husband of a few months blew his brains out. A few years later, I'm in Spain and one evening with Nikki in Madrid, I read about Harlow in the paper. Headlines. Uremic poisoning. Nikki was a year away from her own death, at the hands of the OGPU most likely.

I wonder if Porfirio Díaz had sat in that cushy purple velvet chair that China slept in on the train. The old general could not have curled up so niftily, for sure. She was a dazzling picture. Eventually, China's eyes opened a little, to check my whereabouts, to make sure I'm still on the train; then, she slipped back under. It was after dark when we pull into the DF. This one, I have to keep.

June,1940
Monday

Not much to celebrate these days. Hitler's boys about to walk into Paris. The French have given up. The English pushed into the Channel.

Here, the fiesta goes on. Fireworks and parades. The Mexican shoots off a skyrocket when he fries an egg.

China came back from Guadalajara last night. Pretty exhausted but excited by the reception they got. Many flowers and curtain calls. La Paloma Azul a big hit at the local opera house. I don't know which of us was happier to see her, me or the dog. Tonantzin's tail knocked over a clay statue of Tlaloc on a table. What's that mean, a drought? A flood? These old gods can get testy when you knock them around.

This morning I wake to my girl singing in the kitchen a happy song about *un cántaro,* a little water pitcher. She sings off-key, a sweet flat-footed sound. I spend most of my days off at her place. I stretch out and smell the coffee. Some of her lavendar silks are hanging like happy thoughts on a chair, from the bed post. By the crispness of the air, I know the kitchen window looking south is open. You can see the snowy peaks of Popocatépetl and Ixtaccichuatl, and if you lean far out to the right — Toluca. The air in her small apartment is fragrant and cool. Tonantzin thumps her tail under the bed, her dog sense picking up my mood. She thinks it's time for a run in the Alameda. Since her leg has been fixed, she wants to run in the park all the time. Maybe run back home to Oaxaca.

Another reason I spend so much time here, is because Peggy Arnett has taken to hanging around the hotel. So, I'm grateful about the vet fixing the dog's leg. So what? And the flying lessons are business. That's all.

It occurs to me that the whole view out the window, the magnificent snow capped mountains, the tile roofs of Mexico City sparkling under a perfect sky, the deep blues to oranges and ochres of the scenery — all that would become drab, ordinary and gray, if China did not look upon this scenery. I mean, her perception gives these things color and spectacle. By just looking at it, she fills in the blanks, like a kid with crayons. Makes all of the wonders happen.

And so I feel sometimes when she looks upon me; that I'm somehow made better — by her very glance.

All of which makes me feel even more of a heel; this business with the Arnett dame. Well, it is just flying lessons. Not even that; more seeing the sights. Part of my job. Sure that's right, McGee. She and her big shot oil man are trying to get my commission reinstated. That's what she tells me the other day. Pulling strings. I have to swear that I've been a fighter against fascism. Hey, that's me.

But what about the girl singing in the kitchen?

"It's not all that easy," the guy at the Embassy tells me. "Your Mexican citizenship don't mean dog-doo to the Dies Committee. They've got you on the list, and you take one step across the border and they'll make you an Un-American, Red-lover."

Arnett has this way of smiling like her lips are held back by something even funnier that she can't express right then. "You probably prefer to be paid in dollars," she said after we landed the first time. And she took a crisp fifty-dollar bill from a deck of them in her billfold. I told her I'm doing it as a swap for the vet that fixed Tonantzin's leg. She owes me nothing. "Nonsense," she says and tucks the bill in my shirt pocket. It's like a tip.

Would China even leave Mexico? Dare I ask her?

"I am wanting these things for my country," she tells me seriously. We are on the roof patio outside her kitchen last Saturday afternoon. The twin towers of the main cathedral loom behind us like huge fountains that have somehow been frozen solid; pink lemonade turned into stone. There aren't many tall buildings in this city, so five floors up we can look straight across and out beyond the city limits from almost any compass point.

China sits on the tile ledge around her

flower garden. Her feet are flat on the floor
and apart and she leans forward to rest her arms
on her knees. She wears a white cotton shift,
and she is looking like her mother's side.
Curiously, she looks more Indian these days. It
must be these dances she's doing. Her talk has
become darker also. Angry. She has a long list.
Good medicine. Land reform. Fair elections. Good
water. Good sewage. Good night! I've heard it
all before. The election has pushed tempers sky
high. Cárdenas's candidate looks a sure winner,
but China's father is raising hell down south.
Lot about him in the papers. She steers away
from talking about him. Rather than say something bad, she says nothing and she still has-
n't spoken directly about that kid being killed
in Oaxaca. That's still between us. Well, it's
difficult for her, I guess.

As she talks, the passion rises in her face;
her complexion becomes a mahogany color. A couple of lizards play dart and start in the ivy
behind her on the wall. The flat whiteness of
the cotton petticoat is delicious against the
glossy dark skin of her legs. We're going to a
party at the British Embassy.

Then, she becomes silent. We sit in the late
afternoon hush that comes up from the streets
below. A vendor hawks ice milk. A street car
clangs across the _zócalo_. Far to the west, in
the Colonia Cuauhtémoc, drums beat a monotonous
relay. A political rally or a funeral — down
here it could be both. A tinny bell from the
cathedral strikes the quarter hour. Once more,
China looks like one of those versions of herself that Rivera has put into his murals. The
way her face is down and to one side like someone has just struck her. History maybe.

It's near five o'clock and the light is doing
that trick it does — buildings and streets, city
and countryside all become one; no lines define
one thing from another. Like a French painting.
It must be the atmosphere or the altitude or
maybe all the minerals buried in the deserts

have fused into one large glass dish in which hard definitions are dissolved.

This magic moment has its counterpart. On Friday, we were letting down to Tampico, scooting down the eastern slope of the Orientale. The light was extraordinary. The afternoon rain had just washed everything sparkling clean. The infinite shades of desert and high ground going to velvety purples, greens that hurt the eyes with their greeness. Miguel and I can see all kinds of magic from up here. Regularly, we fly over the mounds of what must be an old city near Tampico. A huge layout but only visible from up here because of the jungle grown over it. No one digging around down there like they are doing at Monte Alban, China's hometown. But there it is, grown over and waiting to be discovered. Streets and temples and old ghosts.

The valleys look buffed and the bony spines of the mountains are shining. We can make out villages and small farms around Tamazunchale where Miguel has cousins. We see a herd of goats and their herders picking along a ridge. What looked like an old temple, Mayan probably. Another guy was leading a string of burros. People going about their business on earth.

What I wanted to say to China on her rooftop, five floors up, was that I don't want to be entirely divorced from this earth, but just fly above it, so I can feel the lonesome separation of it while seeing all of its beauty. As I feel about her sometimes, when I'm on a trip or she's on tour. The separation makes me sad but also joyful because I know I'm coming back down to earth, coming back to her. Being apart but still a part. People like Doolittle and Roscoe Turner are trying to go faster and faster, and planes will keep on going faster. And that means they will also go higher and higher. None of these shapes and colors will be seen anymore. How terrible. For all of us, how terrible to be so separated from the earth where we can breathe the air.

Some of the younger guys say we old-timers fly by "the seat of our pants." That we are a little simple-minded, and all the fancy instruments are beyond us. But that isn't it. It's just that we want to fly with our eyes on the earth, to be able to look down on it in wonder. Tell me this. How many people have seen a whole flock of wild geese in the moonlight — from above? It is some sight, I tell you, Molly.

But how can I say any of this to her as we sit on her patio in the cooling of the afternoon; she would think I've gone loco. So what do I do instead? A crazy thing. I get up and take one of her feet, this long, beautiful foot that is bruised and a little swollen from her dancing — the nail on the big toe badly cracked. I lean down, and I kiss it.

"Hey, *qué estás haciendo*, hero?" She pulls away, embarrassed but pleased all the same, like I had kissed her in some more personal place. But she gets up and pushes me back down in my chair, climbs on my lap and plants a big one on me.

I return her kiss sorrowfully because I'm thinking of our first kiss, at that pyramid in Teotihuacan, and how it may have had the taste of good-bye on it. I'm almost twice her age. I've got this goddamn yearning to get back into uniform. It's like Harlow all over again. Questioning why the gods have put this happiness in my lap.

So, I'll just hold this girl a little tighter and for as long as I can. A band strikes up down in the zócalo. Some kind of political rally or a labor demonstration. Trumpets and a lot of clarinets. Cymbals and drums. Always drums. They are big on drums down here.

The other morning, China walks into the bedroom carrying a tray, and wearing a roomy, orange native gown, a huge purple dahlia stuck in her black hair. "*Hola, cariño, café?*" Her face is glowing, and she flashes a big toothed grin, all for me. All full of happiness because of me, it is clear. So, I reach up and take the

tray from her and take her in my arms and kiss
her. The two of us, right then, are a small victory of some kind and cause enough for celebration.

Before we took off the other afternoon, Peggy
Arnett hands her camera over to one of the
grease monkeys and has him take our picture. We
are standing beside Halstead's company plane.
Louise Thaden won the Bendix a couple of years
ago in one of these sporty ships. Beechcraft
Staggerwing. So, it has some sass to it though
Thaden took a long time to finish. A very comfortable plane with good recovery characteris-
tics; tricky to land because of the heavy nose.
A 420 HP Wright Whirlwind. Electric retractable
gear. Ain't progress wonderful? On my Polikarpov
fighter in Spain, it took 40 turns on the crank
to pull up the gear!! With the flaps down, this
Beechcraft comes in at 60 mph, but breaks ground
at 29 inches, about 80 mph. She'll do more than
200 with 27 on the manifold. By no means a
lady's plane, but then Louise is a damn good
pilot. How much of a lady she is, I don't know.
Halstead's plane is painted a spiffy green
with a trim in the same color but darker. The
oil company's logo on the fuselage. An Indian
head like on the nickel. Cherokee Oil. In the
air, Peggy Arnett rolls the window down on her
side and pokes her Leica out, but she'll never
be able to fit all the territory down there
into that tiny camera. Nor the colors, of
course. We're doing figure eights north of the
city. To the west, a curtain of afternoon rain
is preparing to move in, but we have a good hour
of fair weather. The rain front is a blackish
green, luminous — much like I've seen in a performance of La Paloma Azul. Pull that curtain
back and there's my China — playing Corn Woman.
I am keeping her in mind as I gain altitude,
because Arnett has put her hand on my thigh — to
steady herself or the plane. Or something.
It's a gorgeous day at three thousand feet.
Mexico City sparkles below. Some wool packs of
cumulus are hanging around 4000 feet south of

us. Their shadows slowly drift over San Angel.
Little baby coverlets west of us, over in
Michocan, pulling up the rain that will wash
down the streets and cool off the evening. This
is the rainy season.

This rich dame goes through a routine when
she gets into the plane. She's a little nervous,
I guess. She pulls her seat belt tight, pats her
pockets, checks her person, the seat, the cabin
of the plane — all in some order that seems better done in another place, like her dressing
table. Putting everything down neatly. She also
has a serious problem with the horizon as well,
keeping it level.

She works at it hard enough, leaning forward,
chin out and the jawline set in concetration. I
pass over the control wheel. "This is all so
very new to me," she says, and the plane's nose
starts to dip. Pull it up, I tell her — easy,
not so fast; we almost stall out. In fact, our
first time up, I deliberately put the plane in
a power stall just to rattle her some. Let her
know that flying is a serious matter. But, she
giggled and asked me to do it again. She's surprised me. So, the horizon is steady up. She
wriggles her butt into the seat and grips the
wheel. "I'll just never learn how to do it," she
says and peers over the cowl. Ever so slightly, little by little, the nose starts to dip
down. "Oh, dear." Then, she puts a hand on me.
Pretty good grip. We try level flight over and
over. Some people can fly and some cannot.
Mastery of level flight is beyond the expertise
of more people than you would guess at, Molly.
On the ground as well, if you follow me, McGee.

Once airborne, she usually takes off her
helmet, as if she only supposed to wear it on
the ground. She ruffles her hair which is cut
short, like a second helmet underneath. She's
seen too many pictures of Earhart, probably. She
got herself all suited out in flyer "togs" — so
she looks the part, you might say. The helmet
makes her look like a nun but when she takes it
off, she still looks like a nun. And she talks

veddy proper. Lots of *thank you very much* and this or that is just *per*-fect. "Oh, you're a *per*-fect teacher. I can feel the difference. It's *per*-fect." But the horizon is still coming up. Dipping down.

"Don't you think Mussolini is *per*-fectly dashing," she says out of the blue one day. "Charles and I met him in Rome two years ago." About the time I was meeting his Fiats over Madrid, I was thinking. Then she pulls the switch, like she's reading my thoughts. "Oh, it's *per*-fectly shameful the way you have been treated. A man of your proven abilities." And she goes on this way for a bit. "I know Charles will help you out." Then she asks me about China. I get the feeling she knows all about us.

This other afternoon, we have been flying generally on a northeasterly course, dipping up and down thanks to Arnett's handling which is making me a little queasy actually. Then, we come on the ruins of Teotihuacan. It's always like flying over another world for me — like Buck Rogers breaking through the atmosphere to another planet or what's left of another planet — and in a way — that is the truth. What is below us *was* another world. Another time. Just twelve months ago, China and I watched the sun come up from on top of the biggest of the two pyramids which I am now circling in this Beechcraft. Where we made the sun come up.

Arnett has got particularly interested in this scenery; so — tourist guide that I am — I take over the controls and we buzz down to the carpet and I do a 360 around the larger pyramid like it was a pylon in Cleveland. They've uncovered a little more of this ancient city. Cut the jungle back, cleared out the brush from around the main buildings.

So I've made several passes between the two pyramids which are about a mile apart. A wide avenue was laid out between them, with high terraces rising up along both sides of it. Palaces and such had been here, they say. You can see their outlines from above. Arnett is on the edge of her seat. Why I do the rest, I can't figure.

Showing off, I guess. I haven't told China. Never will.

The stretch of ground between the pyramids looks smooth enough. Risky because of cactus and clumps of greenish mesquite growing all over it. Foolish. What the hell, it's not my plane. I put down the gear and sideslip the Beechcraft over the smaller temple at the end of the boulevard, throttle back; punch the drag flaps and set the plane down right in the middle of this old thoroughfare. If the Toltecs were still around, they'd throw a big fiesta for me. What's-his-name coming back. They'd give me my own personal, engraved flute. All the mangoes I could eat. Or is that virgins?

It's not a bad landing at that, two wheels only. We are lucky that the mesquite bushes hide no rocks. No holes. We taxi the length of the old boulevard. Not a soul in sight. Peggy Arnett is looking out her window. Ooh-ing and ah-ing at the ruins we taxi past. "*Per*-fectly marvelous. You are *per*-fectly marvelous." She's gripping my leg. I am thinking, after the mangoes and the virgins, the Toltecs would have cut out my heart just to see how this contraption works.

We come to the end of the avenue. The big pyramid where China and I kissed looms just off our left wing tip. Only a year ago. All at once, I know I've done something wrong landing here. Though the gods once worshiped here have long disappeared, I feel I have profaned a holy place. And why, you ask? Just so I can get back to the States, which means I double-cross China even as I am lying in her bed, waiting for her to show up with the coffee. Yes, and Tonantzin too. Even, the dog. Even, the goddamn dog.

So, I whip the Beechcraft around and push the throttle into the firewall. Arnett is startled. She had put her other hand on the door handle, like she was about to get out to tour the ruins. Maybe buy them. I grab for altitude, wanting to leave the place behind as quickly as possible. Fleeing the scene of a crime. And I'm a little angry with this woman sitting next to me, but who's flying this crate anyhow?

So, high enough, I wing over into a dive and pull up into a couple of snap rolls, the 400 horses of the Whirlwind screaming like banshees and then I use the extra airspeed for some rolling eights in and out of those cloud puffs that we had seen earlier. I felt better; cleaned up inside and out. When I level out, I look over at her but she's all pink and her eyes are big as saucers. She's shivering but she isn't cold. "Oh my...oh my...goodness." She sees me but she doesn't see me. "That's never happened to me before," she says out of breath. And I'm reminded of Harlow that time and feel even worse.

This party at the British Embassy on Saturday was to celebrate the Tommies getting off the beaches at Dunkirk. That's the English for you, throwing a party to celebrate a defeat. The orchestra kept playing *God Save the King* between dance numbers. But everyone was there, including Avila and Moreno who introduces me to her nephew — who goes by the name of Frank Jackson. China rolls her eyes. It's not his real name, of course. So what, I tell her? She's been *cocinnando un gringo* who goes by the name of Juan Carillo.

"Ha!" She punches me. "You funny man. You mean *cogiendo un gringo* not *cocinnando. Si,* I fooking you but cooking you and eat you later. Yummy-yum." So, how can I not love this girl — she even corrects my dirty language? We keep on dancing. Besides, she sort of knows Jackson because he's the boyfriend of one of her girl-friends who is Trotsky's secretary. Is this a small world or what, Molly?

A line of Alberti comes to mind. We almost had to memorize it in Spain; you'd see it on posters, in the newspapers. "..*nacer ya lleva contra su espalda muro de los ejecutados.*" As I'm holding this beautiful woman, dancing, I think of this poem. No sign of an execution wall behind us, nothing but free eats, champagne and orchestra music. The band slips into "Blue Skies." Appropriate. I want to tell her that I am heavier than air but she has shown me how to fly.

She's pinned a large flower in scarlet velvet to her white lace dress. Just before we left her place, she had suddenly decided to put her hair up on top of her head with a tortoise shell comb. A filmy mantilla fell to her bare shoulders. "I play the *imperialista* this day," she had said, her dark eyes flashing. "*La madonna de la hacienda.*" We laughed. It's a class joke.

"So, how is Jack?" she says with a mischievous grin and rubs against me. She's been humming out of tune in my ear, but her thoughts are elsewhere. "He is liking the party?"

Last night at her place, China makes some of those bloodthirsty sounds that come deep from her long, beautiful throat and which make me feel like a young cuss. We have closed Tonantzin up in the bathroom, because she would have been happy to join us in bed. I expect, in the old days—before Cortés brought Christian decency and civilization to these parts — that might have been a normal part of the exercise. But China and I are busy enough, which is to say, happy enough with just each other. Anyway, the dog croons along with this girl-woman in my arms. Rrrrrrrr-Roy. Rrrr-Roy!!! And then she says things in Zapotec that must be *muy picante* for gringo ears. She's off in the blue skies.

Veracruz
—Friday 6/28/40
Hotel Diligencias

The rainstorm that Miguel and I rode into town has pushed out to sea but this city is like a sauna. I have the windows wide open and the fan turned up to its maximum rpm's, but my *cojones* are slowly being cooked hard. The bells of *La Parroquia* across the way are about to strike 2300. A big sound to stir up the steamy goo. The *portales* around the plaza below are still busy. The ding-donging of marimbas like harmonic butterflies. Laughter and talk — a couple of voices climb into song. Kids screaming and laughing. A guitar here and there being frenzied.

I am lucky to be here, I guess. The old grim reaper cheated once again. A whole string of good-lucks starting with that morning when Udet had me dead in his sights and his guns jammed. He just saluted and flew off. We laughed about that scrap we had over the Meuse at an airshow after the war. Jumpin' catfish, Andy — that was twenty-two years back!

This front that had come through the D.F. an hour before we took off. We had a full passenger list; business is picking up. East of Pueblo, we see a wall of deepening blue ahead, going from light to dark purple to black. Lightning. The storm had pushed up against the western slope of the Orientale and has got pretty intense. Right away, Miguel gets out the frequency book and clicks on the RCA radio compass. This Douglas transport has all the latest, and Miguel has learned how to operate everything. I guess that says something. I'm just the dumb driver.

He's flipping through the frequency book just as we enter the storm. It's like going into a shadowless room with no walls or ceiling or floor — nothing to give you a perspective, a handle on where you are. You could be sideways, upside down. A little drop and rise, playing tag with the air currents. If it weren't for the gyros and attitude indicators on the instrument panel, I could have been flying this DC-2 cockeyed and not know it. I will give them that — these instruments are of some use. It's too bad we can't have similar gadgets to help us out just walking around, getting up in the morning and doing our business. Loving each other. Help me find my way out of here, and still be on the level with China and myself.

Miguel has put on the headphones and clicked the band selector at the twelve o'clock position. Veracruz has a radio beam but we got the mountains between us and it, so he's going for a radio station on our side of the Orientale. I guessed Orizaba and that was right. He gets this big smile on his broad face and starts snapping his fingers, jumping around in his seat. He's got a good signal for sure.

When I pull on my earphones, I get a blast of Cuban style music. Maracas and bongos and a needle sharp trumpet that tickles my eardrums like an angry bee. Lot of Cuban influence in this part of Mexico. Especially close to Veracruz. But we are flying blind. Four feet on the other side of this waterfall we're flying through could be the side of a mountain. We've picked up an errant tail wind, so we're flying into oblivion even faster. I throttle back. Just to save a little gas. Death waiting in the rain. Miguel is pretty sure he's saved, he goes to Mass regularly , and his side of the cockpit dangles and glitters with all kinds of holy medals. We wouldn't know what we hit, water or rock. It's all the same. An old Mayan temple waiting for this blue-eyed wunderkind coming back. Here I come, Montezuma. Your boy eagle returns!

With this radio directional, when you point the plane directly at the broadcast station, the signal almost fades away. The rumba disappears. So, I adjust the radio compass needle and tap a little right rudder to put us on a course a couple degrees just west of the signal, the needle trembles barely to the right of the vertical position and this is just enough to keep my copilot happy. He's singing the words softly — a sweet tenor. I can visualize Miguel beneath a moon-shadowed balcony. The chorus is something about a guy's love being treated like an old sandal. Cubans are a moody lot.

Miguel enjoys the music and the course I'm

flying puts us close enough. We want to fly in
this south by southwesterly direction, because to
our left — somewhere — is Citlatepetl, all 19,000
feet of her. *Pico de Orizaba* to you, McGee.
Miguel nods and squints, to show he appreciates
my sensitivity to his aesthetic needs while, at
the same time, keeping us alive.

Gunfire in the plaza just now.
A political rally. The election is heating up.
Earlier, candidates of the CTM made speeches in
the plaza below. Banners and a band. Free plan-
tains. Toledano's party. Mostly left-wing workers. But they're against Trotsky. They have broken with Cárdenas over Trotsky — want him thrown
out of Mexico. Mr. Lund and his rabbits make a
lot of trouble for everybody. Ansers tells me
that Joe Stalin ordered Siquerios to kill
Trotsky. Or try to.
The CTM is pretty strong here in Veracruz
—lots of dock workers. Fiery speeches. Fireworks
over the harbor. The Mexicans love skyrockets—it
goes with the flowers that are like daytime
fireworks. Pistols fired into the hot wetness of
the night. I could get shot standing in the big
open window in my BVD's. *War Ace Shot In His
Skvvies In Veracruz.* Reed Ansers of the *N.Y.
Times* would have another exclusive.

So, we're at around five thousand feet this
afternoon, coming into Orizaba on a hot Havana
rumba. China tells me that Orizaba is the clos-
est the Conquistadores could imitate in Spanish
what the Aztecs called this place — "Rejoicing
of Waters." Many streams and waterfalls pouring
down the sides of the pico somewhere off to the
left of us. Nineteen thousand feet up, it always
has snow at the peak. Oh, brother! Our Lady,
Tonantzin, thump your tail for us!

Miguel is trying to enjoy the moment.
Hey-hey! He snaps his fingers. His hips move in
the seat. I can see he's a little nervous. He's
a great kid and a damn good pilot. I can't see
a goddamn thing. I don't dare go lower.

Foothills around here come up to our altitude.
I take a chance and turn 90 degrees to the
right. The music gets louder and louder, almost
busting our eardrums. So, I figure we are flying straight across the broadcast signal. I've
checked our charts against the compass course
we've been on and, using some old-fashioned dead
reckoning, together with the blast in our ears,
I figure we might be due west of the city. So,
I kick the rudder back left and come around
exactly to the east, counting off 180 degrees.
Sure enough, the music gets lower and lower,
dims to nothing. Then louder. We're going the
other way, back across the signal. The compass
needle is pointing straight up. I let down
another thousand feet.

"*Gustosos cigarros los de Orizaba,*" Miguel
says a little too gaily. "*La Rica Hoja.*" He
names the brand and makes a smoking gesture.
Beads of sweat glisten on his brow. I guess that
collection of holy medals is working hard too.

"Let's go down for some smokes," I say,
which sends him into a spasm of nervous giggles.
Then he gets serious fast as I drop down a little more. I'm hoping that I am remembering
right, that we did re-set the altimeter before
we took off and that the altitude I'm reading on
the gauge is the actual fact of our distance off
the carpet. Orizaba is 4,000 feet up, so we
could be flying into their basements. No time to
question the instruments now. Trust your compass, like they say. I'm bargaining with all the
gods — get me out of this, and I'll come clean
with China. I'll level with her about Arnett.

The passengers are quiet. I flicked off the
cabin lights when we got into the rain to cut
down the glare. So, they're in the dark, more
ways than one.

We strain our eyes to pick up the lights of
the city. It is down there and ahead. Somewhere.
The needle of the compass is straight up. I'm
afraid to go right or left. To the right is the
lower ridge of the Orientale, that levels off
suddenly at 10,000 feet. Like the prow of a huge

boat. To the left is the wall of the big one
herself — Citlatepetl. All 19,000 feet. The
highest in Mexico. I'm hoping we're in between
these two, in this little notch of 4,000 feet.
The city nestled in the saddle.

And there she is! Miguel snaps his fingers
and makes *charro* yelps. Lights appear like a gas
station coming out of a desert night. It's okay
to think about something else now. I choose
China, of course. I'll see her again. I've made
it one more time. But I'll have to tell her
about Arnett. A bargain is a bargain.

We take Orizaba at roof tops. Our passengers
are buzzing, finally catching on that this is not
the usual beer and tortilla run. But from here,
it's a piece of cake. I still can't really see
much, but I can imagine the big shoulder of the
mountain to our left, towering over us. Almost
immediately we pick up the glow of Cordoba and
I let down another five hundred feet.
Instruments are dandy, but I always feel better
when I can see the ground. We have made it
through the pass and are in the valley, over
Cordoba. Where Mexico became Mexico. Where the
sorceress La Mulata was from. China does a dance
about her. Their version of Sacajawea. She
guided the Spaniards; then sailed away on her
ship. That's her name in Zapotec, China giggled.
Translation: *She who gets fucked.*

We're still in the soup. The radio beam from
Veracruz is off or not working. We can't find it
when we switch the compass over. Miguel knows
instinctively what I'm about and he is also
looking hard ahead and to the side. I ease the
transport down closer to the map. The Cyclones
are whispering to each other so as not to dis-
tract us.

I'm doing some fast arithmetic with the
altimeter. We should have a cushion of about
five hundred feet. I drop another two hundred
feet. Check the compass. Almost due east.

Then, we break through. It's magical. Heavy
rain but some visibility at this low altitude.
Miguel shouts and points. We compare the ground
with the chart and nod. It's the Rio Cotaxtla

all right. After a graceful bend, the river flows directly into Veracruz and into the Gulf. We'll follow it the whole way. In fact, toward the horizon, the waterway becomes a scarf of silver binding up the lush greeness of the low-land. I treat everyone to a view at tree level. You could pick the bananas going by. The carpet sweeping under us at 170 mph. Miguel snaps his fingers, and does the dog yow-yow a couple of times.

Veracruz lies ahead. The airport searchlight rolls around like a diamond-emerald jewel on gray velvet. Slowly stretching out beyond, the endless magenta of the Gulf from which so much misery came to this land.

Miguel has the clip board out and is start-ing the checklist for landing. I switch off the radio compass. He puts down the wheels. I throt-tle back and after circling the field we come in. We do our tab and flaps routine which gives him great pleasure. I've taught him a few things you won't find in the book. The wind from the storm is right for it. When we're about thirty feet from the tarmac, he quickly does the flaps and I pop the elevator tab. We drop right in; eight ball in the side pocket. "Hey," I say to Miguel. "Cheated the Grim Reaper once again." He laughs and slaps his knee. He punches me in the arm—Mexicans have a big thing about *Senor Morte*. Death is a clown masquerading as life. We kiss a perfect three-pointer. Only six minutes behind schedule.

China tells me she's pregnant.

armstrong's return

"We got a couple of old-timers in the Post, Walt; vets from the 1918 war. Still alive. Still coming to meetings." The man's voice has taken on a peculiar neutrality, as if the screen door between them filtered the resonances of his voice to make it colorless. Adams sounded exhausted, and his voice unwound lazily. Hardy wonders if Adams might be slipping into a doze, exhausted by his own anger and anguish.

"I worry about them living," Clarence Adams goes on, "because they will witness all that is going down. Someone like me knows the score; I was born with the score. Nam was the concert. I was born to play it. It was my special music. But these old guys have lived long in disappointment. Every day it gets worse for them, because history was supposed to get better. Their time was to end all the bad stuff—the world was supposed to be made okay. A safe and a sane Fourth of July. And every day since it has got worse and worse. They must be terribly saddened by the vain part."

"The vain part?" Hardy's legs have become cramped. He's been hunched up on the floor of the front porch, next to the screen door since midmorning. He looks at his watch.

"You have to be somewhere?" the voice says in his ear.

"No. Just an old habit." They had told him to keep Adams talking. The longer he keeps talking, they told him, the better the chances. Chances for what? He hadn't asked. So, the two men resemble hikers taking a break, idly chatting as they catch their breaths. But on opposite sides of the path, Hardy thinks. Going in opposite directions.

Adams kneels on the living room floor inside the screen door, and Walt Hardy leans against the doorjamb outside on the porch. He senses the man lounging behind him, feels him looking over his shoulder and down below to Butler Street, to the base of the slope both of them might have ascended. Both can see the jumble of police cars and emergency vehicles. Panel trucks with transmitter dishes mounted on their roofs in which television crews monitor their equipment. Inside the house, the canary strikes a chirp and then another which finally ignites a long trill of such luminous possibilities that Hardy almost looks round to see if the darkened interior has brightened. The bird will be something else to talk about, he makes a note to himself; another subject to keep the conversation going.

The cheerful insouciant notes also sing to a domesticity, or at least a hope for a domesticity, Hardy muses, that Eddie Poremski's widow, now this man's wife, may have let rise within her as she fed the bird, cleaned its cage this morning. Or every morning. He imagines Shirley Poremski-Adams taking out this hope as she might take out a last, single piece of family china and then put it carefully away. Not for any special occasion. This would be the occasion. "What about this vain business?" He asks to keep Adams talking.

Earlier, Shirley had spotted him when he got out of the Lincoln at the police barrier. She had run to him, tripping over the feet of policemen, looking frightened and helpless. "Thank God, you're here," she had said, as if she had expected him, as if someone had put out a call to him and she had been waiting for him to reappear in their lives and solve everything. Shirley Adams had placed her pale arms around him. The woman's crazed state of mind, the disarray of her loosened hair and dressing gown—her very helplessness, gave her a perverse appeal as she turned in her terror from one to another of the men in uniform. She drew Hardy into this group and quickly introduced him. A friend of her husband. Yes, of both her husbands, he sensed the thought behind her wild eyes. He can help them. "Oh, thank God, you're here," she said over and over as Hardy saw other credentials begin to appear, almost print out in the eyes of the cops ganged around them. They had begun to recognize him. The guy on the magazine cover. The guy from the hearings. The can-do guy. She says he's a friend. Maybe, he could be useful.

Adams has been taking a long time to consider the last question. The two men have the high terrace to themselves. The neighborhood is completely still, because families on either side of the house had been evacuated by the time Hardy came on the scene. Since then, the black limousine has become surrounded by garish emergency vehicles—red, yellow, white, and blue. He couldn't leave, he reckons, even if he wanted to.

"Yes, the vain part," the voice inside the house says dreamily.

"You were saying something about the old-timers at the VFW being saddened—I think you said saddened—by the vain part."

"Well, it has never happened, has it? The vain part?" Adams's voice has become a little patronizing. "It's a little like the social contract we were discussing yesterday with one difference. The social contract did exist at one time and for certain people only. Perhaps, no more. Just certain people. But the vain part never did happen. Never. Just in talk, Walt, just in talk. And it goes way back. He's to blame for it. He introduced this whole falsehood, Walt."

"Who was that, Clarence?"

"I never liked the name, you know. Clair-ence. Some guys in the service would call it out like that. Clair-ence. Like queers, you know what I mean? I prefer to be called Jack."

"I didn't know that," Hardy replies.

"It's my middle name. My grandad's name was John. John Adams. He was named from the President but they called him Jack. He rode the Broadway Limited. A waiter in the dining car. An aristocrat through and through. One time, I was just a little kid, we went down to the station here and got on the train when it stopped on the trip east. There he was, my grandad, big white apron down to his shoe tops, black jacket, little black bow tie. Spinning this tray of cups and saucers on one finger. And the diner—the whole train—smelled like heaven. On the move, going somewhere. Oatmeal. Sugary smells. Bacon. Hot breads. Coffee. Tablecloths like quilts. Silver pitchers full of cream. Real cream. Everyone made way for us—just momma and me. Grandad sat us down at this table and set down a plate of sticky buns. The works. You could see that he was in charge. He ran things in that diner. The way he snapped a napkin open, spoke to the white people. He told white people what to order. Where to sit. A little bit later, he had the engineer stop the train at Wilkinsburg. Down the track. Can you imagine the Broadway Limited stopping at Wilkinsburg so this little black boy and his momma could get off and take the trolley back home? Grandad did that. I mean, he ran the train. Jack Adams. Has a sound to it, don't you think?"

A neighborhood dog has ambled across the top of the high terraces and has stopped to inspect them and the porch. The dog looks disappointed and turns away; moves on to something more interesting. "But a funny thing," Adams continues as if rising from a dream. "The people on that train, the white people in the diner, all called him different. They called him George. 'We'll have just a bit more coffee, George.' Or, 'How's the eggs this morning, George?' And when we got off the train in Wilkinsburg, I said, 'Mama, how come they call Granddaddy by the wrong name? How come they call him George?' And my momma says, 'That's just his train name, sugar. That's just the name he uses on the train.' And that's a funny thing, isn't it, Walt, how people can call you what they want sometimes; give you an entirely different name and everything on the train."

Soil and plant aromas rise in Hardy's head as if both flowers and earth have only just first happened on this spring morning. Last night's shower had freshened the season. "We were talking about this vain business, Jack. About someone being to blame for it."

"Why, Lincoln, of course. Don't you remember? It's all Lincoln's fault. '...that we here highly resolve that these dead shall not have died in vain' and so on. And so forth. He started all the trouble, Old Abe. The old-timers have been sadly disappointed, they have waited for it so patiently, because they keep experiencing that vain business. Over and over. Not in vain. Remember? They were led to believe it wasn't going to be that way. Not me. I knew from the beginning that it would all be in vain. But not these old vets. Over and over, the vain part comes up. It's the joker in the deck. The wild card. How many does it take, Walt, for the vain part?"

"Yes, I remember that speech," Hardy says quickly. "We used to stand by our desks and recite the whole thing. 'Four score and seven years ago'...and the rest of it.."

" '...our forefathers brought forth on this continent'," Adams continues in such a way that Hardy knows he is meant to join in, so it becomes, for the moment, really like school days at Park Place, the two of them reciting the words together. He has a quick picture of the blackboard before them, Miss Darnell pointing the way along the speech with the same yardstick she used to measure the growth of the room's tomato plant. Eddie Poremski sat behind and near the windows. Hardy falls behind, stumbles over a phrase and has to catch up to Adams, like not having the words to a hymn and humming along with the congregation. Clarence Adams knows all the words. The two of them recite the speech together, until Adams abruptly quits just at the conclusion. Hardy says the line by himself " '...shall not have died in vain'."

"Oh, it is sad to see these old guys from that '18 war saddened by what goes on. It just goes on and on. I hope they do not go on much longer, because this wagon has broken down. I would not want them to live longer for they will be more distressed."

A metallic sequence, precise and complete, chills Hardy but he dares not look around. He tries to remember the sequence of a pistol's hammer being pulled back and set. Was it *click-clack* or *clack-click* ? Was the man behind him cocking or uncocking the heavy automatic? "But you scared Shirley, Jack. You shouldn't have done that. She's a wonderful woman. All for you. You really scared hell out of her." He tries to joke about it, as if it had all been a joke. Just between us guys—being a woman, she hadn't got the joke.

"Yes, I am distressed by that. She's a lovely lady." Adams sighs deeply. "I'm sorry for that. I was thinking of protecting her from the sadness. The ultimate sadness. No one should have to suffer that."

"Yes, I understand," Hardy says. "But maybe she should have the choice in that. Don't you think? Let her decide?"

From this high porch vantage, Hardy can see several blocks each way on Butler Street. Police have cleared the thoroughfare and kept onlookers behind barriers set up at the far ends. Just below, a military position has been staked out. Men in body armor and helmets crouch behind vehicles, weapons poised above their heads. Across the street, and stretching for several blocks, the rusted, blank sides of the steel mill rise like those of an abandoned fort, huge stacks pointing straight up like spiked cannons; so, it might appear the armed men in the street were protecting the derelict behind them.

Walt Hardy feels like a player who has stepped onto the wrong stage, rehearsed the lines and plot of quite a different drama. He checks his watch. It seems as if he had left Celia days ago. He calls up the warmth and feel of her; their lovemaking. The print of her lips must still be moist upon him, so that on this porch, in this fearful moment, his breath becomes a little ragged. He had felt this fright before, once or twice and, as before, he holds her image close within him as if it were to be his last vision. It had been a talisman that had always worked.

He also thinks of his good intention, the idea that had pulled him from that cozy bed and brought him to this porch high above Butler Street. What was he doing here? A stupid trick, revealed in all its vanity by the man with the gun crouched behind him. Just above the tentlike peaks of the steel mill's roof, he can see late morning traffic move along the highway on the other side of the Allegheny. He cannot see the river, but the endless stream of cars catches the hazy light to lay a dazzling ornament upon the landscape, a busy decoration quite different from the vicinal road just below, long ago by-passed and made bereft by that same suburban migration across the river. People going to work, coming into the city to start their day's occupations; unmindful of what was taking place on this porch above Butler Street. He had whispered in her ear that he had to do something, kissed her murmurs and gently pulled her arms from around his neck. Do something.

The casual dissembling had clicked in easily this morning as it had yesterday when he had come across the blank check. "What's that?" He had just slipped the paper into his pocket with the rest. "Something for my Kansas City talk," he had told her deftly, assured of the lie's success because she would not want to know, turn away from knowing anything about that event; a fund raiser to pay off the cost of his other glib deceptions. On this porch in Lawrenceville, Hardy is sorry that Celia might never know the truth of this most recent deception—that it had covered good intentions. The deception had been too easy. But deception had always been easy.

"Jack, are you there?"

"I'm still here." Adams chuckles. "No, don't turn around. I like you facing out like this. So we can both share everything going on down there. Like buddies."

The man's voice is close to his ear and Hardy wonders if they do resemble a class picture or the members of an odd sport team—only two to a team for this particular game—and posed on top of each other, kneeling and hunched over in a comradely compactness. "Sometimes of an evening, we'd sit here on the porch as the light fades, and you could look through the mill, through the sheet steel like it was made of gauze—and we could see the river. You could imagine how it must have looked from here—the river flowing down there. Indians in their canoes and the like. Or some evenings, myself and Shirley would be the Indians, up here, watching the river drift through the twilight like a dream. Like a magic show and we were a part of that magic. Sometimes, we'd see a boatload of fur trappers coast by and we'd watch them without saying anything but knowing that something had happened. Something had changed, gradual like the river's flow but all the same, not reversible. It's not reversible, Walt. You know what I mean?"

"I know what you're talking about," Hardy says. "I've been thinking something similar."

"Yesterday, we were talking about school days and how we'd stand and tell the class what we wanted to be? You know what I wanted to be? I knew what I wanted to be, but I didn't have the words for it. So, I just stood there like a dummy and the kids laughed. Good natured and dumb—it's the part, you know?" He pauses and takes a breath. "Civil engineer." Each syllable is given careful emphasis. The canary inside chirps. "That's what I wanted to be—a civil engineer."

"Bridges and highways."

"You got it. Emphasis on the ci-vil. You know how many bridges there are in Pittsburgh? Must be a thousand or more. Not just for the rivers. But to get people from one place to the other. From one hilltop to another. And the inclines, all those stairs up and down the hillsides. Reaching across the valleys. They tie the place together so people can meet each other. Not feel so isolated . Not yelling at each other across the divides. Like strangers. Put a bridge across and they get to know each other. Talk easy. Almost in whispers. Like lovers. Like you and me, Walt."

"I was an engineering major."

"Is that right?"

"Yeah, but a different sort. But that was a while back." The neighborhood midmorning hush rises up from the street below like a vapor lifting into the air and into their senses, like the scent from the small garden below the porch. Tulips and hyacinths. Hardy thinks of Shirley Adams planting the bulbs.

"HARDY." The amplified voice from below startles him. A couple of dogs bark nervously. "OKAY...HARDY?...OKAY?"

"I better answer."

"Do that." Adams's laughter is low in his throat.

Hardy leans forward, over the edge of the porch, and waves his right arm in a wide sweep. Every cop in Pittsburgh must be down there. Stores are being robbed, people mugged, pedestrians run over as all the police mill about in this morning convention. All they need are placards to hold up, he thinks. Shirley Adams is not in sight. He eases back on his haunches to rest his head against the wall by the screen door. Utter exhaustion has just poured over him, a fatigue that must have been saved up from years and years. All the energy that had propelled him into this or that campaign, into this or that camp, had also produced a waste that is suddenly voided. He's too tired to move, but he keeps talking. "It's not too late."

"You mean to learn the words for it? How to describe it?"

"Forget that."

"If I only had had the words...ci-vil engin-eeer...is that what you're saying?"

"That's all behind us. Yesterday." Hardy stops abruptly, straining to hear anything behind him. Even the bird is silent. He's afraid he might have angered Adams. "Why don't I come in," he continues after a little. "I have something to show you. A way out of this problem. Won't you let me come in?"

"No, I don't think so," Adams replies thoughtfully, as if he has carefully considered the request, minded all its pros and cons. He sounds regretful, sorry he has to deny Hardy. His tone is that of someone who has given the same answer to the same question, over and over. People always coming to the door, asking to come in, and he has to turn them down, always and regretfully. "I don't think so." But, he sighs and it sounds like he's shifted his position on the floor. "What do you have to show me?"

"It's why I came down here this morning. Nobody called me, Jack. Shirley didn't call me. The cops didn't call me. I came on my own. I want you to believe me."

"Yes. I can believe that."

"I had this idea."

"What's the idea?"

"I wanted to see you. I just got up this morning and said to myself that I had to come see you. Talk to you." The silence between them stretches out, and a heaviness sinks within Hardy, a ballast too heavy for the hope it was meant to steady.

It was an utterly stupid idea. Had he ever been able to change anything for the better? He takes a deep breath. "It's like a bequest."

"A bequest," Adams says evenly as if they have been discussing the subject all morning.

"Yes. I had this benefactor—the woman my dad and mother worked for. She just died. And old, old lady."

"Okay," Adams replies agreeably. "I read about her. One of the mill people. Arnett. "

"Right. Arnett. Well, she always took an interest in me, sent me to college even. Sent me a birthday check every year up to the very last."

"No shit. Every year? Like the old days." The man's voice heartened Hardy. "Down on the plantation."

"Yeah. She was a funny old dame. An old maid—never married. Very conservative, you know."

"That's cool. I place myself to the right of center."

"Is that so?" Hardy replies. "Anyway, she left me this odd-ball bequest. In her will."

"No kidding."

"Yeah, no kidding. Her will said I could go through her house and pick out anything I wanted. Anything." He spins out the narrative to keep Adams listening. Keep him talking and listening, they had told him. Far across the city, a siren wails and suddenly ceases, as if the alarm had been a mistake. A short-circuit of some kind. No one to answer it in any case—all the emergency vehicles were down below.

"Anything?" Adams is saying.

"Yeah. I came across this bundle of old checks in her desk. Every check she had ever sent me. Every birthday and Christmas. All there."

"Like Santa keeping track."

"Exactly. That's what Celia said." Introducing her into the narrative makes it more interesting, family like. Something else to talk about; how they had met, their early days. Then that would introduce Bobby Kennedy. Spin it out.

"I mean this stack of old checks was this thick, and all for little amounts—five, ten, fifteen bucks. Then those for my birthdays—that cost her twenty."

"Yeah." Adams chuckles. "The big one."

"But the very last check in the pile was this one."

"Oh, yeah?"

"See. Look." He holds the check up beside his ear and to the screen. "See, it's blank. Made out to me and signed by her, but the amount left blank. See?"

He could take anything he wanted. Even this check. Made out to him and signed, but the amount left blank. Maybe she had forgot to fill in the amount. It had been meant to be another draft for twenty dollars; another petty benevolence. She had been good at that, shoving small change into people's pockets. Buying her way into their gratitude, even their affections maybe. Even as a young woman. She had poked fifty-dollar bills at that pilot in Mexico for flying lessons. Oh sure, flying lessons, Celia had joked when he told her.

Or maybe, she hadn't forgot to fill the check in. Couldn't decide how much it should be before she died. Maybe, this was her way, leaving it for him—if and when he found the check—to fill in the amount himself. A last joke on everybody, her family. The chauffeur's son would take it all. Then, this idea hit him. Hardy looks down at the check in his hand. Her trustees had been instructed to pay all her debts. All outstanding checks. He could write in almost any amount. What could anyone say about it—the family wouldn't want the publicity? This morning as he dressed, in a fever with his idea, he had pictured Susanna Pell throwing up her hands. "Oh, give it to him," she would say. The rest would go along. It was part of their profile; pay off the problem. Don't make a fuss. One of their PubRel people could turn it into another demonstration of the family's generosity, civic virtue.

"You see where the amount is blank."

"Yes, I see that."

"We can fill in any amount we want."

"We can?"

"For civil engineering. For you and Shirley. You could go anywhere. Be obligated to no one. Go to school anywhere. You could design bridges, Jack. Not just make the cables for them. You could dream them up and someone else would build them this time. Make the cables."

"Kind of like winning the lottery."

"Absolutely. Just like the lottery."

"But, it's made out to you?"

"All I do is sign it over to you. Endorse it to you."

"Just like that?"

"Just like that." A radio plays somewhere in the neighborhood; an announcer gives an hourly traffic report. Parkway West is backed up to Greentree. The accident on Route 65 has been cleared.

"Well, well," Adams finally says genially. "Here Shirley has been filling out those certificates from *Readers Digest* all the time and here you show up with the winning number. Here she's been pasting up these coupons, and you come up on this porch like Ed McMahon. TV down there and everything. Isn't this something?"

"It's just like that," Hardy says. Last night, in Celia's arms, he had thought about tearing up the check, to dispose of it along with the lie he had told her about finding it. The first erasure of all the lies he had told her. And he had fallen asleep with that intention. But, some other part of him—the can-do guy working overtime, even in his sleep—had whispered in his ear to wake him at daybreak. Here's an idea that could solve a lot of their problems, the voice said; Celia's feelings toward him and their marriage at the top of that list. And Clarence Adams. Yes, even Eddie Poremski.

"Like a million dollars," Adams says in his ear. The man's voice is almost amorous.

"Well, maybe not a million."

"You just said any amount." Adams sounds a little disappointed.

"We have to be reasonable, Jack."

"That's reasonable," Adams replies softly. "A million dollars is reasonable."

"Sure, why the hell not?" Hardy says and laughs. He'll enjoy the look on those Arnett relatives. A million dollars for Mr. and Mrs. Clarence Adams. Celia will laugh and laugh. He hasn't heard her really laugh in a long, long time. "I don't have a pen. Can I borrow a pen? You have a pen inside? I'll have to come inside to fill out the check."

"Oh, I don't think so," Adams says calmly.

"Maybe, I could come in and we could look for one. Together. Then we could fill in all the blanks. A million bucks."

"That's shit, man. A million dollars is not going to make

any difference with me. Don't you know that? I'll just have bigger pockets. A bigger bank account. But, I'll be the same. My hands will be the same, man. Don't you get it? You're pushing me, dude." The voice has become a little strained.

"Okay, Jack. It's okay." Hardy takes a couple of breaths. "It's a good idea. Think about it. Will you? Just think about it." Something presses against the screening by his head. It could be the gun's muzzle. Me and Bobby Kennedy, he suddenly thinks. After all these years, finally coming down together on this porch in Pittsburgh. He chokes back a laugh.

"What's the joke?"

He's been deserted by all the old fluencies. The gab that had eased him through one door and into another, from one encampment and then into another has dried up on his tongue. He had talked his way through all those doors, his own belief in the rhetoric coming through and making it believable. The sky above them has been going gray and a translucent lid has fitted over Pittsburgh. He has become a tourist who has lost his phrase book.

"Looks like we're going to be on the six o'clock news," Clarence Adams is saying companionably. "I dig that blonde anchor lady."

"Being on the news does nothing, proved nothing. Take it from me. For one night, maybe. For the week at the most—but then everyone turns around for another beer, goes to the crapper. The commercial comes on. It's all forgotten. The next item is on. Being on the TV will do nothing, Jack."

"Sure, I know that. I was thinking of that guy in Los Angeles. That was something to see a person, a human being beaten to the ground on the TV. By the police. Not a story but for real. A human being kicked and beaten to the ground. Trying to get up and beaten back down. And by the police. Just like that. That's what this country is all about, Walt, and it finally got on the six o'clock news. But, I think you're right, Walt. It's all forgot after a trip to the crapper."

"That's not what I meant," Hardy says quickly. "It's not all like that. That was a bad scene. A bad scene. But it doesn't have to be that way. You could make it different, Jack. With this money you could change things. Build bridges." The laughter in his ear breaks him down; he has been found out. He's talking in slogans.

"Which brings us back at the vain part, Walt. This is where we came in. This is where you came in. Don't you sometimes feel bad?"

A noon-hour whistle raises howls from the neighborhood's dogs. No one else to respond, Hardy thinks. No workers left to open up lunch pails. Maybe, it's a signal that management forgot to turn off, like a light in the office; a cruel reminder of better days. "What's that you're doing?"

"Don't be alarmed. I'm just cutting a hole in the screen," Adams replies. As Hardy looks down, he sees the blade of a pocket knife sawing through the aluminum net.

"That's a good job. This screen door I mean." He had meant why ruin this fine screen door, he would tell Celia later, but his heart is skipping beats. Maybe Adams has changed his mind; he wanted the check after all. He has talked him into it. He'd be able to tell Celia that he had persuaded the guy, and she would put her arms around him, tell him that he had done well. That everything would be okay.

"My Uncle Ben is an outstanding carpenter," Adams is saying. "Outstanding. He built houses, big buildings, all over the country that are still standing. All over America, his buildings are still standing. One whole week-end—just last year—my family came over and we did all the screens for the whole house. Uncle Ben showed us how. We set up shop in the back-yard, set up formers for doors and windows. Screens. We made them of wood, not out of this aluminum shit—but real wood. Wonderful hard pine. Clean. Made them to fit every window and door individually, to custom, which was a challenge, Walt, because an old house like this has no square angles to it.

"But we made the mortises crystal right, everything fitting perfect. It was like a remedy, that weekend, an antidote to all the poison. Do you know what I mean, Walt? All the bad stuff coming down from the stars which are beautiful but deadly close-up. Like Nam. So beautiful but death all around you. So, I made this screen door, Walt, and it is perfect. Can't be made better. It was my way of thumbing my nose at all the shit. Know what I mean? For a little time anyway, just a little bit of time."

"It's a beautiful piece of work, Jack."

"And we had a fine time that weekend. The women turned out wonderful foods. Pies and yam pudding. Shirley's preserves were a special treat. Everyone was so pleased with her strawberry jam. Other delicacies. What a sweet woman she is, Walt. A Christian woman." Adams pauses, as if to admire the hole he has made in the screen. "We did all these windows and doors that one weekend. Made them and painted them. And it seemed to be enough. It was a weekend to remember. I like to remember that weekend. Hold it like a balloon. Here."

"What's that?"

"It's my hand," Clarence Adams says. "Take my hand."

"What for?"

"I want to give you something. That's cool."

"Wait a minute. What about the bird?"

"What about the bird?" Adams says and pulls the trigger.

1, July, 1940
4:20

I'm sitting in the Papillon, across from Sanborns, waiting for China who is rehearsing with the Symphony. Revueltas is taking the Pigeons on tour with the orchestra up to Monterrey. They have a new dance number. *Hommage to García Lorca.* Franco's boys shot him the year before I got to Spain.

It's a pleasant spa, this bar, and we are known here — a couple. Have our own table, like celebs at the Stork Club. This evening, I'm doing *la cena del vuelo* to Mérida. That's what Miguel calls the trip, not because the airline serves a meal in flight but because most of our passengers lose their dinners during the flight.

We've talked some about the baby business. So far, China has said little about getting hitched. She talks about the pregnancy like something for a new dance number. A Mayan priestess gives birth to a serpent that helps the peasants with the harvest. That sort of thing. She's not as rambunctious. Her breasts look a little different. And sometimes I catch her looking at me with the long face; she's been studying me. I'm a little tickled by this old soldier throwing a calf or a serpent or whatever. But it's another door closing on me too.

So, I keep bringing it up — the officer and a gentleman part of me. "You think it's important to marry?" she says. The thoroughly modern girl. "Let's wait until after the election, at least wait until then," she says. Which person is talking now? The daughter of a *cacique* ? Papa will blow this *gringo's* head off for making a baby with his baby? Or, then she says, "Oh, phooey on you, h'Armstrong. You are not a homebodies. My warrior. You will be crossing the border." Is she testing me? She usually smiles when she talks like this, but her eyes are dark with questioning.

And how *do* I feel? I'm barely a citizen, and I'm about to become the father of another Mexican citizen. Am I, Roy Armstrong, late of the US Army Air Service, the hero of Spanish skies — ready for an adobe with a white picket fence around it? An open sewer running through the front yard?

Of course, this thing with Arnett. The gods are waiting for me to pay off that IOU. Today's my birthday. Blow out the candles, Molly.

Once I had just come in from walking Tonantzin in the Alameda, and China was standing in the small hallway that leads to her sitting room, the roof garden behind her. It was like I had caught her in something, like coming on a wild animal on a forest path. She was standing flatfooted on the tile floor, her feet firmly planted. A pose I've seen in her dances, all

of her ready to spring up and become a warrior butterfly or an eagle. The light was behind her, her
hair was fluffed out, a little kinked by the moisture in the air. She was in silhouette, but for the
whites of her eyes. I could tell she was grinning,
ear to ear. But her stance, the way she held her
arms akimbo, the grip of her feet on the floor —
she was ready to scoot one way or the other,
straight up, or disappear into the woodwork, out
of my life. Why does that picture stay with me?

Or the night we are at the Patio Seville in
the Colonia *Roma*. I see people from the *Sinaia*;
it's a hangout for Spanish refugees. Flamenco
guitars and dancing and paella. The room goes
quiet. China's up on the floor, by herself.
They've cleared the floor for her and the guitars are doing that thump-thump business as she
slowly unwinds her arms and hands. She usually
doesn't dance flamenco, says it's *imperialista*,
creole. But this night, she comes right up to
the table. All for me. One knee bent and slowly
moving under her dress lazily, this way and that,
back and forth, timing the explosion about to
happen. Hands raised, fingers like flower
petals. Snapping out the beat. She's staring at
me, a hawk measuring a rabbit. The tension is
wound tighter and tighter. From the dark, at the
back of the place, someone says softly, "*Olé*,"
and it was like everyone had just seen the two
of us roll over in bed. I can almost hear the
whispers in the place: he must be some *grand
gringo* to have that *muchacha* dancing for him.
Then!! *Brra-ratta-tat-tat-ta-tah!* She whirls
away, feet pounding the floor. Back arched tri-
umphantly, the way she is sometimes on top.
Cheers and whistles.

The waiter here has just brought me another
bottle of water and fresh limes, dusting off the
table with his napkin. Keeping the flies hopping
is an approved method of sanitation down here.
The front shutter door has opened and I look up,
hoping it is my girl. An American couple have
rushed in, out of the rain. Probably saw the

place listed in Terry's. In fact the woman carries the guidebook in one hand. They sit at the bar. I saw them a few hours ago over at the consulate. This city is a small town, especially if you're an American. Or ex-American. But, I like to watch other couples in public who are happy with each other, loving, because it makes me think of us when we are together. It's another belonging, I guess. Seeing this couple at the bar, sitting close and talking, her hand on his — I say to myself, yes, I'm part of that, I know how they are feeling. *Qué va.*

I like to look over her things; be among her books and statues. Photographs of other dancers. The evidence of her seriousness. I'm in love with her history as well. Black bowls and candelabra from her part of the country. Big plates over the sideboard. Blue rebozos and rust-colored rugs thrown over the cushions, the sofa. All very comfy, and Arnett can't find me there, either. I was dead tired from wrestling the Ford down from Torreon and I get to the hotel. Angel comes running out of the lobby. He's been waiting for me. *La americana importante* is waiting for me in my room, he says. In my room? He couldn't do anything about it, she'd already bribed the desk clerk, got the key. So, I come to China's. Armstrong, you are one dumb jackass!

Rivera's wife gave us one of her own paintings, and we've hung it on the wall above the sideboard. It is of a dog racing through the jungle. A snowcapped volcano smokes peacefully in the background. The dog is looking out from the painting, a sweet, womanly face. Happy. Not in danger. We don't talk about it much, but Frida gave us the painting after Tonantzin ran off. The painting's supposed to work a magic that makes us know the dog is okay.
I blame myself for Tonantzin running off. I had taken her off her leash in the Alameda, not for the first time. But this time she just starts running full out. Like she was answering a call from far away. Up in the mountains.

She's up there where the gods and heroes play in the snow. Or maybe she's run home to Oaxaca. Away from my falsehood. All slim four legs working. If I had never had that leg fixed. If I had left well enough alone. If I had only hung up a _milagro,_ and let it go at that. If I hadn't listened to Arnett. Giving the dog her fourth leg back — can we tell her how to use it? How not to use it?

I've spent my whole life looking for some family to take me in. The Service was like that. And it's happened here in Mexico. Here in this bar. Sitting next to Miguel in the DC-2. Listening to Angel at the hotel as he tells me about one of his cousins. He's even invited me to his house for a party. His saint's day. I'm a member of the family.

A fly steps around the rim of the little saucer with the limes, looking for sugar. Round and round. That's me. Trying to avoid the sourness that lies in the center.

The other afternoon, we take a picnic up to Chapultepec. Like any momma and pappa, we get on the trolley with our baskets and pans. _Una merienda con China_ is not your usual outing. The afternoon rain had cleared the air; everything nicely cooled off. I think of her dozing in the park, we were in a kind of grotto with big mesquite trees overhead. The sports section of the _Herald Tribune_ was spread over her face. As always, I am struck again by the richness of her. More than ever.

The paper had a piece about Bucky Walters and how he just might pitch the Cincinnati Reds into the series. That would be some matchup — him against Bob Feller and the Tigers. Animals and birds playing games are part of China's history; after all, she makes up dances about such things. But something bothered her.

"Who are these Reds?" she finally asked, her voice muffled by the newspaper. The name has political meaning for her. Part of _gringo_ political naivete that we name a sports team after the left side of the political spectrum, she is thinking. Trotsky's and Stalin's boys suiting up to play a little pepper.

"It's because they're all left-handed," I told her and look over at a squirrel cleaning his paws. For a moment, I can hear the squeal of the streetcars, turning around way down below, preparing for the trip back down Reforma. Then she is up in a burst of Spanish that lays me out — *me puso en ridiculo* — for making a fool with her, though laughing too, getting the joke of it. And we fall to kissing and then other things. The squirrel is fascinated.

"You want to go back to this?" China asked in the park. She had sat up and thrust the newspaper toward me. She had her finger on a small item. A Negro in Tennessee was lynched— the third one this summer, the paper said. Like a score of some kind, carried over from the sports page. Another national pastime. The colored guy had gone in to register because he wanted to vote come November. In Tennessee, for God's sake!! Probably would have voted for FDR. They ought to be able to vote, of course, if they understand who and what they're voting for. But killing someone over it is going too far. They even burned his body. Or tried to.

"Sure, there's a law against that," I answer her question.

"*Pero*?"

Well, it's *complicado, muy complicado*, and I know I have no answer for it. I could have brought up that kid one of her old man's bodyguards had plugged. China continued to look into my eyes—I dared not look away—and it's like she's pulling all the rotten excuses out of my skull through the eye holes. One of those elementary brain surgeries her people used to practice.

So, I looked up at the trees above us, just to change the subject. "*Qué son aquellos árboles?*"

She followed my look. "*Son ahuehuetes.*"

"*Ahuehuetes*? In English, they are what?"

Her expression labors around the translation, childlike. In fact, my question had reduced her to a child. In a flash this grown-up woman — smarter than me in most things — this queen of eagles, had been reduced to a grammar school kid. Well, hell, how am I so smart? Her lips audition a couple of possibilities; her complexion has gone darker. Finally, she shrugged and said, "*Quinza*...the silk worm...?"

"Ah, a mulberry tree?"

"*Si*, mul-berrie." she laughed and set up the small portable stove to make our *quesadillas*. A sense of well-being overwhelmed me.

Well, here goes. Get it behind me. Arnett had been doing these cutsey manoeuvers, touchy-feelies in the Beechcraft at nine thousand feet. Last month, we've taxied up to the hangar lip and shut down the engine. "I have to talk with you," she says kind of quickly. I think it's about some move Halstead has made to get me back to the US, so I sit still to listen. "Oh, not here," she says with that downturned smile and hops out of the plane. She takes my hand and pulls me into the hangar and toward the rear. The little shack the mechanics use for coffee and *quesadillas*. "What's up?" I'm asking, knowing damn well what was up. Jack was honest—he was up! I'm almost mad at the same time. A strange feeling. Let's get this over with, I'm thinking. She's asking for it. "You have to help me with something," she's saying in this funny voice and when we get into the shack, she starts pulling at the buttons of her whipcords, frantically, and for a moment — so help me, Molly — I'm thinking a spider or some kind of bug has got in there and she wants me to get it out. Some kind of bug, McGee.

It was over quick. "You help me, and I'll help you, Captain," she said. She put my hand between her legs. Sopping wet. I couldn't stop if I had wanted to. And, well, I was curious. Does a million dollars make for any differences.

It was like a business deal. She made it seem like that. Her calling me *Captain*. This has nothing to do with me and China, I kept saying to myself all the while. Halstead would pull some strings as I pulled her string. Or she's pulling mine. Her quid for my quo. What a dumb jackass you are, Armstrong.

If I could find the right *milagro,* I'd hang one up for us — for China and me. Because something has broke. What kind of part would it be? A heart? I may have crippled this beautiful thing we have going. And for what? Trying to get back on a team that doesn't want me? That's doing everything to keep this native from returning?

And today's my birthday—forty-one. *Felicidades*, you bum.

Get back to *las meriendas en el parque.* Keeping this memory fresh. China patting out a tortilla on the little portable stove. She puts some *queso Chihuahua* in the middle, strips of cooked cactus, chilli pepper, fresh cilantro. Folds the corn cake and turns it over so it's browned and the cheese melts. She looked especially Indian doing all this, squatting on her heels, hair down, her expression serene. Beautiful. Not the sophisticated grad of a swank New England school for girls I expect to burst through the door of the Papillon at any moment. Not the dancer featured in *Mexico Hoy* last month. The rest of *La Paloma Azul* as well. How the waiters will snap to attention when she comes in. The couple at the bar will turn with astonishment and envy. I hang this image of her in the park in my mind like a *milagro* to cure the awful ache inside these miserable guts.

All hell is breaking loose here with the election coming up. Every general in the army seems to be running for president. China's old man presents himself as the *Nuevo Zapata*. Even as he shoots down nine year olds. We still don't talk about that. Ansers tells me the Nazis are paying for his campaign. My poor country, China says and cries.

How can Roosevelt run for a third term, she asked me? Even in corrupt Mexico, a President can only serve once. But that's a joke. They more or less name their successors. A couple of newspapers have asked Cárdenas to go for another term, and he's refused. I'd vote for Wilkie if I could. Halstead says FDR is Jewish. "His family changed their name from Rosenfeld," he tells me the other day. "That explains a lot."

Explains what? And so what?

We were at this party where Trotsky took China to one side and asked her all kinds of questions about her father. She was embarrassed. Got angry, then her friend Sylvia, the Bolshie's secretary, rescued her. You'd think Sylvia's boyfriend would spell his phoney name correctly. "Excuse me," he says at the party. " But my name is spelled thusly," and he whips out this Canadian passport. *Jacson* without a *k*.

But all names are misspelled these days; everything just off, missing a letter. In Madrid, you'd walk down the Gran Via and everything seemed okay, normal. People on the street, shoppers, office help. Newspapers, magazines fill the kiosks. Street cars running. Political posters plastered on every surface. Everything normal, until you look up a few floors and you'd see the top floor of a building blown away. The crowd waiting for the metro wear uniforms and carry guns. Soldiers taking the subway to the front! Battlefields used to be out in the countryside — that's the history, isn't it? Waterloo and Gettysburg. Even Verdun. Soldiers fighting soldiers. But now the battlefield is a big city with life going on, movies playing, stores having *REBAJAS*. Cafés busy. People shot dead crossing the street with groceries as the traffic lights keep changing. Kids bleeding to death over their spilled school books. Stukas screaming down.

How I hate Stukas. That's what's wrong with

the world — those goddamn Stukas. To begin with, they're an ugly looking plane. Only designed to dive straight down on hospitals and schools and drop that one egg between their wheels. With little accuracy. Just blow something up, no matter what. One afternoon I was bringing a rebuilt I-16 back to the base from Barcelona. I see a Stuka pulling up over a little village. Above Vallecas. No strategic importance whatsoever. Just blowing up something. School, hospital, church. This Kraut is pulling up from his dive. He had had his fun. Doesn't see me until I'm on him. The rear gunner slumps over quick but I keep the Shekas working. The Stuka has leveled out, about to stall and the pilot has pulled back the canopy. He stood up and faced me, about to parachute. The bastard throws me a salute. That was the last war, sweetheart. I edge the tracer lines up just a hair, and he explodes like a bottle of catsup. All 57 varieties. I keep firing. I sew him into that fucking Stuka. No one around, so no confirmation. No thousand bucks. Didn't matter. Money can't buy how I felt.

They have a saying down here...*para mole su pavo viejo* . This old turkey is only fit for making stew. Think of it — 41.
Slam-bang! Here comes my babe.
Something's up!

Aeropuerto
18:50

Another message waiting for me at the airport from Peggy Arnett. *PLEASE* call her.

Here's what happened. China walks toward me slow and steady, down the center of the Papillion. Hair flat and wet down her shoulders. Her face glistens with rain. She's wearing boots

245

and a long pleated skirt, a bolero jacket. She could have left one of her old man's stallions tied up at the door outside. I'm in for it. She's found out about Arnett, I'm thinking.

One of the waiters runs up to pull out a chair for her but she waves him away. Something tells me not to get up, not try a kiss. Fly close to the carpet, an old instinct warns me. She stops at the table and looks down. Nothing for a minute.

"So," she says slowly, "you went again to the American consulate today. Did you get your passport back — your wonderful American passport?" Her English is icy and perfect.

How did she find out? "I went for my mail. Look. *"Mira."* I hold the letter up from Spatz. That cuts no ice. She is giving me that black Zapotec look. But something else is taking shape in the velvet brown-blackness. A softening within the onyx eyes. She is on the verge of tears.

Her head goes back and she tosses her rain-heavy hair. Spanish is safer for her, the fluency gives her strength. *Ahora haga la cama del parto* — she almost sings the refrain and the waiters come together, like they are about to join in. The Ink Spots. *Alza el vuelo. La cama del parto,* she repeats the phrase, holding her arms out. It's a gesture I recognize from one of her dance numbers, something about a water jug. Everyone is looking. The couple at the bar looks amused, watching the natives spat. I am a villain who has *made this bed of nativity* — somehow it doesn't have the same punch in English — and who is about to fly away.

A couple of the waiters are clearing near-by tables of glasses and silverware. Anything that can be thrown. Like rolling down shutters before a storm.

"Oh, sit down," I say , half rising.

China turns and slowly walks out, down past the tourists and the waiters. At the door, she raises one hand to her face. I'm pretty sure, she's sink-ing her teeth into the fleshy part near the thumb. Then, she's gone.

Miguel is in Operations. Checking out the weather. Our flight plan takes us over the Bay of Campeche. We're ETA Merida at 2330. Give or take. The phone rings. Hector answers. He repeats my name. I shake my head. I'm sure it's Arnett again. But what if it was China? She's never called me at the field. Arnett is not so discrete. That million bucks again. Messages from her lying around everywhere. "Wants some more lessons," Rhyl says the other day. If he wasn't the boss, I'd take a poke at him. It only happened once.

Veracruz
9:35

Dandy tail wind gave us an extra push. Damn frustrating. Even if China had a phone, she probably wouldn't answer. We've picked up a few passengers. I'm not even bothering to leave the cockpit. Miguel likes to do the walk-around. He puts his cap on at a sporty angle, buttons up his blouse. he has relatives everywhere who come down to see him fly the airplane.

Veracruz is where I came into this picture a year ago. *Los desamparatos.* Sounds better to be abandoned in Spanish. I've been circling the same field ever since. No where to put down.

Hotel Itza-Mérida
24:20

Coming in over the water, everything dark, the lights of Mérida like diamonds on black velvet, I slid back the little window beside me, just to feel the slipstream on my face. Like the old days. I wish I could do something like that to clear my head as I sit here in the hotel's patio. Put my face into a breeze that will sweep out all the tangles. Sipping aged tequila. The fountain splashes. Outside on the street, a guitar player passes slowly, gradually disappearing around the corner, chord by chord. A dog barks. Tonantzin, where are you? Come back to us.

I don't even deserve the dog.

Sure, I picked up my mail at the consulate. That was the truth. Half of it. I also met with Emory. Someone must have told China. Probably his secretary is another pal of hers.

—Didn't know you were a Yale man, he says looking over his fingertips. I'm suddenly okay; can use the toilet any time I want.

—For only about a year, I tell him. —I jumped into the war and never went back.

—Chuck Halstead told me, Emory gives me the answer before I can ask the question.—He and I have a squash game over at the American Club. Do you play?

Clearly, Emory has changed his opinion about me. I'm invited to play with the good guys. I can see it in his eyes. I'm no longer the annoying old air bum shacking up with *mestizas*. I am a person with important contacts. A somebody. A somebody in oil, you might say.

—You don't play squash? Emory's clearly disappointed.

—I've misplaced my racquet, I tell him.

He nods and tries to be wise and worldly —Not all you've misplaced, Captain Armstrong.

Here comes the lecture. Serving in a foreign army. Flying with commie wingmates for a socialist government. Relationship with a foreign intelligence agent. Even little Nikki is in the file on his desk. Yah-yah-yah. The Dies

Committee has done its job pretty good. Tiresome stuff.

Emory has this high dome of a forehead that adds to his baldness which adds to the total sum of his pale face. Sometimes, coming face to face with another gringo, I am almost blinded by the whiteness, because I spend so much time with Mexicans. People of brown complexion. Miguel. Of course, China. The hotel, the passengers on the plane. Many others. I begin to think I'm one of the natives. Forget my own color. Then, I pass a mirror. Who's that guy? Who is that *gringo*? *Soy yo.*

But I quickly gather things have changed since Emory and I last talked. After the obligatory review of Boy Scout Rules, his eyes narrow and his lips pull back like a gila's — his best smile. The war coming on has changed certain priorities, he says.

—In addition, you've picked up a couple of pretty good endorsements. Chuck Halstead speaks highly of you. Emory winks.

So, screw a guy's girl and he does you a favor. Is that the way the world turns, Molly? Actually, maybe I did Halstead a favor on that straw mat in the tool shed. It was an angry piece of business and once was enough, brother.

Sitting here in Mérida, the words I should have said to Emory come easily. —Look, I'm a citizen of Mexico. What America or the Dies Committee says doesn't mean two snaps of a snake's dick to me. Mexico has made me legitimate when America put me out.

I should have said, you can take these bars and wings and pin them on some other jackass. I've done my share of wingovers for the US-of-Assholes and democracy. That's what I should have said.

The bartender is falling asleep. I could tell José all this—in English. It might unload the cargo. If only China had a phone. —Honey, I love you. I am never going to leave you. Give me another chance. *Mi mundo nuevo.*

Regis Hotel
3 July 1940—Wed.

How sweet last night. I am struck dumb by the changes in her body. I'm responsible for this flower blooming. When I put her on the train for Monterrey this morning, the other Pigeons chatter but eye me. Many smiles. She's told them, I guess. Papahood gets a lot of respect down here.

I've spent the day with Angel and his family. His saint's day. They live in the *Colonia Obrera*. He's especially proud of the electric fan — the only family in the *colonia* with such a device. The hotel threw it out because it had broken down, *terminado*. But one of his cousins fixed it. They get their water from a faucet in the inner courtyard. A kitchen sink and a toilet was installed in their apartment, but running water never got that far. Typical. Somebody got the money. *Mordida*. One by one, each member of his family is brought over to me as I sit in the one chair with a cushion. An older uncle squeezes a small accordion in the corner. I feel like the pope.

When I tell China about my day with Angel's family, she says nothing for a long, long time. The wash on the phone line to Monterrey rises like a surf that could drown us. It's not a translation problem. I know she is trying to force her angry thoughts through a sieve so the words come out calm. Her face has pulled long, turned a deep raspberry color. I can see all this as I look out my hotel window at the dark Alameda. I had only meant to give her a lighthearted account on the generosity of her countryman, inviting me to share his saint's fiesta. But, all I have done is remind her of the poverty and misery of her countrymen. The corruption that has betrayed them. Betrayed the revolution. She's become deeply embarrassed. I know she is thinking all this in the silence between us.

The election is next week, and it will change
nada.Every candidate, whatever the party — labor,
PNR,fascist,agrarian — all claim to be *al servicio
de las masas.* The masses. It's a word to bring tears
to speaker and listener alike. But the masses down
here have only one pot to piss in — and they cook
in it too. *El profundo* is what they call the people at the bottom of the pile, and believe me, it's
pretty deep down.

So, I know better to talk about politics, let
her work it out. I am looking out at the long,
dark stretch of the Alameda. The dome of the
Bellas Artes at the far end gleams in the night
lights. A couple of *prostitutas* pass arm in arm
through a spill of lamplight. Like sisters, and
they could be sisters. Even mother and daughter.
They wear similar hats. The toot of a clay pipe
comes and goes above the grind of trolleys, the
exhaust of motorcars. Always that mournful
melody. Why so sad? Why ask, McGee?

Los fotingos turn Juarez into the Indianapolis
Speedway. A vendor grills meats on a portable
brazier. The aroma spices the breeze, limes and
peppers roasting. The thick perfume of flowers.
Jasmine maybe? A wet smell like old stone and
mortar. Several dogs hang around the vendor,
tails wagging hopefully, for some tidbit to drop.
None of them Tonatzin.

What a glorious sunny, happy day in Oaxaca
when she curled up at my feet in the cafe. When
I introduced her to China who recognized her;
named her. This afternoon, dogs of every *mestizo*
sat around the goat that Angel's children took
turns winding on the spit. A couple of mutts
passed the time with a slow hump in the corner
of the patio, while keeping an eye on the siz-
zling meat.

From her voice, I can tell China's worn out.
The pregnancy is sapping her energy. She will
have to give up dancing for a little, and that
will make her very blue. She's got back to
tonight's performance. The Lorca piece continues to cause disturbances. She said Gold Shirts
in the audience had almost stopped the show.
Boos and catcalls. Fistfights. Ovations. What a

time, when it is dangerous to be a dancer? Or a poet for that matter. But most of the audience cheered them. A kind of referendum. The theatre was not very modern. The lighting equipment was inadequate. She sounded sleepy. She supplies a few more details; then falls silent and I have to ask direct questions to prop up the conversation.

"*Te amo*." It's my last trump.

"Do you?" she replies, cooly. Her English does not have the slightest inflection. It's a question she's been asking herself as well. "Do you love me?"

To come into the Don Quixote room late tonight and to remember that it was here I first saw China, all rigged up as the dog who was the cook, planting those wonderful feet onto the floor, slowly twisting her torso, arms out as the gourds and the little drums kept time. The management has trouble finding substitute acts when the Blue Pigeons go on tour. Tonight a couple of guys in silk shirts did tricks with yo-yos. The tourists were not impressed.

When we finally hang up, the Alameda is like a lost continent. Looks deserted though I know all kinds of business is happening out there. Throats are being slit and wallets lifted and bodies fitted together in different combinations. A mutt of some kind trots down the middle of Revillagigedo. I keep expecting Tonantzin to bound out of the shadows. In the distance, on the far side of the zócalo, one—two—three sky rockets climb into the night and burst. Somebody's birthday. Somebody's funeral. A saint or a sinner. Both.

Aug 27. 1940
Kelly-Fucking Field
Texas, USA

"*Escucha, cariño,*" China's voice is the sound
of a patient teacher, careful that I understand
what has gone before, then she turns the page.
I hear her now in my head. Ever again in my ear,
near me on the pillow? I cast her voice in different places to make many of her so as to pop-
ulate my miserable condition. I'm alone again.
    "*Escucha.*" Yes, I am listening, China. At
last and too late, I am listening. Talk to me.
I missed it the first time around. The second
and third time around. All this year I missed
what you were trying to tell me. It wasn't the
language, but these stone ears on my head. The
stone in my heart. Talking always so sadly about
Mexico. *La Traición,* you called it. Talking
angrily. The Betrayal. And you would become
older. No, ageless. No age but ancient all the
same. Young and beautiful too.

    Of course, her father is a big part of this.
She's told me things. I don't know the whole
story, and maybe don't want to know it. She gets
very upset when she talks about it. But there it
is. "*Escucha, cariño,*" she is saying. I see us
sitting in the far corner of the *zócalo* near the
cathedral. We sit on a wall of what they think
was part of Montezuma's palace, the center of his
capital. It is late. The city has become quiet
and deliciously cool. Once in a great while, a
streetcar trundles by, lit up and empty. A couple of cafés across the huge square are still
open. Some men are playing cards. *Lotería.* Shall
I light this scene with a moon? Why not? The
dark blue *rebozo,* over her head and around her
shoulders, is black in the moonlight. Was she in
mourning, even then? But her face within the cowl
of material is illuminated by the light in the
zócalo. The angled planes of her cheeks, the
heavy line of her mouth. The whites of her eyes
turn in the darkness. *Qué bonita!*

Here in these spartan digs of the BOQ, I taste the rich flan of her voice. She speaks Spanish and some Mayan, and, in my reverie, I understand every word. Surrounded by the ruins of the Aztec empire. Moonlight highlights hunks of masonry that emerge from the old palace floor like warriors stuck in their own myth. Like Roy Armstrong, McGee.

How is it that every woman important in my life goes off to pursue a dream that excludes me? Milly to raise perfect biscuit dough. Harlow getting her lines perfect. Nikki pushed down the chute of a perfect world. China dancing the perfect Mexico. I am left standing on this tarmac in San Antonio. All by myself. Do we need another Lone Eagle?

What is the word China used? *Nit-laca.* *Nitlaca.* We are humans as well. (Wait a minute — I say. Spell that for me. Here — she says, rising to bend over me and takes my journal from the bedside, and, childlike, holds the pencil in her fist, writes out N-i-t-l-a-c-a. Uses one whole page. Dots the *i* with a tiny circle. She is leaning over me, the sweet *rebozo* of her aroma lightly falls around my shoulders. Her breasts nuzzle my neck. There — she says — I am writing in your pages also. I am here.)
And in my heart, *cariño.*
Just now, I have looked back through all these pages to find this word. *Nitlaca.* We are humans. I kiss the page, the word on it, as I remember her writing it down that Sunday morning. Cathedral's bells had woke us.

So that's the excuse, is it? We are humans. I hear her say, *La Traición* is five hundred years old now. How can such a long history be made right? The betrayal started here. She looks around the ruins. Did one of those stones just move a little bit? Pulling itself out of the spell Cortés put on the place. This is where falsehood began, *cariño.* And this is where it must end.

"You tell me of the fiesta, the saint's day, at the hotel porter's home. The sewage in the courtyard, the lack of water. The poor conditions. This is the 20th Century, h'Armstrong! You see how these people live? And this is in the city. It is 1940! Imagine the life of the *campesino*. Twenty years after the Revolution, and people like your hotel porter still live like dogs. *La traición*."

I should have heard the steel beneath the delicious sounds of her voice. It's difficult to listen to a beautiful woman talk politics. That's always been my problem. Are they really serious? China still reminds me of the rich girls in the movies; home from their fancy schools and chatting up the kitchen help before joining the cocktail party in the drawing room. Plotting with the servants to take over the salon. How could I take her seriously? Oh, my, McGee.

Can't remember if this scene in the *zócalo* was before or after she's pregnant? We had many such talks in all kinds of places. Our little *mestizo*. Our little mistake. I try to explain the pun, but she wasn't amused. She didn't get it. Didn't want to get it. Sometimes, she would close up her expression and I can feel the centuries roll out between us. But, I hold this scene in my mind here in Texas. It is all one. Us talking late in the *zócalo*. Us all the time. Together and intimate. The babe within her. The three of us like a family. The damp, musty smells of the ancient capital rise in the hush around us. Hell, I'll even put a dog in this scene. There's always a dog, wherever you look in Mexico. This one trots along the far side of the square, making her own nightly rounds. China pauses, and we watch the dog stop, look our way, then turn down *cinco de febrero*. Is that you, Tonantzin? Did you recognize us? Yes, Tonantzin replies, but you have given me four good legs; so, now I must use all of them. *Adios, amigos*. Later, China and I will walk hand in hand to her place and kiss ourselves to sleep. And I will hold her in my arms as her breathing goes deep and trusting. I am left awake and by myself.

The last several weeks, I'd come across a blank
spot in her. Even then, she was getting ready to
disappear, head for the mountains. Do what she had
to do. Like Tonantzin. She was part of something
that maybe had never included me. She had been
trying to tell me all along. The dancing was a way
to spread the word, sending messages. All the
places she danced, something else was going on.
Backstage. Then, the baby. Must have complicated
things for her.

Well, I'm back in the States. Roy Armstrong
returns. But a MP stands guard at the door of my
room. Right now, outside of this room. Not
exactly the way I thought it would happen, and
certainly not the way China must think it happened. If she thinks about it. I hope someone
sets her straight, so she won't think I'm a
one-hundred percent louse. That I ran out on
her. The papers were full of Avila and Moreno,
so she would have read that part. Maybe she knew
about it beforehand?

But here I am, across the border. Back in the
USA! Turn down that fanfare, boys, I can't take
all this fuss.

How can it be put right, she was asking that
early morning in the zócalo? After being lost for
five hundred years, how can her country be found?
Returned. Her idea of it. The election proved to
her once more the betrayal of the Revolution. The
people were governed by *rateros y rameras*.
Thieves and whores, she said. Her father among
them? Yes, she nodded. Yes, he worst of all. Her
tears glittered like diamonds. Hard and cold.
She had finally passed judgment. Her features
carved in reddish brown stone. In the name of
justice, she said, we must act even if the act
does not bring justice. Some day what we do will
bring justice. We keep acting until justice
comes. We are laying stones in a marsh and we will
keep laying stones in a swamp and, then, one day,

a stone will stay on the surface. Then we will build on that stone. Her language wears the same seriousness as when she talks of dancing. She's not fooling around. The dog cook and the corn god had been dancing for more than just your usual storytelling. I missed it all, *el tonto*. Her friendship with Sylvia. This guy Jacson — however he spelled his name. She had met him in Paris with Sylvia, she said. That was all. But was that all? Some day, maybe she will explain it to me.

Yes, some day.

"The Mexican government has a warrant out for your arrest," they tell me yesterday. Col. McKnight, some brass from G-2 and a gumshoe from the FBI. We're sitting around the colonel's office and I'm being brought up to date — the breathtaking adventures of Juan Carillo. Outside, Kelly Field is busy. Kids learning how to fly. "They say you're an accessory to Trotsky's murder."

"They've been misinformed," I say.

"But you did know this guy — what's his name?" One of the army brass asks. He wears artillery tabs.

"Jacson-Mornand...alias Frank Jacson." The FBI fills us in. "Without the *k*."

"How'd you meet him?"

"We met at a dance. It was the social season."

"Who introduced you?" Now there's a question that makes a pilgrim pause.

"His aunt," I finally reply. The FBI guy is taking notes like a freshman.

"This Senora Moreno?"

"Yes, Mrs. Brown." They're not laughing.

"The same woman you say forced you to fly her and Gen. Avila out of Mexico?"

"The very lady. I'll do most anything when a Mauser pistol is shoved in my ear."

G-2 suspects I'm not telling the whole story. And he's right! Mrs. Brown meant business. I had just seen her use that cannon. Second nature for her. Like she was adjusting the foundation supporting her hefty bosoms. Just a minute — Halstead said — who do you think you are? BLAM! The pistol hardly bucked in her hand. Just like that. BLAM! One shot and it's Charlie Halstead meet Sgt. Death. How much of a big shot are you now? Right through the heart. BLAM! I play the scene over again. She turned around and fired point blank, like he was a fly that was bothering her. I'll always take orders from someone in that frame of mind. You can bet your last potato, Molly.

"It was Mr. Halstead who asked you to meet him at the airport? For what reason?" They know all about Halstead.

"He employed me from time to time. I flew his guests around Mexico in the oil company's plane. Sightseeing and the like. He called me and I assumed he wanted to arrange another trip."

What I really assumed was that he wanted to take a shot at me. Arnett must have spilled the beans about our episode in the hangar. Jesus, what a dummy. What can I blame this on? The weather? Her money? Are rich women built different? Well, I know some of that answer, I guess. What is it with us, so easily led around by our dicks? Stop bawling, Armstrong. So you got medals — you're still a dope.

But Arnett was getting clingy. Leaving messages for me everywhere. Hung around the Regis. Once not enough for her? So, she must have told Halstead. I get the news from my boss. "Halstead wants to meet you tomorrow afternoon," George Rhyl says.

"I'm on the Tampico run tomorrow afternoon."

"I just took you off the Tampico run," George says. "You meet him where and when he says." I forgot Cherokee Oil pays some of the airline's bills.

So, the secret is out. I'll have to tell China, I thought. Good-bye to happiness. The gray Dodge had just pulled into the field and parks inside the hangar. I'm standing outside by the Beechcraft. I've had the plane warmed up in case Halstead wants me to fly him somewhere.

Just in case that's all this meeting is about. Arnett is with him. She looks unhappy. But then, she never looks very cheerful. My breath catches in my throat. Then all hell breaks loose.

A wing of Ryan trainers has just lifted off outside the colonel's window. The army brass are grinning and looking at each other sideways. "Mrs. Brown, or whatever her name is, was this man Jacson's mother," G-2 tells me. "Moreover, we suspect the three of them — she, Jacson, and the general — were NKVD. Russian agents sent to Mexico to kill Trotsky. Orders from Stalin." He has looked for confirmation but FBI keeps a poker face. "We're not sure of their real names. She was born in Cuba."

"That's true of David Siquerios. Also NKVD," FBI says. "You knew him?"

"We slept together." I enjoy their expressions. "On the *Sinaia*. Bunkmates."

"You seem to have hobnobbed with some fairly dubious characters," another says. They pass the joke around. These guys are the Eddie Cantors of the Officers Club.

"We all met on the boat coming over," I say. "Orphans of the storm."

"What brought you to Mexico?" the civilian asks. He doesn't look up from his notebook.

"The climate," I say.

"What Capt. Armstrong means," McKnight jumps in. He opens up a folder on his desk. I note he uses my commission. "He means the climate of the times. If you gentlemen will review his record," and he does so. No need to go into that *here*. My war record. My efforts to get back into uniform. Every visit to the Embassy had been marked down. Emory has forwarded everything. They kept track of me all that time. Everything in a folder on his desk. Some letters from Hap Arnold and Spatz which I didn't know about. My old wingmates came through after all! McKnight's an okay guy too; the government had him flying airmail a few years back, and he stuck it out just to stay in the service.

"Also," he's saying as he holds up another paper. "Here's a telegram from Cherokee Oil. They're happy the plane is in one piece. So no charges there. And let me say, Captain Armstrong, that was one helluva piece of flying."

In all modesty, I have to agree. It must be a record. Nonstop — Mexico City to Laredo. And with a pistol at my head. Consuelo was damn serious. She would have killed us all. It didn't matter to her. She was furious with Jacson, her boy, for messing up the job. Her kid had fucked up and mama was mad.

She and the General had been waiting outside Trotsky's house. Car idling. When they heard shots, they knew the thing had gone sour and took off for the airport. Jacson was supposed to use only the pick-axe. A wild guess — they could hitch a ride somewhere. And there I was, waiting for Halstead.

When I got the Beechcraft to altitude, I leaned the mixture, and started to figure how I was going to get us out of Mexico — all the way to the border. The tanks had been topped. Having your own oil company sees to that. But we had to make every ounce count. Thaden and Blanche Noyes flew all the way across the US in one of these staggerwings. But they had extra tanks. Also, they stopped to refuel. In Kansas, I think. But they made it by reducing power to less that two-thirds. It took them fifteen hours, but they won the Bendix!! So I was trying to figure how to stretch out 174 gallons, 20 or so per hour. Headwinds across the nose the whole way. The chart showed Laredo to be the best bet. They had a field — a strip left over from Pershing's expedition down here. I mean Mexico. I leaned the mixture until the prop turned over just enough to keep us airborne. We landed in Laredo on fumes after dark. The field had a few lights.

I'll always remember Halstead's astonishment when Consuelo plugged him. Something he hadn't planned on and couldn't buy off. What's this, he was thinking? This is not the way it's supposed to be. BLAM!

The FBI guy is not ready yet to give me the green light. "What troubles me is that you flew agents of a foreign power surreptitiously into the United States. You say they forced you to do so. But, you cannot prove this, can you? Your relationship with this China Suarez, your socializing with Leon Trotsky, your past connections with the communist dominated government of Spain — well," he has to pause and take a breath. My sordid history is just too much for him. I am thinking of that line from Alberti's poem. Truly, I have been born with the wall of the firing squad on my back. And guys like this pull the trigger. What is it all worth anyhow? You think you are doing the right thing, and guys like this FBI gumshoe call it treason. *La Traicion,*as China would say. None of it comes out right. No wonder Tinker flew West. There's no way home for any of us.

"Would you tell us again, just what had brought you to the airport on the afternoon of August 20?" He takes another breath. "You say, Cherokee Oil let you use their plane to give flying lessons? You say you were waiting for one of these people on the afternoon of August 20?"
Outside, the wing of trainers buzzes the field. They set up a humming inside me. Damn, they sounded good. The second day here, McKnight takes me over to a hangar and shows me the new P-38 fighter, a twin-engine design with the cockpit in a pod set between tail booms. Fast and sassy looking.
"No, I didn't say that. Mr. Halstead wanted to talk to me about a charter flight of some kind. That's what I figured."
"Why didn't he call you on the phone?"
"The Mexican phone service is notoriously unreliable," I replied and looked out the window. "Maybe, he tried." It is a cloudless sky over Texas.

"For whom was this charter to be?"

"I never got the name." The guys in Operations had begun to look strange at me. Arnett was leaving messages there every day. Some of them could have been cousins of China's. I was looking bad.

"And it was Mr. Halstead who asked you to meet him?" The FBI agent was putting together his case.

All at once, I can see what FBI is driving at, and it's not me. The design in his head; the lines being drawn from dot to dot. Trotsky's rantings about American and German grabs at Mexican oil were in the papers all the time. Everyone said it was Trotsky who had convinced Cárdenas to take over Standard Oil, Cherokee and the rest, in the first place. So, FBI is wondering, could a guy like Halstead and Joe Stalin be in the same bed? Have mutual interests? And how about the Nazis? They had been bankrolling China's papa. And why? Oil, baby.

"Do you have any reason to think that Halstead had something to do with the Trotsky murder?" He was an earnest type. Nebraska corn seed still in his trouser cuffs.

"Beats me," I said. "I'm just a taxi driver. You heard all kinds of things." Without shame, I add, "Mexico is a mystery for an American like me." McKnight's eyes do a slow roll.

"Sorry to put you through this again, Capt. Armstrong," FBI is also using my rank now. "But could you just go over these details once more? You were waiting with the plane at the airport. You had warmed up the engine?"

"That's right." Ready to go, parked outside the hangar on the edge of the field. In fact, I had just watched Miguel take off on the Tampico run. He had the DC-2's wheels up almost before he broke ground. I taught him that. I remember thinking; that Aztec eagle is going to make a hot pursuit pilot! But then, a great sadness came over me, because I wasn't on that plane, heading for Tampico with him. Something told me I would never fly that route, with Miguel beside me, again. And, of course, this meant something much more. I might never see China again. My stomach turned to lead.

"Go on." I have stopped talking.

"I see this touring car, top down, turn into the area near the passenger station. It careens at a high speed. Looks to be out of control. Then heads in my direction."

Avila is at the wheel. He barely can see over the wheel. Consuelo sits beside him, directing him this way and that. She must have seen the Beechcraft parked outside. No one around. What if I hadn't been there? Would she have tried to fly it? I wouldn't put it past her. Wouldn't surprise me if she knew how. She's got on a purple beret and a frilly blouse cut deep, but she's all business.

Also, the gray Dodge has already pulled up and parked in the hangar mouth. It had come through the service gate by the fuel storage. Halstead at the wheel, Arnett next to him. They sit there and talk. Like an argument. I am more than certain, this is some kind of a showdown for the three of us. So, I've got two carloads of crazy people coming at me.

The Defender of Madrid gets to me first. He brakes and stalls the car's engine. Consuelo is out quickly, and he scurries around after her. *"Ah, es Capitán Carillo,"* she says. *"Qué afortunado."* She motions the general to get into the plane.

"I'm waiting for a passenger," I say. Halstead is just getting get out of the Dodge inside the hangar. Arnett leans out the window and yells something after him. That's what it looked like.

"Si, correcto," Consuelo is saying. "We are passenger." And at this point, I tell everyone this morning, she pulls out this huge pistol from her handbag. It had an oversize magazine snapped into it with rounds enough to fire until Wednesday.

"So you complied?" FBI asked.

"You bet your last cookie," I say, leaving out the rest of it. Halstead is trotting up with this perplexed, aggravated look on his face. He resembles a line judge at Wimbledon who has just had his call overruled. What is *this*? Who are these *people*? I could see it on his face. He is about to say, look here, he wanted to say, this is very irregular. Who are you to interfere this way? To be in my way. This is our business. This is my plane. This is my pilot. My Mexico. My world.

"What in hell is going on here?" is what he did say. You could tell how weary he was of people like this foolish woman in this silly purple hat making his days so unnecessarily difficult.

If I had had any thoughts of disobeying Consuelo Moreno up until then, the look on her face that instant quickly discouraged them. She just turns around and takes aim. Like she's just remembered to powder her nose. BLAM!

"They got in and you took off."

"Just like that." Well, not exactly like that. As we get out to the runway and I wait for the green light — I forget to put on the radio — and I see Arnett has Halstead under the arms and is dragging his body toward the car in the hangar. His white Panama keeps falling off, rolls around her feet and she stops to put it back on his head once, then again and finally clamps it between her teeth, like a terrier bringing slippers. I have a last glimpse of her, legs braced and straining with the effort pulling him along the tarmac toward their car. I've got the throttle pushed to the firewall by then and we break ground.

"Did they say anything during the flight? About the Trotsky murder?"

"They talked about how this Jacson guy had bungled the job. That's all I could understand. The rest of the time, they spoke Russian. General Avila became sick and threw up."

"And in Laredo you say they took a taxi."

"That's right. Just got out of the plane and walked over to the operations shack where a couple of cars were parked. I guess one of them was a taxi. It was dark and I can't be sure."

"And that's the last you saw of them?"

"Yes." Naturally, I didn't tell the brass about Consuelo's adieu. When the engine cut off, almost on its own, she leans over and gives me a big mushy kiss. "*Hasta la vista,*" she says. "We are part of history, Carillo." She smelled like a ripe papaya in the sun. Some momma.

All of us sit silent for a while in the colonel's office. The students overhead bring their trainers in low over the building making a spoon in a cup on his desk rattle. Happy vibrations. I'm still a Red who's an enemy of his people. Yet, here are these letters and documents that say I'm some kind of a hero.

The colonel's telephone rings. He listens for a minute. Looks at me. "Sure," he says. Then he gets up and goes to the office door. "This should clear up everything," he says and opens the door. In walks Peggy Arnett.

8/28/40
Thursday
16:10

I'm going to miss wearing this old straw sombrero. Bought it in the market at Mérida, near the church. A very fine weave. The same day, that night I wandered into the Don Quixote and saw China dance that first time. It's been lucky for me.

No MPs on guard at my door now. I wish they were still standing guard! They've just built this barracks. Not even locks on the doors yet. The whole airfield is being put together. The winds of war blowing. But MPs or locks, it wouldn't matter anyway. Arnett will pull out her bankroll and push on through. Like she did yesterday. And aren't you an ungrateful wretch, McGee? The way she went to bat for you. But, she wants something, I'm pretty sure. But what?

Another roll in the hay? We have a five o'clock date.

"Lets have a drink," she said. "We have to talk." And it was pretty funny how she brought all that brass to their feet. Tiny as she is. Like royalty coming in a room. The Arnett millions pulling them up by their ears like hound dogs. Every man suddenly standing stiff. Well, Jack and I know about that, don't we? I couldn't help thinking at the moment, that I knew a whole lot more about her than they did. *Qué piojo!*

She saved my goose yesterday. Jumped on the Missouri Pacific and came up to San Antonio. Emory at the consulate had told her what was happening. "What a witness!" McKnight clapped me on the back. "Did you see the look on the FBI when I introduced her? You are a lucky man, Armstrong."

After they all troop out, McKnight takes me aside. "Your girlfriend has gone to ground. That's the report I have."

"She's my wife. As I remember, that automatically makes her an American citizen."

"They need some details. Like, where were you married? What bureau has the certificate?"

"It was a small ceremony. Early in the morning," I say. The two of us on top of that pyramid, dancing and kissing. The truth settles upon me as I make it up. I am truly wedded to China. "A family affair with a local priest. They didn't go in for paper work. You have to take my word for it."

"Hey, Roy, I believe you. But it's the bureaucrats. There's a lot that bothers them. Her father assassinated. Her disappearance. One report puts her in the mountains with some rebels. Then, you flying out the people that knocked off Trotsky. It's not your usual domestic situation, you have to admit." He smiles at me. My mind is still buzzing with Arnett. The way she showed up so cool and calm. No nervousness. Like steel rolling out of one of her factories.

"You know, a lot could happen if you could

demonstrate your good citizenship," McKnight says after a minute. He was handing me the papers that set me free. Return my citizenship, but not my honor commission. The field has gone quiet. No flights. Classroom stuff must be going on. Navigation and the like. All those new instruments. I feel old and tired. Why do I even want to try.

"And how do I do that?" I ask, knowing the answer.

"Sign on with us here. Forget about combat. You're over the hill, Roy. Like me. Stand up to it. You could teach these kids a lot. There'd be a pair of oak leaves in it for you. That's what I'm told. We've got a hell of a dogfight coming at us. You know what the Germans are like. You've gone toe-to-toe with them. Face it. You can't go back to Mexico." Was he reading my mind? "They'll throw you in the clink. Ever seen a Mex pokey? You'll rot."

He leans forward all chummy. "I heard from Jimmy Doolittle today. He phoned me this morning. He told me to ask you to do this job for us, for the Air Corps, as a personal favor to him."

McKnight was remarkable the way he held his eyes level. That Doolittle had called him about me was a most outstanding piece of bullshit, but the lie showed how desperate they were to have me. "Find my wife," I said finally.

"We'll do our best."

"Better than that."

"Look, she's disappeared. Everybody is looking for her. The Mexican government. Her old man's people. A couple of private armies. It's like the Keystone Cops down there." He sees my look. "Okay, okay. We'll send in the Marines, if we have to." It's a bad joke, but I let it go. He's shoving these other papers across at me. He's had them prepared all along. Well, what choice do I have? He's right, I can't go back to Mexico. I'd be on the lam down there. One more exile. I could do stunts in Hollywood—working for wages. Teaching youngsters a few tricks would make me feel part of the action.

Close to the show. So, I sign. I'm back in the
Service. Isn't it just like... Arnett coming.

Later...

Esta encinta
"And you're saying it's mine?"
She nods and for a moment I think her watch
face is going to wind up and cry. But she pulls
up straight and sits all prim on the edge of the
chair. Hands in her lap around a white leather
purse. That's been the message she'd been trying to leave me, she says. That she was *preggie*.
That's the way she puts it. She fits a cigarette
into that slim ebony holder and snaps a silver
lighter to it. Holds the whole rig up like she's
about to conduct some music. About to conduct *my*
music.
She's a sight in this bare officer's quarters. Holds herself tight as the blanket corners
on the cot, but she could be perched on a chair
in some fancy club. She's wearing a jacket and
skirt; linen. Her blouse buttoned up to the top.
Shoes; sensible, good leather and fancy tooled.
She has the look of a wealthy tourist waiting
for the tour to begin. Which, in a way, is what
she is.
But, I'm not one of the sights. "I don't
believe it."
"Believe what you want," she replies.
"What about Halstead?"
"Halstead was a fool," she says, and blows
out a thin line of smoke. She means more than
him, it sounds like. All men are fools. Well,
I can't argue with that much.
"Any fool can do it," I say.
"Oh, well, all right. Maybe, once or twice,"
she snaps. "We had our little experiments. But
it was all business. You see, Captain, *I* am
Cherokee Oil. Charles was just my stand-in. He
was necessary to have in business. In business,
no one listens to a woman. Those are the rules.
I've learned to play them." She looks around.

"Is smoking permitted in this place?"

"Sure," I say; then catch on. I find a saucer and hold it out to her. She delicately taps the cigarette ash into it. I'm left holding the saucer. "Me too—another experiment?"

She gives that funny smile. Now I know who she reminds me of. Will Rogers! The way he smiles. Lips turned down. "It was thrilling. *Per*-fectly thrilling," she says.

"More necessary than thrilling, maybe." Her eyes suddenly fix on me. Cool. She's taken stock of the place. Not a whole lot to inventory. My wallet and some Mexican *pesos* beside my journal on the table. My old sombrero on the bed. Borrowed togs hanging in the open wardrobe. She's checked out the cot too. "I thought we had a *per*-fectly fine time of it."

"Well, I guess you were kind of an experiment for me too," I tell her. "I'd never done it with an industrialist. And fucking a war hero must have been a novelty for you."

She doesn't move a hair. Takes a pull on the ebony holder and the smoke curls up into her nostrils. "Please believe me, Roy. I enjoyed the interlude immensely." Something is amusing her. "You must admit there's a certain comic aspect to our situation. If Halstead were alive, I would let our engagement come to full term, so to speak. No one would be the wiser. He'd marry me and then, I'd go to Reno. After the baby was born." She looks wide-eyed. A dumb chorus girl look. Even her shoes do a tap or two on the linoleum floor. But she's no chorus girl, and she's not dumb. "But Halstead is dead, so you see my predicament?"

I'm thinking if Mrs. Brown hadn't been so trigger-happy the other day, I'd be out of this free and clear too. Well, not entirely free. But I'd still be in Mexico. China. Where are you? "Did Halstead know about us?"

"It was none of his business. Whether he did or not, was of no importance."

"But why did the two of you show up at the airport? Why did Halstead ask me to meet him?"

"About your citizenship, of course. Your

commission. I had Halstead meet with the ambassador. He got in touch with Roosevelt. You had been cleared. I was in touch with someone close to Congressman Dies. You were being dropped from his list."

"Jesus, was I that great?"

"I thought it was the least I could do," she says and looks down, like Lillian Gish in a silent movie. I have to laugh and so does she. All of a sudden I feel a little sorry for her and I don't want to. She's had to put on some act or other all the time. Running her daddy's business. Has to hire a jerk like Halstead to be a stand-in. But it's a mistake to feel sorry for her; she shifts gears quickly. "I was of some service to you yesterday. You needed me as a witness." Her chin is thrust out. She's here to collect.

"But, I am already married."

"Yes, yes. Call it what you will. I know all about your little *novia*. You know, of course, she's wanted by every kind of police in Mexico. The talk is that she pulled the trigger on her father herself. Nasty business." She wrinkles her nose. "But, she does sounds interesting." Her eyes measure me. She's maybe overlooked something in the merchandise, then they flicker away. "They say she's run off with bandits in the *Madre del Sur*. I couldn't quite follow everything. Quite a scandal." She takes a tiny lace handkerchief from her purse and squeezes her nose with it.

I picture China on horseback. I never saw her ride a horse. She's probably a fine horsewoman. Part of the animal. Like everything she does. How about the baby — our baby? Horse riding might cause problems.

"So, now, Captain, I need your help. I'm prepared to be generous." She motions for the saucer again and flips out the cigarette stub. It smolders — someone else is supposed to snub it out. I do that. "What I propose won't interfere with your romance. If you do ever see her again. In fact, you both will be set up for life." She grips the small purse in her lap.

"More flying lessons?"

"Don't try to be humorous, Captain. You don't have the wit for it," she says and crosses her legs. Her idea is that I'm to meet her in San Antonio tomorrow and we get married before a JP. She's spent the day setting it up, hired a lawyer, bribed a few clerks. And that will be the last I'm to see of her. She's going to reopen the old family place in Pittsburgh and have the baby there. I'll be the soldier boy in the background, serving my country as she gives birth. I'll be a name on the the birth certificate. Maybe, she'll import me for the christening. I'll be in uniform of course. Her friends will think it *per*-fectly romantic. Peggy and her war hero she met in Mexico. A flyer. Flyers are all the rage right now, thanks to Lindy. *Per*-fectly thrilling.

"After an appropriate time, I'll go to Reno. Unless you are killed or something." Or something. Widow of the hero shot down in flames. Would she bury me in Pittsburgh? Think of it, Roy Armstrong, buried in Pittsburgh, in the family plot. Home at last.

"What about doing something," I say. "A doctor in Pittsburgh or somewhere. You must know someone."

"Of course." She sits up straight. I can't remember why I was so hot on her. Don't want to remember probably. I can't even visualize what she looks like under those clothes. In fact, I never did see much of her. It had been efficient and practical. Just enough exposure to get the job done. Both of us wanting to get it out of our systems. That's how it felt.

"Yes, I could have an operation, but, frankly, I'm curious about giving birth. The experience appeals to me." She flutters her eyes. "Motherhood. That's what every woman wants to experience, isn't it?" She doesn't sound serious. But who can tell?

"So you lease me, like one of your oil wells or...?"

"Don't be tiresome."

"But I might not be the father," I say. "You and Halstead also..." and why stop there, I'm thinking? A toreador or two? Or a painter like Rivera? Just for the experience? I suddenly have a picture of her and Trotsky going at it and give a laugh. She looks perplexed.

"But you could be. You have a moral obligation, at least. Don't you think?" She stands up. Clearly, the board meeting is adjourned. The vote has gone her way.

Talk to me about moral obligations? I've been in a lot of moral obligations and they've all come out wrong. China said she loves me for that, that I signed up for the moral obligations. But what do I have to show for it. And now Arnett's turning that knob.

Then, there's those "experiments" with Halstead? Maybe it wasn't just business or just once or twice. Maybe she combined business with pleasure a whole lot. The time I went to his place; the atmosphere seemed downright cozy between them. She walks to this table where I write this. She sits down and opens her purse and takes out a check book. She takes out a slim gold pen and uncaps it.

"Just to show my good faith," she is saying. "I'll give you a — well, shall we call it a retainer?" The idea amuses her. She looks startled when I put my hand on hers, stop her.

"Let me think about it," I say. "Marriage is a serious business. Lets have that drink, and we can talk more about it. The officer's club has just opened."

"What's this?" she asks. She taps my journal.

"Just a record book, " I tell her.

"You keep a diary?" She gives a girlish laugh and looks surprised. That I can write.

"Just since I left Spain."

"Isn't that amazing?" she says and lifts up the cover a little, as if to take a peek; then, lets it drop. "Truly amazing." I usher her out of the room. I need to shower and shape up, I tell her. Give me a half hour and we'll meet at the club. She's looking hard and holds the purse tight to her chest.

One morning, China, you and I got some burros and rode up to the top of Monte Alban.
Oaxaca lay below on the valley floor. This is
your territory. You may be hiding out in these
mountains as I write this. With your mother's
people. I want to hold this moment, the picture
of this other time, hard in my mind before I
meet Arnett at the bar. Like a talisman. My
offering of corn and pulque. Against temptation.
What she offers could be easy to do. Just like
the time in the hangar. Who will know, she kept
saying. I should have put up your picture
before. It might have helped.

The purple velvet of the mountains comes down
to Oaxaca from the north. The pyramids are being
dug out. An ancient observatory has been uncovered. This whole city carved and built on top
of a mountain a thousand years before Cortés.
Before Montezuma and the Aztecs. Wide stair-
cases. Enormous plazas. Temples. Tombs. Some
kind of ball court. My people, you said. You
took me to one temple with man-size figures
carved on the sides. They looked like guys doing
the frog kick underwater, but you said they were
dancers. See, you said, and there in broad day-
light, on the old stone floor of that temple,
you danced. And you didn't have to make it up.
You knew their dance. You knew how to place your
feet, bend your knees, hold your arms up and
out. The dance was within you. No music, just
you alone moving in the mountain light to the
cries of hawks overhead. The bushes around us
buzzing with toads. A light, cool breeze sometimes lifting your oil-black hair. Your warm,
cinnamon arms held out. The feast of your long
thighs. Now I see you dancing for another. Our
child.

This stone observatory had been built in the
center of the old city. The whole city revolved

around it. That whole culture had turned around this observatory as the universe it was built to study also turned around it, all with a precision that matches all the fancy instruments today. But the observatory never moved. Like a huge stone arrowhead, it points northeast. Come to think of it, in the direction of this BOQ at Kelly Field where I am writing this down. Isn't that strange? The Zapotec calendar was chiseled into the walls. Days and months. Years. Centuries. Not a linear measurement that goes from left to right or even from south to north. But the whole 360. Here, you pointed to some large dots and bars like shrapnel marks in the stone—we are here, you said. You and I, h'Armstrong. Forever, right here in this calendar, you said. And we held each other. Your eyes dark in the sunlight and your mouth full of laughter. It was hard to fit my lips around yours. To take in all your laughter. Slowly you let me.

Sometimes a somber *rebozo* fell over you. Sitting in the Papillon or riding in a streetcar. In your apartment, as you brushed your hair. The obsidian eyes would lose their fire as if dulled by the reflection of something past or present, historical or current. Which would make me wish, at that very moment, that my appearance into your life, that night at the hotel, had not caused you more anguish and pain, and sometimes — as if these thoughts jarred your reverie, you would suddenly turn to me, and your face would break open into a mischievous, sunny expression. I would feel like one of these archaeologists, digging around Monte Alban, coming on a valuable object which my ignorant handling breaks open so the innocent treasure within lies exposed, vandalized. I am no better than one of Cortes's thugs.

I could probably find one in San Antonio. I should hang up *un milagro* in the local church. If we had done only that for Tonantzin would we be different now? Never got her leg fixed. The three of us still together? Hey, the four of us! Those little tin pieces send up prayers for body parts; arms, legs, feet, a liver. What about the spirit? I'd have it made special. Something out of silver, something that will never tarnish, that will reflect our sunny afternoons, our starry nights — restore them? Our souls together? Bring back your breath softly to feather my shoulder. Your eyes looking so seriously into mine. Your anger and sorrows? Your sense of justice? How to put all that into a *milagro*?

You will forgive me. You will say, that I am like one of your ancient feathered gods, tossed about by evil winds and flying off course. Pushed behind the sun where it is always dark. But you will perform a magic. You will be the dog-woman cooking up this fine meal, patting out the corn tortillas. The smoke of your cooking fire will cloud the sun and the aroma from the black pot will reclaim me, and I will follow that aroma like a radio beam back down to earth. To you. Safe landing. Coming home, *cariño*. You have made me into a human being. *Nitlaca*.

Hardy sleeps through the afternoon to wake to the evening song of birds. The ache in his right ear has eased, and his hearing has cleared up, the klaxon set off by Clarence Adams's pistol shot has quit ringing. He lies looking up at the lapstraked ceiling, following the play of the fading light upon the varnished wood as he listens to robins settling down for the night. A pot is scraped in the kitchen. For just a moment, he thinks, it could be almost any time of his life in Pittsburgh. He could be waking from the fever of pneumonia when he was nine, from his first drunken spree when he was sixteen. Homework might wait for him on the kitchen table. For a moment, he has become ageless; then, he stirs and sits up and feels his real age. What about the bird? He still couldn't come up with a good answer. Adams had known he had no answer.

Twilight. Celia's favorite time of day, and her preference had always puzzled him. She was so optimistic, so practical. Early evening seemed so melancholy to him with its harmony of sadnesses, but he had often come on her standing by a western window, enthralled within the amber light. He puts her somewhere on Route 70. She would be driving into these same shadows as they come toward her, one bare arm perched cockily on the car's open window. Hardy finds himself crying. He has slept a monumental sleep like Rip Van Winkle's, one of those intervals we all have experienced that cannot always be measured in hours or even on a linear scale but vertically or centrifugally—he was all turned around—so we think it is only fair that we should wake to find things different; new signs hanging in the place of old, debts forgotten—even death reversed. That's what we expect on rising only to find nothing has changed. It is a heartbreaking fiction, a palliative drunk deep before waking to the dry and barren reality of ordinary circumstances.

Hardy remembers John Glenn and Robert McNamara lifting their ends of Bobby Kennedy's casket as the tears streaked their faces; a silent, manly show of grief that had made it all right for the rest of them in that cathedral to weep. Lately, he had seen McNamara on television, being interviewed because of his memoir on Vietnam, and the man was still crying as if he couldn't stop the lament begun decades ago. Had a spell been put upon them all, not to be broken until the prince awoke? It would seem so, in McNamara's case anyway, Hardy thought, and he would have to admit to the same indulgence in himself from time to time. But this evening he cries because a difference has taken place, a rearrangement of his life, like coming home from school that day to find all the furniture in this room had been changed.

His new reality had been wakened by the liquid warble of birds, but it was the scrape of the pot outside the door, that homely and familiar sound, that had stung his eyes. The man cleaning up in the kitchen is no longer his father. It was almost funny. Armstrong's journal had produced every child's fear—to be exposed as an orphan. And at his age! An orphan! Returning to attend one funeral, he had come upon another. Yes, maybe more than one. Ruth Hardy's comical disappearance, always a hurtful puzzle to him, has been explained by a truth that was even more hurtful. But the figure of the man on the other side of the door, methodically cleaning up the kitchen, makes him cry.

The seamless silence of all their evenings has been

explained. What had always seemed to be the awkwardness of two men living alone without a woman's presence had, it turns out, been normal for their circumstance. He must wonder if Bill Hardy had only been serving an appointed—even salaried appointment as a father, and doing this duty with the same meticulous attention he gave the family limousines. If you were Walt Hardy, such an idea might hurt you beyond any imagination, and you would have to drum up times of real affection, a hug during a ball game or a hasty kiss at bedtime. Then into his review comes Miss Arnett's face as he had waltzed her around the room. Or when she would call to him to come into her bedroom, put down her book and stare at him as if he had undergone some radical transformation since the day before. A crazy old lady look, he'd tell his roommates during bull sessions, and then she'd hold out this godawful candy—an offer far more inadequate than he could ever realize. Had she been about to say something those times? Struggling within herself for the right words and then settling for a piece of chocolate. *You must give me this dance, Walt.* He listens intently to her voice in his memory for some nuance unheard in his adolescent discomfort. Miss Arnett. Could he ever call her anything else?

He hears the man in the next room, carefully doing the dishes so as to not disturb him. Surely, all their years together must count for something in the heart, more than just a custodianship. He wonders if Bill Hardy had come to love him at all and what the level of that love would be if it could not rise on the ordinary tide of blood. Tears seep slowly once again, but he cries for the old man now, for he's being left behind once more. Diminished? No, if you are Walt Hardy, you swear to yourself that you will not let that happen.

Because, Armstrong's journal has somehow cut him loose from a past that had kept him earthbound, that has tied him to a nostalgia and a loss that had never been his to claim. A curious freedom with its own penalties for the weightlessness it grants. Others have not been so lucky with their epiphanies—Robert McNamara for instance. Their revelations only appear to put them deeper in debt to a past they cannot disavow, shake off. So he was oddly gratified by the hurt that Armstrong's journal has caused him; he sensed the healing qualities the punishment carried within its chastisement.

"What's the name of that comic," he says to Celia later this evening, "who keeps slapping his own face and says, 'Thanks, I needed that.' "

She says nothing for some time, and he even shifts the phone to his left ear, thinking she might be talking too softly for the deafened one to hear. In actual fact, he had caught her off-guard and she is trying to pull herself together. Finally, she gets back to what she has rehearsed. "Of course, I hadn't planned to call you yet," she answers. "But it was on the TV when I checked into this motel." Bill Hardy has moved decently into the living room after handing him the phone in the kitchen. "I was planning to put a little more distance between us. Wait until I got settled, got a job."

"Where are you?"

"Outside of Richmond, Indiana."

"You can't seem to get out of Indiana?"

"I'll make it this time." Her quick laugh makes him feel a little better. "Picking up where I left off. But, it was on the news. Your sitting with him and all. How is she? Shirley?"

"All right. The family is with her. His and hers. A bunch of them are staying with her."

Hardy will look at the clean plates stacked on the table. He had volunteered to wash up after their meal, and they had made a pretty good exchange about him doing the dishes, did he need an apron and so on—two grown men making a sport of their blocky strangeness. Trying to be as usual. But it hadn't been the same. They had tried to make a good run of conversation out of it, like a newly divorced couple still being civil in their new relationship. Or, like two buddies in a camp. Had it ever been different?

He will wait until the day he leaves Pittsburgh before he brings up what he has discovered. And Bill Hardy will surprise him. "Yes, Mr. Halstead was your father," he will say with a shrug as if the fact is of no great import; a secret he has held for so long that it has worn thin, not worth keeping any longer. He will almost seem relieved as the title is lifted from his squared shoulders. "But you see..." and then he tells Hardy everything. No, not everything, Hardy thinks, because the old man does not know everything. Only *he*, Walt Hardy knows everything and it's a kind of fairy tale. The Little Match Girl and Her Three Fathers. Celia will laugh. But, as they dry the dishes this night—just before she calls him—they still play out the old myth. Do you call that glass clean, the old man jokes? Give it here! Let a man at the job!

"It was on the news here," she says again. She might be going through her purse for a tissue or a mint. He would imagine all this. "You must think I'm a shit." She doesn't sound too remorseful.

"You missed a great lunch." Bill Hardy has settled down in front of the TV.

"Like what?"

"Corned beef hash with a poached egg in the middle. Canned succotash. The hash came out of the can too. Not like the old days when he..."

"Yes, I remember."

Then, the distance between him and Celia would come unspooled , a long ribbon of silence that neither could cut off, until she abruptly tells him she has to go. Go where?

A year later, they would have much more to talk about, and their conversation would be easier. Her job in Las Vegas, and the racy, slightly dangerous characters who employed her to keep their accounts. Shouldn't she be a little careful? Not to worry; they treated her like a kid sister, she would say, giving him examples of their bemused gallantry. The books had to be clean—honest, that's why they hired her. He would relate the different steps of his appeal. What his lawyers said and did. His job offers. She would relay the funny, often macabre stories she heard, repeat these tales, the outrageously funny, dirty jokes with the breathless gasps of a schoolgirl. So he would feel she yet remained a spectator, still in the audience and still a little shocked by what she witnessed. Even to find herself talking about it.

"I find it curious that you are able to work for these characters," he says once.

She gets his meaning. For a moment, he's afraid he's gone too far. But, she finally answers, "I'm satisfied that they've done nothing illegal. I certainly am doing nothing illegal for them. Know what I mean?" She changes the subject. "How's Bill?"

She has come to refer to him by name. In fact, Hardy can tell her, he had stopped off in Pittsburgh lately to see him. He had stayed downtown in a hotel, not at the carriage house, which seemed to have disappointed the old man. He had got in stuff to cook breakfast. But, they had a few hours together, and Walt had taken him to dinner at a new restaurant that had opened up in the old market district. "He didn't like the menu much," he tells Celia. "Kept joking with the waitress and asking for fried steak."

"What did you talk about?"

Hardy knew her question has another object. Not so much what but how did he talk. "We enjoyed ourselves. I told him I loved him, it seemed to embarrass him." Actually, Bill Hardy had covered his hand with his own, quickly pulling it away when the girl brought their plates. Celia says nothing and he doesn't quite know what her silence means. "Hey, I've got a line on a couple of jobs as a consultant."

"What are you being consulted about?"

"Would you believe parking lots? That's the latest. How big the parking lot should be for a shopping center in Louisiana?" The idea seemed to amaze her, and her end of the line whispered to itself in the desert. This would be when he called after the closing on the house in Maryland. He was telling her the balance less his lawyers' fees was in the mail. "Your life there sounds exciting," he would say finally. The empty living room echoed his voice; all the furniture was in storage or sold.

"How do you mean?"

"Well, the lush life. High rollers. You know." With the phone, he walked across the bare parquet floor to the window. He still held the instrument to his left ear out of habit. Hearing in his right ear has almost completely returned. Sometimes, stalled in traffic or browsing a newspaper stand, the blast of Clarence Adams's pistol would blank out the light. Make him momentarily blind. As he talks to her, rabbits play hide and seek in the tall grass where they had once talked of putting up a swing set.

"I've had my chances," she would say at last and laugh. Outside her window, the neon play of the casino marquees gives the night a peachy ambiance, rather like the light in a funeral parlor. But her apartment, on the outskirts of town, was tidy and with a balcony that looked west. The sunsets were the best yet, she would tell him, and she would even call him sometimes to describe the light as it changed. More than once, because of the time differences, these descriptions would wait for him on his answering machine, and he would sit in the darkness of his apartment when he got home and listen to her voice carefully record the varying shades of purple, the crimsons and how the sand slowly went to gray. She would describe everything faithfully as if she were recording a lesson assignment.

Once she asks, "Did you ever figure out how she got Armstrong's journal?"

"I think she must have stolen it. Came back to his room after they talked. At that Army barracks in Texas. Probably worried about what he had written down about her. She could have waited until he was out of his room. In the shower or whatever. Or, she could have paid someone to do it. That would be like her."

"Your mama."

"Give me a break.

"Maybe he sent it to her?"

"Why would he do that?"

"For you."

Hardy lays back on the sofa. "That's quite an idea. I'll have to think about that," he says finally.

But on this night in Pittsburgh, during the first of these phone talks, Celia has been gathering the loose threads of their conversation. She asks about the event on Butler Street. "How come you went down there?"

"Just to see him."

"Why?" She wouldn't let him off so easy. She knew him; nothing wasted; every movement had its meaning. Hardy, the can-do guy. Celia looks over the printed materials arranged on the table next to the motel bed as she waits for his answer. The place has its own restaurant.

"Why?" Hardy would repeat the word but not the question. To tell her the truth might drive her even farther away, push her off the map. He had torn up Peggy Arnett's blank check, let the pieces of it litter the streets as he drove back to Point Breeze. It was a summons he was tearing up; no more than a parking ticket in a town he was never going to drive through again. "I can't tell you why. I just felt drawn to him, that's all. Call it telepathy. "

The answer was not good enough. Celia hears a familiar resonance in his voice, that brassy ring of dissemblance. "I'm starving," she says. "They have a Thai restaurant here."

"Don't go," Hardy would say.

"We'll talk again. Don't worry."

"Will we?" A sob comes out of nowhere, catches him unawares. She must have heard.

"This is hard for you to understand, I know. I do love you, Walt. This isn't good-bye."

"Sure sounds like it. Listen. Just a minute. I want to tell you something." He could tell she hasn't completely turned off.

"How it felt," he would say. Celia would wait a little more, sits back down on the motel bed in Indiana.

Hardy remembers how Adams's hand had felt. He wanted to make every word count with her. He remembered the large, toughened palm as it pressed his. He almost described the texture to her. Celia would shrug off the description as sentimental. Did he really feel those words? Or was he just trying to keep her attention? The calluses of a working class hand—is that what he wanted to lay on her? He could hear her saying all that, just as the old Hardy joins the laughter of a sitcom. It's a hearty, deep laugh, like Nixon's, he thought, and not for the first time.

"Well, so?" her voice would insist. Her patience is running out.

"Like a hand-off of something. Like he was giving me something. He had said—*Here*—and I thought then he meant for me to take his hand, just take it, you know? But I think he meant something else. Take this, like he was—well, like I said, giving me something."

The wall clock continues its casual give-and-take. Tick-tock. Maybe another dimension was being calculated, Hardy would think. Not the hour or minute, but larger than all of that, to include the silence that stretches out between them, the space and the figures within that space. Everything broken down, split into segments, seconds, degrees; reduced to a fraction. Analyzed. A relentless, banal measurement.

"I have to go," Celia says after a bit and she hangs up without giving him a chance to say more.

But she would call him again in several weeks to give him her new phone number. She had relocated herself. She had never intended to disappear, she told him. She had just found the apartment with the balcony facing west. She wanted him to know how her new place looked, the different rooms of this new life. She wanted him to know how happy she was, setting up her new life—she was okay—like a kid going away to school, away from home for the first time. He could hear this headiness in her voice. So began many telephone calls, back and forth; each speaking from different time zones but within the same familiar zone of their old affection. The history of it.

"So now what?" She would ask him about a year later. He had caught her as she was dressing to go out to dinner. By this time, Hardy would have appreciated another change in her voice; a more confident sound; even youthful. A lilt that he reasoned had sprung from the fun she was having with her success. "You sound sleepy."

"It's been a long day," he would say, thinking his night was ending while hers was just beginning. The court hearing had been tedious and even its exultant finish, the liberating verdict, had come with its own tax on his energy.

"So you and North and Poindexter all get off. Nobody goes to jail, as Clarence Adams said. Remember?" Then she would add very quickly. "But, I'm happy for you, Walt." Her voice would have gone up, and he would hear something of the old days in it, when they had talked to people in those back rooms in the Catskills about the impossible happening. He could remember how Cee's voice would lift; when she had trusted him and when she believed all the numbers that he was bending might give up an important, justifiable sum.

"I read you are going to write a book?" She would almost be giggling.

"There have been some offers, but I don't think so."

"You would make a great movie. Who would play you? Clint Eastwood?"

He enjoys her jab—how he has missed that. "I have another idea." Right then, Hardy would be tempted to suggest he come for a visit. Just to celebrate the verdict, his innocence proclaimed if not restored. How about it, now that he was officially innocent? Outside his condominium's window, Washington sparkled against the day's snowfall. The city's lights turned the avenues and buildings into a huge confection. The hopeful music of the Christmas season was everywhere; not be escaped.

But the ease of the impulse was suspicious, made him hesitate before he said anything. For just a little too long. Maybe the idea had been lofted into the air, a balloon escaping his grasp, for he could sense Celia turning away as if she might have pulled his idea down out of the atmosphere and was trying to find a kindly way of disposing of it.

"Still there?"

"Still here." Actually, she would have turned away to her closet, to its back wall and the array of shoeboxes, row upon row, from floor to ceiling. They resembled the doors of safety deposit boxes in a bank vault, and she did sometimes chide herself for this indulgence, these self-awarded prizes. Like that Marcos woman in the Philippines. All acquired since she came to Las Vegas. Just to make a choice of shoe, as she would be doing while talking to him on the phone gave her a little thrill. Like a miser. But, she didn't even play the slots, nor follow up on tips her employers gave her on games and fights. She could have some fun. Sometimes she felt a little embarrassed by the collection. But only a little.

And then, Walt Hardy would begin talking on an entirely different line which was so unexpected that Celia sat down on the bed to listen. Everything up to then had been the usual line of narrative; once-upon-a-time stuff, and then what happens next? The story took a surprising turn of cards which changed the game. Turned toward an ending different from what she expected. She would have crossed one leg across the other to massage the pad of her stockinged foot as she listened. Where did he get this idea? Was there some church group behind it?

"You know, I've always wanted a brother," he shifted the subject slightly.

"How about a sister?" Celia automatically asked, then was sorry she snapped. Thoughtless. Let him have a brother, what difference would it make? She decided against a pair of gold sandals. Too formal.

"Okay, a sister. Either. It would be family. I could look up them up."

"You're not even sure it would be your family. What if Halstead was the lucky fellow? Really was your daddy?"

"Close enough to a family. China Suarez was a little famous. Must be something down about her."

And that led her to bring up Bill Hardy—the other family. Hardy told her about the last time he had seen the old man. His job as assistant curator of the Arnett mansion had given him a whole new character. He had become almost loquacious. "It must come from talking to the tourists," Hardy tells Celia. "He stands by the front door, in the entrance foyer, and greets them, has this long speech that he's memorized about the place. He even makes a few jokes. Never knew he had such a sense of humor." But he does not describe to Celia how he felt when they parted this last time. It was midafternoon. They had just left the little snack bar that had been made out of the ginger-bread playhouse Peggy Arnett had used as a little girl. "This coffee could be a little stronger," Bill Hardy had apologized for the place.

"Not up to CCC standards," Hardy had joked.

"That's for damn sure," the other said and looked away. Found something of interest out in the garden. The azaelas were in bloom. And then—and this is the moment Hardy didn't pass on—they had walked over to the old carriage house where he had parked his rental car on the apron outside the empty garage. The Lincoln limousine had been put up on blocks in a shed which also housed the family's horse-drawn carriages. As he pulled away down the driveway, he had looked back through the rearview mirror just as Bill Hardy gave one big sweep of an arm. He had waved back. But the perspective had seemed to tilt, go vertical. Curiously, it was as if he had been watching the fig-ure that retreated in the mirror from above, as if he were rising about Bill Hardy, the carriage house, the grounds of the estate, and the mansion. He said nothing about this image to Celia, because he would have added that it had reminded him of times when a helicopter had lifted him up and away from a figure on the ground, standing in a clearing, sometimes waving good-bye and becoming only a face looking up at him and growing faint.

The silence stretched out between them, across the conti-nent. Finally, Celia said in a small voice, "Meanwhile, you can show the Mexicans your way with parking lots?"

"Hey, I have something better than that. How about sewer lines? Sanitation systems." He tells her about the Arnett Family Foundation. Susanna's account of the clinics and hospitals. "I could help put things together."

"With your other family, you mean."

"Or just on my own. Maybe, I could do it on my own."

"I like that better."

"What the hell, I have this degree in engineering. About time I used it."

"He'd be your age. Your brother." She paused and laughed. "That would be the job. That search. Where'd you get this idea? I mean the sewer lines and the rest."

He couldn't think of an answer. "I'm leaving tomorrow."

"So soon," she would say. She will believe him at last.

"Well, what's keeping me here?" He hadn't meant to say that; it just came out. So, he will be a little relieved to hear her laughter in his ear. "What's so funny?"

"You're looking for that girlie," she will say. She is bent over to look at her toes, all lined up neat and nicely manicured. How could she be both sad and happy, all at once?

"What girlie?"

"That jungle twinkie you used to read about. You know the book you were trying to find in the library that day. When we looked through the mansion. What was her name?"

"Rima," Hardy will say, catching up with her amusement. Fresh snow had begun to fall outside his window. *Green Mansions.*

"That's the babe," Celia will answer. "You're going down there to go look for Wonder Woman, swinging through the jungle."

"I won't find her. That's just in a book."

"Well, then you'll have to come back to me, won't you?" She surprises herself.

"You mean it?"

"Yes," Celia will say. "I like the sound of this guy you're talking about."

Then, they would begin to compare the two different winters outside their windows and talk of the time, a bitter January, they had been driving home from Kingston and they had crossed the Hudson River at Poughkeepsie. They will talk of how they had stopped the car half-way across the Mid-Hudson Bridge, and got out to look at the river frozen over, and they both will remember how the ice had glistened in the moonlight like cake frosting, and how a large chunk of it had broken off to float downstream in the shipping channel that had been kept open, a piece of hard meringue so enormous they guessed some of it would still be left when it reached the sea. They had watched it drift toward the bend in the river above Marlboro where it had seemed to bob about, almost indecisively, before passing out of sight.

ROY ARMSTRONG
FAMED FLYER, 88

Roy Armstrong, a retired major in the USAF and one of the more colorful figures in American air history, was reported to have died in Alexandria, Va. yesterday.

His age was given as 88, and authorities of the Cedar Retirement Homes here where Maj. Armstrong spent his last years say that death apparently was by suicide.

As a seventeen year old, Major Armstrong dropped out of Yale University to enlist in the fledgling US Air Service and learned to fly in France,one of the first American pilots of World War I to do so. He shot down at least seven planes in legendary "dog fights", including a sky battle with Ernst Udet, the German ace and later Hitler's Luftwaffe Marshal.Neither man could best the other after nearly an hour of conflict, ending in a draw when the German's guns jammed and the American ran out of gas. Armstrong was awarded several decorations for valor, including the Croix de Guerre.

After the Armistice, then Capt. Armstrong is supposed to have loaned his services to several countries involved in civil wars, but his most notable appearance was as a member of the Patrulla Americana, the group of American volunteers who flew for the Loyalist government in the Spanish Civil War. His skill and daring accounted for at least eleven fascist planes downed and many more probables.

When he wasn't flying in combat in some part of the world, Maj. Armstrong also did stunt flying in several motion pictures, most notably the dogfight scenes of the Howard Hughes epic, "Hell's Angels." Together with his friend, Roscoe Turner of Thompson Trophy fame, he recreated WW I aerial combat for the camera that remain the"classic ultima of the genre" according to air historian, Martin Provensen.

Maj. Armstrong also pioneered Mexican airline routes in 1939-40 while waiting for restoration of his American citizenship and his Army commission, both stripped because of his flying for the Spanish Republic.He had been under investigation by the powerful Dies Committee, and suspected of having ties to the Communist Party, as were many of the American volunteers in the Spanish conflict.But intercession by important Army Air Corps figures and others restored both his citizenship and commission. He was assigned to the Air Corps Training Command during World War II.

But his combat days were not yet over. During World War II, on an inspection tour of fighter units in the South Pacific, Maj. Armstrong is reported to have flown several sorties in a P-38 fighter in the Solomon Islands and to have downed four enemy planes. He also demonstrated to the younger pilots of the Pacific Theatre how to reduce their planes' fuel consumption with a minimum loss of performance. The result was a tremendous saving for the war effort and brought him the Distinguished Service Cross as well as a Presidential Citation.

After his retirement, Maj. Armstrong spent many years in Mexico, in San Miguel de Allende, where he organized expeditions to search for the fabled "Gold of Montezuma", treasure the Aztec ruler was supposed to have hidden from Cortes in the mountainous regions south of Mexico City. These ventures came to nothing. During his last active years, he ran a flying school near Falls Church, Va.

From his home in Pittsburgh, Pa., retired General Jimmy Doolittle, 93, paid tribute to his former friend and fellow airman. "He was one of the best."

There are no survivors. Burial to be in Arlington National Cemetery.